I0706263

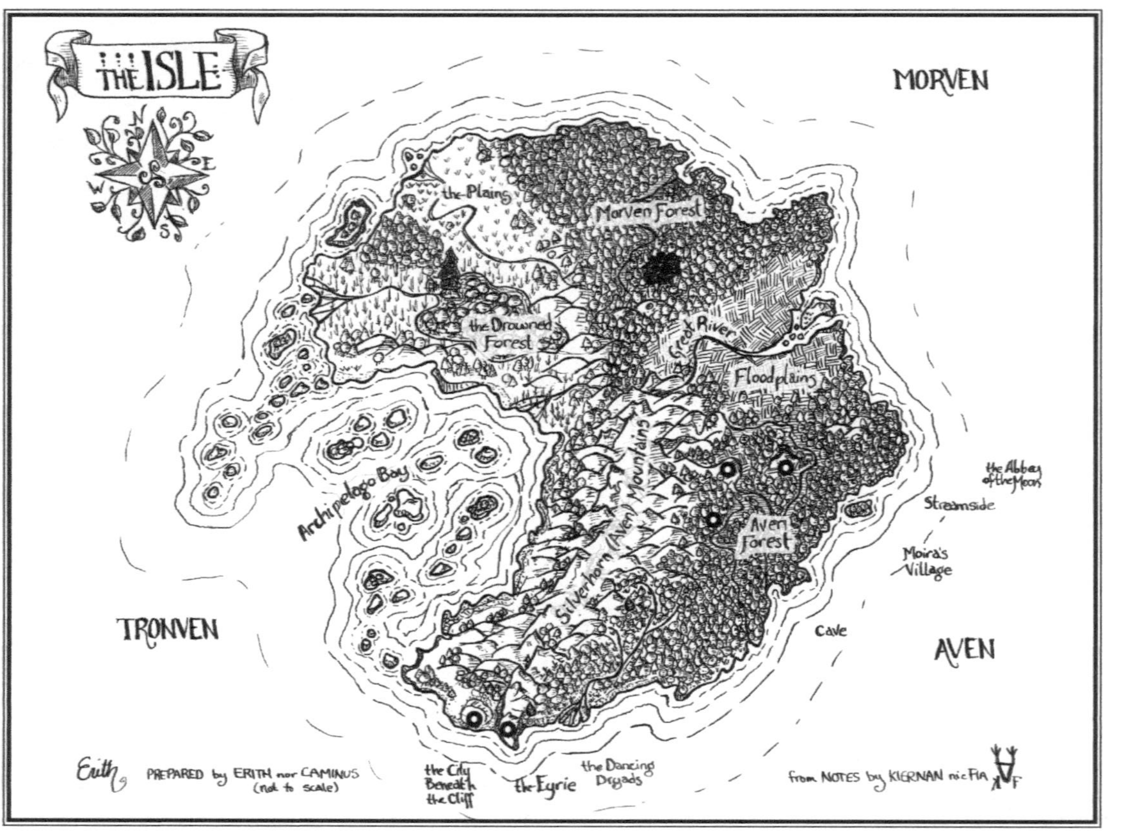

THE ISLE
N
E
S
W
MORVEN
the Plains
Morven Forest
the Drowned Forest
Great River
Floodplains
Archipelago Bay
Silverhorn (Aven) Mountains
the Abbey of the Moon
Streamside
Aven Forest
Moira's Village
Cave
TRONVEN
AVEN
Erith
PREPARED by ERITH nor CAMINUS
(not to scale)
the City Beneath the Cliff
the Eyrie
the Dancing Dryads
from NOTES by KIERNAN nic FIA

A VISION OF AIR

Three Realms, Nine Monarchs

A VISION OF AIR

written by

NICO SILVER

illustrated by

NIK SYLVAN

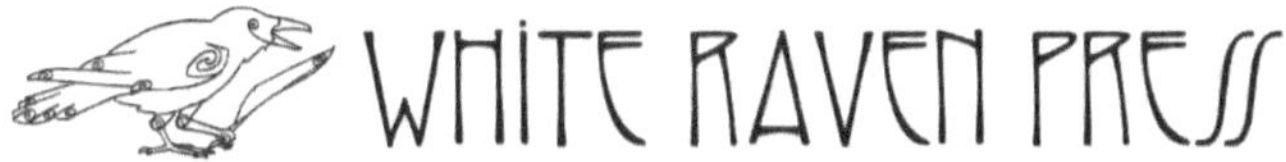

WHITE RAVEN PRESS

2nd Edition, 2023 (previously published as by Nicole Silver)

ISBN 978-1-998212-10-1

White Raven Press
North Cowichan, British Columbia, Canada

Cover illustration: "Fionn and Kier: Before Falling" © 2023 by Nik Sylvan.

Cover design and border by Nik Sylvan.
Title typefaces: Rivanna NF Pro by Nick Curtis and Eva Antiqua by Spiece Graphics, used under license via MyFonts, www.myfonts.com.

*for Papa Tolkien and Papa Lewis
(who probably would have hated all the smut):*

This is all your fault, really.

Author's Note

THERE IS A LOT of enthusiastic, consensual sex in this book between two men in love. It gets pretty graphic, so if that's not your thing, maybe this book isn't for you.

There are also scenes of sexual harassment, dubious consent, and sexual assault (this does not happen between our main characters, who are sweet and gentle with each other). These scenes are not meant to be titillating; they're terrible and that's how they should be viewed.

There are scenes of violence, which include broken bones, blood, and death-by-thrown-knife.

There is a lot of swearing, including (especially) the f-word. Kiernan swears a lot, sorry.

And, finally, there is no happily ever after – yet. This is book one, and it ends with our heroes in an okay place, but there is more to come. I promise there will be a happily ever after for Kier and Fionn before the series finishes.

1: THE ABBEY

1
Fionn

Very little ever changed in the Abbey of the Moon. It was something I could count on, like I could count on the sun rising in the morning or the Abbess being disappointed in me.

Like I could count on my visions being useless, showing me only episodes in the life of some fey boy I didn't know and whom the Abbess said I would likely never meet.

The only things that changed were the things that changed everywhere. The weather might be fair and bright, or it might bring a soaking downpour. The roster of novices shifted, new girls arriving one month and others departing in tears the next. But for me, life changed very little.

And the Abbey itself was always the same. It squatted disapprovingly on its hill, overlooking the fields and gardens that clustered at the base of its walls, and the forest beyond. It was square gray stone with a tower at each corner and one in the middle that only the Abbess was allowed inside. It smelled musty in some places, mildewy in others, and damp and soapy in the bathhouse and laundry.

The sisters also did not change, or at least not much and not often. There were nine senior sisters, all under a vow of silence, each ruling over three junior sisters, under a vow to never look upon a male body, who in turn held sway over a varying number of novices who took both vows to prove their worthiness to dwell under that grim roof.

And over all of them was the Abbess. She was as stern and gray as the Abbey itself, but required neither to keep silent, nor to avoid looking at men, because otherwise she would have been unable to negotiate with outsiders for wages for the work the Abbey took in or prices for the produce it grew.

And then there was me. I was, quite literally, the odd man out. I was Vogel – bird folk – to begin with, in an abbey of Alfar. I leaned toward animism in a place devoted to a demanding goddess. And I was a seer among those who were not even allowed the most basic of magics.

And most of all, I was a man in a stronghold of women. Granted, we bird folk don't have any obvious external sexual characteristics, so I could have walked naked among the sisters and not aroused any scandal or lust. Those sisters sworn to never look upon a male body were unaware that they broke their vow nearly every day, because under my shapeless clothing, my functional male parts were tucked neatly inside my body, to be revealed only when called into action.

Or when I thought too much about how nice it would feel to be touched in kindness; in the Abbey physical contact was only for punishment.

Or when I looked at the handsome, and very naked, young man on a cot in my infirmary, as I was that afternoon.

Fortunately, my tunic covered me from neck to knee, and my loose trousers from waist to ankle, leaving only my feet and back bare to allow my claws and my wings and my tail freedom to move. Also fortunately, I had very strong belly muscles and could clamp my sheath closed, holding my erection in until it was so painful I could have screamed.

It helped, too, that the naked man was unconscious. It seemed very wrong to think wicked thoughts about someone who couldn't consent to being ogled.

So I ignored my discomfort as best I could and focused on my patient. The sisters hadn't told me how the young man had come to be in the Abbey, where only women – and one Vogel man – were allowed. They had only told me the young fey – Sidhe to judge by his pointed ears and delicate antlers – was in need of healing.

And that he was not to be allowed to leave my tower.

I knew the Abbey's wards prevented the use of magic, kept out intruders, but I didn't know how they did so, or what would happen if someone tried to get in, as I supposed this man had done. But I *did* know him. I had never met him, of course; I had never met anyone besides the sisters and the novices. But he was the fey boy I'd been having visions of – entirely useless visions, as far as I could tell – my whole life, the young man the Abbess had told me I would never meet. So, the source of the pressure in my belly wasn't just that I was looking at a very attractive young man, though he was that. It was that in some of those visions, including the most recent, I and this young fey had been… intimate.

Toe-curling, throat-scraping, back-arching intimate.

Those visions I had *not* reported to the Abbess, as I had never reported any of the times I had *seen* myself with him. I didn't know why I had always left myself out of my reports to her; I only knew those visions felt private, and I had never wanted to share them. So, I had not blurted out that this fey was the one I'd been having visions of for as long as I could remember. That I knew what he had looked like as a boy, as a youth, and as a man. That I knew what kind of clothes he usually wore, and what he liked to eat. And I knew what he looked like laughing, and crying, and in the throes of intense pleasure. My possible future relationship with him was a secret, and though I had been brought up by the Abbess to never keep secrets, *that* one I had always chosen to hide.

So, I had said nothing when four junior sisters carried the young man into my infirmary, their eyes bound with dark cloth so they couldn't accidentally look upon his very obviously male body. Because even clothed he was incredibly masculine.

"What happened?" I had dared to ask the Abbess, when the sisters had deposited the man on the cot and retreated back the way they'd come. I preferred not to draw the Abbess's attention at all if I could avoid it, but she was there in my infirmary and if I was to treat this man, I needed some clues, at least.

She had looked down her long nose at me and narrowed her cold gray eyes. She was the only person I knew who could look down on someone while actually looking up, because I was tall and thin, as I was told all Vogel were. Of course, the only bird folk I had actually seen was myself, reflected uncertainly in a basin of wash water.

"He ran afoul of the Abbey wards," the Abbess had said, her voice emotionless as always. Somehow, no matter what the subject or the words she used, she always made me feel insignificant. So I didn't ask for more details, nor did I ask what the man was doing to have run into the magic that protected the Abbey from intrusion.

"He will wake in pain," said the Abbess, and I snuck a glance at her face, and thought I detected a look of satisfaction there, behind the emotionless mask. I looked carefully away.

"He may be blind," she added. "He is lucky to be alive at all." She had stared at me, as if daring me to ask more, or to confess my deepest thoughts.

I knew better than to do either, and she stepped past me to the door. "He is not to leave this tower," she said.

"Yes, Abbess," I murmured, keeping my eyes down.

"This door will be locked. I will have food sent at mealtimes. A novice will come to empty your chamberpot."

"Yes, Abbess." My voice didn't change, but I felt dismay wash over me. I seldom left my tower, but I liked to have the option, to be able to visit the bathhouse, or the latrine – how I hated using a chamberpot – or the small kitchen garden in the courtyard.

"When he can walk, you will be allowed to take him to the bathhouse. After dark, when the sisters are asleep. In the meantime, you will have water and soap."

"Yes, Abbess." I had clasped my hands in front of me and bowed, and the Abbess sniffed and swept from the room. The sound of the lock snapping to had echoed in my head like a slap to the ear.

And then I was left to my own thoughts. My forbidden, lustful thoughts that I couldn't seem to keep from creeping to the front of my mind. I had managed to push them aside while I wrestled the young fey out of his filthy clothes and examined him for injuries. I found nothing obvious, only a green leafy tattoo around one wrist and something that looked like an archaic symbol for the head of a stag just above the cleft of his buttocks. His perfect, muscular buttocks.

But when I had stepped away to fetch a candle, to see how my patient's eyes would react to light, I had turned back to look at the man from across the room, and I felt my breath rush out and I could only stare.

This scene, this exact present moment, I had *seen* in a vision. The young man, mysteriously injured, naked, unconscious. It hadn't been an erotic vision, and the situation shouldn't have been arousing, but seeing him there, bronze skin gleaming, every muscle looking like it had been brought into being by a divine sculptor, I couldn't help the stirring beneath my belly muscles, deep in my sheath where my erection was growing, threatening to push its way out.

I shook my head sharply. I didn't *know* this man. Not really, no matter how much it felt like I did. And just because I'd *seen* him in my visions, over and over again, didn't mean…

But truth be told, I had no idea what the visions did or didn't mean. Because even though the Abbess had given me mindfulness exercises, meditation techniques, and breathing patterns she said would hone my abilities, I really knew nothing about being a seer.

Even the Abbey library was little help and could only tell me about some famous seers who had once existed. There was no information on how to *be* a seer.

So, I clenched my belly muscles harder, straightened my spine, and brought the candle over to my patient, who didn't stir, even when I pried one of his eyes open. Only the regular rise and fall of his chest told me he was even alive.

"Well, that's not good," I said softly, when the man's pupil didn't contract when I brought the lit candle closer. The other eye produced the same non-reaction. I hoped it was only damage to the eyes and not something worse, because eyes would often recover where brains seldom did. At least both his pupils were the same size.

There was little else I could figure out until the man woke, so I took the pail of warm water the sisters had brought from the bathhouse, and the soap and washcloth, and bathed the young man as best I could, pretending he was any other patient I might have tended in my years at the Abbey. I made myself focus on the cloth and the water, and not the smooth skin I was cleaning with it, and I refused to let myself remember my most recent vision, that had seemed to last hours and left me with a large wet patch on the inside of my trousers.

When the young man was as washed as I could manage, I wrestled a clean tunic onto him, almost dropping the unconscious fey to the floor more than once. He was heavier that he looked, all solid muscle despite his small size. I covered him with a blanket, wound a bandage over his eyes so the dim daylight filtering through the tower windows wouldn't damage them further, and retreated across the room to a tall wooden stool and my basket of silk for spinning. I took up my drop spindle and waited.

I HAD WORKED my way through a good portion of the basket of deep gold cloud silk, spinning and winding a shiny, soft, improbably thin thread, before the young man on the cot stirred.

I set aside my work and hurried to my patient, but he only mumbled something about burning light – a reference, perhaps, to what had happened when he clashed with the Abbey's wards – and turned his head the other way on the pillow. He did not wake.

I bit my lip and looked more closely at the young man's face. I had been afraid, really, to see him properly, in case I was wrong and this wasn't the man from my visions after all. Or in case it *was*. I wanted so badly for it to be the same young man, but I was also afraid of it. I wasn't sure if I wanted the change the fey brought or if I wanted to retreat to the sameness of Abbey life.

The fey stirred my thoughts like a hurricane, leaving a

whirlwind of wants, of wishes and longings that I had always before been able to ignore. I had always told myself I loved the peace and the solitude the Abbey gave me. The predictability. But now, locked into my own tower, a place that had always been my refuge, I began to wonder if I had always been a prisoner. I had always known that the magical wards that cocooned the Abbey of the Moon were as much about keeping the sisters and the novices *in* as they were for keeping intruders out. I had just never considered how that applied to *me*. I had never been able to simply leave, but now it wasn't just one more thing I could ignore to get through the day, the nineday, the moon, the year. My life.

I tried to force my thoughts back to pleasant things, to the contentment brought by spinning the finest-quality thread and yarn of anyone in the Abbey, or the joy when the herbs I harvested and prepared brought health to a patient. Or the soft gleam of the young fey's curly dark hair. I took a cloth from the table and wetted it, wiped sweat from my patient's brow, and dared to tuck curls of hair away from the young man's face, to untangle them from the small antlers that sprouted from his forehead.

Curious, unable to help myself, I dared also to run my fingers over one of those antlers, to trace its solid, not-quite-smooth shape. It felt nice.

The fey stirred on the cot, pulled in a noisy breath, and moaned quietly.

I snatched my hand away and the young man quieted, turning his head on the pillow again.

"I wonder who you are," I said softly. Spending so much time alone, I tended to talk to myself a lot. "And what you were doing trying to get into this place." I frowned and put the damp cloth back on the table. "Not many come here on purpose," I said. "Usually they're sent here." I bent and picked up the man's dirty clothes from the floor and carried them to the hamper against the wall.

"Because they've misbehaved." I tossed the clothes in after emptying the pockets – only a few coins and an ornate key. "Or because they've one child too many for their family to feed."

I bent again, picked up the well-made and well-worn boots, and set them next to the door, tucked the leather arm guards into their tops, and then tried to decide what to do with the belt, the sword, the matched pair of knives. I had never seen such weapons in real life before, and they fascinated me.

The young man made a noise in his throat again, a restless sound, but didn't stir.

I hefted the sword, drew it a few inches from its sheath – as if I even knew what to do with a sword – and slid it back. I looked around, as if a good place to store it would appear among my cabinets. None of the familiar furniture had big enough cupboards or drawers; they were meant for holding herbs and roots, jars and muslin bags. The only blades they could contain were small ones for harvesting mushrooms or chopping dried plants.

I glanced at the door out of the tower. It had a small window with the curtain drawn over it for privacy and to keep the sisters from spying my patient by accident. Then I looked at the door at the top of the open staircase that rose against the curved outer wall.

"Stay here," I said to my charge, even though the young man couldn't hear me, and was unlikely to be capable of going anywhere even if he could, if the Abbess's evaluation of his likely pain was correct. Then I headed for the stairs and up.

The door led to the next floor in the tower and my sitting room. There was a low couch in front of the fireplace, a bookshelf that didn't have nearly enough books on it, and a big table, curved to fit against the wall, that held my small loom and an assortment of yarns and threads on big spools. A partly woven cloth in shades of blue webbed the loom.

I frowned, looking around my room, shook my head, and continued up another stairway to another door, another floor of the tower, my bedroom. I had a large bed and a small wardrobe, a desk, and a chair.

"The wardrobe?" I muttered to myself. "Or under the bed?" I looked from one to the other, examined the sword in my hand, then dropped to my knees and slid the sword, the knives, and the arrangement of leather straps that would attach the whole thing to its wearer into the narrow gap between bedframe and floor.

I stood up and resisted the urge to lie on my bed, to sleep and forget the beautiful young man in the infirmary downstairs. Or, more likely, to be unable to sleep *because* of the young man in the infirmary downstairs, and to succumb to the temptation to think about him, to touch myself and find at least some release from the pressure under my belly muscles.

I also resisted the urge to climb one last stairway to the roof of my tower. It was my one true refuge, that roof, the only place I felt I could really escape the eyes of the sisters, of the Abbess, and I only ever went there after dark, when the rest of the Abbey slept. When I could lie on my back and stare at the dark sky and the stars, and pretend I could fly, that my stunted wings weren't as useless as my visions.

"Dammit," I said, feeling a childish thrill at the swear word. I wasn't even supposed to *know* swear words, let alone pronounce them out loud. It felt good, that small bit of defiance, like it could get me through the rest of the day without falling into the despair that was becoming more and more common the older I got.

I would be thirty-three on the solstice, only a few sunrises away. For bird folk, and fey, and most of the other non-human peoples of the Isle, thirty-three was the age of majority, the end of youth and the very beginning of adulthood.

I did not feel very much like an adult. I had grown up sheltered, unexposed to anything a normal child would experience, and as a result, I felt like I would be treated as a child forever. I frowned again, shook my head, and turned for the stairs – the steps down, not the ones to the roof.

The young man on the cot had pushed the blanket off and the tunic had slipped up to expose his muscular thighs. Any higher and it would have exposed a lot more.

I had to force my breathing to remain even, and gently tugged the garment back down, trying not to imagine what the young man's skin would feel like under my hand. Trying not to remember that, thanks to my visions, I already *knew* what that strong leg would feel like under my palm. I spread the blanket back over the young man and dared, again, to push hair from his face. It was soft, that hair, curling darkly around his ears – the ear uppermost had a deep nick out of it, two gold rings, and three gold studs. A matching stud protruded beneath the young man's full lower lip. His dark hair tangled with the base of his antlers and curled down the back of his neck. It looked like it had once been short, I had *seen* it shorter, but had grown out, unruly. I wanted to bury both hands in it, to lean over and inhale its scent.

I clenched my jaw and only stroked the hair lightly back from his cheek.

He had a strong face, the young man. High, sharp cheekbones, curvy lips, a strong chin edged with soft dark hair that matched that on his head but wasn't quite enough to be called a beard. I wished I could see the young man's eyes. They were green, I knew, green so intense it looked unlikely against his skin. Both eyes were ringed with green, too, like makeup, except it didn't wash off. A tattoo, maybe, like the curly branch and leaf on his left wrist, or the stag on his lower back.

I felt a flush rise up my neck and turned away. The pink would show up like a fire beacon on my fair skin, and even though the bandages would hide me should the young man wake, I felt suddenly shy. What would I say to this person I knew, yet didn't know?

But, "I wish you would wake up," I said, though I was terrified of that very thing. I turned to look at my charge again. "I can't help you if I don't know what's wrong with you."

I sighed and went to one of the cabinets along the tower's only flat wall – the one that joined it to the rest of the Abbey. At least I could prepare something for pain, something to give the young man when he woke. I selected jars and carried them to the nearby table, crushed herbs, mixed them and poured them into a bag of loosely-woven linen. Then I fetched water from the pails the novices had left by the door, filled the kettle, and put it on its hook in the fireplace, and built a small, hot stick fire under it.

I was just pouring the hot water over the bag of herbs when my patient stirred again, moaned, and said, "I feel like I just rolled out from under a stampede of swamp deer," in Islish.

I whirled around, almost spilling the kettle in my haste. "You're awake!"

"No," he said. "I'm pretty sure I'm dead." He shifted on the cot. "Though I never imagined being dead would hurt so much."

2
Kiernan

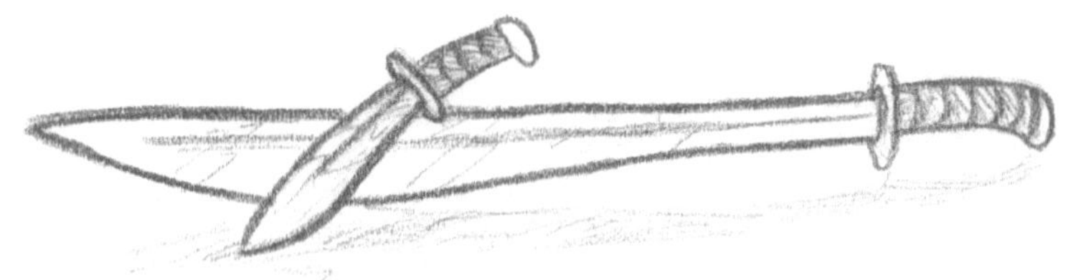

I OPENED MY EYES but couldn't see. Was it night? It didn't feel like night, didn't *smell* like night.

It smelled like stone, and herbs, and a small hot fire; like sweat, and something pleasant, musky and a little sweet. I reached up to touch my eyes and found the source of the darkness: there was a bandage wrapped around my face.

"No!" said a voice. "Don't take it off. Your eyes were damaged. They need darkness to heal."

The voice was as pleasant and sweet as the unidentified smell. It was somewhere in the mid-range, and a little husky, so I couldn't tell if the speaker was male or female, both or neither.

"Where am I?" I said, my voice coming out hoarse.

"Here, drink this," said the nice voice, and I felt a hand behind my head lifting it up, and a cup pressed to my lips.

"What is it?" I got out before hot liquid lapped against my mouth and I had to sip or else let it spill down my front. It tasted sharp and bitter, but not unpleasantly so.

"It will help with the pain," my unseen companion said. "Drink all of it, or it won't be as effective."

I obeyed, reaching up to grasp the cup and covering the other person's hand in the process. Their fingers were cool in comparison to the heat of the ceramic vessel and its contents, their skin soft and smooth. I traced one finger with my own, discovered it was tipped in a long nail or claw. That told me nothing, really, except that the person was probably not human, though even that was not certain; some humans grew very long fingernails.

When I finished the drink, I asked again, "Where am I?" This time, my voice sounded more like it should.

"This is the Abbey of the Moon," the voice said. "Do you remember how you got here?"

"I don't even know where *here* is." I frowned. Something in the name was familiar, though I couldn't say what. The other person seemed nervous, and I thought a joke might put them at ease, but the only jokes I could think of were inappropriate for polite company, and I didn't know, yet, what sort of company the other person was. And since my life seemed to be in the other's hands, it was best not to make a bad impression.

"It's in Aven," the voice said. "A half day or so from the coast, depending on how you travel."

"Fuck." The Monarchy of Aven was not home. It was not anywhere near home, whether I was counting mother's monarchy or father's stronghold by that name. "I wish I could remember what I was doing here."

"What *do* you remember?" The voice had moved away and I could hear the sound of a ceramic cup set down on a wood surface, a soft clicking as the person moved, as if they had nails in the soles of their boots or long claws that tapped the floor with each step.

"I don't know you. I don't know why I'm here. Why should I trust you?" The words were pointed, but I said them with a smile, demanding, but still trying to be friendly.

The sound of shifting fabric, a creak of wood like a stool being sat on, something soft and soothing and repetitive that I couldn't identify. I had been trained to move in utter dark and wasn't bothered by the lack of sight – if I didn't think about it too hard – but this was an environment I didn't know, full of unfamiliar things.

"What's that sound?" I said. It stopped as soon as I mentioned it.

"Which sound?" It started again.

"That one."

"I'm spinning," the voice said. "If you can hear that, then we needn't worry that your ears were damaged. I can barely hear it and it's in my hands." There was a soft noise, like a chuckle from someone not used to laughing, and I liked the sound of it. "Or not in my hands, as it's currently hanging by a thread of cloud silk."

"Fuck," I said, but not with any force behind it. I touched the bandage over my eyes, but didn't try to remove it, even though I desperately wanted to. I did want to keep my vision more than I wanted to see the person I was talking to, who had such a sweet voice and soft touch.

"I remember being in the forest," I said. "My stag wouldn't leave the shelter of the trees, so I had to leave him there. No doubt he's gone to try to find his way back to my mother's court." I scowled, but hid it behind my hand, pretending to scratch my nose. The other was such a comfortable presence that I forgot myself and almost gave too much away.

"The court my mother attends," I amended. It was a lie, but if my instincts were wrong and I couldn't trust the kind-voiced person who had given me a very effective tea for pain, then it wouldn't do to have them know who my mother was.

"You ride a stag?" my companion asked, wonder in their voice. "The fey I've seen from the wall ride horses."

"They would be Alfar, if we're in Aven. The Alfar love their horses."

"You're not from Aven, then," the voice said.

"Obviously." I smiled to take the sting from my reply. Who in the Nine Monarchies wouldn't know the moment they laid eyes on me, saw my coloring, my clothes, my antlers? "I'm Sidhe." Then I scowled again but didn't hide it. "Half Sidhe, technically. My father is human."

"I don't know very much about the world outside the Abbey." Was that embarrassment in their tone? I felt a little bad, then, for being unkind. "And what I do know comes from books in the Abbey library, most of which are at least a hundred years out of date as far as currents events go."

I turned towards the voice again, curious about the mild self-scorn I heard. "I remember leaving the woods," I said, when my companion didn't volunteer anything further. "I crossed some fields, gardens. Then the stone wall. There was a huge gate, with a smaller one to the side. And then a flash of light. And I was here. And blind, apparently." There had been pain, too, much worse than I'd woken up with, pain that felt how I imagined being hit by a lightning bolt would feel.

"The sisters didn't tell me how they came to find you, nor did the Abbess inform me why she let you stay, why she had you brought to me for healing."

"The sisters? You're not one of them, then?"

"I am not." The voice sounded amused, but I couldn't work out why.

"A novice?"

"No." The faint sound of spinning stopped.

"Then why are you here, in an abbey, if you're neither?"

"I'm a seer," they said, as if that explained everything. "I've been trained to heal, and to control my visions, though I don't *see* much of use to anyone, it seems."

I really wished I could see the other, read their expression. Everything they said just confused me more. Why would a seer be hidden away in a religious abbey instead of training under another seer? So I said, "I've never heard of a seer being sent to an abbey to train. Not even to a moon abbey."

"How should I have been trained, then?" The voice seemed skeptical that I could know what I was talking about, but there was a hint of uncertainty there, too.

"I haven't met a lot of seers," I said. "But I've always understood that they're taken to a more experienced seer once the visions start. Their families usually have someone lined up soon after they're born. Once they're trained enough to continue on their own, most seers serve their monarch, though a few become ambassadors, and some of the less talented may return to their home cities and serve there."

"Oh," said the voice. This time, there was nothing in it to read.

"What color are your eyes?" I asked. If this person really was a seer, I already knew the answer. If it was the wrong answer, then either my companion had been deceived their whole life, or else they were trying to trick me.

"Silver, of course," the other said. "I'm all silver. Silver hair, silver… well, everything."

"Skin, too?" I teased, wondering what that would look like.

"No." They laughed, but it was tentative, like they were still thinking though what I had told them. "I'm pale, but not that pale."

"You sound lovely," I said, then realized that kind of

remark might not be welcome, and I couldn't see their reaction to be able to tell. I cleared my throat. "How long have you been here?" I shifted on the cot, trying to find a more comfortable position. The tea had helped a lot, but there was still deep ache in every bone and muscle.

"My whole life," said the voice. "I was born here." There was something in their tone. Regret, maybe, or longing. "I've never been outside the Abbey walls."

Loneliness, I realized. It was loneliness I was hearing. Something deep in my belly made me want to make this person feel better, to reach out and comfort them. Something that felt like a connection, as impossible as that was.

"It must be peaceful," I said, searching for something good to take the edge of sadness away.

"If you consider routine peaceful," said the voice. They sighed, a soft and fleeting sound. "Perhaps, if the Abbess was kinder, the sisters less distant, it might be a pleasant life."

"How old are you?" I couldn't have begun to guess, other than adult, probably, and young, definitely.

"Thirty-three come midsummer." A shifting of clothing as they moved on their seat. "How old are you?"

I knew better than to trust someone I'd just met – fuck, I knew better than to trust my own kin – but I very much *wanted* to trust his person, and not just because they seemed lonely and isolated.

"Thirty-six." I grinned, knowing the effect would be cheeky and not a little cocky. "Past my majority, but not by much."

The other laughed, soft and pleasant, but melancholy.

"What's your name?" they asked.

Being half-human, I could lie, where a full Sidhe could not – no fey could lie outright – which was a fact my royal mother took frequent advantage of when sending me on errands. But

I despised lying on principle, even the sort of deception my fey relatives could use to get around their compulsive truth-telling. I also knew it could be dangerous to be too open. I might be right, and this young healer might be trustworthy, but they might also be accustomed to reporting everything to their Abbess. So I gave only *most* of my name, the version of it I used those few and fleeting times I escaped Mother's court.

"Kiernan Druison," I said.

"Kiernan," the other repeated.

I liked the way their voice made my name sound. Impulsively, I added, "You can call me Kier, if you like."

"Kier." I could almost hear the smile in the other's voice, and I smiled back. "I'm Branfionn," they said.

"No surname?"

"Not that I've ever been informed of."

"Branfionn nor Aven, then."

"I don't know what that means." They sounded embarrassed.

"Your name, Branfionn, is Sidhe," I said. "And nor Aven means 'of Aven' because that's where you were born."

"Oh," they said, the embarrassment replaced by something that might be delight. Again, I wished I could see my companion's face. "My name is Sidhe?"

"It is. You didn't know? You're not Sidhe, then?"

"No," they said. "It's the name I was given. By the Abbess, I suppose, but she's Alfar."

"Odd." I added that small mystery to the others surrounding this young seer-healer. I pushed it aside and said, "Can I call you Bran? For short?"

"I… no," said Branfionn. "But you can call me Fionn."

I smiled. "If you're as silver as you say you are, the name suits you. It means 'pale' or 'white'."

They laughed and I smiled wider, though I didn't really

know why. I just couldn't help responding to their delight.

"I am very pale," Fionn said.

"Are your eyes truly silver? Or only very light? Our seer in Morven Forest has eyes that gleam like coins in the sun."

"I don't have a mirror," said Fionn. "But I'm told they truly are silver, yes."

"I wish I could see them. Our seer used to tease me, when I was a boy, for staring at her eyes. I used to ask her how I could make mine look like that." I remembered, then, what state my eyes *were* in, and touched the bandage, like I needed to know they were at least still in my head.

"Your eyes will heal," said Fionn. "I have good hope."

"You hope? You don't know?" And I felt sudden panic building, where before it hadn't bothered me to be temporarily deprived of one of my senses. The thought that I might never see again terrified me, even though I knew there were many who lived long and full lives with no sight.

I sat up, struggled with the blanket, and Fionn was suddenly there, hands on my shoulders, steadying me. "Hey," they said, softly. "Hey now, you shouldn't try to get up yet."

"What if I never see again?"

"You will," said Fionn, firmly, all their tentativeness gone, replaced with something strong and sure, something that made me want to trust them completely.

"You just said…"

"There is always a chance of the worst, yes. I won't lie to you about that. But I have seen nothing that says you won't recover if you rest and stay in the dark."

"How long?" I let Fionn push me back down onto the cot, feeling comforted by the press of their hands against my shoulders, on my chest. Fionn tucked the blanket back around me and brushed my hair out of my face.

"I'm sorry," they said. "I don't know for sure. I think a day or two, but maybe a week, or longer." They fussed with the blanket some more. "The Abbess said, *you* said, there was bright light when you ran into the wards." Their hand pressed against my forehead as if checking for fever, then brushed another curl of hair from my cheek.

"And?" I turned my face into Fionn's gentle touch, then realized what I was doing, and held very still. Their voice, their soft hands, the musky sweet scent that I realized was their skin, were becoming increasingly attractive. I knew almost nothing of my caretaker. I didn't even know what they *looked* like, or if they were male or female or something else. Not that a person's sex or gender had ever mattered much to me.

"A bright flash of light, over and gone, is most likely to cause temporary damage, while a more sustained exposure, even at lower intensity, is more likely to be permanent," Fionn said, sounding like they were reciting a lesson. They tucked another curl of my hair aside. "Now that you're awake, I'll make you some eye drops to contract your pupils, to help stimulate them into working on their own again."

Their gentle hand smoothed the blanket over my chest and I relaxed under the touch. I found myself wanting them to touch me more. "Thank you," I said. Then, "Wait, did you say I ran into the Abbey's wards?"

"So the Abbess told me."

"But why?"

"I presume you were trying to get in and didn't want – or couldn't – to wait for someone to give you permission."

"Why would I be trying to get into an Abbey?" I was speaking mostly to myself, trying to make sense of the situation I found myself in, but Fionn answered anyway.

"I can't imagine," they said. "There's nothing here to steal except a lot of wool waiting to be spun, a little bit of cloud silk, and a whole lot of very old books on very boring subjects."

That startled a laugh out of me. "Are you calling me a thief?" I said.

"No, I…"

I laughed again. "I'm teasing," I said, and reached out, hoping to find Fionn's hand. I found only air, but before I could draw back my reach, Fionn's hand found mine.

"There." I felt the slender length of Fionn's fingers, their fragility and strength, and the softness of the inside of their wrist. "Friends?"

Fionn inhaled sharply and I wondered if they were unused to being touched. "Friends?" Their voice was uncertain.

"Sure. Don't you have any friends among the sisters? The novices, at least?"

"Friendships are not encouraged here." They sighed. "Or closeness, or kindness. Only attention to duty and service to the Lady of the Moon." They withdrew their hand and I felt vaguely abandoned. "You should try to sleep some more," Fionn said. "Tomorrow we'll get those eyedrops made and see if you can walk."

"Will you stay with me?" I felt suddenly very young, like the child sent to live with strangers the first time my mother tired of me and rushed me away to live with my father's people. I realized how completely alone I was here and even if I couldn't trust Fionn, at least they'd be company. And could steer me to a chamberpot to piss if I needed it in the night.

"I –"

"Surely you have more than one cot in an infirmary?"

A sigh. "This isn't the main infirmary. I only rarely have patients all to myself."

"Why now?"

"You're a man."

"I'm a… okay…" I didn't see why that would matter. A sick person was a sick person and it wasn't like I was currently capable of assaulting any novices, even if I'd wanted to.

"This is an abbey of women," Fionn said. "They follow a virgin moon goddess, and most of them have sworn never to look upon a man again." They snorted, but I couldn't guess which part of that statement they found amusing.

"How did I get here, then?"

"The sisters were blindfolded. And the Abbess is not under the same constraints as her flock."

"And you aren't, either, presumably?" I was trying, without actually asking outright, to find out if Fionn was a man or a woman or neither. I wasn't even sure why it mattered – it wouldn't affect how I treated them, and a person's tackle and manner of dress had little effect on whether or not I found them attractive. Knowing one way or the other would have no effect at all on the fact that I wanted Fionn to brush my hair out of my face again, to take my hand, to smooth the blanket over my body. But I still wanted to *know*.

"As I said," said Fionn. "I'm a seer, not an acolyte." But they sounded uncertain again. And also amused, as if they suspected what I was trying to learn and weren't going to make it easy.

"So, you're allowed to look at me?" I pushed the blanket down and plucked at the coarse tunic I was wearing. "Presumably you saw me naked?"

There was a pause and I listened to Fionn's careful breathing, like they didn't quite know how to reply. Or like a change in breathing might give away something they didn't want me to know. I wished desperately that I could see Fionn's face. Were they blushing? Did they, could they possibly, feel the same spark of attraction that I felt?

"I suppose I must be," Fionn finally said. "Someone had

to get you out of those filthy clothes."

"Where are they? My clothes?" I said, and an edge crept into my voice, the uneasiness returning to my gut. "Fuck. Where's my sword? My knives?"

"Your clothes are in the hamper, waiting to be washed and mended. Your sword is… safe."

"Where is it?" I pushed myself up, swung my legs over the side of the cot, and tried to stand. The floor was farther away that it should have been. I felt Fionn's hands under my arms, lifting me back onto the cot, slender but surprisingly strong.

"Don't get up," they said. "Please. Your sword is safe. I have it. I… I hid it."

I tried to breathe evenly, to force myself calm. That sword was important. It was a Sidhe sword of moonsilver, and had belonged to my ancestors, and I still had trouble believing my mother had allowed me to have it, had *given* it to me, of her own accord. "You hid it? From me? Why?"

I let myself be pushed back down on the cot. Again. Fionn lifted my feet onto the mattress, tucked the blanket back around me, and smoothed it across my shoulders. Again, I let myself relax under the touch. I wanted more.

"I didn't hide it from you," Fionn said, fussing with the blanket where it lay across my chest. "I hid it… I don't know why I hid it." Their voice was uncertain. "I suppose I thought the Abbess might want to confiscate it, and if she didn't see it out in the open, she might… not think about it." Their fingers moved from my chest to my face again, tracing my cheekbone tentatively. "I can get it for you, but there's nowhere in this room to keep it out of sight."

I untangled my hand from the blanket and placed it over Fionn's. They shifted to pull away, but I squeezed their fingers. "That feels nice," I said. I let go, rested my hand on my chest, and Fionn stroked my cheek again, then my hair, traced a finger along one antler. The feeling was startlingly erotic, and I felt myself respond. I couldn't remember anyone ever caressing my antlers before. I shifted on the cot, trying to hide my growing erection with no way to know how much was even visible in the first place.

Fionn kept tracing the shape of my antler, and if they realized the effect it was having, they didn't say. "It's under my bed," they said finally. "Your sword and your knives."

"What?" I dragged my thoughts away from the tingle that Fionn's touch was spreading though my body.

"Your sword, your knives, your belt. They're hidden under my bed. On the top floor of the tower."

"Up there?" I pointed at the ceiling.

"Yes."

"The Abbess doesn't search your room?" I moved my hand under the blanket, trying to be subtle, and pressed my cock close to my belly so it wouldn't push the cloth up.

"Not that I know," Fionn said. "As long as I do what I'm told, she leaves me alone." They stopped tracing my antlers and tucked the blanket back around my neck. "And there's no way into this tower except though this room. Unless you can fly."

"Thank you," I said.

Fionn made a noise of assent in their throat and stepped away. "Try to sleep," they said, and moved away.

"Will you stay?" I said. "You never answered."

"There's only the one cot."

"You can share this one." I wanted to know what Fionn would do if I implied that I found them attractive.

"I'm thin," said Fionn. "But not that thin."

"You're thin," I said. "And tall. I can tell that from where your voice is when you speak and how you have to bend to reach me."

Fionn sounded amused when they replied. "Tall and thin. Not very heavy. Shall I describe myself some more?"

"I'd like that."

They snorted. "Maybe tomorrow."

"I don't care, you know."

"Don't care about what?" Fionn's voice moved away. It sounded like they were tidying things away. Something on the table, their basket of spinning, the stool they'd been perched on.

"I don't care what you look like. If you're tall and thin or short and stocky. If you're male or female. If you're Sidhe or Alfar or Huldr, or any kind of fey at all."

"What if I was human?"

I paused. "My father is human, remember? I spent as much of my childhood around humans as I did around fey." I laughed. "As long as you're not bird folk, I don't care what you are."

Stillness was the only reply.

"Fionn? Did you suddenly disappear?"

"Is there something wrong with bird folk?" There was a note in Fionn's voice that made me realize, all at once, that I'd said something very, very stupid, but I couldn't seem to keep my mouth shut.

"You know, flighty, bird-brained."

A gust of breath, like Fionn was snorting out their nose.

And I suddenly realized. "You're bird folk." I wasn't sure if sound was even coming out of my mouth. "Oh, fuck, Fionn, I'm sorry. I…" I took a deep breath.

"I think perhaps you should call me Branfionn from now on. Or maybe just Healer." There came the soft clicking as they walked away, and I realized that the sound was the claws on Fionn's toes connecting with the stone as they took each step.

"I was only joking, Fionn. Branfionn." I tried to sit up, hoping the healer would return to my bedside to make me lie down again. But the steps only receded farther, changed sound as Fionn reached the stairs. "It was a joke. The Sidhe say the Vogel are bird brained and flighty. Because they're bird folk, and they fly?" I repeated it, as if saying something mean over again could possibly help.

"It isn't a very funny joke," said Branfionn, and then there was the sound of a door closing, and a lock clicking to, and I was alone.

"Fuck," I said softly, to no one.

3
Fionn

WHEN THE DOOR was locked behind me, I turned and looked around my sitting room. It was blurry, though I wasn't really seeing anything anyway, so it hardly mattered.

I blinked tears out of my eyes. I would *not* cry. As a child, tears had only brought me a stinging slap or extra chores. I leaned back against the door, slid down it until I was sitting, knees tucked to my chest, and wrapped my arms around my legs.

It was disappointing. Of course, I never should have expected Kiernan Druison to be perfect. I shouldn't have had any expectations at all. I didn't *know* Kiernan, no matter how many of the other man's most traumatic life events I'd *seen* in my visions. So the fey had turned out to be an ass. A bigot. A brainless jokester. What had I lost? I'd had nothing before I'd met Kiernan, and I had nothing now.

But it *felt* like I had lost something. Like I'd lost a part of my future, the possibility of something beyond the Abbey, the potential of friendship, of toe-curling sex, of…

I could hear Kiernan moving downstairs, slowly, the sounds of his bare feet audible because he seemed to be dragging them over the stone floor. Because he couldn't see and would have to feel his way around carefully.

"Fionn?" came Kiernan's voice, uncertain. "Branfionn, please come back. I'm sorry."

I pushed myself to my feet, stood undecided for a moment, then fled up the next stairway to my bedroom. I locked the door and threw myself face-down on the bed. Tears still burned in the corners of my eyes and for a while I considered letting them come, allowing myself to be weak, to bawl into my pillow and let out all the disappointment, the sting. The loneliness. To cry as I hadn't done since the first time the Abbess had sent me to bed without supper.

I had neglected my chores, had let myself be distracted by the courtyard garden, and had wandered, looking at all the different plants, talking to them as if they were other children, friends. And how pathetic was that? A child who had to pretend the vegetables in the garden were his playmates.

When the Abbess found me, hours later, lying on my back under the pea trellises, singing a made-up song to the fragile new pea-pods, she had pulled me to my feet by my hair, had landed a stinging slap on my cheek, and told me I'd have to do all of today's chores tomorrow, and all of tomorrow's, too, and no excuses.

And she'd hauled me to my tower, already turning into an infirmary though my training had only just begun, tossed me inside, and locked the door. I hadn't had any food or water, or even a chamberpot.

Even at four years old I had been so ashamed, when I couldn't hold my waste in any longer, that I had to relieve myself on the previous day's laundry and hide it at the bottom of the hamper.

I had cried then, in fear and shame and loneliness, had curled up on the roof, great sobs wracking my body. I was too thin, even then. I might not have stopped as soon as I did, except the fear that the Abbess would know I had been crying overwhelmed the ache in my chest. I had stopped, had gone back down to my bedroom to wash my face, and had finally fallen asleep.

I woke, now, eyes dry but aching, chest aching. The pressure behind my belly muscles was gone at least, as if I had never felt the intense arousal, my attraction to Kiernan as overwhelmed by disappointment as my childhood sorrow had been submerged beneath fear.

My stomach rumbled, and I realized I had been too far up the tower to hear the novices bring food. I thought about going to see what they had left, but I couldn't face Kiernan. Not yet. Not while I was still feeling so fragile.

I made myself sit up and drink from the cup of water I kept next to the bed. The sky outside the windows was dark, with not even a glimmer from the Abbey below. I pulled the quilt off the bed and climbed the stairs to the roof.

Up there, I felt close to the sky, like having wings might actually *mean* something, even if they were too small to allow me to fly. I spread out the quilt, lay down, and folded it over myself. The moon was waxing, almost full, and the sky was full of stars. In the clear air above, two feathered serpents – each about the length of my arm – circled once to make sure it was really me, then dove down to find themselves places to burrow into the quilt.

"Hello, little friends," I said, barely above a whisper, and they chittered at me, one from a spot close to my neck, and one from the bend in my wing.

As always when I came up here, I felt myself relax, my hurts and wants and sadnesses becoming insignificant next to the glory of the night sky. I pushed away the thought that I had been looking forward to bringing Kiernan here, once he could manage the stairs, to share my refuge. I had thought, maybe, I'd have the courage to kiss him here, where I had always felt safe. It would have been my first kiss. It would have been special.

A tear escaped the corner of one eye and slid down my cheek, followed by another.

"No, dammit." The swear didn't feel as daring as it once had on my tongue. "He won't make me cry." But it wasn't just that Kiernan had hurt my feelings with a bad joke. There were years of disappointments pushing out those tears and Kiernan's thoughtlessness was only the one that made them all too heavy. I curled on my side, ignoring the sleepy protests of the serpents, and buried my face in the quilt until the tears stopped.

When I looked up at the sky again, the moon was gone, dipped behind the trees, below the horizon, leaving the stars to blaze even brighter. My eyes stung and my face felt tight, but the ache in my chest had eased. I rolled onto my back again, the serpents murmuring their protest and shifting position to get comfortable. I tucked my wings carefully under myself and slipped my hands behind my head.

Then I felt the sudden pressure in the back of my neck, the tightness in my scalp, and my back seized and I arched against the stone, my eyes rolled back, stared into nothing. And then, I *saw*.

It was a place I had never seen before, could never even have dreamed existed. A city was built out of a mountain that dropped, cliff by precipitous cliff, down to the sea. Against the sky, figures spread their wings wide and soared.

Closer by, on a narrow strip of sand that grew even narrower until it vanished against the base of the cliff, walked a woman. She had wings, huge gold-and-red feathered appendages that she held half-spread to help her balance against the wind. A small flock of feathered serpents, moving and darting so quickly they couldn't be counted, twisted through the air around her.

She was pregnant, and walked with both arms wrapped around her belly, smiling at the serpents, the sand, the sea, the world in general. This vision carried no sound, but the woman was singing between smiles, her mouth opening wide with each note, then narrowing, then closing so she could smile again.

She stroked her belly, said something, then turned to look behind her.

A man approached. He might or might not have had wings. He wore a hooded cloak so large it dragged in the sand behind him and could have hidden both wings and tail, had he tucked them close to his back. He appeared to be hunch-backed, and he held his hood against the winds, kept it pulled down to hide his face.

When he reached the woman, he spoke, gestured, and she shook her head. He grasped her arm and she tried to pull away. The feathered serpents swirled around her, around him, hissing and biting, until he knocked one away viciously and it hit the sand and didn't rise. The rest of them fled into the sky.

In the vision, the man pulled a long sharp knife from beneath his cloak and stabbed the woman.

I was only an observer in this vision, disembodied, but I tried to scream anyway.

The man had been careful where he aimed the knife, had slid it between the woman's ribs to pierce her heart. He caught her as she fell, laid her on the sand, and bent over her with the knife.

When the man stood, the woman's body was neatly

carved open. Blood smeared her and the object the man held up. It was pale and rounded, pliant like the egg of a turtle. He set it on the sand while he pushed the woman's body toward the incoming tide, left her to the sea and the scavengers, and the small flock of feathered serpents that tugged at her hair, her clothes, trying to get her to rise, to sing to them again.

I *saw* glimpses of the road to the Abbey, a figure on horseback, cloaked and hunched, that could have been the same man or might not have been. And the Abbess, gray and stern, but looking younger than she was in the present. Not a lot younger, because she was fey and aged slowly, but enough to be apparent that this was not a vision of the future, but of the past.

The Abbess held a bundle wrapped in cloth, carried it across the Abbey courtyard.

Inside the Abbey, inside the vision, the Abbess crossed the courtyard, skirted the laundry, and entered the building behind. I had never been through that door. I had been told it was a sauna for the private use of the Abbess and the nine senior sisters.

And it did seem to be a sauna, the heat provided by an upwelling of hot water from the earth – the same spring that fed the laundry and the bathhouse their heated, ever-replenished water. Next to the spring, looking very un-sauna-like, was a sort of nest, built of unfired clay and lined with linen towels and down feathers that might have come from the chickens the novices plucked to feed the Abbey's inhabitants.

The Abbess unwrapped the cloth from the object she held. It was an egg, the same egg that had been cut from the bird woman's body, and it was large enough she needed two hands to hold it, heavy enough it took her some effort to keep it aloft, though not as heavy as it looked like it should be. It was pearlescent white, speckled blue and silver. It was so beautiful

I would have wept if I'd had a body to cry with.

The Abbess put the egg into the nest and smiled her cool, mirthless smile.

The vision shifted, not in place, but in time. Sisters came and went, the Abbess tapped at the egg and pressed her ear to it to listen, steam billowed and ebbed, and finally – surrounded by all nine senior sisters and the Abbess, the egg rocked in its nest. It rocked again, and then was still.

They waited, tense, for a countless stretch of time. And at last the Abbess climbed up to the egg, scowled at it, and kicked it viciously. It cracked, and she kicked it again. A shard flew off and nearly struck one of the watching sisters. One more kick and the egg shattered, pieces falling to all sides. Cradled in what was left, in the rounded bottom of the egg, lay a tiny child, pale and silver and frosty blue, with naked pink wing stubs, large soft toes, and eyes far too big and too bulbous for something so small and delicate.

The Abbess smiled her stony smile, plucked the child out of the remains of the egg, and pinched its large, pointed ear until it flailed its arms and wailed.

I couldn't hear the sound – though not all of my visions were soundless, many were – and I had never heard any child cry, let alone a newborn, but I felt I knew exactly what sound it made, and what that wail felt like when forced out of my tiny lungs.

Then the vision was gone, leaving only a burning headache behind my eyes. For a long time I couldn't move. I was exhausted. My back was cramping and my muscles ached. My tail had fallen asleep. But I was caught in sorrow and wonder.

Someone had murdered my mother, had cut me unborn – unhatched – from her belly, and somehow my egg had made it to the Abbey, where the Abbess had kept it warm and safe until I was developed enough inside it to hatch out of it. I had grown up feeling alone, unhappy, unwanted, but I had at least grown up. I had lived because of the Abbess.

Finally, I stirred, made myself stretch, and sat up, pulling the quilt around me. The pair of feathered serpents had left during my seizure and had not returned, and I felt very alone again. It was still dark, but I had spent enough time on this roof that I could tell by the position of the stars that it was getting close to morning.

At least now there were no chores for me to neglect, not while Kiernan was locked in the infirmary with me. I stood, gathered up the quilt, and left the roof. I wouldn't go all the way back down, not yet, not until it was time for the novices to bring breakfast.

I knew I should sleep. Even brief visions tired me, and that one had lasted hours. My body ached and one of my wings twinged whenever I moved it. So I spread the quilt back over the bed, took off my tunic and trousers, and climbed under the covers, too tired to even wash my dirty feet first.

And then I lay there, staring up at the high ceiling, full of wonder and sadness and the sheer strangeness of witnessing my own birth. I knew, from a book I had stolen from the Abbey library, that the Abbess would have banned had she known it existed, and that now hid in plain sight on the bookcase in my sitting room, that Vogel infants developed within eggs that were incubated inside their mothers' bodies. When the time came to be born, the eggshell was absorbed, and the child was born like any other baby from any of the Isle's other peoples.

But sometimes, a mother under extreme stress might expel her egg early and the embryo was trapped in the shell. The egg contained all the nutrients the growing infant needed – bird folk had belly buttons just like fey or humans, only ours had once connected to a yolk sac in the egg, instead of a placenta in the womb. If the egg was kept warm enough, moist enough without being too wet, it might survive long enough to hatch.

Even then, the result could be death, because infant bird folk were not equipped, as actual birds are, to fight their way out of the shell. As it aged, the eggshell became harder, tougher. If it was cracked too soon, the child would not be developed enough to survive, and if too late, they would suffocate.

I was lucky to have survived. I sat up, needing to tell someone about the wonder I had *seen*, and the horror, the grief I felt that my only glimpse of my mother had been to witness her murder.

And then I remembered. The only person I might have wanted to share my vision with had made an ignorant joke about my people. Kiernan already thought bird folk were beneath him. Telling him that I had *hatched* instead of being born would only give him something else to look down on me for.

I lay back down. Had it really been that bad, the joke? I didn't know any other Vogel. Maybe my people really were all bird-brained and flighty. But then I thought of the wondrous city in the cliff that I had seen in my vision, and the Vogel woman walking on the beach – my mother – singing to her unborn child, and I refused to believe that.

Kiernan could stuff his opinions up his pompous ass. I would do my duty as a healer; I would treat Kiernan like any other patient, would do my best to see the young man healed and well. But there would be no friendship. No kisses on the roof. Nothing more.

I closed my eyes and an earlier vision came to the fore of my memory, unbidden. Kiernan's breath on the back of my neck, his rich smoky voice drawling – because that vision had had sound –"I'm going to seduce you, pretty bird." I felt the pressure return behind my belly muscles, felt myself stirring.

And then I remembered another vision, one I liked to call to mind sometimes when I was feeling lustful, one of Kiernan looking up at me from between my thighs, grinning and flicking his tongue out to tease…

"Goddess Above," I whispered. "I don't want to remember *that*." But I *did* want to remember. I wanted to picture – to feel – how Kiernan had run his tongue over the tip of my erection, slid his whole mouth over my hard length, and sucked.

"No," I whispered, but I moved my hand to my belly, to stroke over my pubic bone, tracing with one finger the almost invisible seam there. I felt feathers and fine hair and muscles part, and my erection slid out into my hand.

Maybe I could sleep if I could just relieve the pressure, I told myself as I moved my hand under the quilt, as I stroked myself, harder and faster, forcing an orgasm as quickly as I could.

It didn't feel good, when I spurted semen all over my belly, but it left me tired and empty, and I made myself get up to wash at the basin near the fire. When I got back into bed, I fell asleep almost immediately.

4
Kiernan

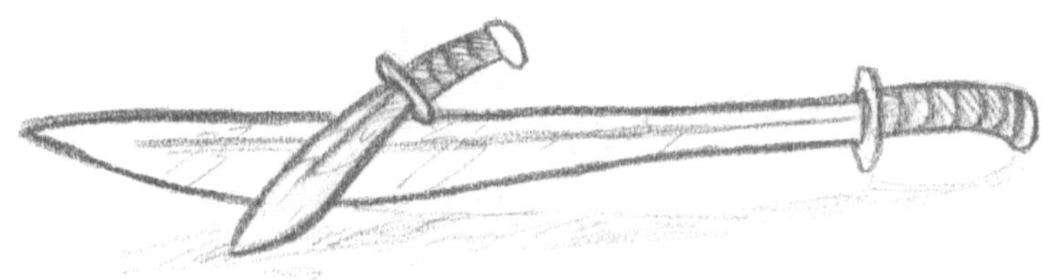

I LISTENED TO Fionn's soft clicking footsteps retreat across the room and up the stairs. I felt sick.

"Fionn?" Why had I said it? Fionn was right; the joke wasn't funny. It was unkind. *Worse* than unkind. And I should have known better, because I had spent my life pretending to laugh at unkind jokes made by one side of my family about the other side. And both humans and fey had plenty of such jokes about each other.

I pushed myself off the bed, almost screamed when my feet hit the floor and my legs took my full weight, and pain lanced up them, and they buckled. I caught myself on the edge of the cot, forced myself to take three agonizing steps towards where I knew there had to be a table, and leaned on that. My arms trembled and ached and threatened to let me fall, but I gritted my teeth and held on, forced my bare feet to slide across the floor, forced my legs to take as much of my weight as they could bear.

"Branfionn, please come back," I said, managing a few

more steps in the direction I knew the stairs to be. "I'm sorry."

I was about to push away from the table, to try to reach the stairs on hands and knees if I had to, when I heard movement behind the upper door. I stopped, waiting to hear the snap of the lock, the creak of the old hinges.

But nothing happened. Then I heard the soft clicking footsteps again, moving farther away, until they were too faint to hear anymore. I heard a more distant door open and close, another lock click to between me and the kind young person I had hoped to befriend.

Pain stabbed up my calves and I tried to shift more weight onto my arms, braced on the table. One wrist gave out and I caught myself on my elbows, just saving my knees from cracking against the stone floor.

"Fuck." I lowered myself until I was kneeling on the floor and moved back in the direction of the cot, found it by crawling into one of its legs face-first, and hauled myself back up onto the thin mattress. Everything hurt. Every muscle, every joint, every bone ached deep into its marrow.

"I sure could use some of your wonderful pain-relieving tea right now," I said, knowing Fionn was too far away to hear me, and would probably have let me suffer even if they did hear.

But no, that was unfair. Fionn was a healer and had been nothing but kind. They could probably hate me with a raging ire and still do their best to ease my suffering.

I tried to get comfortable on the cot, to sleep, to kill the time between now and whenever Fionn decided to come back. They would have to come back eventually.

I had finally managed a fitful doze when a noise at the door roused me again. Quiet footsteps caught my ear, and then a soft tapping.

"Hello?" I said, pushing the blanket aside and trying —

and failing – to sit up.

"Branfionn?" said a female voice. "We've brought supper."

"Branfionn is upstairs," I said. "You can leave it on the table."

"We cannot look upon you, fey man, and we will not venture in blindfolded with you alone in the room with us."

"I'm not going to do anything," I said. "I can't even get out of bed."

"Nevertheless," said the voice. "We will leave the tray outside the door." There was a clatter and the sound of footsteps retreating.

"Wait!" I called. "Can't you slide it *in* the door?" The footsteps were gone. "How am I supposed to get it from *outside* when I'm locked *in*?" I said to the empty room.

Wonderful smells wafted under the door. Steamed greens and warm bread. Sharp cheese. Even roasted meat. My stomach rumbled, ached, and then cramped. How long had it been since I'd eaten? I didn't know. Sometime before I'd apparently tried to get into the Abbey using magic and had been struck down by the wards. Whenever that had been.

"Wonderful," I said. "Now I hurt *and* I'm hungry." I forced himself to sit up just to prove I could. Then I turned over, lay down again, and pulled the blanket over myself. I tried to tuck it in and thought of Fionn's gentle hands smoothing the wool fabric over my chest and making sure my feet were covered.

"And on top of all that, I've alienated the only person besides myself who might have felt the least bit sorry for me." I rolled onto my back again and opened my eyes under the bandages. My lashes scraped against the fabric, so I closed them again.

Should I have guessed that Fionn was bird folk? Had

there been any clues? I could only think of the soft clicks that accompanied their footsteps, but there were fey and other peoples who had claws long enough to make sounds like that.

What did Fionn look like? They would have wings, of course, and a feathered tail. I had only met bird folk once before, but I remembered that they were tall and slender, huge wings folded against their backs, tails sweeping behind their thighs almost to the ground. They'd had scaled legs ending in elegant feet, each with two large, clawed toes in front and another at the heel. They'd all had hair shorn short, of course, and had feathers around their faces – how many grew there, and how many were added adornments, I didn't know.

They had all been colorful, too, skin a rich golden-tan, and feathers red and yellow, blue and green.

But Fionn had told me they were pale, silver to match their eyes. I tried to picture what that must look like. Fair skin, silver scales on their shins, long slender fingers tipped in elegant pale claws. Long, slender limbs that were stronger than they looked. Short silver hair and glorious pale wings. How had Fionn been able to keep me from noticing their wings? Wouldn't their size alone have stirred the air as they moved?

I touched the bandages over my eyes. Tomorrow. Fionn had said they would make the eyedrops tomorrow, and then it would be a day or two more for my eyes to finish healing, and then I could see what the young Vogel looked like. Assuming my eyes *did* heal. My fey ancestry meant I healed quickly, but I had no idea if that applied to something like damaged eyes the way it did to cuts and bruises and broken bones.

"I'm so fucking sorry, Fionn," I said. "I'm just a stupid half-human errand boy for the Queen of Morven Forest. I know nothing about bird folk, but I want to learn. I want to know all about *you*." I made a fist and resisted the urge to punch myself in the face. I'd never been one for self-harm but I felt the need to atone somehow.

Eventually, I slept again, badly, waking frequently to shift position, to try to make my aching body more comfortable.

And then, sometime long after dark, I woke with a sudden feeling of urgency. I sat up, clenching my teeth against the deep ache in my limbs. I tilted my head, listening. There was nothing but the faint sounds of night insects outside the tower. Had I heard a distant scream, or was that only in my dreams?

But the feeling of urgency persisted, gnawing at my belly, and I swung my legs over the side of the cot. Somewhere above me in the tower, someone was feeling intense distress. *Fionn* was feeling distress.

My legs wouldn't hold me at all, so I crawled across the floor, found the wall, located the bottom of the stairs, and dragged myself up. The door at the top was locked. Of course the door was locked; I'd heard Fionn secure it. I knocked, at first softly, then louder.

"Fionn? Are you okay?" I didn't want to be too loud, didn't know how loud I'd *need* to be, for Fionn to hear me at the top of the tower. I didn't want to wake anyone else in the Abbey. But the urgent feeling, the need to do *something* to ease Fionn's distress, churned in my guts. "Fionn!"

There was no response. I reached up, felt the door handle, traced my fingers over the lock plate. It was old, simple. I could pick it, if I had something to pick it *with*.

I turned back towards the room, as if I could peer through the bandages and spy something I could use to open the door. The thought of crawling back down the stairs, of exploring the room on hands and knees to – maybe or maybe not – find a makeshift lock-pick made me want to throw up. But I eased myself down one step, bit back a yelp when pain stabbed up my backbone, and down another.

And then, all at once, the urgency, the distress, was gone, and I found myself wondering what the fuck I had thought I could do, even if I had been able to reach Fionn. And why had I been overcome by that strange feeling to the point I would push through intense pain to try to get to them? To Fionn who was angry at me, who probably wouldn't want my help anyway?

The idea of making my way back to the cot was even more overwhelming than the need to help Fionn had been. Moving was too much. So, I sat on the hard, cold stone, leaned against the wall, and wrapped my arms around myself. I thought I might cheer myself up by making a little flame appear in my cupped hands, like I used to do as a child when I was feeling upset about something. I wouldn't be able to see it, and it wouldn't do much to keep me warm, but the heat would be comforting on my chilled fingers.

But nothing happened. No heat. I resisted the urge to tear the bandages from my eyes so I could see if the flame had appeared, but I knew it hadn't. There was no heat, no scent of warmth, no tiny updraft of air, no crackle. Nothing.

I forced myself to breathe carefully, slowly, to reach down to the land, up to the sky, and around to the distant sea, to consciously connect with the three sacred Realms as I hadn't needed to since I first learned how to summon magic. I couldn't reach any of it. All I could feel was a cold wall where there should have been a rushing energy.

The Abbey wards had stolen my magic, had stolen a deep, essential part of myself. If I hadn't been in so much pain, I would have noticed sooner.

"Fuck," I said quietly, leaning my head back against the wall. I wanted to scream, to let panic overtake me, to march out and find the Abbess and demand to know how to get my magic back. But I was too tired, too bone-deep exhausted to do anything but force my breathing to calm. And I only managed that because panicking would be too painful.

I sat and waited and might even have slept a little, and finally, when I heard a distant rooster crow, felt the faint heat of the sun find its way through one of the deep windows to touch the skin on the back of my hand, I heard footsteps again.

Faint clicking, soft padding, the sounds of Fionn descending the stairs and crossing the floor filtered out past the door. Then the lock clicked, and the door hinges creaked, and Fionn said, "Oh!"

"Hi." I didn't move. I wasn't sure I *could* move. A thin breeze from somewhere higher up the tower carried the musky sweet scent of Fionn's skin to my nostrils, and I breathed it in.

"Why are you on the stairs?" asked Fionn, stepping carefully around me to bend and put a cool hand on my forehead.

"I'm sorry," I said.

"What?" Fionn sounded distracted, like they had much more on their mind than a displaced patient.

"I wanted to say I'm sorry." I turned my face towards Fionn's touch, but they'd already withdrawn their hand.

"You crawled up the stairs to apologize?" Fionn didn't sound convinced. They didn't sound like they wanted an apology, either.

"I woke up in the middle of the night." I considered my options. I could lie, make up some plausible reason I might be sitting here, and avoid the whole awkward truth about what I'd felt. And then when I was healed, I could leave and forget all about Fionn and go back to my normal life.

Or I could be honest and confess that I felt some kind of connection between us that I couldn't explain, that made no sense, and wait for Fionn to tell me I was imagining things, that whatever I thought I felt was a side-effect of my encounter with the Abbey wards.

But if the connection I thought I'd felt was real, if I *had* felt Fionn's distress, then the only choice was the truth.

"I felt… You were…" I stopped, not knowing how to phrase what I needed to say. "Fionn, I…"

"Branfionn," the healer said, coldly.

I would have stared at them if I could have. I lowered my face into my hands.

"I *felt* you, last night," I finally said, and Fionn's sharp inhale gave me the incentive to continue. "Something was causing you distress, and I wanted to make it stop."

"I'm sorry my feelings inconvenienced you," Branfionn said. "Now let's get you back to bed." They pulled my arm over their shoulder and hoisted me up.

It took me several breaths to recover from the agony that stabbed through every limb, but I managed not to scream, to only let out a hiss between my clenched teeth. I allowed Fionn to help me down the stairs, across the floor, and to the cot. They helped me lie down, and pulled the blanket over me, but didn't smooth it over my chest, or tuck it in around me.

When the ache subsided, I tried again. "I wanted to help you, Fionn. Branfionn. Healer. Seer. Whatever you want me to call you." I stumbled to a stop, then carried on. "I could *feel* it, feel *you.* We're connected somehow. I don't know what it means, but I wanted to help."

I bunched the edge of the blanket in my fists.

"And…" I hesitated again but then plunged on. "My magic's gone. I can't even make a flame in my hand." I held out my hand, palm up, as if to demonstrate. "It's a child's trick, and I can't even do that."

Fionn sighed, sounding exasperated. I heard them moving around near the big table, smelled herbs and water, and heard them move over to the hearth to start a fire to heat something.

"You haven't lost your magic," they said. "The Abbey wards don't allow any magic inside the walls."

"Not even healing?" I struggled to sit up when Fionn put a hand behind my neck, took the cup they pressed into my hands, and gulped the hot liquid. It burned, but I drank it all anyway, knowing it would make the ache bearable, and I let out a long breath as relief spread through my limbs and joints.

Fionn took the empty cup. "Was it bad? The pain?"

"I barely slept. I couldn't get comfortable. But I managed." I didn't want to lie, but I also didn't want Fionn to feel bad. I didn't know why I even cared, but I did. A lot.

"I should have given you more tea before I left."

"It's okay. I understand why you left. I didn't think. I'd never have made that stupid joke if I'd known you were bird folk."

Fionn was back at the table, moving things around as if gathering ingredients, but they paused. They said nothing for a heartbeat, two, then three. Then they replied, "Does it matter that you wouldn't have said it to my face if it's still something you think?" They resumed what they were doing, and I smelled the sudden sharpness of a crushed herb.

"No," I said. "You're right. But I don't think that. I don't think all bird folk are brainless and flighty. I don't *know* any Vogel besides you, and I only met a few others once, and they seemed intelligent enough."

Fionn moved towards the hearth again and metal clattered as they put something over the fire to heat.

"Then why would you say it at all?"

"I don't know." I turned my head on the pillow, facing towards Fionn even though I couldn't see them. "I guess… if I laughed at the jokes my fey cousins made about dumb, short-lived humans, then I could pretend I'm not half-human myself.

They could forget, I could forget, and I could fit in." I turned my face back to the ceiling, squeezed my eyes closed in shame. It was not a feeling I was accustomed to, and I had done things most people would feel more than a little shame for.

"And," I went on, "When my human half-brother said something about how effeminate and fussy the fey were, if I laughed he could ignore my pointed ears and pretend I was human too, and maybe he wouldn't gang up on me with his friends, to teach me a lesson about being too haughty by beating the crap out me."

"What does that have to do with hateful jokes about bird folk?" Fionn's voice was softer, understanding, maybe, but not forgiving. They moved away from the hearth, and I turned my face to follow.

"I guess I got used to pretending jokes like that actually *were* funny," I said. "And maybe… I thought if you were human or fey, that you'd laugh and we could… share the joke." I pushed the blanket aside and sat up. "But I should have known better. I shouldn't have said it, even if you were fey or human, or something else. And I'm sorry."

Fionn didn't answer, but they turned back to the cot and I felt them move closer, felt the faint stir of air and breathed in the scent of their skin.

"Tilt your head back and close your eyes," they said, and I did as I was instructed. I felt Fionn's slender fingers touch the bandage, unwind it carefully, and then withdraw.

"Don't open your eyes," they said. "I'm going to pry them open one at a time to put the drops in, and I need you to keep them closed otherwise. Okay?"

"Okay."

Fionn's fingers on my eyelid were gentle but strong. "This will burn, but you mustn't blink. The drops need to soak in to do any good."

"Okay," I said again. What could hurt as much as the stabbing pain in my legs last night?

So quickly I couldn't react if I'd wanted to, Fionn pried open my eye, dropped liquid in, and forced the eye closed again. They pressed the lid down with their thumb and massaged my eyeball.

"That wasn't so bad."

Fionn only snorted, then applied the drops to the other eye, put their thumb on the lid, and massaged. They kept their thumbs in place, one on each eye, pressing and rubbing my lids gently, and wrapped their fingers around the sides of my face.

It felt pleasant, even vaguely erotic. Until the burning started.

I was wrong. It wasn't as bad as the agony in my limbs. It was *worse*. I wasn't quite quick enough clamping my jaw shut to keep the scream in entirely, but I did manage to bite it off short. My eyes burned, growing hotter and hotter, radiating out from where Fionn's thumbs rested on my lids until it enveloped both entire eyeballs.

For a terrifying moment, I was sure Fionn was trying to blind me permanently, that I had been very, very wrong and they could never have been my friend because they were my enemy.

Then the sedative that had been in the pain-relieving tea finally took effect and I slumped over, letting darkness carry the burning away.

5
Fionn

IT WAS A RELIEF for me almost as much as it must have been a relief for Kiernan, when the sedative did its work, and the young fey lapsed into unconsciousness. I felt bad, of course, for not telling him about the extra ingredient in the tea, but I had been worried that Kiernan might refuse it; he seemed like the type who would rather suffer than relinquish control.

I eased Kiernan down onto the cot, swung his legs back up, and tugged the tunic into place, trying very hard not to look at his legs while I did so. How did a person end up with calves and thighs so perfectly sculpted?

When I had Kiernan covered with the blanket again, tucked in neatly, I turned back to my patient's eyes. I checked that the curtains were drawn over the high windows – all save the one that didn't close properly – and gently pried one eyelid open.

The white of Kiernan's eye was red and inflamed, but his pupil contracted against the relative brightness as I watched, and contracted even more when I brought a lit candle close.

The other eye was the same. I fetched a dish from the table and dropped a little balm from it into each of Kier's eyes. The redness faded as the liquid touched it.

I stroked Kiernan's forehead gently, watching as his face relaxed from a drugged state to real sleep. He had apologized and sounded genuinely upset to have said something so wrong. Perhaps he could be trusted after all, or at least he could be something like a friend.

Footsteps sounded in the hall, and I stepped hastily away Kier, and waited in silence as three novices brought pails of water and empty chamberpots, sloshing some of the water onto the floor, awkward with their eyes covered against a glimpse of the fey man on the cot.

When a junior sister deposited a tray on the table, I spoke up. "Your pardon, sister?" I said, clasping my hands in front of my abdomen and bowing my head, even though I knew she couldn't see me.

"Yes, Seer?" she answered, keeping her face directed at the floor.

"Could you inform the Abbess that I've had another vision, please?"

"Of course, Seer," she said, and turned to leave.

Once they were gone and the lock engaged, my shoulders slumped and I leaned on the table. I heard a noise behind me and turned to find Kiernan's vivid green eyes half open, watching me.

"Did you drug me, or did I pass out?" he said, voice groggy.

"A little of both." I forced myself to stand up straight. "I should have covered your eyes. Too much light is still dangerous."

"In a minute," said Kiernan. "I spent all my time conscious listening to your voice. I want to see what you look like." He didn't try to sit up, he just regarded me seriously, eyes moving over me and making me feel too warm.

I tried not to squirm. I made myself stare back, steady and calm.

"Well," I finally said. "Do I meet your approval?"

A slight quirk of the lips that wasn't quite a smile touched Kier's mouth. "I was right," he said. "You're as lovely as your voice."

"I'm told most men," I said tartly, "Wouldn't be terribly pleased to be called lovely."

Kiernan's lips quirked again, but this time it did seem to be a smile. "So you *are* a man. I wasn't sure."

I jerked my chin up a little. I'd never thought it would sting to have my masculinity questioned. "Does it matter?" It came out like a challenge.

"Not to me." Kiernan continued to look. "I can see why I couldn't tell you had wings. They're too small to stir the air much."

I looked away, something in my stomach aching. "Yes," I said. "That's me: useless visions, useless wings."

There was silence from Kiernan. When I tried to move past the cot to the hearth, he reached out and grasped my hand.

"I don't think useless is the word I'd use," he said.

"No?" I glanced back and tugged at my hand. He didn't let go. "What word would you use? Stunted? Ineffectual? *Decorative?*" I glared at the other young man.

"Beautiful," said Kiernan. "Breathtaking. Lovely, like the rest of you."

"Piss off," I tugged harder at my hand.

"So you *can* swear. I was beginning to wonder." He pulled back on my hand, forced me closer a step, then another. He still didn't sit up. "I'm not making fun of you. You *are* lovely.

Your eyes are lovely, and your hair – I've never seen a Vogel with long hair. And yes, your wings are lovely, too."

I stared back at him until I had to look away. There was nothing in Kiernan's eyes, or on his face, that said he was lying or poking fun. He seemed to be entirely sincere.

"Stop," I said, but I couldn't put much conviction in the word.

"And anyway, if your visions are so useless, why do you need to let the Abbess know whenever you have one?"

I tried once more to pull my hand away, but Kiernan laced our fingers together. "I don't tell her about all my visions," I said. Then I pressed my lips together. I shouldn't have said that. The Abbess had saved my life. Surely, I could trust her more that I could trust a stranger?

But Kiernan still didn't *feel* like a stranger.

He stroked his thumb over the back of my hand and I shivered. Just that simple touch was radiating heat through me again. "What visions do you keep from her?" he asked, his voice gone low and soft. I shivered again but hid it by pulling my hand sharply away. This time, he let go.

"That's none of your concern," I said, and regretted it when the openness in Kier's eyes was suddenly shuttered. I turned back to the table, where the tray the sisters had brought held bread and cheese, fruit, and a pot of tea.

"You must be hungry," I said.

"I am." It sounded like he meant hungry for more than food.

"Do you think you can walk?" I asked, without turning around.

"Let's find out," he said, and I heard the cot creak and my patient's sharp, pained inhale. "It hurts," he said, "but not as much as last night."

I still didn't turn. "Last night," I said. "You said you felt a… connection with me?"

"Yes." Kiernan's voice was closer. "I wanted to help you. I wanted to stop whatever was bothering you. I wanted…" He paused and I waited for him to go on, forcing myself not to hold my breath, not to turn around.

"You wanted?" I whispered, when he didn't continue. I felt the air stir against the feathers on my lower back, and then Kier's hand was there, just barely brushing against them. I couldn't keep my breath from going ragged, struggled to make it even again, to keep the pressure in my belly from growing. He had made a mean joke about my people and, even if he had apologized, I still shouldn't feel this way about him.

"I wanted *you*," Kiernan said, his voice as ragged as my breathing. Then he said, right in my ear. "I'm going to seduce you, pretty bird."

I whirled around, the voice from my vision and the one from just now joining into one and the same. "What?"

Kiernan was so close we were almost touching, and even though the fey barely came up to my chin, I still found myself intimidated. And very turned on.

"Goddess Above. I had a vision of that," I breathed.

It was Kiernan's turn to look surprised. "You had a vision of *me*?"

I could only stare.

"What?"

I stared some more, afraid to speak, to confess everything he had meant to me over the years.

"Fionn?"

"I…" I slipped past him and away, crossing the room to perch on the stool I used when I was spinning. "I've had visions of you since I was a boy," I finally admitted. "I think my *first* vision was of you."

He looked confused. "Why didn't you say something

sooner? Is that why I feel connected to you?"

"I don't know, Kiernan. I don't know anything. I only know that I've been here, away from the world, for thirty-three years, and for at least thirty of those years, I've been having visions of you. Sometimes I see things as they're happening. And sometimes I see things that happened in the past."

"And sometimes you see what hasn't happened yet."

"Visions of the future are uncertain, because there's no guarantee that they *will* happen, only that they *could*," I explained. "But yes, sometimes I have visions of what has yet to occur, of what could possibly occur."

"What have you *seen* of me? Have you *seen* my death?" Kiernan took a step closer, a fascinated look on his face.

I shook my head. "No, not your death." I looked at my hands, and when I looked up again, he was closer yet. "The first time I *saw* you in a vision, I was three. I don't remember much from that long ago, but I remember that vision."

"What did you *see*?" He stopped, looked like he was going to reach out, but then just stood still.

"You were a boy. Maybe six years old."

"You *saw* as it happened, then?"

"I suppose. I'm told that that's often the way with traumatic events. Ones that don't have world-shaking effects, at least." I sighed. I had never been good at explaining things.

"You saw six-year-old me being traumatized?" He tilted his head in curiosity, then his face went pale.

"Kiernan?" I watched him, concerned, wondering what *he* remembered, what he thought I'd *seen*.

"What did you see?" he said. "Tell me."

"A woman. Beautiful, frightening. She had antlers and long dark red hair. She was… angry, I think. She… she put her hand on your forehead and with her other hand…" I reached out towards Kiernan, not wanting to say any more. His jaw was tight, his eyes bright. He held very still.

"Say it," he said.

"She took hold of one of your antlers," I whispered. "They were only little spikes, your antlers. You were only a small boy. And she… she… wrenched… and tore your antler off." I blinked, surprised at the tears running from my eyes. I had cried when I had *seen* the vision as a child, too, after I was done screaming. It was the only time I could remember the Abbess not punishing me for crying. "And then she did the same with the other." I closed my eyes, not wanting to remember, knowing how much worse it must be for him, to whom it had actually *happened*. I opened my eyes again to look at Kier, who did *not* cry, but whose face went harder and harder, until he might have been made of stone.

"And after that?" Kier's voice had gone gentle, and suddenly he was close, one hand stroking my hair, the other wiping tears from my face.

"That's all I saw." I sat stiffly, then allowed myself to relax, to let him tuck my face against his chest.

"She combed my hair over the stubs where my antlers had been," he said. "And she combed it over the points on my ears." His voice was still soft. "And she put me on a horse and sent me away to live with my father." He stroked my hair and I buried my face into his tunic front, breathing in the salty warm scent of him.

"That was the first time my mother got bored with me," he said. "I lived with my father for three years, until my antlers grew back, and grew too big I couldn't hide them anymore and my half-brother decided to beat me for it almost every day." He slid both hands into my hair and tilted my head up to meet his eyes.

I blinked away the rest of my tears and faced his bright

green gaze.

"When I was nine, I stole a horse," he said. "And rode back to Morven Forest. My mother acted like I had never been gone."

I reached up to touch one of his antlers and he jerked away, then relaxed and bent his head to allow me to touch him.

"I should warn you," he said. "My antlers are more sensitive than you might think."

"I'll be careful," I said and stoked very gently with just the tips of my fingers.

"That feels good," he said, and bent his head closer, until I could feel his breath on my face. I stared into his eyes, captivated by the color. The green of fir needles, of holly leaves in shadow. The green of the deep forest.

"Did you mean it?" I whispered. "When you said you were going to seduce me?"

"Yes," he said. "Unless you tell me you don't want me to." His words made my breath hitch and my manhood twitch and harden in my sheath. I clenched my belly muscles tight as his lips got closer.

And there were footsteps in the hall and a rap on the door. I almost fell backwards off my stool, but Kiernan caught me.

"You're practicing walking," I said frantically, grabbing a walking stick from a rack near one of the cabinets and thrusting it into his hand.

I slipped away towards the door, closing my eyes as I walked, reaching for calm, applying one of the Abbess's breathing exercises.

At the door, I said, "Yes?"

A voice replied, "The Abbess will see you. I'm to bring you to her."

"Let me get my cloak." I turned to see Kiernan hobbling around the room, leaning on the stick. "Have some breakfast,"

I said, gesturing at the tray. "And don't leave your eyes uncovered too long. They still need rest."

Then I reached down my cloak from its peg by the door and slung it on, letting the hood cover my hair. When it was on, I was a shapeless gray figure, even my bare feet, even my wings, hidden. Then I waited for the sister to open the door.

THE SISTER LED me down the hall and outside, to the Abbess's rooms at the base of the central tower.

I knocked and waited. A moment later the door opened and the Abbess stepped out, thin and severe in her coarse gray habit, her only adornment a large silver pendant of the moon that seemed to change phases as the light shifted, waxing and waning before my eyes.

As a child, I had asked when I would get such a pendant and was disappointed to learn that because I was a boy, the answer was "never."

"Branfionn," said the Abbess. She gestured for me to follow as she walked away from the tower and towards a set of stairs that led to the top of the wall.

"Abbess."

"You've had a vision," she said. "Am I to assume it's not another one of your silly glimpses of the life of some spoiled fey brat?"

"It was not, Abbess."

"What, then? Something useful, at last?" Her voice was sharp. I didn't think she was intentionally cruel, but I'd never been certain. I reminded myself that she had saved my life, that without her, I would have died, trapped in my egg.

"It was a vision of the past, Abbess," I said.

"So not useful then," she said, and sighed, as if she had been infinitely patient and was just now becoming short. "Let's hear it, then."

"I *saw* my mother, Abbess." If I hadn't been following so closely, I might have missed the hesitation in her stride.

She led the way up onto the wall, above the roof of the main dormitory. Below were the laundry and the bathhouse, and the so-called sauna where I now knew I had been born.

"Did you?" she said, her voice neutral. "And you're so sure it was her, and not some other bird woman?"

"I *saw* her killed," I said. "And an egg cut from her body."

"How unfortunate for her. And how do you think you know it was your mother?"

"It was my egg," I said. "It was me."

"Again, how can you be certain?" The Abbess's voice betrayed a hint of annoyance, and something else I couldn't identify.

"I *saw* the egg hatch, Abbess," I said. I took care to not seem to be very concerned, to be merely curious. "Here, in the sauna." I paused. I had believed, after I had had the vision, that I should be grateful to the Abbess, but walking behind her now, she made me uneasy. She had always made me uneasy.

"You saved my life, Abbess," I said, letting no emotion into my words. "I am forever grateful for that. For my life here at the Abbey."

We approached another stair and began to descend again, back to the courtyard.

"Don't forget that, my little seer," said the Abbess, never mind that I was taller than her, and had been for years. "You owe your life to this Abbey."

"Yes, Abbess," I said.

"I appreciate you bringing this vision to me."

I bowed when we reached the bottom of the stairs.

"Tell me how your patient fares," she said.

"Well enough. Still in pain, but it is much less. His eyes are recovering. I think he can make it to the bathhouse tonight. The hot water would be good for him."

"Very well," said the Abbess. "I will send some sisters to fetch you when the rest are asleep. You will not loiter too long, however."

"Of course, Abbess."

"Has he told you why he attempted to get in? Is he a thief we need sent to the King's guard for imprisonment?"

"I don't believe so, Abbess, but he doesn't remember."

"Are you sure, or does he merely not want to admit guilt?"

"I believe he is beginning to trust me, Abbess. I don't think he's lying when he says he remembers nothing after reaching the gates, and nothing about why he came here in the first place."

"Well, he couldn't lie, could he?" she said, and I bit my tongue to keep from speaking. I should tell her that Kiernan was only half fey and that he could, in fact, lie. But I said nothing. I wasn't even sure why. My loyalties were at war in my mind. I *should* trust the Abbess, who had saved me and raised me and given me a home. But I *did* trust Kiernan, who wanted to seduce me, and who was the last person I ought to place confidence in.

"No, Abbess," was all I said.

She stopped in front of her tower door and paused. I waited to be dismissed, head bowed. I startled when she put a finger under my chin and made me look into her eyes.

"There are ways a seer can help a person recover a damaged memory," she said.

"Oh?" I kept hope from creeping into my voice. "Can you teach me?"

"Alas, no. I am not a seer. But try your mindfulness

exercises, your breathing techniques. See if you can look into this young fey's mind and extract the memory that will tell me what he was doing at my gate."

She kept me fixed with her cold gray stare a few heartbeats longer, then stepped away, back into her tower, and shut the door in my face.

6
Kiernan

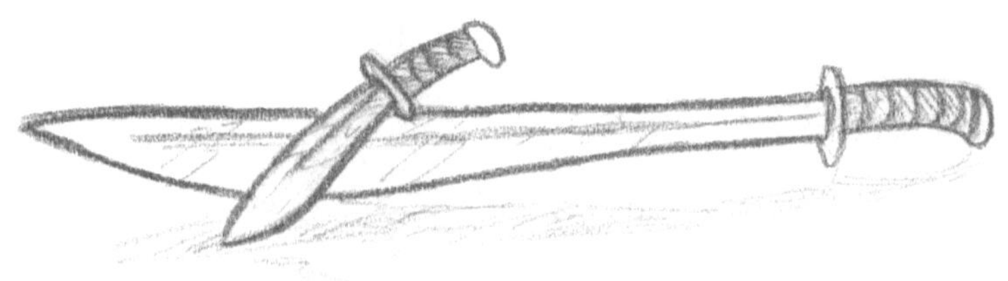

WHEN FIONN had gone, I hobbled over to the table, dragged out a stool, and sat down. I laid a thick piece of cheese on a slice of bread, added a handful of tiny strawberries, and took a bite, chewing while I looked around the room.

It looked about how I had expected it to look, going by the things I had heard and smelled while blinded. It was a rounded tower room with one flat wall, one door into the rest of the Abbey, and another door at the top of the stairs.

Narrow, deep windows pierced the wall close to the high ceiling, and shelves and cabinets stood at intervals around the room. There was the table I sat at, the cot, and Fionn's tall stool and basket of spinning. Across the room from the door, a screen hid a table with a washbasin and a chamberpot.

Everything was tidy and put away, almost too neat. I wondered if Fionn was simply a very organized person, or if the sisters had beat it into him from infancy.

The only things that had been left out on the table besides the breakfast tray were a small pile of coins and an ornate key.

I picked up the key and turned it over in my hands. It seemed familiar, but I couldn't have said why. I put it down and reached for more bread and cheese and poured myself a mug of tea. It was cold, but it tasted good and I was thirsty. The sedative Fionn had given me had left my mouth feeling sticky inside.

Breakfast eaten, I looked around for something to occupy myself. I should cover my eyes and lie on the cot like a good patient, but I had never liked being still for too long. As a boy, I had forever been running off into the woods to explore, and my lessons with a teacher – whether at my mother's court or my father's stronghold – were tedious at best, even if my teachers said I was intelligent enough to excel if only I would pay attention.

The only lessons I had enjoyed were the ones about battles and strategy. And later, the more physical ones, like sword skills and knife-fighting, unarmed combat or endurance.

I fiddled with the key again, then got up and wandered over to Fionn's spinning basket, tossing the key from hand to hand. The drop spindle was plain wood, unadorned but smooth with use. The fibre in the basket was cloud silk in a deep honey-gold shade that would fetch a good price. Not that the Abbey would see any of that money. They would be paid for the spinning of it, but whomever had provided the silk would take it back and sell it on, or perhaps pay another craftsperson to weave it into cloth. Cloth that would adorn only the wealthiest and most esteemed fey noble. I wondered if Fionn knew what it was he was spinning, or if he would even care.

I wandered to the stairs, then climbed them slowly, refusing to let pain keep me from moving. At the top, I examined the lock, then the key I still held in my hand. I fitted the key into the lock and turned it, expecting nothing. It clicked, and the door swung open a handspan.

I stared at the door, ajar and unlocked. Had I actually *heard* Fionn lock it this morning? I couldn't remember. I pulled the door to and turned the key again. The lock clicked.

"Shit," I said, then shook my head. Fionn had simply forgotten to take the key with him, that was all. Even the most organized person could forget something once in a while.

I thought about opening the door again, of stepping through into Fionn's rooms. I was intensely curious, but as a very private person who had seldom had the luxury of space to myself, I knew how much Fionn probably valued his privacy, and I wouldn't violate it, no matter how much I wanted to know if Fionn's personal space was as tidy as his infirmary. Was it a sparse place? Or was it cluttered and messy?

I pulled the key out of the lock and went back down the stairs before my curiosity could get the better of me. I was determined to see the inside of those rooms, to find out how many chairs Fionn had, and how soft his bed was, but I would do it by getting myself invited in.

I dropped the key back onto the table and poked at the coins. They were all small denominations of common Islish currency and told me nothing. Each Monarchy minted their own coins – it was a matter of prestige – but they also shared a common currency to make trade easier. Just like language: each people had their own, but everyone also spoke Islish.

Finally, with nothing else to do, I started opening drawers and cupboards, but I had no idea what most of the herbs and preparations were for, and the small sharp tools I found weren't good for anything other than preparing medicines.

At last, completely bored, I went behind the screen and used the chamberpot, then washed my hands. The water was cold, but there was more in buckets next to the door, some of it warm. There was a bar of soap and a pile of washcloths next to the basin.

I turned my head and sniffed an armpit. I didn't *stink*, but I didn't exactly smell fresh, either. So I poured warm water, stripped off the tunic Fionn had dressed me in, and began to wash.

I was just thinking about how I had almost kissed Fionn when I finished washing my belly and moved on to my groin. The brush of the cloth and the memory of Fionn's half-closed eyes made my cock twitch and I wondered if I would have enough time to jerk off, to ease the ache of desire, before Fionn came back. I certainly didn't want to get caught touching myself, though the thought of what Fionn's face would look like when he realized I was stroking my own cock just about did make me want to be found, after all.

And why the hell had I walked up behind Fionn and told him I was going to seduce him, right into his pretty pointed ear? I wanted to, for sure, and I wasn't above being forward, but pushy didn't seem the right approach for Fionn. Subtle was probably a better choice, yet the way Fionn had *reacted* — not insulted, or disgusted, or afraid. No, he had seemed aroused. And I was sure Fionn had wanted that kiss that had almost happened as much as I had wanted it.

I finished washing my legs and feet and was just wrapping my fingers around my erection when I heard Fionn's soft clicking footsteps in the hall, and the tower door opened. I cursed under my breath — no relief for me, then — and grabbed the tunic to pull it over my head.

"Kiernan?" said Fionn.

"Just washing up," I answered. I heard the door lock us in, heard Fionn remove his cloak and hang it by the door. I picked up my wet washcloth and towel to put into the hamper and stepped around the screen.

Fionn was standing by the table, chewing thoughtfully on a slice of bread. He looked like there were a lot of thoughts churning around in his mind, things that caused his eyebrows to draw together and a crease to form between them.

"You forgot to take your key with you," I said and Fionn looked up, a question in his silver eyes.

"I don't have a key to the outer door," he said, swallowing his bread and taking a sip of tea.

"The key to your rooms, I mean." I picked up the key from next to the pile of coins and handed it over. "I… I tried it. I didn't go in. I was just curious what it was for. And bored."

Fionn looked at the key in his hand then back at me. "This one isn't mine," he said. "I found it in your pocket when I put your clothes in the hamper to be washed. The coins, too."

I sat down. "Why would I have a key to your rooms in my pocket?"

Fionn frowned, took a key out of his own pocket, and compared the two. "They're similar," he said, "But not exact." He held them up. The teeth almost matched, but not perfectly. He studied them, looked at me, then glanced at the door. He drew the curtain aside, peered out, then fitted the ornate key into the lock, and turned.

The lock clicked open and Fionn stood without moving, staring out the window into the hall. Then he re-locked the door, pulled the curtain across, and turned around.

"Try your key," I said.

Fionn tried, and nothing happened. He stared at both keys, then at me.

I stared back. "Why did I have that? Are you sure it was mine? It didn't…?"

"Didn't what? Appear in your pocket when I checked to see if there was anything there that shouldn't be washed alongside your trousers?"

"But why? What the hell am I doing here?"

Fionn walked back to the table, sat down, and set the key next to the coins. He layered a piece of cheese on a slice of bread, but then left it on the plate. "Are you sure you don't remember anything else about why you were here?"

I shook my head.

"The Abbess said seers can sometimes help people recover memories," Fionn said.

"I've heard that."

"Do you know how?"

I shook my head again. "I saw our seer do it once, when one of the guards was found unconscious at his post."

"What did she do? The seer?"

"She put her hands on his face. Like this." I reached across the table, put my thumbs side-by-side in the middle of Fionn's forehead and arranged my fingers along his temples and cheekbones.

"She closed her eyes," I said. "And then, I don't know." I let my hands drop back to the tabletop. "It took a while to work. A couple of hours later, they found the guard trying to sneak away. It turned out he had gotten drunk and fallen asleep at his post, and then forgot all about it."

"Do you want me to try that on you?"

"Yes." I said it so quickly, so strongly, that Fionn stared at me for a moment. He nodded.

"Okay," he said. "Tonight, we're allowed to go to the bathhouse. The heat will be good for your healing. After that, when we're sure everyone is asleep, we'll go up to the tower roof, and I'll try… something. See if I can help untangle your memory."

"Why not now?"

"Because…" Fionn hesitated, poked at the bread and

cheese, and sighed. "Because sometimes I think the Abbess can see everywhere the Abbey wards encompass, and only has to choose to focus her attention there." He studied his hands. "The wards are cast from the roof of the central tower, and I think… I'm pretty sure they don't cover the roofs of the other towers."

"That must make it very uncomfortable when you want to jerk off." I grinned, but Fionn didn't smile back. "What?" I said. "Don't tell me you've never touched yourself. Thirty-three years alone here and you've never –"

"Of course I have," he said sharply, cheeks bright pink. I let my grin soften when Fionn couldn't meet my eyes. I felt a little bad for teasing him. Again.

"Under the covers," Fionn said. "When I know she's busy. Or on the roof. Not that it's any of your business."

"It could be my business," I said softly. "If you wanted it to be." I smiled wider when Fionn blushed again.

Then I touched the back of Fionn's hand. "I'm sorry," I said. "You're just so pretty when you blush." Fionn's eyes snapped up and I almost had to look away from the glaring silver gaze. "Why don't you trust the Abbess?" I asked gently, knowing he might welcome a change of subject.

"I should," Fionn said. "I'm only alive because of her." He told me about his recent vision and didn't pull away when I took both of his hands and held them, stroking them with my thumbs. Fionn's skin was so soft it was hard to resist touching him, and his fingers were slender and elegant. I wanted to put them in my mouth.

"But the Abbess frightens me, too," Fionn said. "And…" He hesitated and looked away.

"And what?" I kept my voice soft, trying not to be pushy again.

"And I don't want to tell her anything about you, to share

you. I… I want you for myself." He blushed again at that and pulled his hands away.

I sighed, missing the feel of Fionn's fingers against my own already. "Okay," I said. "Tonight. So what do we do in the meantime?"

"Rest. Cover your eyes again. Wait."

DARKNESS WAS A LONG time coming, but eventually it crept in and the Abbey fell silent. I lay on my back on the cot, bandage draped over my eyes, waiting. Fionn perched on his stool and turned raw cloud silk into thread.

I sat up and pulled aside the bandage, watching Fionn's clever fingers, unfaltering on the thread, never letting it draw out too thick or too thin. It was mesmerizing. I could watch him spin all day, except I kept thinking about those fingers touching me, not the silk.

"Not many have the skill to spin cloud silk," I said, and Fionn glanced up, continuing his work by feel.

"I've had a lot of time to practice," he replied.

I looked away from Fionn's hands to the fall of silver hair over his shoulder. "Do you know what cloud silk is? Where it comes from?"

He looked away to wind thread onto the shaft of his spindle and set it whirling again. "From a moth, I assume. Or a spider."

He didn't know. I tried to think of the best way to tell him, and wondered how he would feel about that knowledge once he had it.

"Bird folk all wear their hair shorn close," I said, deciding on an indirect approach. "I was surprised to see yours long."

"Would you prefer it short?" Fionn said, watching his spindle. A bit of pink touched his cheekbones. Was he flirting?

I chuckled. "I like it long," I said. "I want to bury my hands in it." I smiled wider when Fionn's spindle wobbled on the end of its thread and he had to grab for it and set it spinning straight again. His cheeks grew pinker.

"I used to think the Vogel kept their hair short to better show off the feathers around their faces."

Fionn glanced up again. "I know so little about my own people," he murmured.

"I'm told the patterns of feathers mean different things, like a whole language that's never spoken out loud. And there are craftspeople who specialize in making adornments to supplement the people's natural feathers."

"What kinds of things might they say?" Fionn asked, winding on a length of thread and starting another.

"One might tell that the wearer is a married woman," I said. "Another might say the person is single and looking for a partner of either sex, or none."

"I wonder if my feathers say anything."

I studied Fionn's face. He only had a smattering of feathers that kept his hair naturally swept back. I had no idea how to read them, but I said, "Probably that you're a single male virgin just reaching his age of majority, who prefers…?" I paused, left the rest as a question. Something about the word "virgin" plucked at my memory, but nothing surfaced. It made Fionn frown.

The young Vogel looked away again, back at his hands and his spinning. "Men," he said softly. "Who prefers men." His cheeks flushed again.

I smiled. "Me, too," I said, though really I preferred anyone who saw me as myself and not as my mother's or my father's son.

"You said you *used* to think that's why bird folk kept their hair short," Fionn pointed out. He was quick. I hoped it wouldn't take much for him to figure out where I was leading, unless he didn't want to see it.

"As it turns out," I said. "Short hair isn't a fashion choice."

Fionn glanced up again, and now I felt myself flushing at the other's scrutiny.

"The Vogel are a vassal monarchy to the Alfar," I said, and Fionn nodded, frowning.

"So the history books in the Abbey library aren't *that* out of date, at least."

"No," I said, "I suppose not. It's been that way for some time." I paused, considering, then said, "The bird folk, the Vogel Monarchy, is required to pay a yearly tribute to the Alfar Monarchy. It's… my mother says it's to keep them from getting too rich. My father says it's to ensure they remember their place."

"It keeps them poor and dependent," said Fionn, winding more thread onto his spindle. He appeared calm, but I thought it was just a facade, that something else lurked in his thoughts.

"Yes," I said softly. I took a deep breath. "Part of that tribute is cloud silk. It's only produced by the bird folk, *can* only be produced by bird folk, but they aren't allowed to keep any for themselves for their own use. They aren't even allowed to spin it for themselves, because that would make it worth more, would give it more value, so they would need to pay less to the Alfar."

"That's horrible," said Fionn. "There are enough resources on the Isle for everyone; why can't the Monarchies just share equally?"

I shrugged. "Everyone wants more than they have. The Alfar, the Sidhe, the Huldr, they all have the power to take more from others." I got up from the cot, walked painfully over to Fionn, and touched his hair hesitantly.

He didn't pull away, he just kept spinning, so I stroked his hair. "Do you know that your hair isn't really hair?" I said.

"Of course," he said. "Vogel hair is more like feathers, fine long filaments. Filamenta is the proper term."

"Under the right circumstances," I said, "The right handling, filamenta can lock together and make a very thin, strong thread."

His spindle wobbled again, and he didn't seem to notice.

"Fionn," I said, stroking his hair again. I relished the feel of the soft strands under my fingers. "Each year, every citizen of the Eyrie and the entire Vogel Monarchy is required to cut their hair to within two fingers' breadth of their scalp. Those who don't comply are imprisoned and their hair is shorn by force. They present their hair to the king, and there is a big parade, and then the king uses it for tribute to the Alfar Monarchy."

The thread Fionn was spinning snapped, and the spindle hit the floor with a clatter and rolled away. He gasped like he couldn't get enough air, but he didn't look up.

"All this time," he whispered. "I've been contributing to the subjugation of my own people. I've been spinning their fucking *hair* into a luxury thread for rich fucking fey."

Two swear words in one sentence, but Fionn pronounced them as if they were any other word, and only the trembling in his muscles told me how distressed he was. That and I could *feel* it in my belly, just as I had the night before.

"I'm sorry," I said.

"You're sorry for a lot of things," he said, standing and moving abruptly away. I was left with three long strands of silver caught between my fingers. I wound it around and around and it seemed to adhere to itself, making a shining ring around my finger, bright against my skin.

"I would change it if I could," I said. "The world. I would change it all."

Fionn looked back at me, chin high. Then his shoulders sagged. "I believe you." He looked at the nearly empty basket of golden cloud silk. "It's so cruel," he said.

"The world is cruel," I answered. "Perhaps you should be glad you haven't had to see it."

"I have seen it," Fionn said. He took a step closer, and his foot bumped the spindle and sent it rolling farther away. He ignored it. "Some of it. In visions." He took another step. "Is everything in the world terrible?" One more step and I took a step, too, and we stood face to face. I looked up into Fionn's bright eyes, saw confusion and longing and hurt.

"Not everything," I said, and reached up to stroke his cheek, trace the shape of his ear, and the curve of his lower lip.

"Some things in the world are very nice," I whispered, and his lips parted under my touch. I was just about to pull his face down to mine when there was a tap at the door.

"Healer?" said a voice. "Seer? We're to escort you to the bathhouse now."

7
Fionn

WE LEFT THE TOWER covered crown to sole in concealing gray robes. I could have worn my usual cloak, which was nearly as concealing, but I didn't want Kiernan to feel like he was being singled out, even though he very obviously was.

Two senior sisters led the way, and two followed, to make sure we went directly from the tower to the bathhouse. The shortest route would have been across the courtyard, but that would have meant passing by the Abbess's tower and it seemed even the senior sisters preferred to avoid her scrutiny whenever possible.

So instead we followed the long, dim hallways of the Abbey, down one side of the blocky structure, around a corner, and down another. Only then did we emerge, to follow the wall behind the central tower to the bathhouse.

At the door, one of the sisters gestured to the blindfolded junior sister who scurried along behind her, clutching her robe hem, and the younger woman said, "Three turns of the glass, and we will escort you back."

I nodded and opened the door for Kiernan. When it was closed behind us, the lock scraped across and we were alone. A large time-glass sat in a recess next to the door and I lifted it and turned it over, and the sand began to fall.

"We'll have to watch it and turn it again when it empties," I said, then took off my robe and hung it up.

Visiting the bathhouse was one of the few genuine pleasures of Abbey life. There was a deep pool with benches lining both sides, and the hot water that came up from the earth flowed through it, ensuring the water was always fresh and clean. There was a shelf of soaps and lotions, mostly unscented, but still lovely on the skin. I always came late at night, or sometimes very early in the morning, so I could be alone. I could almost relax here.

"That looks heavenly," said Kiernan, stripping off his robe and hanging it next to mine. I turned away as he began to pull his tunic over his head.

"Does my naked body offend you, pretty bird?" Kiernan said and I looked sharply up. He was grinning.

"Stop," I said. "You know very well it doesn't." I pointed at a laundry bin. "Put your dirty tunic there. There are clean clothes on the shelves for after."

Kiernan did as he was told. "Are you not bathing?" he said, gesturing at my still-dressed state. "Or do you not want me to see you unclothed?"

I jerked my chin up, felt my cheeks flush. "I don't really care," I said. It wasn't true, but I wouldn't let him know that his gaze made me feel flushed all over, made me wonder if my body was nice to look at or unappealing. I'd never had anyone to compare myself to before, and next to him, I was too thin and too tall. Too pale. Too bird-like.

I turned towards the laundry bin, stripped off my tunic, and tossed it in, relaxing a bit when I heard water splash and

Kiernan sigh in relief as he sank into the hot water. I stepped out of my trousers and turned around to find his deep green gaze watching my every motion.

"What?" I said, the word coming out belligerent. I didn't care.

Kiernan grinned. Again. "You're lovely," he said. His eyes drifted lower and I forced myself to move, to step towards the pool where I could hide under the water. I stopped again when Kiernan's eyes paused and stared.

"What?"

Kiernan shrugged. "I guess I thought, when he said you were a man, you meant physically, that you'd have…" He stopped and looked up at my face. "It doesn't matter. I still think you're lovely."

I clenched my jaw and stepped into the water. "I *do* have," I said. "Vogel sex organs are kept inside." I put one hand flat over my lower belly muscles, where my sheath opening was. "Until we need them."

Kiernan's gaze followed my hand, studied me. I slipped under the water, forcing him to look back up at my face.

"You keep your cock put away until you need it?" Kiernan said. "That seems very practical." He leaned back and stretched out his legs. The pool was wide enough that his shorter legs didn't reach all the way across. Even I couldn't quite extend a leg all the way to the other side. "Except for one thing."

"What's that?" I said, closing my eyes and trying to relax now that Kiernan wasn't inspecting me.

"How do you piss?"

My eyes snapped open again. "What?"

"When you need to urinate, do you have to take your cock out? That doesn't seem so practical."

"Have you ever had a bird shit on you?" I said sharply, the

forbidden swear feeling daring on my tongue so close to the Abbess's tower, even though my companion seemed to swear with everything that came out of his mouth.

"Who hasn't?"

"Have you noticed that part of it is white and part dark?"

"Not that I make a point of inspecting bird shit, but okay."

"The dark part is feces, and the white part is urine. Bird folk elimination is the same."

Kiernan considered that information. "So, you piss out your ass?"

"Something like that."

"Can I see it?"

I closed my eyes again. "You want to see my urine? Or my feces?" I knew very well that was not what Kiernan was asking, but I couldn't resist making him ask outright. I wanted to hear the filthy word. I wanted to make Kiernan ask to see my hidden parts.

"No, thank you," he said. "I want to see your cock." He paused, as if waiting for me to react, but I kept my eyes closed, and somehow managed to keep breathing evenly. "It seems only fair," he said. "You've seen mine."

I squeezed my eyes shut tighter, pretending to be unconcerned, but his blunt statement made me twitch inside my sheath. I *had* seen Kiernan's manhood, but I had tried very hard not to look at it.

"It only comes out when it's erect," I finally said. "When I'm aroused."

A ripple of water lapping at my chin told me Kiernan had moved, but I didn't realize how close he was until I opened my eyes again. He stood, the water up to his chest, and leaned a hand on the edge of the pool on either side of my head.

"I can take care of that for you, pretty bird."

I felt the pressure increase behind my belly muscles, felt

the seam of my sheath strain.

"Stop," I said, barely above a whisper. "I told you the Abbess can see anywhere the wards cover."

"You said you thought *maybe* she could." Kier ducked his head so his breath whispered against my neck and I shivered despite the warmth of the bath.

I looked across the room, anywhere but at Kiernan. "The glass," I said. The sand was getting close to running out, and it needed to be turned.

"Already?" Kiernan straightened up and climbed slowly out of the pool, stiffness still evident in his movements.

I watched, pretending not to, studying how his muscles moved under his skin, noticing how his buttocks bunched and relaxed. The pressure in my belly increased and I pressed both hands down.

When Kiernan turned around from adjusting the glass, I had to force myself to look away from his erection. He didn't seem the least bit embarrassed by it. In fact, he hardly seemed to notice.

I stared at the ripples on the surface of the water until he sat back down across from me.

"What are you afraid of?" he asked. "The Abbess? You're not an acolyte of the Moon. What can she do to you?" His voice was gentle.

I shook my head. "You haven't had to live here. The Abbess can be… terrifying."

"So leave," said Kiernan.

"And go where? Do what? I know nothing of the world outside these walls."

"Go to the Eyrie. By Isle law, you should be at the Vogel King's court anyway. If he knew you were here… If *anyone* knew you were here, that's where you'd be sent."

"I'm alive because of the Abbess," I said. It had seemed so

clear, after I had the vision of my egg, of my birth.

Kiernan leaned back against the wall of the pool, and I felt the other man's foot brush against my own, then scoop under, and suddenly he was leaning forward, my ankle in his hands.

"What are you doing?" I tried to pull my foot away, but he held it still, balanced my heel on his knee, and shifted his grip. Then he dug his fingers into the pads of my toes. "Goddess Above," I whispered. It almost hurt, but it felt *good*.

"Have you never had anyone touch you in kindness?" Kiernan said, working his thumbs over the bottom of my foot until I wanted to slide under the water and melt away.

I didn't answer. I *couldn't* answer. "That feels nice," I finally managed. I didn't try to pull away when he let go of my foot and pulled the other onto his knee and rubbed it.

Then one of his thumbs slipped between my toes and a shivery sensation stabbed from my foot all the way up my leg to my crotch. I sat up with a jerk.

"Sorry," he said. "Does that tickle?" He slid his thumb between my toes again, slowly.

I swallowed, hard. My erection was pressing so firmly against the opening of my sheath I wasn't sure I could keep it in much longer. "No," I said, breathless. "It doesn't tickle. It…" I had to stop talking or risk letting out a moan. Weakly, I tried to pull my foot away.

Kiernan looked confused, and then realization came over his face and turned it wicked.

"Branfionn, do you have an erogenous zone between your toes?"

I clenched my teeth, then carefully unclenched them. "I don't know what that means," I said, though I was pretty sure I could figure it out from the context.

His thumb slid between my toes again. "Does me touching you here turn you on?" he said. "Do you want me to stop?"

"Yes," I gasped. I supposed I'd never really touched myself between the toes before, except maybe when washing them before bed. "And no."

He rubbed again, gently, and I felt my sheath seam part. I pressed my hands over it and pulled my foot suddenly away.

"But you mustn't. Not here." I stood suddenly, climbed out of the pool to turn the glass, and when I got back in, I sat as far as I could from Kiernan.

"I want to kiss you, pretty bird," he said.

I opened my mouth to answer, but he stopped me. "I know, not here. I just want you to know."

I looked at him across the pool. "I wonder how many other people you've said that to."

He shrugged. "A lot, I suppose. I've kissed a lot of people. Fucked a lot." He closed his eyes, then opened them again. "I like fucking."

I looked away.

"If you'll let me, I'll show you why."

I couldn't answer that. I wanted to. I wanted something more than visions of what *might* be to get me though the lonely days at the Abbey. But I also didn't want to be one more conquest for Kiernan to include in the words "a lot."

"You should wash," I said, gesturing at the shelf of soap. "Before our time runs out." I selected a bottle for myself and ducked under the water to wet my hair, then worked the liquid soap into it. When I sat up from rinsing, I saw him doing the same.

Then we dried off, dressed in fresh tunics and trousers, put our long concealing robes on, and waited for the sisters to let us out.

Just as the lock snapped open, Kiernan reached out and touched my arm. "Later," he said softly, "On the roof. I want to make you feel good."

Then the door opened, and I had no time to answer.

KIERNAN HEADED FOR the stairs as soon as we were back in the tower and the lock snapped into place, but I stopped him with a hand on his arm.

"Wait," I said. "Wait until the sisters have had a chance to fall asleep."

"Why? Surely they know you go to the roof."

"They know. I just don't want… I don't want the Abbess to know I took *you* there." I was so conflicted I wanted to scream, but I *was* certain I wanted to keep my feelings for Kiernan a secret from the Abbess.

He cocked his head but didn't ask any more questions. He sat at the bottom of the stairs and watched me pull a tunic out of the laundry hamper and stuff a cloak inside it.

"What are you doing, pretty bird?"

"Don't call me that," I said.

"Why not? You are."

"I'm making a dummy to put on the cot."

"So if the Abbess decides to spy, it'll look like I'm asleep down here."

"Yes."

"And if she's watching right now? And sees you deceiving her? Won't she want to come and see what's happening?"

I stopped what I was doing and smoothed my hands over the blanket with the dummy tucked beneath, as I had smoothed the blanket over Kiernan's chest.

"I have to hope she only looks once in a while," I said. I didn't want to think about the Abbess watching my every move. If I thought about that, I would be paralyzed. I adjusted the blanket, stepped back, and turned to Kier. "I couldn't bear it if I let myself believe I have no privacy at all." Then I stepped around him and led the way up the stairs. "Quickly now," I said.

I could almost feel his curiosity as we passed through the sitting room, but I paused only to pull the blanket off the couch and then led the way up the second stairway. In the bedroom, I took the quilt from the bed and kept going, forcing him to follow or be left behind.

On the roof, I closed the door behind him, spread out the blankets, and sat cross-legged. He sat facing me, like an attentive student.

"I really don't know how to… to fix your memory," I said. "But I'll try."

Kiernan nodded and held up a hand. A tiny flame danced in his palm, and I felt my breath catch. Magic. I had read of magic, of course, but I had never seen it. It was forbidden in the Abbey, prevented by the Abbey's wards.

"You were right," he said, smiling at the look on my face. "The wards must not cover the roof." He closed his hand over the flame, then held both hands out, cupped together, and a bluish light gathered in his palms like water.

"It's beautiful." I reached out to touch but made myself stop.

Kiernan smiled wider. "Hold out your hands, just like this," he said.

I echoed the posture, hands held out, cupped palms up and together, like I was scooping up water to drink. He poured the glow out of his hands into mine. It tingled but didn't burn.

"It's called wisplight," he said. "It's the same kind of light will o' the wisps use to lure unwary travelers into the swamp." He moved his hands away and the light stayed pooled in my palms. "Only I won't drown you and devour you." He leaned forward, tipped my chin up with one finger, and breathed into my ear. "I might devour you," he said, making my heart beat suddenly faster. "But I'll keep you alive so I can do it again."

I trembled and the wisplight dribbled out between my fingers and disappeared.

"Don't," I said.

"Why not?" Kiernan traced my cheekbone and I felt my skin flush in response. "She can't see us here."

"I'm…"

"Are you afraid of me?" he said. His fingers found the curve of my ear and traced it up to its point, then back down.

"Yes," I said, but I made himself look at his bright eyes. His eyebrows were raised so high they almost disappeared under his hair. I bit my lip. "But I…" Then I leaned forward and pressed my lips to his.

For a moment, he didn't move and I thought I'd made a mistake, that for all his flirting and his filthy words, he didn't want me after all. But then his mouth parted against mine, kissed me back, and I let him take over. I'd never kissed anyone before and I was afraid I'd do something wrong.

It was terrifying, letting him kiss me, and it was exhilarating. I tried not to embarrass myself by moaning when his tongue slipped between my lips to probe the inside of my mouth. I failed, and he chuckled and kissed me harder.

When we sat back, the rest of the wisplight was gone, and I stared at my hands.

"Do you want me to teach you?" Kiernan said, and I met his eyes.

"To kiss?" I said. Had I been that bad? That obviously inexperienced?

He laughed. "To make wisplight."

"I don't have magic."

"We all have magic, to some degree. And you're a seer, so

you should have plenty."

My eyes widened. I had never considered that I might have magic. I nodded.

"The first thing fey children learn is how to connect to the Realms," he said. "So, we'll start there. Close your eyes."

I closed my eyes, breath too fast, heart too loud. My body didn't seem to know if I should be turned on or serene.

"Breathe deep, slowly, calm your body and your mind." His voice took on a solemn tone, and became more resonant, like he might begin to sing.

I breathed, relaxed my muscles, and tried to calm my mind.

"Now center yourself, here." Kiernan put a hand on my chest, pressing next to my heart and a little below. "And breathe. Imagine the sky above you is swirling with energy, with magic, and breathe it in, deep into your center."

I breathed, and felt my body grow warm.

"Now breathe out, and imagine that energy, that magic, leaving you, moving deep into the land below you." His voice held me mesmerized and I followed the instructions.

"Breathe in and draw magic back up from the land. Breathe out and see the magic flowing out to the sea around you."

I breathed.

"Breathe in the magic of the sea and breathe it back out and up to the sky."

I breathed and felt a jolt of heat, of energy. Of magic.

"Breathe in from the sky, out to the land," he said. "In from the land, out to the sea." I breathed. "In from the sea, out to the sky." His hand moved away from my chest. "You are at the center of the Three Realms, a bright spark of fire named Fionn."

I wanted to speak, but no words seemed right, so I just

kept breathing, feeling the magic of land, sea, and sky swirling through me.

"Now," said Kiernan. "Imagine your hands filling with light. Redirect some of the magic flowing through you into your hands and make it glow."

I tried to do as instructed. The palms of my hands tingled.

"Open your eyes, pretty bird." His voice was soft.

I slowly lifted my eyelids and looked at my hands. They were full of bluish light, so full it ran over the sides to vanish when it hit the quilt.

"Oh," I said.

"See," said Kiernan. "You do have magic."

"I have magic," I whispered. "I never knew." I felt full, like my whole body was glowing and not just the light in my cupped hands. I closed my hands, and the light vanished. When I met Kier's eyes, he was smiling. I smiled back, and it grew until I knew I must be grinning like a fool.

"I fucking have fucking magic," I said, because it seemed too momentous for ordinary words.

"What else do you suppose your Abbess was keeping from you?" Kiernan said gently.

8

Kiernan

THE LOOK ON Fionn's face when he opened his eyes and saw his hands full of wisplight made all the pain and aching of the past couple of days worthwhile.

I wanted to make him smile like that again and again, but it was sobering to think that he had been kept from learning even the most basic children's magic. It was one more thing that made me uneasy about this place, that made me need to remember why I was here, and what I had come to do. Because the longer I was trapped in the Abbey, the more I realized I could not have ended up here by chance.

"Do you have to do that every time you do magic?" asked Fionn.

"Do what? Connect to the Realms?"

He nodded.

"In a way," I said. How could I explain a lifetime of learning in a few words? "As children, we learn to connect that way, to learn how magic feels, and how to regulate the way you draw on it. But the more you do magic, the less you need to think about it."

"And anyone can do this?" He conjured a small pool of wisplight and poured it from hand to hand. He was still smiling.

"Most people – humans, fey, Siegel, anyone – can do a little basic magic like wisplights or small flames. Some can do much more."

Fionn looked up from his hands and his silver eyes reflected the blue of the light. "What can you do?"

I held out a hand, and a small bright flame danced in it. "My strongest connection is with the land, the forest especially. But I can do some magic from all the Realms."

"What is forest magic like?"

"I can speak to trees, to animals. Sometimes they'll do things for me, though I don't like to force any living thing against its will. But if I need to, I can make things grow, move earth, create wind, call water." I shrugged and closed my hand around the flame. It was too much to fit into one conversation.

"You always have your visions up here, don't you?" I asked. "On the roof?"

"How did you know?" Fionn let the wisplight in his hands dribble away where it winked out before it hit the quilt.

"Because it's part of your magic as a seer."

"What else do you suppose I can do?"

"Many seers are also healers, like you. They know healing magic, magic to ease pain and prevent infection. Most seers can tell truth from lies, and read emotions, and some can speak mind-to-mind, without need for spoken words."

I touched Fionn's hand and he didn't pull away, so I laced our fingers together.

"And most seers can read memories, heal them if they're lost or damaged." I paused. "I've heard that the Vogel can speak to birds." I glanced up over Fionn's shoulder as a thin, slender shape swooped out of the sky and down into a fold of the quilt. "And feathered serpents. Maybe even dragons." I wasn't even surprised to find that he had made friends with serpents.

"That's magic?" He stroked the back of the serpent, which had curled up on his knee. Another swooped out of the sky to land on his shoulder.

"It is," I said. "So, you know you have *some* magic, at least." I smiled. "Do your serpents have names?"

Fionn looked at the thin creature under his hand. "She's Smoke," he said. "Because her scales are mostly gray." He twisted to look at the serpent on his shoulder, reached up to pet her tiny dragon-like head. "And this one is Flame, for her red wings."

"She's an unusual color for a tree serpent," I said. "And just a baby."

"They hatched last year," Fionn replied. "There was a whole clutch of eggs, over there." He pointed to a spot where a stone had a dip in it, a little hollow against the parapet. "I watched them all spring, and when they hatched and the rest flew away, these two stayed."

"I'm glad." At least he had two small friends to keep him company.

"Shall I try to free your memory?" said Fionn after we watched the sleepy serpents for a little while.

I nodded. "If you'd like. It might help to connect to the Realms, like I showed you."

"Yes," he said. "I'll try that." He arranged his fingers on my forehead and face like I had told him I saw our seer do. He closed his eyes.

I closed mine, too, and waited for something to happen. Fionn's cool fingers felt good on my face, like just his touch could heal. And maybe it could.

"I wish I knew what I was doing," he said. "I see… memories like threads, all tied up in your mind." He sighed, and I felt it like a warm breeze on my face. I wanted to lean towards it, but I held still.

"I think… maybe…," he said. I felt a gentle pressure behind my eyes, felt something slip free.

He dropped his hands. "I don't know if that did anything," he said. "I'm sorry."

"I felt… I don't know. Something." I took Fionn's hand again and stroked it with my thumb. "Thank you."

"Do you remember anything?"

I shook my head. "I think it takes time for the memories to work themselves out." I squeezed his fingers. "I'll let you know if I remember."

Then I leaned forward and slid my fingers into his hair on the side opposite from where the tree serpent perched. He turned his face toward my touch, and I wanted to moan out loud.

"I don't want to want you," he said, voice quiet.

"Why not?" I asked, keeping my voice soft, too.

"I'm afraid," he whispered. "I'm nothing to you, but you… I've *seen* you my while life. And I… if we…" He stopped and drew in a breath. "You'll leave, and I'll be alone again, and it will hurt so much more."

"Then come with me." I didn't know why I said it. Even if Fionn wasn't, by law, supposed to be attending the Vogel Court, I couldn't take him to my mother's court, where he would be looked down on by the Sidhe. And I couldn't take him to my father's stronghold, where anyone not human was suspect. It wouldn't be safe. It was barely safe for me.

Fionn looked up, met my eyes, fear and hope battling on his face. "I know nothing of the world."

"Then let me show you this one thing," I said. "Just for

tonight. Let me make you feel good, so you won't forget me when I'm gone."

"You want me to remember you?"

I let a smile curl up one side of my mouth. It was exactly the kind of thing I might say to any attractive person to get them to sleep with me, but I realized that this time I actually meant it. I wanted Fionn to remember me, and I wanted to remember him. "Yes," I said, and leaned forward again to brush my lips against his. "I want you to remember me." I pressed a little harder.

He made a soft noise in his throat and leaned into the kiss, responded so fiercely I felt our teeth knock together. His desperate longing made me want him more. It made me want to give him everything I could, to take him away from this terrible place and show him life could be full of joy. Here, now, all I had to give was pleasure, so I would give him all the pleasure I could.

"Come here," I whispered against his mouth, and pulled him closer, laid him on the quilt, carefully tucking his wings under him, and looked down at his face. The feathered tree serpents chittered in complaint and moved away. I stroked Fionn's face, his hair, kissed his neck, nibbled his earlobe.

When I paused, he said, "I don't know how."

I licked his lower lip. "Don't know how to what?"

He looked away and traced a fold of the quilt with one finger. "I don't know how to touch you."

"Pretty bird." He met my eyes again. "You know how to touch yourself. We're not so different, so touch me that way, if you want to." I kissed him, slid my tongue into his mouth, then looked at his face again. "But tonight is for you. You don't have to touch me at all if you don't want to."

"I want to, Kier," he whispered. He reached up, brushed a curl of hair behind my ear and stroked an antler. "I want to touch you. I want… I want to taste you." His cheekbones flushed pink, bright in the light of the nearly full moon.

My breath hitched. My chest felt tight. My pants would have felt tight if they hadn't been the shapeless coarse weave of Abbey trousers. My cock twitched.

"Let's get this tunic off you," I said, reaching for the tie that held the loose top around Fionn's waist. He reached for the button at his throat, and together we pulled the fabric away.

"You too," he said, and helped me pull my tunic over my head.

For a moment, I just looked at him, studying the shape of his lean muscles, the pretty bluish freckles on his shoulders and chest, his arms and his cheeks.

"I never noticed," I said.

"What?" His eyes snapped open, and he looked worried.

"You don't have nipples." I stroked a palm over his chest. His skin was so *soft*. "But you do have a belly button." I poked my finger gently into the place in question and he squirmed.

"I'm not a mammal," he said. "Of course I don't have nipples." Then he hesitated. "Is that bad? Do you…?"

I put my fingers on his lips and shook my head. "It was just an observation," I said, and stroked the skin of his chest again. "I like you exactly as you are."

I found the waistband of his trousers and tugged at the drawstring. He clung to my shoulders as I pushed them down and away, then insisted on removing my pants before letting me touch him again.

I pulled a fold of the quilt over us both. It wasn't cold, but it wasn't quite warm, either, and I wasn't sure if Fionn's shiver was from being touched or from the night air.

Then I slid my hand over his belly, over his pubic bone. "Is this okay?" I said, when I found the seam of his sheath and traced it with my middle finger.

"Goddess Above," he whispered, arching under my touch. "Oh, yes."

I pressed my finger down just a little as I ran it over his seam. Moisture leaked out and I stroked again and was rewarded by his sheath opening and his cock sliding out, already hard, into my waiting hand.

"You're wet, pretty bird," I said, curling my fingers around his length and stroking. His erection was slippery, and it felt amazing. I wanted to moan just from touching him.

He looked worried again, like he was afraid I would find him repulsive. "Bird folk self-lubricate," he said, his voice small and uncertain.

I stroked him again and again, until he arched his back and cried out.

"That seems very practical," I said. "And it feels very nice. Is there anything else I should know about bird folk before I make you come?"

"Before you what?"

I hid a smile in his neck. He was so sweetly innocent. "Before I give you an orgasm," I said.

"Oh," he said, rocking his hips in time to the movements of my hand. "There is one thing." He arched again and dug his fingers into my shoulders.

"What's that?" I licked his neck, followed the muscle to his shoulder, then traced his chest, his abs, his belly, until I was whispering into his thigh. "What do I need to know, pretty bird?"

He whispered. "We… we orgasm differently."

I lifted my head, looked up the length of Fionn's body, and met his eyes. "Do you?"

He bit his lip. It made him look young and vulnerable, and I felt an unexpected urge to protect him.

"When you… when you come," he said, hesitating over the unfamiliar word usage, "it's one… one moment."

"Mmm," I said. "Sometimes a long moment, sometimes a short one. Sometimes very intense, sometimes less so. But yes, I come all at once."

"I… Vogel orgasm in pulses," he said.

I flicked my tongue out and stroked it across the tip of Fionn's cock and smiled when he gasped.

"I might need a little more detail," I said, kissing the inside of one of his thighs, and then the other. "To make sure I pleasure you adequately."

"We… we orgasm in pulses," he repeated, his hands groping for me, his fingers tangling in my hair. "One pulse is a… a basic physical release. Some semen is emitted, and it feels… okay. Two is good. Three is very good. More ejaculate is produced with each pulse." I could tell he was struggling to get the words out, to keep them coherent, and I hid another smile against his skin.

"Like multiple mini orgasms?" I asked and flicked my tongue again. He moaned.

"Something like that," he gasped out. "But… once the first pulse happens you can't stop… you just have to keep going until it's over."

"Can you have more than three pulses?"

"I never have."

"But can you?"

Fionn's fingers tightened in my hair. "According to… a book I have… yes. More than three is… mind-blowing."

I smiled. "So, I should aim for four, then." I slid my mouth over his erection, felt him arch against me, and sucked.

"Goddess Above," breathed Fionn. "I'm… Kiernan… Oh…" His words dissolved into soft moans.

"You taste sweet," I said and then he grabbed both of my

antlers and thrust against my mouth, and I couldn't say anything else. I sucked until I felt his cock throb – pulse – against my lips and then I swallowed the sweet spunk that flooded my mouth.

"Don't stop," pleaded Fionn. "Oh, Goddess, please don't stop."

I didn't stop. He tasted good, felt good, *smelled* good, and I wouldn't have stopped even if he hadn't been begging me not to. But I did move one hand away from his thigh, slid my fingers against the base of his cock, and covered them with slick moisture from his sheath. When he pulsed again, spewing more semen into my mouth, I slid my fingers lower to massage his asshole.

He twitched, but when I moved my fingers away, he said, "No, that feels good." Then he pulsed again and clung to my antlers.

"Don't stop," he said, when he could form words. "Please don't stop."

I pressed my slick fingers against his asshole, and he arched his back and thrust against my mouth. "Don't stop," he whispered, so I kept sucking, kept licking, kept pressing with my fingers, until I was sliding my mouth over him and pushing my fingers inside him, over and over.

And suddenly he twisted, buried his face into the quilt, and yelled into the fabric. When the fourth pulse was over, he collapsed, limp, and I gently removed my fingers, slid my mouth away, and swallowed.

I crawled up to lie next to him, and he looked at me through half-open eyes.

"I counted four," I said. "Was that mind-blowing?"

"Goddess Above." He sounded sleepy. "Yes."

"Mmm. Good," I said, pulling him close. He rolled over, tucked his wings tightly against his back, and rested his cheek on my shoulder.

"Can I touch you?" he said softly, placing a hand hesitantly on my chest.

"Please," I said, burying one hand in his hair.

He was hesitant, but determined, kissing and touching his way down my neck to my chest, and pausing to study my nipples. He touched one with his tongue and I made a noise in my throat. "That's nice," I said, cupping my hand on the back of his head. He grew bolder, took the nipple between his teeth, and pulled. It sent a jolt through me and I wanted him to bite harder.

"I want…" said Fionn.

"What do you want, pretty bird?" I said, watching his face as he traced the shapes of my muscles, outlining each one with his finger, then his tongue.

"I want to taste you." He ducked his head and touched his tongue to the tip of my cock. I stifled a moan.

"Yes, please," I said. "I want that, too."

"You're salty," he said. He glanced up at my eyes, then back down. He traced the length of my erection with his fingers, then with his tongue. "Your skin feels like cloud silk." Then he slid his mouth over my cock, slowly, like he wasn't sure about what he was doing.

"That's nice," I said, my voice gone low and rough. "Goddess Below, that feels good."

Fionn's mouth slid up and down and he seemed to become more confident, until I was arching against him, clenching my fingers in his hair, and biting back moans with every breath.

I wanted, desperately, to fuck Fionn's mouth, but I didn't want to frighten him with my intensity, so I held back, letting him suck and lick and stroke until I had to turn my head to muffle my shout in the quilt. I felt Fionn's surprised jerk as I spurted into his mouth, then his soft lips slid away.

"Was that okay?" he said, crawling back up the quilt to lie next to me. I pulled him close again, wanting his warmth, his gentleness.

"More than okay," I said. "Much more than okay." I stroked his hair until I felt him relax into sleep, then stared at the sky for a long time, poking at my memory until the tangled threads seemed to fall into order and I knew why I'd come to the Abbey of the Moon.

I knew why I'd tried to sneak in undetected, and what task I was supposed to accomplish once I got inside.

I buried my face in Fionn's hair, breathed in the musky sweet scent of him. I knew, I remembered, too, why he was here, one lone Vogel man, one single seer, in an abbey full of moon-worshipping Alfar women. I knew why his unhatched egg had been brought to the Abbess, and I knew what she was planning for the next night, the full moon, the solstice, Fionn's thirty-third birthday.

What I didn't know was how to tell him any of it, or if he would even believe me. Or what the fuck I was supposed to do now. Because I couldn't – I wouldn't – do what I had been sent to do.

9
Fionn

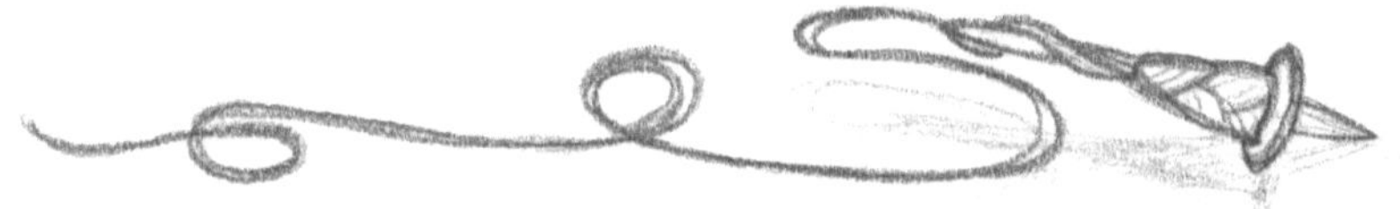

I WOKE WITH MY HEAD pillowed on Kiernan's shoulder, with his hand stroking my hair and the feathers of my wings.

"Awake, pretty bird?" he said. His voice was subdued, like something was troubling him.

"Is it morning?" I mumbled, rolling over to look at the sky. It was still dark and even though it felt like the night had already been long, the stars showed it was barely half over.

"Not yet," said Kier. "We have time." He turned his head, and I felt his breath on the top of my head, his lips press on my hair.

"Did you sleep?" I pushed myself partway up to look at his face. His eyes were closed, and a frown made a line between his eyebrows.

"No."

"What's wrong?"

His eyes opened. He looked tired. Worried. Sad? "I remembered," he said.

My first reaction was delight, so I smiled, but his frown

didn't go away and the smile faded. "You remembered something bad," I said.

He touched my face, tracing my cheek, my jaw. "Well, it's not good."

"Tell me."

"You won't believe me."

"You don't know that."

He sat up and reached for his tunic, but I took it from him and set it aside. I put both hands on his chest, resting them gently. "Stay. Stay naked a little longer," I said, not sure I was even making sound come out of my mouth.

The plea earned me a half smile from Kiernan. "You like me naked, do you?" he said, teasing.

"Yes."

"This isn't going to be easy to hear, what I remembered."

"Try. Please."

"You might get angry."

"At you?"

"Maybe."

I dropped my hands from Kiernan's chest and rested them on my knees instead. "Is it so terrible?"

He sighed. "You've read history books about the Isle? About the Nine Monarchies?"

"Of course. There have been nine rulers almost since history was first recorded."

"So you know that each of the three fey monarchs conquered the other peoples of their Triarchy, their third of the Isle? So the humans and the other peoples are vassal monarchies?"

"Yes. Some say the Triarchies correspond to the three sacred Realms, but that's always seemed more like wishful thinking to me."

Kiernan laughed, but he didn't sound very merry. "My

mother's people rule Morven Forest with their Queen of the Sidhe, and the humans of the riverlands and the Hirsch of the plains are her vassal monarchies."

I nodded. "Here in Aven there is an Alfar King, who rules the Aven Mountains."

"And his vassal monarchies are the humans of the foothills and the Vogel of the Eyrie, the bird folk."

"And Tronven is the Huldr Monarchy."

"With the Siegel – the sea folk – and the humans of the coast as vassals."

"What does this history lesson have to do with whatever terrible thing you've remembered?" I moved my hands from my own knees to Kiernan's, and he touched my fingers, clasped and gently squeezed them.

"For generations, that's how the Isle has been ruled. Sometimes one of the vassal monarchies will rebel, like my father's people did before I was born. He and my mother married to end that conflict. I'm not sure his people have ever forgiven him for that, even though they still revere him as a hero."

Kier squeezed my fingers again. "The fey monarchs have plotted against each other for as long as they have been rulers over their Triarchies, but they've always been too evenly matched for any one of them to conquer the whole Isle."

"What does this have to do with you and the Abbey?" A fear was growing in my belly, a feeling that I'd *seen* something relevant, but I couldn't think what it was.

Kiernan stared at where his hands covered mine. "The Alfar King has found a way to gain power. Enough power to let him meet both the Sidhe and the Huldr in battle and defeat them."

"How?"

"Magic."

I considered his words. I still didn't see what any of this might have to do with a quiet abbey near the coast, far from the politics and conflict of the capital, or the borders. "I suppose you would have to go to war, then?" I said. "But the Vogel, Siegel, humans, Hirsch… we've all been vassals for longer than anyone can remember. It hardly matters to anyone but the fey who rule over them."

"It does," he said. "If it comes to war, the innocent, the ordinary people, will be hurt the most. Fionn, the Alfar found a way to use the vilest magic to subjugate *everyone*. They will take what they want from all the peoples of the Isle, and the weakest of their vassals will feel it hardest, soonest."

He paused and shifted away from me to lean against the low parapet wall. "The magic they discovered requires a sacrifice to gain the power they seek. To keep that power will need more and more blood. If they succeed, they are the only ones who will benefit, but only until the evil consumes them."

"This is too far beyond me to comprehend," I said, trying and failing to really understand what he was telling me. "Evil magic and conquering." It sounded like one of the epic tales I had read in the Abbey library, like something from before the days of the Nine Monarchies, when the Isle was in chaos and war was constant.

Kiernan moved closer again and put his hands on my face to make me look into his eyes. "To gain this power requires a sacrifice," he said. "A perfect life, spilled out in blood to the Goddess of the Moon on the night of the solstice."

"Here? You believe this ritual will be conducted *here*? Tomorrow night?"

"My mother has a spy in the Alfar court. I was sent here to stop the sacrifice."

"Your mother isn't a Sidhe courtier, is she?"

"No."

"She's the Queen of Morven Forest."

"Yes."

I pulled away, out of his reach. "I see. Well, if this ritual is to be so terrible, I suppose I can help you stop it. If you're sure it will affect my people." I felt as if I'd been slapped. It wasn't as if Kiernan had actually lied about who his mother was, but it felt like an important omission, even if it was an understandable one. We were still strangers, after all, whatever closeness we had begun to feel.

"Fionn, it will affect *you*." He leaned forward and reached for my hand, but I shifted farther away. I wasn't sure how I felt, besides confused.

He sighed. "The sacrifice is to be someone the Moon Goddess would find perfect. Thirty-three, a number of magic and the age of majority for most of the Isle's peoples. Born on the summer solstice, sacrificed on the summer solstice. A seer, pure silver, a virgin. And since the Moon Goddess is a protector of women, the sacrifice would have to be a man."

As Kiernan spoke, I felt ice settle in my belly, colder and colder. Every descriptor he added described me and only me. I could feel the horror that must be showing on my face.

"You're wrong," I said. "The Abbess saved me. She cared for me. You're wrong." I knew my voice was edging into hysteria, but I couldn't help it. Kiernan had brought change, and I had hoped it would be good change, but this… He was trying to overturn my whole world. But I didn't feel angry. I felt devastated.

"The Abbess *did* save you," Kier said, his voice gentle, almost pleading. "And she did care for you, after a fashion. But it was because you represent her people's chance to conquer, to be ascendant over all the other peoples of the Isle."

I made myself breathe, made myself find calm. I had to remember what I knew of myself, what I had *seen*. I refused to believe I had lived my whole life just to be a pawn in someone's insane bid for power. I shook my head.

Kiernan smiled sadly. "I was sent here to stop the sacrifice. To either steal the sacrifice away so my mother could claim the power for herself, or to make sure the sacrifice never happens."

"Is that why you wanted me to leave with you? So you could deliver me to your mother?" I wanted to scream, to cry, to hit Kiernan with all my strength, but I made myself be still, to speak coldly.

"No, pretty bird. I hadn't remembered any of this. I wanted… I only wanted to help you."

I scowled. "How?"

"How what?"

"How are you to stop this supposed sacrifice from happening?"

He looked away, staring at the moon as it sank in the sky. "I'm supposed to kill you before the ritual takes place."

I scrambled backwards across the roof until I found my back pressed against the door. He watched me but didn't move.

"I'm not going to *do* it, Fionn."

"Why not? Isn't it your sworn duty to your Queen?" I couldn't keep the spite out of my voice, though I'd meant to keep it cold.

"Because… I won't be my mother's assassin. Because there has to be a better way. Because I *like* you. I want… I want to *help* you."

I opened my mouth to reply and felt the sudden tightness across my forehead and behind my eyes. My back spasmed and I smacked my head against the door. The world went gray and I heard Kiernan's voice, concerned, but couldn't make out the words.

And then I was falling. The tower stones sped by past me and I beat my wings frantically, trying to slow my descent. But I wasn't alone. My arms held another person and I stared down into a pair of deep green eyes, warm and trusting. And Kiernan and I plummeted from the tower and I couldn't stop it.

Before we hit the ground, darkness came and I was curled up in a nest of blankets, looking at his face in candlelight. He was smiling, his lips slightly parted. "I love you, pretty bird," he said.

Before I could reply, we were falling again.

My head was pillowed in Kier's lap when the rooftop came back into focus. The back of my head hurt where I'd hit it and a headache stabbed behind my eyes.

"What did you see?" he said, stroking my face. I thought vaguely that I should want to flee. There was a reason I should be afraid of Kiernan, but everything was muddled.

"We were falling," I said. "From the tower." I shook my head. "That's all." I couldn't mention the darkness and his words to me.

"You were only gone for a moment." He slid out from under me and laid my head on a pillow of our bunched-up clothes. "I didn't know you had seizures when you had visions. Our seer just kind of… goes away." He frowned and shook his head. "I'll get you some water." He slipped in the door.

I sat up slowly. I ached. I remembered why I was supposed to be afraid. Kiernan had been sent to kill me. I wouldn't consider the idea that the Abbess also wanted to kill me. To sacrifice me. That was too big a thought, and I was only one insignificant Vogel seer.

Kiernan returned with the cup and pitcher from beside my bed and I took the water and drank. I hadn't realized how dry my throat was until the liquid slid down it.

"I'm sorry," he said.

"For what?"

He sat down, put the pitcher to one side, and leaned his head in his hand. "For telling you something terrible. For being here for such an awful reason. For making you trust me and then giving you a reason not to."

I just shook my head.

"I need to get you out of here," he said. "I won't let her sacrifice you. Even if it didn't mean war and death for the whole Isle, I won't let her hurt you."

"Kiernan," I said. "It's okay." I put my hand on his, realizing that even if I should be afraid, I couldn't be. Not of this man who had made me feel so good and had let himself be so vulnerable in turn. "It will be okay. Somehow."

"We have a key to the tower. Let's go now." He took both of my hands in his and squeezed.

"Okay," I said, not knowing what else to say. "But you need your clothes first."

"Do you know where they are?"

"In the laundry, probably."

"Can you get them? Safely?"

I nodded. "Stay here." I found my tunic and trousers and pulled them on. "I'll be right back." I didn't look at Kiernan as I hurried in the door. If I looked at him, I would never be able to do what I needed to do.

"Be careful, pretty bird."

I almost turned back.

In the infirmary, I took Kiernan's key from the table, pulled on my cloak, and left the tower, locking it behind me. I wasn't sure, as I did it, if I was locking the sisters out, or locking Kier in.

It was still quiet, everyone asleep in the dormitory, and when I glanced up at the sky, I could see there was still a lot of night left. How could one span of time seem so endless?

I went straight across the courtyard and around the Abbess's tower instead of taking the long way through the halls of the Abbey. The laundry was next to the bathhouse, making use of the same upwelling of hot water. Inside, it was damp and warm and smelled like soap and something that made my eyes sting. A shelf of clean, folded bedding and other linens ran along the wall next to the door, and there, at the bottom of a pile of sheets as if someone had tried to hide them, was a bundle of deep green and warm brown fabric. I pulled it free, tucked it inside my cloak, and left the laundry.

In the courtyard, I skirted the Abbess's tower again, hugging close to its wall. I glanced longingly at my own tower, where Kiernan waited for me on the roof. Then I straightened my shoulders and walked quickly around the last curve of the central tower to the door. I hesitated, then lifted my hand. But I couldn't bring myself to knock. I looked up at my tower again.

Kiernan had been kind. He hadn't always told the full truth right away, but he hadn't outright lied. I liked him, perhaps too much. I felt myself falling when I looked at Kiernan, when I thought about him, when I remembered the visions I'd had of him, of the two of us, together. I dropped my hand to my side.

I wanted to scream.

I was just turning away from the Abbess's door when I heard the creak of hinges. I turned back as the door opened and the Abbess stood there, looking at me from cold, colorless eyes.

"Branfionn," she said, no surprise in her voice.

I looked at the stone cobbles. "Abbess," I said, forcing my voice to be even and strong. "The fey has remembered."

"And *what* has he remembered?"

"He says he was sent here by the Queen of Morven Forest."

"The Sidhe Queen."

"Yes."

"I should have guessed. For what purpose did she send him?"

"To stop… He claims there is to be a ritual conducted here, that he was sent to stop it from happening." My belly clenched, not in suppressed desire, but in anguish. I shouldn't have come. Kiernan had trusted me, had only wanted to help me.

But Kiernan was wrong. He had to be.

"And what else does he claim?"

"Only that it is a ritual that threatens his people, and he means to ensure it doesn't happen."

The Abbess considered me, cold eyes boring into me, as if daring me to leave out any details. I suppressed a shiver. I *should* tell her the rest, that Kiernan believed *I* was to be the sacrificial offering. But I kept silent and waited.

Finally, the Abbess nodded. "Return to your tower. Do not let him leave. You must keep him occupied until after the solstice tomorrow night. Drug him if you must."

"Yes, Abbess," I said. "May I ask…?"

"May you ask what?"

"Is there to be a ritual?"

The Abbess looked at me closely and I avoided her eyes. "There is," she said. "One that will bring glory to this Abbey and to all of Aven. And to you, little seer."

I bowed my head. "I do not need glory, Abbess."

"Of course not," she said. "But it will reflect on you nonetheless."

"What will happen to him, Abbess?"

"To your patient? You haven't grown fond of him?"

"No, Abbess. I only wondered."

"He will be sent back to his Queen to tell her of the glory that has come to Aven. In the meantime, he must not interfere."

I bowed. "Of course, Abbess." I turned to go.

"Branfionn?"

I paused, suddenly afraid. "Yes, Abbess?"

"The key?"

"Key, Abbess?" My stomach cramped.

"The one you used to get out of your tower. The one the fey presumably had hidden somewhere. Give it to me."

"Oh, that key. Of course, Abbess." I handed it to her, knowing it was useless to argue. I was supposed to have been locked in, but very obviously wasn't. I could hardly claim there was no key.

The Abbess gestured and I walked back to the other side of the courtyard, into the Abbey, and up to my tower door. She followed, watching my every step. When I stepped through my door, she closed it and locked me in.

I leaned on the table, just breathing, until the Abbess's footsteps were gone. Then I put Kiernan's clothes next to the pile of coins, took off my cloak, and headed for the stairs. I didn't know how I could face Kiernan again, or what I would say. I didn't know if I'd done the right thing or the wrong thing. I only knew I'd done something that would make him upset.

When I stepped out onto the roof, Kiernan was lying flat on his back, still naked, a feathered tree serpent curled up next to each shoulder. He smiled at me. "You took a while," he said.

"I was getting worried."

"The Abbess caught me." I held up a hand when he sat up, worry in his eyes. "It's okay. She only sent me back. But she took the key."

His shoulders sagged. "So much for a quick and easy escape tonight. Now we'll have to wait for her to fall asleep and then pick the lock."

"I got your clothes."

"Thank you." He took my hand and I allowed myself to be pulled down to sit on the quilt. "I'm glad you're okay."

My stomach cramped again. I wanted to blurt out what I had done, but I was confused and scared, and I didn't want Kiernan to be angry with me, to hate me. That I had changed my mind at the last minute wouldn't matter, because the Abbess had found me anyway and I'd told her... not everything, but enough. Too much. I didn't know.

Kiernan put his arms around me and I leaned against his strength, craving his touch even if I didn't deserve it. Even if he was seeing my distress and thinking it was because we couldn't leave tonight, and not because I was conflicted.

"Let me make you feel good again, pretty bird," Kier said. "While we wait for an opportune time to escape," and I shivered. I didn't deserve to feel good, but I wanted it. I wanted it more than I'd ever wanted anything.

"I want..." I said, but I wasn't even sure what I'd been about to say.

And once again, Kiernan replied, "What do you want, pretty bird?" and stroked his hand down my back, smoothing my hair and my feathers.

"I don't want to be a virgin anymore," I said, and blushed, feeling the heat rush up my neck and onto my face. I hid myself against Kier's shoulder.

He touched my cheek, stroked the side of my face. "Do

you want me to fuck you?" he said gently.

"Yes."

"Are you sure?"

"Yes, I'm sure, Kiernan. I want you to… to…" I stopped. I wanted to pronounce those words, those filthy swears the Abbess would have beat me black and blue for saying. But I couldn't.

"You want me to shove my cock up your ass?" said Kiernan, as if knowing what I wanted. His voice was soft, and he said the words just like any other words, like they were caring words.

I shivered again. "Yes," I said. "And… maybe…"

"Maybe what, pretty bird?" Kiernan's hand cupped my face, his thumb stroking my cheek, but he didn't try to make me look at him.

"If there's time… can I…?"

"Do you want to fuck me, too?"

"Yes," I whispered.

Then he did tip my face up to look at him, and he kissed me, gently but somehow fierce, claiming my mouth with his own. He kissed until I felt I would go limp with it, then pulled away.

"You're going to have to take your clothes off again," he said, and I laughed in surprise, some of the tension draining away. I stood up and undressed slowly, letting him watch me instead of trying to hide. By the time I was naked, Kier was hard and watching him get that way made me swell, too.

Kiernan held out a hand, and I took it, and knelt on the quilt, and let him pull me closer. We kissed, and this time I couldn't have said who started it, only that our tongues slid together, and our lips moved hungrily until we were both breathing hard.

When we pulled apart, I discovered I was flat on my back

with Kiernan leaning over me.

"Pretty bird," he whispered, and stroked a hand over my hardness, making me arch towards him. He leaned away, stroked me until his fingers were glistening with my lubricant, and then he spread it on himself. Watching him spread my fluids on himself made me so hard I ached, and I said, "Now."

"Are you comfortable?" Kiernan asked. "Are your wings okay?"

I nodded. I bit my lip and reached out to touch Kiernan's hip. He stroked my leg, bent my knee and tucked it under his arm. When he leaned over me again, my spine curved and I felt my cheeks spread apart.

I looked into Kier's eyes, green as the forest, and reached down to take hold of his hardness, to guide it to my anus.

"Ready?" he said, his voice a soft breath in my ear.

"Yes," I said. "Oh yes."

"Say it," Kiernan said, low and smoky. "Tell me what you want me to do to you."

For a moment, I couldn't force the words out and I just stared at his bright gaze. Then I said, "Fuck me, Kiernan. Please."

He smiled and pressed against me, and I felt myself pushed open. I gasped and bit back a cry and he paused. It hurt. It burned, but it felt good. "Don't stop," I whispered, and he pushed again, harder, split me open and slid inside.

"Okay, pretty bird?" he said, curling his fingers around my erection, stroking as he thrust, and the pain went away and there was only pleasure. My first pulse splattered my belly and the second my ribs.

"Don't stop," I said, digging my heel into Kiernan's back.

"Not stopping," he gasped. "Almost done. But not stopping until you tell me to."

My third pulse sent semen as far as my neck and for a

moment I didn't think there would be a fourth, that I was finished and satisfied. But then I felt Kiernan throb inside me, heard him moan and his fingers tighten, and suddenly the fourth pulse swept over me, and I yelled into Kiernan's mouth and spurted semen over both of us.

10
Kiernan

FIONN WAS ASLEEP AGAIN, large eyes closed and silver lashes brushing his cheeks. I had to resist the urge to touch his face; I didn't want to wake him. He looked so peaceful, and so tired.

I should have taken more time with him, should have stroked and caressed and kissed until neither of us could stand it anymore, instead of shoving inside of him as soon as we were both hard. But it was what Fionn had wanted, what he had asked for, and I found myself, over and over, wanting to do whatever Fionn asked.

It was a strange feeling, unfamiliar. I was used to taking whatever I could get as quickly as I could get it, and to being so used in turn. I wasn't used to caring that much about my sex partners. And I *did* care about Fionn. So much it confused me.

The little tree serpents, Smoke and Flame, crept back from where they had waited on the parapet, and curled up in Fionn's hair. Flame looked at me and chittered. I had no idea what she was trying to communicate, but I reached out and stroked her head with one finger. She closed her eyes and hummed.

"I wonder if I could understand you," I said, quietly so I wouldn't wake Fionn. "You're a *tree* serpent, after all, and I'm a forest Sidhe."

I stroked her head again and she curled up tighter in Fionn's hair. Smoke slid closer and bumped my hand with her head, so I petted her, too, and she hummed and curled up next to her sister.

I reached for my magic, found it strong and green and waiting. Then I reached out again, brushing my mind gently against those of the two serpents. They startled, made little noises in their throats, and I suddenly knew they were sleepy and happy, but annoyed that I was poking at their thoughts. I smiled.

"Watch over him, if I can't," I whispered, and Smoke opened one eye to look at me.

We watch, silly, she said then she closed her eye and went to sleep.

I sighed and leaned back to watch the stars slowly turn overhead, wishing the night could last forever, that I could sit here with Fionn always, content and peaceful. In the morning, we would have to find another way to leave the Abbey. There had to be a way. Perhaps, while the Abbess and her sisters were busy preparing for their ritual, they would be less watchful.

As they prepared to sacrifice the only seer born to the Vogel in seven generations. Their perfect, beautiful sacrifice.

Except he wasn't so perfect now, was he? Fionn was no longer a virgin, no longer untouched in the eyes of the chaste Lady of the Moon. The Abbess had made a grave error in letting him stay locked in the tower with a fey who'd fuck anything on two legs capable of giving consent.

I laughed, trying to be quiet, but once I started, I couldn't stop. Though it may have been my shaking and not my voice that woke Fionn.

"What is it?" Fionn rubbed his eyes and yawned.

"Sorry pretty bird. I meant to let you sleep."

"Why are you laughing?"

"It doesn't matter. Get some rest while you can."

"I can't now. Tell me what's funny."

I squeezed his shoulder. "We may not have escaped, but we've spoiled the perfection of the Alfar's sacrifice."

He frowned. "But you think *I'm* to be offered on the altar."

"Yes, and you're not a virgin anymore."

He stared at me until I felt I needed to do something to break the tension, then he snorted.

"Will you tell the Abbess and stop this supposed ritual, then?" Fionn smiled.

"I doubt that would stop her," said Kiernan. "Though it might make her angry. We still need to get you out of here."

He sat up, and the sleepy serpents wiggled to stay in his hair, and finally draped themselves across his shoulders when they were dislodged. He bit his lip and I reached out and touched it, so he removed his teeth.

"I'm still a virgin in one sense," he said, and my eyebrows shot up.

"What way is that?" I trailed my fingers over Fionn's chin and down his neck. I wanted this night to go on and on and never end. We still had time. Tomorrow we would escape.

"I haven't… been inside you," Fionn said, looking away, then jerking his chin up and meeting my eyes.

"Do you want to fuck me?" I said. I felt myself responding to his words, to the look in his eyes, going hard at the thought of him on top of me, inside me.

"Yes," said Fionn, the trembling in his voice evident even

in that single word. He leaned towards me and brushed our lips together. I pulled him closer and let him push me back onto the quilt. The tree serpents complained and launched into the sky.

Fionn's eyes were full of longing and something else I couldn't read. I didn't have long to think about it, though, because his mouth was on mine, on my earlobe, my neck, my chest. I buried both hands in Fionn's hair and clenched my fingers when his mouth closed over one nipple and sucked.

When he lifted his head and looked at me, all I could see in his gaze was desire, so hot his silver eyes seemed molten. "Let me touch you," Fionn said. "Let me… let me be in charge."

I smiled; I couldn't help it. "Touch me," I said. "Tell me what to do." Then I gasped as Fionn's mouth found my erection. "Take me," I said, my voice barely audible.

He looked up, something almost wicked on his face that I hadn't seen there before. "Say please," he said, fingers cupping my testicles and squeezing gently.

"Please."

"Please what?"

I grinned. "You're a very good student, and a fast learner."

He squeezed harder, until it almost hurt. "Please what?" he said again.

"Please fuck me, Fionn," I said. "Seer, healer, silver man of the bird folk."

"Don't tease," said Fionn, taking his hand away.

"Goddess Below," I gasped. "I'm not teasing." I reached for him, found his cock hard and already emerged from his sheath, and stroked. "Please don't stop touching me."

"Do you want me?" he said, watching my hand slide over his slick hardness.

"I want you, pretty bird."

"Roll over."

My eyes widened, but I smiled again. I rolled over and looked back at Fionn over my shoulder.

He was breathing hard. He looked scared and very, very turned on.

"Please touch me," I said, and he jerked his eyes away from my ass to meet my gaze.

Hesitantly, then with more confidence, he stroked both hands down my back, over my ass, and down my thighs, then back again.

"That's nice," I said and in response Fionn nudged my legs apart and leaned over me.

"Tell me you want me," he said, his voice pleading. Then, more demanding, "Tell me you want me to fuck you."

"I want you, Fionn," I said. "I want you to fuck my ass until you have the best orgasm you've ever had."

He made a desperate noise in his throat, and I lifted myself onto my knees and pushed back against him, felt him hard and slick.

"I'm ready for you, pretty bird," I said, and Fionn moaned.

"Now?" he whispered.

"Now. Please."

He shifted his weight onto one arm, and I felt his cock press between my ass cheeks, slide until it found my asshole, and press forward.

"Will it hurt you?" he said.

"Just fuck me."

"Goddess Above," he breathed and thrust forward all at once, pushing me open and sliding in. His first pulse came before he was even all the way in. He cried out quietly.

"Goddess, I'm sorry," he said.

"Don't stop, pretty bird," I said. "You can fuck me as hard

as you need to."

Fionn thrust and thrust again, and the second pulse came almost as quickly.

"Goddess Above," he said, clinging to my hips. "I should be touching you."

"Take what you need," I said. "We can worry about me later."

"No," he said, slowing his movements. "No. I want to see your face."

I twisted my neck to look over my shoulder again.

"No, roll over," he said. He pulled out and made a desperate sound. "Hurry, please."

I rolled over, wrapped my legs around his waist to pull him closer, and he fumbled to get himself back inside. I reached down and guided him.

"There you go, pretty bird," I said.

Fionn gasped and thrust, wrapped his fingers around my cock and stroked me. He had his eyes squeezed shut.

"Kiernan," he said. "I…" Then he arched as his third pulse hit and I almost came, too, as I felt the hot throbbing inside me.

"I think that's all," breathed Fionn. "I think…"

I stroked a hand down his back, marveling at the softness of his feathers. "Stop if you need to," I said gently, though I didn't want him to pull out and leave me empty. I wanted to be fucked until I had my own orgasm.

When his eyes cracked open, I added, "Tomorrow I'm going to lick between your toes," and he moaned and thrust into me again.

I met each thrust with one of my own, making Fionn's hand tighten on my cock, pushing me closer and closer.

"I can't…" said Fionn.

"Stop if you need to," I said, trying to force myself to come before Fionn was finished with me.

"Can't stop." His thrusts came harder, deeper, more frantic. He spread his wings and beat them against the air as if they could give him more leverage. And maybe they did, because I felt like I was being fucked as deeply and as thoroughly as it was possible to do.

And I could only hold on to his hips, digging my fingers in as I watched my beautiful lover above me, wings beating, pelvis thrusting, until I wanted to scream. I bit my tongue until I tasted blood and suddenly spewed semen all over myself as I felt the deep pulse of Fionn's cock in my ass.

And then Fionn collapsed on top of me.

"Hey, pretty bird. Are you okay?" I said as I caught him and lowered him gently to the quilt.

His eyes opened, but only halfway. "Goddess," he said. "I thought I was going to pass out." I propped him up to make him drink a cup of water. He was limp, his movements languid. He looked utterly spent and completely fulfilled. I wanted to lie limp next to him, to revel in the aftermath of one of the most intense fuckings I'd ever been given, but morning would come soon, and one of us should stay alert.

"If you ever give me five pulses," said Fionn, blinking his eyes in slow motion. "I shall probably expire from ecstasy."

I snorted. "Let's get you to bed, pretty bird." I stood on wobbly legs; I couldn't remember the last time I'd had three incredible orgasms in one night. I bent and scooped Fionn up, blankets and all. He was lighter than he looked, and I wondered if Vogel had hollow bones like birds did.

I carried him down the stairs and laid him on the bed. Then I went to the hearth and got a washcloth, wet it in the basin, and returned to the bedside to clean my spunk off of Fionn's lovely soft skin. He watched me from sleepy eyes but didn't say anything.

Then I cleaned myself off quickly, dug my clothes out of the bundle on the bed, and dressed. I pulled the quilt over Fionn, made sure his feet were tucked in, and smoothed the covers over his chest.

"It will be morning soon," he said.

"It will. But you can sleep a little." I kissed his forehead and when I straightened up, his eyes were closed again.

"Kiernan?" he said, though he didn't really sound awake.

"I'm here."

"I love you."

My breath caught and I couldn't answer. And how *would* I answer, anyway? But Fionn turned over, curled up, and seemed to drift even deeper into sleep.

"Oh, pretty bird," I said gently, my heart aching. "That's a very bad idea." Then I left the room, shutting the door quietly.

Downstairs, I lay on the cot and stared at the ceiling. I should sleep while there was time. My body was still sore from my encounter with the Abbey's wards, and fucking all night hadn't helped.

Not that I regretted it. Fionn had been so perfect, so beautiful, wings spread as he fucked me. I wanted that again.

I rolled over to stare at the door. Soon someone would bring breakfast and if Fionn wasn't here, they'd leave without bringing the food in. But even though I was hungry, I wouldn't wake him just for that. No, I would wait until the sisters and the novices were busy and then I'd pick the lock on the tower door, and I'd go get Fionn, and we would slip out before anyone came to fetch their sacrifice.

I wouldn't think, yet, about what we would do or where we would go once we were away from the Abbey.

I sat up when I heard footsteps in the hall, expecting a tap on the door and a polite refusal to come in without Fionn being present. So I was surprised when the door opened without a knock and a tall, severe looking woman in a shapeless gray habit stepped through. Behind her stood four sisters, blindfolded.

The Abbess, because it could be no one else, looked at me and I could read nothing at all on her face. Her fair skin, pointed ears, and pale eyes marked her as Alfar. She was sharp-featured and beautiful, and must have been ancient, to actually have lines of age around her mouth.

I fought the urge to look away in deference, and instead met her stare with one of my own.

"So," she said. "My little seer tells me you remember why you attempted to break into this Abbey."

I tried to think of what to say, how best to answer. Fionn had only told me he'd been caught by the Abbess, not that he had told her anything. The thought that she might know everything I'd told him hurt like a backhand to the face, but I wouldn't let it show.

"I'm here to stop your foul ritual," I said, fighting to keep my voice even. I would be willing to bet everything I had that the Abbess was not subject to the same nulling of magic that everyone else in the Abbey suffered. Even without my own magic, I could feel her power and see it shining in her eyes.

"Indeed?" she said.

"Yes."

"And yet you have not attempted to remove my sacrifice from play," she said. "Which would have been the logical first move."

"If you thought I would kill him, why did you lock me up

with him?"

The Abbess paced closer and behind her the blindfolded sisters moved into the room, leaving a tray of food, pails of water, and a pot of tea, and collecting empty buckets, chamber pots, laundry, and dirty wash water.

"Because you cannot harm him within my walls," she said. "He is protected by my magic."

I felt cold. I hadn't ever intended to kill Fionn anyway, but the thought that I'd have been doomed to fail from the start was not comforting. And I believed the Abbess. Not only because she couldn't lie, as a full fey, but because I could feel the threads of her magic winding through the tower.

"That may be," I said. "But I *have* spoiled him for you."

She laughed. "And how do you think you've done that? You can hardly change what he is or when he was hatched. He is perfect."

"He is not a virgin," I said, pronouncing the words slowly and clearly, and watching the Abbess's face begin to show a hint of worry.

"Did you smuggle a woman in with you?" she said. "Or are you one yourself?" She stepped closer, reached out before I could flinch away, and grabbed my crotch. "As I thought," she said. "He is still pure."

"I didn't say he'd been with a woman," I said, shoving her hand away.

She laughed.

"I said he wasn't a virgin." I sneered at her, suddenly furious that she had kept such a gentle person as Fionn locked away his whole life just so he could be used as a pawn in a game of conquerors. "I fucked his ass until he screamed in pleasure," I said, voice hard. "And then I let him fuck me."

What little color had been in the Abbess's face drained away. "You little shit," she said.

"Yes, I am," I replied. "My Queen knew exactly who she was sending to spoil your fun." Then I froze at the sound of the door closing at the top of the stairs and the soft clicking footsteps that came down. How long had Fionn been standing in the doorway listening? I felt suddenly sick but forced myself to keep staring into the Abbess's cold eyes.

"Kiernan?" said Fionn. "Is it true? Is that why you wanted…?" He stopped and bowed his head to the Abbess.

She looked at Fionn and back at me. "It is of no matter. Branfionn knows his duty to this Abbey, and he knows Sidhe avoid the truth like a cat avoids water."

"Sidhe can't lie any more than Alfar can," I said.

"But you're half-human," said Fionn, his voice small and lonely. My heart ached, but I couldn't explain, couldn't swear that I hadn't fucked him to ruin the sacrifice, that I hadn't even been thinking about the sacrifice at all, with the Abbess standing there, listening.

"Is that so?" said the Abbess. "Branfionn, you do have a part to play in the coming ritual, and you must be ready. The King will be joining us. Rest, eat, and don't believe anything this half-breed tells you. I will send for you this evening."

"Yes, Abbess," Fionn said.

I couldn't make words come out. Fionn might as well have punched me in the gut, but I supposed the words he'd heard me say hadn't felt any better.

The Abbess swept out of the room, the sisters following behind like they'd been caught up in the wind of her passing. The door locked and the footsteps receded.

Fionn walked to the table and busied himself pouring tea. He didn't look at me.

"Pretty bird?"

"Don't call me that." Fionn's voice was quiet but even, no emotion evident.

"Fionn?"

"Is it true?" he said, a hint of anger creeping into his voice.

"Is what true, pretty… Fionn?"

"Did you fuck me just to spoil this sacrifice you think is going to happen?" So Fionn hadn't overheard the Abbess admit he was to be offered to the Moon Goddess. "It's why you came here, to stop this terrible ritual you think is going to destroy the world."

"No, Fionn. I…"

"So, it was just a convenient side effect, then?"

"I wasn't even thinking about rituals or sacrifice when we… when I said I wanted to make you feel good."

"How can I believe you? How can I be sure you just didn't… didn't want me because if you failed to kill me, then at least I wouldn't be perfect anymore. At least I'd be *spoiled*." His anger was evident in his movements now, and tea slopped over the side of the cup as he poured.

"Fionn," I said. He stopped moving but didn't look up.

I sighed and pushed myself off the cot. "Fionn, you are the most beautiful person I have ever seen."

He did look up then, hope and sadness warring on his face.

"Last night… You were magnificent. I wanted you because I … because you make me feel… Goddess Below, Fionn, you *asked* me to fuck you, and I want to give you everything you ask for."

He shook his head. "I want to believe you." He lifted a cup of tea and stared into it. "I just… I'm so confused."

"I know, pretty bird, and I'm sorry. But I'm no danger to you. I want to help you."

I took the cup when he held it out to me.

"The Abbess told me she intends to let you leave in the morning. To report back to your Queen."

I sipped the tea. For once it was hot, if a little too sweet. I sipped again, then drank until the cup was empty.

"You believe her?" I said.

"She's Alfar," said Fionn. "She can't lie." I could almost feel the implication that I, only half fey, *could* lie.

"True," I said, and sat on a stool and rested my arms on the table.

"I'm sorry," said Fionn.

"For what?" The room went fuzzy around the edges. I tried to stand but my legs simply wouldn't lift me off the stool. "Fionn? What did you do?"

"I'm sorry."

And the room went black.

11

Fionn

WHEN KIERNAN slumped forward onto the table, I couldn't stop the sob that tore out of my throat. It felt like the worst kind of betrayal, even if I was doing it for his own good. If he tried to escape, the Abbess might not kill him, but she *would* hurt him. If he could just wait until after midsummer night was over, he would be allowed to leave unharmed.

That much, at least, I was sure of. As for the rest – the supposed sacrifice, the bid for magic power – I didn't know any more than I knew two days ago. I wanted to believe Kiernan; I wanted to believe he really *wanted* me and hadn't just been trying to ruin the sacrifice, to *spoil* the victim. To *sully* me so I would no longer be acceptable to the Lady of the Moon.

But I knew the Abbess couldn't lie; I knew she had saved me, had nurtured my egg and had broken it open when my infant self would have been trapped inside. She had fed me and clothed me, had given me work, trained me as a healer, had given me the run of the Abbey library. Everything I was and everything I had was thanks to her.

I got up and paced across the room, unable to sit still any longer. Kiernan looked smaller, younger, less imposing, sprawled unconscious across the table. He looked vulnerable and beautiful.

I had to turn away, to choke back another sob. I would *not* cry. Not now. But I couldn't help returning to the table to look at him, to touch his soft, unruly hair and run a finger along one of his antlers. I closed my eyes and I could see his face, looking up at me in wonder, in desire, in awe even. I remembered his moan as he climaxed and how he'd caught me when I collapsed after fucking him, exhausted, satiated… dangerously close to falling in love.

I shook my head. I couldn't think about that now. Now I had to prepare to assist the Abbess with the midsummer full moon ritual. The Alfar King would be there, and everything had to be perfect. I had never been allowed to participate in a full moon before, but because of the King's presence, this time was to be special. For the first time since I'd been in the Abbey, it would not be a woman-only rite.

So, reluctantly, I left Kiernan slumped at the table and went upstairs to my sitting room. I sat at my worktable where a cloth of sky-blue cloud silk was nearly finished on the loom. It was a task the Abbess had set me moons ago but hadn't told me what it was for. Now I knew; it was for me, for tonight. For a while, I was able to lose myself in the meditative act of weaving and finished off the last handspan of rows. When I reached the end of months of work, I pulled the cloth free and held it up. It formed a long rectangle, tapered almost to a point at one end, and was deliciously soft and drapey.

I wove in the loose ends of thread with a needle and moved the loom to the floor so I could lay the fabric out on the table. From a plain wooden box, I took a length of banding, woven in the same blue cloud silk as the cloth, and measured and cut and stitched it to add strapping in strategic places on the cloth. Then I added my one treasure: a set of silver buttons.

That finished, I stripped off my clothes, climbed the stairs to my bedroom and washed next to the hearth. I braided my hair: two long braids on each side of my head that I wound around the rest of the silver mass to contain it. I used an extra length of the blue cloud silk thread, leftover from my weaving, to tie the braids securely.

Then I went back down to my sitting room and held the fabric up to myself. It felt soft on my skin. Soft like Kiernan's mouth, like his breath on the back of my neck. I shivered and pushed the thought aside. I buttoned the shorter, narrower band of silk around my neck and the longer, wider one around my waist, pulling the cloth around my hips. The fabric, now a short tunic, left my entire back bare, but it hardly mattered, since my buttocks were hidden by my tail, anyway. I wished I had a mirror so I could see how the garment fit, but mirrors were temptations to vanity, according to the Abbess, so I would just have to imagine it.

When I went back down the stairs, I thought for a moment that Kiernan was watching me and my breath caught. I would have liked to ask how he thought I looked, if he liked the blue cloud silk on me. But it was too late for that. It had only looked like he had opened his eyes, but it was just a trick of the shadows.

I glanced at the window above the stairs and saw the sun was going down. It had taken longer than I'd expected to finish the weaving and sewing. But that was good. It meant I could spend less time waiting and worrying, wondering if Kiernan was right after all, and I was about to walk willingly to my own bloody death. Less time wondering if I should have tried to flee this place with him, instead.

I stopped by the table again, to brush Kiernan's hair out of his face. I bit my lip, pulled in a long breath and let it out. Then I fetched Kiernan's boots from next to the door, picked up his bundle of clothes, and climbed back up the stairs. I paused in the sitting room to take a book off the shelf, then continued up to the bedroom. I set the boots next to the bed, then laid out Kier's clothes, piece by piece, on top of the quilt. I pulled his sword, his belt, his twin knives, from under the bed and arranged them next to the clothes.

The leather on the hilts of his weapons was almost a match to the blue of my tunic, and they bore the imprint of his fingers. I touched one of the daggers, fitted my hand to the grooves and found my own grip narrower that his, my fingers longer. I imagined his hands on the leather and wanted them on my skin.

I shook my head and picked up the book. It had the long and scientific-sounding title of *A Guide to the Reproduction and Sexual Habits of the Peoples of the Isle*, and no author was listed. I had been in the library once, years ago, reading a history of Aven, when I'd heard giggling. I followed the sound, peered cautiously around the end of a bookcase, and saw four junior sisters bent over a book, pointing and covering their mouths to try to stifle their laughter. I watched, staying out of sight, until they had hidden the book and scurried away to finish their daily chores. Then I took the book from where they'd hidden it and smuggled it back to my tower. I knew I would never be punished, would never even be suspected of theft, because the sisters would never dare report the forbidden book missing. Most likely, they would assume one of their own was responsible, anyway.

I kept the book not because it was about sex, but because it was the only book I'd ever found in the library that told me anything *useful* about my own people. It explained why, unlike the mammalian peoples of the Isle, a bird man's penis was hidden, and how his sheath worked. How *my* sheath worked. It told me about self-lubrication, and that my orgasms would happen in pulses. It told me all the ways my body was different from the bodies of fey and human and Siegel.

From the book I had learned how long my mother would have carried me in her body if I hadn't been cut out of her still in the egg. And I learned, from a too-brief chapter near the end, that while a male and female were necessary for reproduction among all the peoples of the Isle, sex for pleasure could occur between any two – or more – be they man, woman, or other.

That book was how I had learned I preferred other men, when I'd never met another man my whole life.

Now I hoped that somehow leaving this book for Kiernan would tell him… I don't know, *something*. I thought about leaving a note, an apology, an explanation, but I couldn't. I didn't know *how*; I didn't know what to say, what words would help anything I was feeling make sense. So I opened the book to the chapter on bird folk, turned to the page that showed a cross-section of a bird man's reproductive apparatus, sheath and all, and I placed it on top of Kiernan's shirt.

Then I went back downstairs, put on my cloak, and waited.

When the senior sisters arrived to escort me to the Abbess, I didn't look back. If I did, I was afraid I would scream and throw myself at Kiernan and beg the sisters to leave us alone.

So I walked, back held as straight as I could make it, and

followed the sisters down the stairs and out to the courtyard. To my surprise and dismay, it was full of people. No junior sisters and no novices were anywhere to be seen. Instead, there were armored men on horseback filling the space. How could I not have heard them arrive? How could I have missed the sound of restless horse hooves and quiet conversation, no matter how politely silent the men seemed to be trying to be? They looked impatient, ready to leave at a moment's notice, and I wondered if they had been there long, or if they had only just arrived.

I felt their eyes on me, saw them glance at the sisters as we crossed the courtyard and I was glad for the concealing drape of my cloak, and even – for once – for the smallness of my wings, that they wouldn't be noticeable under the heavy fabric.

We walked quickly, and when we reached the central tower, all nine of the sisters filed through the door after letting me go in first, then someone locked the door behind us. Three sisters went first up the stairs, then me, then the other six sisters. I wanted to loiter, to look around me and see what the Abbess's sanctuary looked like.

I had only been here in her office once before, when I was a child and had snuck in to look at the big ledger where the Abbess recorded everything that happened at the Abbey. I had read something about how birthdays were celebrated in the different cultures of the Isle, and wanted to know when I was born. I could have asked, but I had been afraid the Abbess would dismiss my questions as irrelevant, since we didn't celebrate birthdays at the Abbey. So I had crept quietly in one day, and read the ledger, and learned how old I was and that I had been born on the summer solstice. The Abbess had recorded it as the day of my birth – not that I had hatched from a premature egg – so I had spent most of my life thinking

I had once had a mother who had been a Sister of the Moon.

From my quick glance as we passed through, the room looked exactly the same: sparse and utilitarian. The next floor was similar. It was a sitting room equipped with a small number of pieces of uncomfortable-looking furniture that hardly looked used. More stairs and we passed through the Abbess's bedroom which had only an enormous, plush-looking bed in it, hung with rich curtains of silk and velvet, and equipped with more pillows that any one person could possibly ever need.

Next came a floor that held boxes and crates. I wanted to ask what they contained, but even if any of the sisters had been inclined to answer, they were sworn to silence. Finally, we came to the uppermost room in the tower. It was bare of furnishings, save tall candlesticks around the perimeter, and the floor was painted with the phases of the moon.

The Abbess stood in the middle of the room, facing a tall Alfar man with honey-colored hair and dark blue eyes. He wore a circlet of silver on his head and was dressed in cloth-of-silver and blue velvet, with yellow cloud silk peeking out of his collar and cuffs.

The sisters sank to one knee before the man, pulling me down with them, and I realized that this was the Alfar King, Monarch of the Aven Mountains, and Overlord of the Triarchy. "My King," said the sisters, breaking their holy vow of silence to give the King his due reverence. I spoke the words along with them.

"This is the boy?" he said in a voice that had something like the smoke and resonance of Kiernan's, but with the coldness of the Abbess's, and a haughtiness all its own.

"It is, my King," said the Abbess.

"Let's have a look at him, then."

"Rise, Branfionn," said the Abbess, and I stood up,

looking carefully at the shiny toes of the King's black leather boots.

"You gave him a Sidhe name?" said the King, surprise and mild disgust in his voice.

"It seemed… appropriate, my King," the Abbess responded. The King said nothing, then snickered.

Two of the sisters stood close to me, each one with a pinching grip on one of my elbows. It hurt, but I was glad, because I was suddenly so nervous I was shaking. What if he decided I was unsatisfactory? That I was not good enough to assist him with this ritual?

After a moment, the sisters let go of me, and stepped back, pulling my cloak off and leaving me exposed, only the thin cloud-silk tunic covering me.

I kept my eyes on the floor and clasped my hands together to keep them from trembling too obviously as the King walked a circle around me. I watched his shiny black boots disappear to one side and reappear on the other, then stop directly in front of me.

"Look at me, bird boy," he said.

I looked up and met his hard blue stare. His eyes would have been beautiful if they hadn't been so cold, so frightening.

"Yes, my King," I said, hoping my voice was actually audible.

"Remarkable," he said, but to the Abbess, not to me. "You've found a fucking Vogel seer. I won't ask how you did it."

"He has been here since infancy, my King," said the Abbess.

"He's a pretty thing." The King reached out and grasped my chin and I realized I had to look up at him. I'd never met someone taller than I, not since before I reached my full growth.

"Pity he needs to be kept pure," the King said, turning my face from side to side and looking over every inch of me. "I wouldn't have minded taking him to bed once or twice."

I slid my eyes away from the King' scrutiny to look at the Abbess. She was staring at me, as if daring me to speak up, to admit I'd already lost my virginity to the half-human Sidhe who was supposed to have killed me.

I said nothing.

"Well, let's get on with it," said the King. "I've been waiting a long time to show the Sidhe and the Huldr just how far beneath us they are."

I felt my knees go weak at his words and thought I might fall when he suddenly let go of my face, but I clenched my teeth and stayed upright. I knew I mustn't show weakness.

"Of course, my King," said the Abbess. "If you would stand in the center of the room."

The sisters drew me to one side so the King could move to the very middle of the room, then arranged themselves around the perimeter, forming a circle of alternating sisters and candle holders.

"My senior sisters will channel the magic we raise into you, my King, as I channel it to them." She turned to me and her cold eyes seemed to look right into me. I held off a shiver. "Come with me, Branfionn. Our business is on the roof."

"Yes, Abbess." I forced the words out of my mouth. With every passing moment, I felt more and more sure that Kiernan had not been entirely wrong. I still couldn't believe the Abbess would save me as an unborn child only to kill me thirty-three years later, but it sure felt like *something* sinister was going to happen.

I followed her up the last set of stairs and onto the tower roof. Unlike my tower, which had a door in a partial wall, this one had a trap, leaving a clear view all the way around. I had never seen the Abbey from this angle before, and I couldn't help turning to look. I could see everything: the four straight sides, the corner towers, the courtyard and gardens, the laundry, the bathhouse, even the gate and the men on horseback waiting below.

I looked over at my own tower, then away. The partial wall that held the door blocked much of my view of my own roof and would have hidden me – and Kiernan – from view had anyone thought to spy on us last night. What I could see of the roof was empty.

"Will your patient make his way to the roof, do you think?" asked the Abbess. "I should like him to watch his daring plan fail in the most spectacular way."

"I don't know, Abbess," I said. "He was unconscious when I left."

"Was he lying, little seer?" she said, fixing me with her cold glare. "About taking your virtue?"

I didn't answer. I didn't know *how* to answer. A "no" would tell her I had gone against all she had taught me about goodness and propriety, that I had given in to my baser urges in my desperate loneliness and longing for kindness. But it might also cause her to give up whatever scheme she had up here, to change her mind about this power grab for the Alfar throne.

But a "yes" would get me punished if she sensed it was a lie.

"I…" I stammered. "I don't know what that means, Abbess."

She smiled with no warmth in her face. "Good. No decent dweller in my Abbey should know about such filth."

"What am I to do, Abbess?" I asked. "What is my part in this ritual?"

"Only to sit there." She pointed to a slab of stone in the

center of the roof. "Clear your mind as you do when you have visions."

I couldn't help thinking how little the Abbess knew about having visions if she thought a clear mind had anything to do with it. Most visions were confusing muddles of images and even the straightforward ones were never clear. How had I believed she was a mentor to me for so long?

"Do you wish me to *see*, Abbess?"

"Only clear your mind, boy, and prepare to be a conduit for such magic as has not been seen in these lands since the last Vogel seer died."

"Abbess?" I felt cold, and not only because the summer air was promising rain and my tunic provided little protection from the breeze. If I was to channel magic, then Kiernan must be wrong, yet I couldn't help but be afraid. Because he had been right, at least, about the *aim* of the ritual.

"Sit," said the Abbess, so I sat.

"Clear your mind," she said.

I tried to clear my mind, to push aside my fears and doubts, my regret at drugging Kiernan and leaving him alone in the tower. The best I could do was to sit very still.

Then the moon, which had been creeping higher as we spoke, cleared the treetops, full and bright, and pierced through the thin clouds.

The Abbess raised her arms and called out in a language that sounded like Alfar, but a dialect I had never heard before. In the room below, the unfamiliar voices of the nine senior sisters, sounding uncertain from long disuse, echoed her.

For a long time the Abbess stood, chanting to the moon as it rose higher in the sky. When it was nearly overhead, she turned. In her hand – though I had not seen her produce it, nor even move her arm to reach for it – was a sickle-shaped blade, a silver crescent that gleamed in the moonlight.

"Clear your mind, little seer," the Abbess said, and stepped behind me, out of my line of sight. She ran her free hand over my hair, then suddenly gripped and pulled, hard.

Somewhere, on the edge of my awareness, I thought I heard my name.

"Goddess Above," I whispered. Fear held me prisoner, kept me from pulling away, and the Abbess pulled my head back and back and I saw the sickle blade from the corner of one eye, moving closer.

And finally, I tried to pull away, to tear my hair free of the Abbess's grip and stand up from the altar stone. But I couldn't move. Something held me still on the slab of stone, would only let me bend slowly backwards under the pressure of the Abbess's grip on my hair until I felt cold rock against my back and I met the Abbess's even colder eyes, upside-down. My wings were bent awkwardly under me, my tail at a painful angle.

I heard my name again, screamed across a distance that seemed insurmountable.

"I'm sorry, Kiernan," I whispered.

"What was that, little seer?" the Abbess said. "Have you a final prayer before your perfect magic joins that of our King?"

Kiernan would have had something to say. Something irreverent, or filthy, to spit in the Abbess's face. All I could think to tell her was, "He told the truth."

She blinked at me. "Who did?"

"Kiernan. The fey. He told the truth. We were lovers. All last night. Three times." Tears burned the backs of my eyes and left hot trails down my face. "I'm not a virgin."

"You're a filthy little shit," said the Abbess. "A degenerate, primitive, barely sentient creature, just as you always have been." She lowered the knife to my throat and I thought I heard my name again, from somewhere very far away.

"But you are still close enough to perfect to draw down the power of the Lady of the Moon, to allow our King to conquer the rest of this degenerate land."

I could see, now, the fervor of a fanatic in her eyes, and I wondered why I had never seen it before.

"I'm not ready to die," I said. "I've only just discovered how to live." And before she could answer, before she could bring the knife down onto my throat, my two little tree serpent friends were diving at her, knocking her hands away, and suddenly I could move.

I stood up from the altar and looked frantically around. The Abbess stood atop the trap door, fending off Smoke and Flame, and there was no other way out of the tower.

And then I heard my name again, clearly, "Fionn!" shouted with a smoky, resonant voice, a voice I'd heard saying my name in the midst of pleasure. I turned towards my tower and he was there, dressed in the green and brown of the forest, holding a long sword that shone even brighter than the Abbess's knife.

"Kiernan!" I screamed back. The tower was so close. So impossible to reach. Only the distance that three or four rooms were wide, but too far to jump across.

Kiernan stood on the parapet of my tower, holding out his hand. "Jump, Fionn," he called. "I'll help you."

Below in the courtyard, the King's men looked up, waiting to see what would happen. And on the top of the tower, I felt a breeze, a warm wind that sparked with magic, green and yellow, alive and tugging at my hair.

"Please, pretty bird."

The tree serpents, unable to hold off the Abbess any longer, swooped past me, chittering at me, tugging at strands of my hair as they went.

Come, said Smoke, into my mind.

You must, said Flame.

The Abbess's footsteps sounded loud on the stone. I felt her magic reaching for me, trying to drag me back to the altar stone, to hold me down.

So, as a darker, thicker cloud covered the moon, temporarily darkening the sky, the tower, and the surrounding land, I did the only thing I could think of.

I jumped. I spread my stunted wings, my too-short tail, and hoped that by some miracle I would make it across the impossible distance between the towers. To where Kiernan waited for me.

A sudden gust of warm, magic-filled wind swept under me, tugged at my wings, seemed to lift me, just a little. Smoke and Flame twisted and glided through the air, calling out in encouragement.

Behind me, the Abbess cursed in every word she had forbidden me to speak, and others I'd never encountered before.

I beat my wings frantically. And I fell.

12
Kiernan

I WOKE WITH AN AWFUL taste in my mouth, like I'd been drinking my father's soldier's wine for three days straight and then puked it all up again, and a sick feeling in my belly. Only the first of those was from the drugged tea.

I levered myself up off the table, climbed unsteadily to my feet, and found a pail of fresh water near the door. I hoped it wasn't also drugged and gulped at it until my mouth and throat felt cleaner.

"Why, Fionn?" I said out loud, but I was pretty sure I already knew. He was lonely and had only ever had the Abbess as company. Even the sisters and the novices were barely real, only silent presences that watched him, always.

He might have believed, for a little while, for that one glorious night, that I cared for him, and wanted to help him. But when I opened my big stupid mouth and boasted to the Abbess that I had defiled her sacrifice, when I had said it in such a derogatory way and Fionn had overheard… It was no wonder he thought I had used him, that I had only wanted to stop the ritual, to carry out my assignment, and maybe get a bit of ass in the bargain.

"Fionn?" I didn't expect an answer, but I suppose I hoped for one, hoped he was still in the tower and hadn't gone with the Abbess. I climbed the stairs, expecting the door at the top to be locked, to have to pound on it to get Fionn's attention. But it swung open as soon as I put my hand on it.

Things had been moved, the loom with the partly-woven cloth was empty and on the floor, thread and snips and needles scattered the work surface, leaving an untidiness that didn't fit with what else I had seen of Fionn's personal space. I climbed the next set of stairs, and found that door unlocked, too, and Fionn's bedroom uninhabited.

On his bed, on top of the soft blankets where I had laid him to sleep, where he had whispered that he loved me, probably not even realizing he had said it out loud, my clothes were laid out as if waiting for me. As if he had set them there for me to dress. My sword and knives were there, too, arranged with care next to my clothes.

I kept going up to the roof. If Fionn was still in the tower, he would be there. I hoped he would be there, waiting for me, waiting to escape with me. When I opened the door, I heard the stamping of hooves and the jingling of bits, the soft impatient voices of men at arms forced to wait but afraid to speak up in complaint. I slipped to the floor before I crawled out of the shelter of the door and its wall, and peered over the parapet.

The courtyard was full of armed Alfar on horseback. King's men. I turned away and lay flat, wondering what the fuck to do now. It was unlikely the men would look up and see me, though not impossible, and I didn't want to be seen. Not yet. And not by them.

I crawled back to the door and descended to Fionn's

bedroom. I wanted to crawl into his bed, to get lost in the sweet, musky scent of his skin that would no doubt linger on his sheets. I wanted to not have to think about any of this. Instead, I sat on the very edge of the bed and reached for my shirt, only to find it held down by a large book, laid open in the middle of the green fabric.

The page showing was a diagram of a Vogel man, as if cut in half to show the inner workings of his sex organs. It showed his sheath and how it protected his reproductive anatomy, and despite the sick feeling in my guts that grew worse with every moment, it made me smile.

Fionn had blushed when he told me about this book, his pale cheeks touched with delicate pink, the tips of his perfect ears growing red. I had no idea what he meant to tell me by leaving it for me to find, but at least he had been thinking of me. At least he had been remembering last night.

I yanked off the terrible, coarse Abbey clothes and pulled on my own. They had been cleaned and mended and the fabric felt so good on my skin I sighed out loud. Who would have thought something as simple as nice cloth could make such a difference?

Then I tried to think what to do. I could pick the tower lock and slip out, but with that many men between me and gate, I didn't think much of my chances. Not without access to my magic. And I still didn't want to leave Fionn. Not only would that mean I had failed to stop the ritual and condemned the Isle to decades of war, but I would have failed to save someone I cared for.

And I was forced to admit I *did* care for Fionn. I thought about how he had told me he didn't want to want me, because it would make parting more painful, and I realized I was *enjoying* wanting him, caring about him, because I wasn't afraid of pain. I was afraid of the emptiness that had been my experience of relationships and sex before I'd met him.

"Fuck."

The only place I could use magic was on the tower roof, so whatever I was going to do would have to start there. But then what? The forest was too far away to call on and the gardens and fields at the base of the wall too small.

Possibly, I could set something on fire to cause a distraction. Or maybe reach around the wards and ask the earth beneath the Abbey to rise up. Or maybe I could just as likely sprout wings and fly us away from here.

And then there was the problem that I didn't even know where Fionn was. He had said the Abbess cast the wards from the roof of the central tower, so it would make sense that that's where the sacrifice would be carried out, but that wasn't exactly within reach.

I went back to the roof to look for the moon. If the sacrifice was in honor of the Lady of the Moon, it would happen after moonrise. I had until then to come up with a plan. It wasn't yet risen above the treetops, but it would be soon. I could see its glow already turning the edge of the forest silver.

I crouched behind the partial wall, my back against the door, and waited. I don't know what I was waiting *for*, but I there wasn't anything I could do until something happened that I could react to.

Just when I thought I was going to have to hurl myself from the top of the tower just for something to happen, I heard a small noise that wasn't the men in the courtyard. I closed my eyes and listened to the sound of a trap door from the direction of the central tower. Unlike the other towers, it lacked a partial wall and door, but was instead entirely flat on top. The trap banged open and I heard footsteps. One set shuffled, like the sound the sisters made with their leather slippers as they entered to leave our food and water, like the Abbess's feet had made when she delivered the tea that left me unconscious. The other set was soft, almost inaudible from this distance, and accompanied by little clicks of claws tapping against the stone.

I heard voices but couldn't make out the words. The Abbess's cold, stern voice, and Fionn's, husky and tired. He didn't sound afraid, only uncertain. He still trusted the Abbess. The trap door banged shut.

I wished I had my bow, to shoot the Abbess where she stood, before she could hurt him. But my bow had been strapped to my stag's saddle, and might still be there, for all I knew, wherever the daft old deer had wandered off to.

Then I heard chanting as the moon cleared the treetops. I crept to the edge of the wall, staying low to let the parapet hide me as I peered across from Fionn's tower to the Abbess's. She stood facing the moon, arms spread. Fionn sat unmoving behind her, on a stone altar in the center of the roof, and I resisted the urge to call out to him. I could see the tendrils of the Abbess's magic twining around her, around Fionn. I would need to distract her.

The moon rose as the Abbess chanted, and she raised one hand higher, holding something that caught the light and glinted silver. A curved, wicked-looking blade, its shape a crescent moon, if the moon were deadly sharp. She left the edge of the tower, turned to Fionn and swept around behind him. My breath caught in my throat, and I couldn't have screamed if I'd tried. And I did try. No sound came out.

The Abbess seemed to stroke Fionn's hair gently, but it turned into a cruel yank that pulled his head back, stretched his throat taut. She moved the knife closer, and two thin shapes darted out of the sky, chittering at me, tugging my hair and my clothes, and suddenly I could speak, could yell.

"Fionn!"

No one reacted, save the King's men, who only glanced up in bored curiosity.

The Abbess hauled on Fionn's hair until he lay flat on his back on the stone, his silver tail twisted cruelly to the side, his lovely wings bent awkwardly beneath him. I could see that his eyes were wide and afraid, even from this distance.

I stood and screamed, "Fionn!" Smoke and Flame swooped and dove around me, frantic.

The Abbess still held her knife poised but didn't strike. I heard Fionn's voice again, still quiet but choked with tears, and the Abbess listened and replied in a tone of disgust.

"Help him," I whispered, and the two little serpents streaked through the air towards Fionn, flinging themselves at the Abbess as she brought her knife down to Fionn's throat.

I reached over my shoulder and pulled my sword free of its scabbard. The ancestor who had it made could command not only the magic of the land, but also the sea and the sky. There was no one here I could attack, so I wielded it like a child might wave a wand to focus their magical intent and I called on the air, the wind, to push the Abbess back, to keep her from Fionn. It was a gamble, using her own element against her, but it was the only thing I could do from here.

Fionn stood up and looked around, as if seeking a direction to flee in. There was nowhere to go.

"Fionn!" I yelled, and he saw me.

"Kiernan!"

I stepped up close to the edge of the roof and held out my hand. "Jump, Fionn," I called. "I'll help you." I only hoped the serpents could keep the Abbess occupied long enough.

Below, the King's men watched, but didn't seem inclined to move. Perhaps they had to wait for orders. Or perhaps they weren't paid enough to care. And for all they knew, this could be part of the ritual.

The Abbess advanced on Fionn and I could feel her power, could *see* it, gathering around her. The serpents left off trying to keep her away and dove around Fionn instead, tugging his hair. And he screamed – in terror maybe, or in defiance, or frustration – and flung himself off the tower.

He spread his perfect little silver wings and I pointed my sword and called the wind, tugged it right out of the Abbess's control because she wasn't expecting me to try, and I sent it to catch him, to sweep under his wings and lift him. I could only keep the wind moving above the wards, above the top of the towers and Fionn had jumped away and not up, and so the wind could only carry him a little, could only pluck at his feathers and keep him airborne until his weight dipped him below the level of the parapet.

He was close. So close. I looked into his beautiful eyes, wide and afraid, but full of hope, of trust. He was falling, but he was so close. I threw myself belly down on the edge of the parapet, dropping my sword and reaching desperately.

I caught his wrist. I held as tight as I could as he fell, as he hit the side of the tower and cried out in pain. I would not let go.

"I've got you," I said. The serpents dove around me, around Fionn, scolding me, telling me to pull, to hurry, to not *dare* drop the seer. So I pulled. If Fionn had been human or fey, or anything but a hollow-boned bird man, I don't think I could have lifted him onto the roof. But he was slender, and light, and he beat his wings as hard as he could to add some lift, and I got him up and over and pulled him on top of me, onto the tower's roof.

"I've got you," I said again, and wrapped my arms around him. "I've got you, pretty bird."

"I'm sorry," Fionn said, into my neck. "Kiernan, I'm so sorry." He was crying.

"It's okay, pretty bird. It's okay." I stroked his hair, tucked his face into my shoulder, and held him while we lay catching our breath. And the tree serpents flung themselves at Fionn, chittering frantically.

You must flee, they said.

I heard a shriek from the central tower and felt a pressure in the front of my head, and rolled, pulling Fionn with me into the shelter of the door and its wall. A force hit the stone where we had been lying and shook the whole tower.

"We have to go," I said.

"Where?" said Fionn. "How? The courtyard is full of soldiers."

"Do you trust me?" He had no reason to, not really, and I couldn't blame him when he hesitated.

"Have you had visions of things that happen after today? Visions of us?"

"Yes," said Fionn. "But visions of the future…"

"Are only possibilities. I know." I touched his face, traced his delicate cheekbone. "Trust your visions, Fionn, if you can't trust me. Trust that we live past today. Okay?"

He nodded. "Okay."

The tower shook again, and I could just hear footsteps far below, pounding up the tower stairs. I got to my feet and pulled Fionn up after me, keeping us in the shelter of the wall. I bent for my sword, sheathed it on my back and moved towards the farthest edge of the tower, where it looked over the forest.

"Hold onto me," I said and wrapped both arms around Fionn, pulling him against me, chest to chest.

"Kiernan?"

"Trust yourself," I said, and I stepped up onto the low parapet. Below was only a garden full of pea vines and beans, turnips and carrots and beets. I kissed him, gently, firmly, trying to tell him everything I wasn't ready to tell him with words. And then I threw us both off the tower.

Fionn screamed but opened his wings and spread his tail and tried to break our fall, to slow our descent. The air ripped through his feathers.

"I've got you," I said, and twisted around, spread my fingers, and called the wind again. It was easier, here outside the Abbey, and the air pushed against us, slowing us.

It wasn't going to be enough.

I called out to the land, to the pea vines and the bean tendrils, to the weeds that even the most industrious field workers hadn't been able to eliminate, and I asked for help. Below us, the garden erupted into growth, tendrils and vines and leaves grew, thrust up into the sky and broke our fall.

It still hurt. It still knocked the breath out of me, and I was sure I'd have a black bruise across my back soon, where I'd landed on my sword.

It hurt like hell, but the fall didn't kill us, and it didn't break our bones.

When I opened my mouth to speak, only a groan came out. I tried again. "Pretty bird?"

"Yes?" Fionn's voice was hoarse from screaming.

"We have to run now. We have to get to the forest."

"Okay."

We climbed to our feet, leaning on each other. From the other side of the Abbey, I could hear yelling, and I breathed a prayer of thanks to whichever deity might be listening that Fionn's tower was on the opposite side of the Abbey from the gate. From the top of the wall, I could see faces watching, Novices, maybe, or sisters.

"I thought they swore never to look upon men," I said, trying to stand up straight enough to run.

"They did."

"I guess a lot of them are going to be sent home soon, then."

Fionn looked up at the Abbey. "I suppose so."

The feathered serpents swooped around us. *Run*, they urged. *Flee.*

We turned our backs on the Abbey and ran.

It hurt. I had been knocked out by the Abbey's wards, my joints and muscles left in deep aching pain. I had then spent an entire night fucking my brains out, and another drugged into unconsciousness. And then I fell off a tower. I was not in the best shape of my life. In fact, I was very close to pushing my body as far as it would go. Much more punishment and it would simply refuse to work anymore.

As for Fionn, he had probably never needed to run before, or at least not very far. His feet were shapely, but built for grasping and slow, stately walking, not for fleeing at high speed. But he ran next to me, spreading his wings to give him a little lift with each stride.

Hand in hand we fled across the Abbey's gardens and fields, past surprised rabbits and mice raiding the crops at night. I wanted to yell at them to flee, to get away before the King's men arrived, but I only had breath for running.

I heard the hooves of horses and the bellows of the King's men, but horses dislike being made to run at night, and I heard them neigh in complaint, and imagined them tossing their heads and shying at shadows.

I reached out to the land as we ran, and asked for help, to hide us and protect us, and when the Abbess threw a bone-stripping wind after us, a wall of earth rose and deflected it, creating a whirlwind of dirt and rocks that hid us from her.

We ran until I tripped in my exhaustion. I fell, and almost pulled Fionn down with me. He pulled on my arm and the serpents whirled around us.

Flee! said Flame.

This way, said Smoke, and the little snake-dragons streaked for the trees.

"We're almost there, Kier," Fionn said, so I forced myself up, made myself run again and there it was, the forest.

We reached the trees, pushed through the brush and under the shelter of the canopy. I knew we needed to keep going, but I couldn't seem to catch my breath. I looked at Fionn, but he was staring in horror back the way we'd come. I turned.

The Abbess sent fire.

All I could do was grab Fionn and fling both of us out of the path of the fireball and watch as it hit a tree and the conifer burst into flames.

I reached for the land, for the forest's magic and the trees made a wall behind us, but the flames spread, fueled by the Abbess's anger.

"No." I didn't realize I'd said it out loud until Fionn looked at me.

"We have to keep going," he said. "We have to go far enough she won't follow."

"We can't let it burn," I said. "*I* can't let it burn." I stumbled closer to the fire, so close I could feel it scorching on my skin. I called the sky, the wind, the air, to starve the flames. I don't know if it was the Abbess's magic, or my exhaustion, but calling the air only made the blaze flare higher.

So I called the land, the earth, where my deepest strength lay, and flung a wall of dirt at the flames. They stuttered, dimmed, and then flared up again.

"Kiernan," Fionn said. "We have to go."

"I can't let it burn, Fionn," I said. "You wouldn't understand, but I have to stop this. My magic comes from the forest. Maybe not *this* forest, but that doesn't matter. I can't let it burn." I looked at his face, trying to make him understand. "Keep going," I said. "I'll find you."

"No," said Fionn. "I won't leave you. Let me help. Tell me what to do."

"Just keep watch. Tell me if the King's men enter the forest."

I dropped to my knees and pressed my hands to the damp earth, closed my eyes and sent my thoughts deep into the soil, reaching, sensing, asking. Begging. And I felt it, felt it surge up in a blast of magic so strong I knew I could never contain it. But I didn't need to contain it, only direct it. It hurt, it ached, and burned, but I didn't stop. I kept calling, kept begging.

And it came. From between my hands, a geyser of water shot up, knocking me backwards. It was even hotter than the water in the Abbey bathhouse, but it could still smother fire.

I clawed my way back onto my knees, raised my hands, and flung the magic, the water, towards the burning tree – the many burning trees, because the flames had spread, were still spreading. There was a hiss, a roar, as if a huge dragon of steam was screaming its anger, and the flames disappeared.

Steam shot up instead and I screamed at it, grabbed it with what magic I could still muster, and directed it towards the King's men, the Abbey, towards anyone who might have pursued us.

For a passing moment, I felt sad for the horses, for any animals that might not have fled at the approach of soldiers, for the birds that might be in the way, but then the magic swept away all emotions.

I could feel Fionn and the tree serpents safe behind me, and that was all that mattered. I felt the Abbess and the King vanish into the safety of the Abbey, leaving the men to their fate. Some of the men closer to the Abbey turned their horses and fled, and some made it to the shelter of the walls. The ones closer to the forest were caught in the blast of superheated steam and died.

And then, suddenly, the magic was gone, and I felt only a deep ache where it had been, and everything went dark.

I came to, feeling movement. Someone was carrying me; someone hairy and very strong, who smelled like something familiar, though at first I couldn't say what. I think I fucked someone who smelled similar, once, or had been fucked. A long time ago. It had been nice. I had been so sore after that I could hardly walk.

Then the blackness came again.

I heard Fionn's voice. "Thank you," he said. "I don't know how to thank you."

"Think nothing of it," said another voice, a woman. She did not sound cold and cruel like the Abbess, like the Queen of the Forest, but warm.

I drifted again. I remembered falling, Fionn's arms around me. Falling from the tower. Falling in love. I wanted Fionn's arms around me again. Fionn, who could be gentle and fiercely passionate in the same moment, who tasted sweet and liked that I tasted salty. Who cared about me.

Black, then gray, then black again. Then it was morning, and my head hurt like nothing I'd ever felt before. Like stabbing and pressure and aching all at the same time. I tried to sit up and suddenly lost everything in my stomach, but someone was there, holding a basin for me to vomit into.

"It's okay. You're safe."

"Fionn," I said. My voice didn't sound like my own. It was raspy, like I had been screaming for days.

"Drink this," said Fionn, and held a cup to my lips. I drank and the cool water eased the burning in my throat.

"The last time I drank something you gave me I woke up

a very long time later and you were gone," I said. My voice still didn't sound right, but at least my throat felt a little better.

"I'm sorry, Kiernan. I didn't –"

I cut him off with a gesture. "Don't," I said. "You don't need to apologize."

"I do."

"You don't."

He frowned and I realized my eyes were open. I didn't remember opening them.

"The fire?" I asked.

"You put it out," Fionn said. "It had the Abbess's magic in it, and it could have burned the whole forest, but you stopped it."

"That's good." I turned my head cautiously and my stomach lurched, but I didn't throw up again. "Where are we?"

"Safe," said Fionn. "Try to sleep some more."

"Are you sure?" I tried to sit up and immediately regretted it. I clamped my mouth shut and swallowed hard, and nothing came spewing up.

"Yes." Fionn fidgeted with the edge of the blanket, then smoothed it over my chest. "You stopped the fire and the people who live in the forest… they brought us to a safe place."

"It was our fault the forest almost burned in the first place."

"They have no love for the Abbey, or the Abbess." Fionn smoothed the blanket again. "Or the Alfar King of Aven, for that matter."

I closed my eyes and tried to relax. To calm myself, I reached out for the Three Realms. And just like in the Abbey, I couldn't feel them.

"Fionn?" I tried to keep my voice calm.

"I'm here."

"Please tell me this safe place of yours has wards that prevent magic."

"I… It doesn't." Fionn's voice was a whisper.

"I can't feel my magic, Fionn," I said, trying not to panic. Panic would do no good. And how could I panic properly anyway, when I could barely move? "Fionn?"

"I know," Fionn said gently. "I know." Then he leaned over and kissed my forehead and the blackness rushed in again.

II: AVEN FOREST

13
Kiernan

For the second time in a few days, I found myself waking up in a strange place with no magic and Fionn watching over me.

The first time, Fionn had been a stranger, and my magic was only suppressed and not gone. This time, Fionn was… something more, and there was nothing preventing me from reaching my magic. It just wasn't there.

My body ached from too much exertion but the hollow feeling where magic should have been was much more terrible.

Fionn hovered as if he was afraid I would panic, or worse, and I knew I should be feeling either amused at his concern or irritated at being treated like an invalid. I found it hard to feel much of anything except empty.

When he asked me for the third time if I wanted a glass of water while reaching to adjust the way the blanket lay over me yet again, I said, "Fionn, please just stop." I couldn't keep the emptiness out of my voice, but I think Fionn must have heard it as something else, because the look he gave me was hurt, and I felt bad.

"I'm sorry," he said, and straightened up from where he'd been bending over me. "I'll leave you alone." He didn't look at me as he headed for the door.

"Wait," I said.

He stopped but didn't turn and I realized I didn't know what to say next. Did he know I couldn't feel my magic? Is that why he was being so smothering? Or was he just trying to look after me because I was sore and tired?

"Can I meet our hosts?" I finally said, because I had no idea how to say what I was actually feeling. The room we were in was small but comfortable, part of a larger house, and I hoped we hadn't taken over someone's personal space. I'd rather have a tent in the forest than impose on someone's privacy, no matter how much pain I was in.

"They've gone to the next village," Fionn said, finally turning back to me. "They needed some supplies, and Col – he owns this house with his wife Moira – thought he'd see if anyone was talking about what happened at the Abbey."

"Col and Moira are werewolves," I said, but Fionn shook his head.

"Col is." He left the doorway to sit on the side of the bed, started to reach out to touch my forehead like he meant to check for fever, but then withdrew his hand. "Moira is human. And a witch." He met my eyes and smiled, tentatively, unable to hide the sparkle in his gaze. "She's a seer, Kiernan, and a healer, too. She says she can teach me, a little. She's already taught me how to –" He stopped suddenly and looked at his hands, guilt replacing excitement on his face.

I untangled my arm from the blanket and took his hand in mine. "She taught you how to put a patient to sleep with magic," I said, and he bit his lip. With my free hand, I touched his chin so he would look up at me.

"Yes," he said softly. "I should have asked you."

"It's okay," I said. "Just stop making a habit of knocking me out."

His eyes widened and he opened his mouth, probably to apologize. I put my fingers on his lips and smiled.

"I'm teasing you, pretty bird."

"Oh," he said against my fingers. I moved my hand to his cheek.

"Are you okay?" I asked. "Did you get hurt when we fell?"

"A few bruises," he said. "That's all. I landed on you."

"You can land on me any day," I said, and he laughed. Why did I want so much to chase away the worry and care from his eyes?

"How are your feet? You ran a long way barefoot."

"They're okay," he said, but his eyes slid away from mine.

"Let me see. I can rub them for you."

He bit his lip again. "You just want to touch me between my toes."

"You have pretty toes."

"Kiernan?"

"Mm?"

"Moira said you almost… I can't remember the word she said, but you used too much magic."

"Hollow?" I said and stopped to clear my throat. "Did she say I burned myself hollow?" And there was no more avoiding that empty feeling inside.

"Yes," he said, searching my eyes with his, like he was afraid of what I might do. "But she thinks you stopped just in time, that your mind shut itself down before you… before you were hollowed."

"Is she sure?" I felt around in my head, in the depths of

my being where magic should be. I felt like I'd been scraped out with a rusty carving knife.

"I don't know. She said… she said it will take time to be sure." He put his hand over mine on his face, then pulled them both away to kiss my fingers. Suddenly I wanted to lose myself in him, in his touch and his gentleness, so I could forget what I was missing.

"She does think your magic will come back, but you mustn't try to use it or you could… you could be hollow permanently." He spoke with his lips against the palm of my hand, and it sent a distracting tingle down my arm.

"Will you kiss me, pretty bird?" I said, and he studied my eyes again.

"Always," he said. "Kiernan, I –" I stopped him by pressing my palm against his mouth.

"No," I said. "Don't tell me that. Not yet." Of course, I couldn't be sure of what he'd been about to say, but I could guess. And I couldn't deal with being loved. Not yet. Not here. Not hollow and damaged as I was. And not as the only person he'd ever fucked.

He moved his lips like he wanted to say it anyway, but he didn't. Instead, he moved my hand away and helped me sit up. When I was upright and leaning against the headboard, he pressed his lips softly on mine and something dark and frightening seemed to vanish from the edges of my thoughts.

I opened my mouth to him, teased his tongue with mine, until he shifted position to press against me.

"You're hurt," he said, when we finally parted. "You should rest."

"I am hurt," I replied. "But you heal me." And maybe that sounded dumb, but it was true.

He blushed, soft pink tinting his cheeks and making his pale freckles stand out.

"Let me see your feet," I said, and he scowled. "Do you have any lotion? Something for dry skin?"

"Fine," he said. "You can rub my feet if you promise to rest."

"Only if you lie down with me."

He looked at me with narrowed eyes, like he suspected me of trying to get away with something.

"We'll see," he said, and got up to get a jar from a small table near the door. "Moira uses this on her children's paws, while they're learning to turn into wolves."

I took the jar and sniffed it. It was made of some kind of thick plant oil steeped with herbs. "Swordleaf?" I asked.

"It cools sore skin." He settled himself on the end of the bed opposite me and let me put his feet in my lap. I spread on some lotion, and he flinched. The bottoms of both his feet were scratched and red, the skin dry and cracked. I rubbed very gently, and he relaxed.

"Can bird folk wear shoes?" I asked as I rubbed and stroked the arch of his foot.

"I suppose," he said. "If my claws could stick out."

I moved my touch to the pads of one of his big front toes and he stretched his foot and sighed.

"Leather wraps, maybe," I said. "But you can't stay barefoot if we're going to travel."

"Can't we just stay here?" He closed his eyes and more of the tension eased out of his posture. I switched to his other foot, rubbing the lotion thoroughly into his skin and massaging the pads.

"Perhaps," I said, but I knew we couldn't, and I was sure he did, too. Sooner or later, word would spread that a new Vogel seer had been found. And sooner or later, my mother – my Queen – would expect me to report back.

"Did I tell you how lovely you look in that color?" I said,

and he smiled and smoothed the blue cloud silk over his chest and belly.

"Do you like it?"

"It's not very practical," I answered, "But I like it very much."

"Moira says I can spin for her, to earn our keep. And she's given me some cloth to make new clothes for myself. Practical ones." He peered at me from under his lashes and tried to hide a smile.

"You like her."

"She's very kind."

"In my experience, seers usually are." I lifted his foot, bent over, and kissed his arch. "Perhaps because they can sense emotions in others."

He laughed. "That tickles."

"Does this tickle?" I slid my tongue between his toes, and he gasped.

"Kier." His voice was breathy, and his eyes drooped closed again. "You know what that does to me."

"Yes, I do," I said and licked between his toes again.

"If you keep doing that, I'll grab you by the antlers."

"Promise?"

At that he did open his eyes, and stared at me, lips slightly parted.

"Come here," I said, laying his foot on the bed and sliding my hand up the back of his leg. "Or else I'm climbing down to your end."

He stared at me a moment longer then sat up, swung his legs over the side of the bed, and moved closer.

"You should rest," he said. "You should see the color of the bruise on your back."

"I'd rather not. Come here and lie next to me."

Unlike the cot at the Abbey, this was a proper bed and big

enough for both of us. It was even long enough for Fionn's legs. He lay next to me and pulled the blankets up to cover us both. I turned onto my side to look at him.

"Thank you," I said.

"For what?"

"For getting us to safety when I couldn't. For watching over me. For caring."

"Those aren't things you need to thank me for."

"Thank you anyway." Then I kissed him again. I intended to lean over him, to push him down against the pillows, and taste every bit of his skin. But weariness hit me and instead I relaxed into the softness of the bed, and he leaned over me, kissed my forehead, and my eyelids, and each ear.

"What happened?" he said, touching the deep nick on the outside edge of my left ear.

"It's not a nice story," I said.

"Will you tell me?" He bent down and traced the edge of the cut with his tongue, and I shivered. It felt awfully nice for something that had once brought such pain.

"I have two older sisters," I said. "From my mother's previous entanglement. From before she married my father."

"Which she did to end the human uprising in Morven."

"Mm. Before that, she had a lover from among the Huldr. She was, I'm told, as in love with him as my father was later obsessed with her. And they had two daughters before he left her to return to his own people."

"Are they much older?"

"They are. Older and envious that our mother was married to my father, while their father was only her lover. Never mind that they're my mother's heirs and full fey, while I'm neither. She didn't even acknowledge me as legitimate until I reached my majority, and she decided I was useful."

Fionn made an encouraging noise to let me know he was

listening, even though he was busy licking my neck.

"One day, my sisters decided that since I was half human, I ought not have both antlers *and* pointed ears. First, they tried to pull off my antlers, as they saw Mother do when I was younger. When that didn't work, they decided to cut the points off my ears."

"Oh, Kiernan." Fionn pushed himself up to look at me and his eyes were sad, full of moisture.

"They would have succeeded, if our seer hadn't happened along and stopped them."

He kissed my ear again, as if to soothe the old hurt.

"It was a long time ago," I said and turned my head to claim his mouth again.

"There has to be a better way for the world to be," he said, as he tugged my tunic over my head and ran his hands over my chest. "Or somewhere better we can go."

"I wish there were," I said, finding the silver buttons at the neck of his tunic and tugging them open. He undid the buttons at his waist and pulled the fabric away.

I caught my breath and held him away from me so he wouldn't move, so I could just look at him. He was bruised, and scraped, and held himself stiffly, but he was still perfect. He shoved my hands aside so he could reach the tie of my trousers and I helped him take them off.

I was already hard, and had been since he started kissing my neck, and he smiled when he saw my cock sticking up. He bent over me, put his mouth tantalizingly close to me, and kissed just the tip of my cock and made me moan. He slid back under the covers and pressed his whole body against mine.

"You're going to take me to the Eyrie, aren't you?" he said. "To the Vogel King?"

"It's where you should be," I said, running my hand down his side. "By Isle law." I rolled him away from me enough to stroke a hand down his belly and find the seam of his sheath with my finger. He sighed and titled his pelvis against my touch. "But I won't take you anywhere you don't want to go."

I stroked more firmly, feeling the moisture of his lubricant slick on my finger and he made a noise in his throat – one of his sweet, wanting sounds – and pushed harder against my hand until my finger dipped inside his sheath and stroked the hard length of him, and his cock slid out against my palm.

I kissed his forehead, then his throat, and curled my fingers around his erection. "Tell me what you want," I said.

His fingers combed through my hair and made fists, pulling my mouth to his ear, so I traced it with my tongue and nibbled his soft earlobe.

"I don't know what to do," he said. "I don't know what I want."

"What do you want right now?" I said, against his neck.

"I want to taste you," he whispered, removing a hand from my hair to press it against my chest and push me onto my back. "And I want … I want to feel your mouth on me."

"Then turn around," I said. "Put your head on my thigh and give me your thigh for a pillow."

"Oh!" he said. I don't think it had occurred to him that he could have both the things he wanted at the same time. He pushed the blankets aside and turned around on the bed and as soon as he was in reach of my mouth, I licked him. He gasped.

"That's it," I said and lifted my head to rest it on the soft inside of his bent leg. "Lie on your side." And then I didn't say anything else because I was too busy sucking.

"Goddess Above," he said and moaned softly as his first pulse came quickly. I reveled in the sweet taste of him, his intoxicating scent, and I sucked harder, sliding my mouth over him, almost off of him, and letting him plunge deep again.

For a while, I thought he'd forgotten he wanted to taste me, too, and I didn't mind. Just having him here, his legs twined around my head, his soft sounds of pleasure filling my ears, was all I needed. Then he pulsed again and muffled his cry against my erection. He grabbed my ass and dug his fingers into the muscle, as if he was worried I'd move away from his tongue, his lips, his open throat.

He moved away enough to say, "Don't hold back. I know you do, sometimes, but don't."

I didn't reply, I just took him deeper down my own throat.

"You can fuck my mouth," he said, almost whispering the word "fuck." I responded by thrusting against his face to see what he would do, if he would pull away. He groaned and clenched his fingers on my ass and pulsed again, filling my mouth with a sweetness like honey.

And then I didn't hold back. I pushed my pelvis against him, thrust my cock into his mouth and down his throat and he made hungry noises and thrust himself against my mouth in turn.

I groaned deep in my chest and sucked him and spewed semen into his mouth. I felt him swallow, and then he moved his head away, tilted it back and said my name over and over again as his fourth pulse claimed him and left him helpless to pleasure. I had to swallow quickly, and swallow again or let his spunk leak out of my mouth onto the sheets.

Complete exhaustion hit me then and I could barely move. Fionn lay limp on the mattress, then slowly crawled up the bed to lie next to me, where he pulled my head onto his shoulder and stroked my hair.

"Will you rest now?" he said.

"Will you?" I managed after trying several times to make sound.

He kissed my hair between my antlers. "I'll stay with

you," he said. "We can rest together."

"How long will they let us stay here?"

"You're not resting."

"Neither are you."

"I don't know," he said, kissing my hair again. "Until we're healed, I suppose. Long enough for me to sew proper clothes, for me to spin enough wool to last a while. Maybe long enough to learn a little about being a seer."

"Fionn, my pretty bird," I said, and I realized I was about to say something I couldn't take back. Something I wasn't ready for. Something he'd already said to me, though I don't think he remembered.

"Yes?"

"You're going to be a great seer," I said instead.

He smiled. "I don't have very useful visions."

I nestled closer to him, pressing my face into his chest and wrapping an arm around him. "Your visions might not have been useful to the Abbess, or to the Alfar King, but they *were* useful to you. To us."

"Were they?" He sounded sleepy and I could feel his breathing evening out.

"You *saw* me," I said. "So you knew you could trust me when we finally met."

"But I didn't trust you. Not like I should have."

"It was enough," I said. "And you *saw* a future for us. Maybe that was only possibilities, but possibilities are better than certain death."

"Maybe," he said. "Maybe you're right." And I'm pretty sure I felt it when he slipped into sleep, relaxing at last, limp and languid.

I stayed awake a moment longer, enjoying the smell of his skin, intensified from making love, and the softness of him next to my cheek. I reached out for my magic again – not to try to use it, but just to see if it was there, like poking a wound to make sure you still have feeling.

Nothing.

I hoped Fionn's new friend Moira, witch, seer, and wife of a werewolf, was correct, and the loss was temporary.

And then my exhausted body wouldn't let me stay awake worrying anymore and I slipped after Fionn into sleep.

14
Fionn

S OMEHOW, DEEP IN slumber and worn out from our escape from the Abbey, some part of me was still aware when Kiernan finally relaxed and drifted into sleep. And maybe that part of me was the same part that had kept me hovering near him since we got here, that part of me that needed to be sure he was okay, because I woke up.

For a while I lay next to him, enjoying a moment when I could just hold him close and listen to him breathing, and not have to do or say anything, to wonder if I was acting in a way that would put him off. I was still sleepy – sex seemed to make me sleepy anyway, and each pulse took more energy out of me, so that after four, I was barely wanting to move at all. But for all my content at just feeling him next to me, I couldn't hold off worry, thoughts of all the spinning there was to do, the questions I needed to ask Moira and Col, the things I just didn't know about the world I was soon to face.

Where should I go when we eventually had to leave this idyllic village in the forest? Was there anywhere I would be safe? And would Kiernan come with me, wherever it was I ended up, or would I be alone again?

Eventually, the worries got the best of me, and I eased out from under Kiernan's arm and out from under the blanket. I climbed over him, careful not to jostle him – he stirred and mumbled and rolled over but didn't wake – and rummaged in the blankets to find my tunic.

I looked at him a moment longer, his head turned against the pillow, dark lashes thick against his cheeks. The green outlining his eyes made him look truly a creature of the forest and the tattoo on his forearm, resting on top of the blanket, looked almost like it had grown there.

I wanted so much to tell him how I felt, even though it also terrified me, but he didn't want to hear it. Because he couldn't answer in kind or because he was as afraid as I was? Asleep, though, he couldn't tell me "No" and I whispered, "I do love you Kiernan Druison nicFia, and you can't stop me." Then I slipped out of the room, out of the comfortable little house, and onto a lawn made of wildflowers.

The werewolf village didn't look like a settlement at all. There was a small, fast stream that ran through a grove of broad-leaved trees and the houses were nestled under the canopy, each nearly hidden from the others. Some, like Moira and Col's, had space cleared around them, like miniature meadows, while others had brush and trees growing right up close to the walls, so they were nearly invisible from any distance away. Here and there, where the stream ran through flat land, there were gardens, lush with vegetables and fenced against deer.

Paths meandered between the trees, dirt-packed or moss-cushioned, and thin streams of smoke showed where fires were lit in some of the other houses, to make tea, perhaps, or heat a meal.

It was quiet save for birdsong and the music of the stream, and more peaceful even than the Abbey on the best of days. I could imagine living in a place like this and being happy, and wondered if Kiernan could ever be content somewhere so small and uneventful. He might be from the forest, but he was used to the glamor and bustle of a fey court.

And I realized how little I really knew of him. I had seen visions of him, of significant events in his life, and I had learned a few things since I'd met him. He was strong and brave, for all his small size. He could lie, but he didn't like to. He could use a sword, twin knives, or his fists. He liked to fuck.

I knew our bodies fit together in ways I'd never imagined possible, but I didn't know if *he* had felt this way before, with someone else. I didn't even really know how he felt about me, except that he cared, at least a little, and he enjoyed making me feel good.

I shook my head as if I could dislodge the unwelcome thoughts and stretched in the sun, trying to wake my weary body and my sluggish brain. Then I turned for the path to the weaving shed, where baskets of wool waited to be spun, and a length of cloth waited to be made into clothing. And Moira had said I might try my hand at her large loom, to see how I liked it compared to the small one I had used at the Abbey.

Someone was waiting for me when I turned the corner, leaning against the door and smiling.

"Hello," I said, and stopped uncertainly. He was big, tall, a dark-haired werewolf who seemed not too much older than me. He had been with Col and a few others when they'd found Kiernan and me after the fire.

He smiled wider, and dimples appeared next to his mouth. "Hello." He had a nice voice, deep and gravelly. "I'm Dag." He held out a hand and I clasped it tentatively. His hand dwarfed mine, but he held my fingers carefully and stroked my palm. I pulled my hand away.

"My name is Branfionn," I said. "I'm staying with Moira and Col."

"I know." He didn't move out of the way, he just looked down at me. I didn't know what to do, how to act, and without him giving me any clues, I was helpless.

He looked me up and down, his gaze lingering on my legs, and I wished I had fled the Abbey in my shapeless gray tunic and trousers, instead of the thin blue cloud silk garment that didn't even reach my knees.

"So," I said, and pointed past him. "I came to do some spinning."

His smile grew again. "That's why I waited here for you," he said. "I knew you'd come, sooner or later." He pushed away from the door and took a step closer. I wanted to back away but didn't know if that would be rude. People in the outside world and the sisters in the Abbey didn't follow the same rules of behavior.

He cocked his head a little to one side, as if to look at me from a new angle. He was very handsome, with eyes as dark as his hair, and little freckles across his cheeks and nose.

He reached out and lifted the bottom corner of my tunic. "This color looks good on you," he said. "Though the shape doesn't leave much unseen."

I stared at him. Was he being forward, or only making conversation?

"It's all I have," I said. "I wasn't actually able to pack a bag before fleeing for my life." The words came out tart, but I wouldn't be sorry for that.

He moved even closer; so close I could feel his body heat. "I meant no offense," he said. "I like it on you." He lifted a strand of my hair and rubbed it between his fingers. "But I'd like it better off of you."

I opened my mouth, but no words came out. If it had been Kiernan, I'd have said something cheeky back and then let him undress me, but this wasn't Kier.

"I'm sorry," I stammered out at last. "I can't…" and I started to back away.

"Don't go," he said, sliding a hand behind my back and pressing closer. "I only want to kiss you."

"I can't…" I said, but I still didn't know how to finish the sentence.

"He doesn't love you."

"What?"

The suddenness of his statement caught me by surprise.

"The fey. He doesn't love you. He can't."

"What are you talking about?" I tried to pull away, but he held me firmly against him.

"Even here in this tiny village deep in the Forest of Aven we meet all kinds of people, and I know the type of man who'll fuck anyone who asks." He dipped his head close to my ear. "He could never resist taking you to bed."

"He's not that type," I said, even though I knew he was, by his own admission.

"Of course he is." Dag pressed his face closer into my neck and dragged in a deep noisy breath. "He might try to hide it, but I've known men like him." He lifted his head from my neck and looked into my eyes, stroking my ear lightly with his fingers. "He'll fuck you till you can't walk," he said. "But then he'll find someone else who catches his eye. You're Vogel. People like you and me, bird folk, werewolves, humans, we're beneath him, lesser than his kind, or so they think."

I tried to pull away again. "You don't know him," I said.

He shrugged. "Can I kiss you?"

"No. I –" I looked into his eyes. He didn't seem angry or

mean, or even crude. He seemed, almost, kind. Concerned. "If I let you kiss me, will you leave me to my work?"

His mouth curled in a smile. "Sure." He leaned closer. "I can't guarantee I won't be back for more later, though."

"Fine," I said, and he leaned in, pressed his mouth to mine, and I tried not to shove him away. He held my body close to his, his hand in the small of my back keeping me pressed against him, his fingers on my cheek, holding my head so I couldn't pull away.

I felt his teeth bump mine and his tongue was hot in my mouth.

He pulled back. "You could try to enjoy it," he said.

"I —"

"I'm not stopping till you kiss me like you want it."

I didn't get a chance to say anything else as he swung us around, pressed my back against the door, and pinned me there with his body. I felt tiny next to him, nothing like how gangly and awkward I felt next to Kiernan.

His mouth was hard on mine at first, and then suddenly gentle, and I tried to relax, to pretend I was kissing Kiernan, that Kier had told me he loved me and wanted no one but me. And it must have worked, because he held me a moment longer, then pulled away from my mouth to kiss my neck. And I felt as flushed as I had that time Kiernan had told me he was determined to seduce me.

"I want you, little seer," Dag said, and I tried not to flinch as he called me the same thing the Abbess had called me. At least it reminded me he wasn't Kiernan. "You're so fucking pretty," he said, and kissed me again, and I felt him hard against me, aroused, and he slid his tongue into my mouth and moved his hand to the back of my thigh.

I was finally able to push him away. "That's enough," I said. "I have work to do." Then more boldly, I added, "You said you would leave if I kissed you, and I have."

He grinned and stepped away. "I don't give up easily," he said and turned towards the path. "See you around." And then he was gone.

Smoke and Flame dropped out of the trees to twine around my arms, and I said, "You could have come to my rescue."

Big, said Smoke.

Scary, said Flame.

"So was the Abbess," I said. "And you attacked her for me."

You liked? one replied.

You didn't like? asked the other.

"I –" I wasn't sure how I felt. He had been forward, pushy, but so had Kiernan, at first. He had felt different from Kier, kissing him had been different, but not bad. I just didn't want anyone else, even if Kiernan probably wouldn't care who I fooled around with.

Because I couldn't help thinking that Dag hadn't been entirely wrong. Kiernan had told me himself that he liked fucking, that he'd been with many others before me, and I could hardly assume he'd never want anyone else but me now. Never mind that I'd had visions of us together in the future. Just because I never *saw* him with anyone else didn't mean he wouldn't. I'd never *seen* him with anyone else in the past, either, and I knew he had been.

I stood a moment longer on the threshold of the weaving shed, then finally went inside, selected a drop spindle and a basket of wool, and carried them back to the house. I was supposed to work in the shed, where all the tools and supplies were to hand, but I didn't want to be too far away from Kier, especially not while I was feeling so confused.

So I moved a stool into the room where he still slept and

sat and spun and watched over him. Or I told myself I was watching over him and was definitely *not* hiding from a handsome werewolf in a place where Kiernan would wake up and protect me if I needed it.

THE WOOL SLIPPED through my fingers, twisting into a thin, strong yarn. Spinning wool went much more quickly than spinning cloud silk – the result needn't be so thin, nor so smooth. It was easy to relax into the work, to perch on the stool and let my thoughts drift.

Kiernan stirred in his sleep, making a small noise in his throat and rolling over. The blanket slipped, leaving his shoulder and a wedge of his back bare. I thought about getting up to fix it, but it was summer, and warm. I could see the dark purple bruise where he had landed on his sword, already yellowing around the edges. I would have to ask Moira if she had any well-heal to make a salve, or something with which to make a pain relief tea.

I hoped this wasn't going to be a pattern in our lives: Kiernan getting hurt saving me, and me watching over him and tending to his injuries. I didn't mind taking care of him, but I didn't like to see him hurt in the first place. And I didn't want to always need rescuing.

He groaned and rolled over again, nestled his face into the pillow and shifted to get comfortable. Then he opened his eyes and saw me watching him.

"What's wrong?" he said, and my mind immediately jumped to my recent encounter with Dag.

"Nothing," I said, "Why do you think something is wrong?"

"You look sad, and your lips are swollen."

I caught the spindle with my feet and pressed a hand to my mouth. He laughed.

"They're not," I said. My lips felt normal to my fingers, but they did feel hot, like they did when Kier and I were together.

"I like seeing your mouth like that," he said. "All pink and soft and plush. But since I've been asleep, I can't help but wonder who you've been kissing." He was smiling as he said it, but I felt a surge of guilt.

I had no argument; I just stared at him.

"Pretty bird," he said. "You can kiss whoever you want." He sat up slowly, shifting and stretching his shoulders. "You haven't made any promises to me."

I still stared, desperately trying to think of something to say. Finally, I blurted out, "I didn't want to," though I wasn't sure that was even entirely true.

"You didn't want to what? Promise yourself to me?" He was teasing, but it still made my stomach lurch. Maybe it was stupid, hasty, way too soon, but I would have promised myself to him in a heartbeat.

I looked around for something to throw at him that wouldn't hurt, and he laughed again.

"I admit, I might be a little jealous," he said. "Of this handsome werewolf you've been snogging while I was asleep."

I snapped my eyes back to his face. "How –"

"Come here, pretty bird," he said, and patted the bed next to him. I didn't move, and he sighed. "We're staying with werewolves, so if you kissed someone, chances are it was a werewolf. And I'd guess handsome because no one ugly would have the nerve to try to kiss you."

He patted the bed again, and I set the spindle aside but still didn't get up.

"Did he force you to kiss him?"

"No… he…" I looked at him helplessly.

"You said you didn't want to."

"He was waiting for me and he… he was very persistent. I said I would kiss him if he left me alone."

"Was he a good kisser? Did you enjoy it at least? You don't end up with swollen lips without a good hard snog."

I blinked and looked down at my hands. "He wasn't you," I said.

I heard fabric moving and wood creaking and then Kiernan was there, one hand stroking my hair, the other tilting my face up to look at him.

"It's okay. You can kiss other people," he said. "How else will you know what you like if you don't try new things?"

"Do you *want* me to kiss other people? To… to *fuck* other people?" He wouldn't let me turn my face away, so I focused my eyes over his shoulder.

He sighed, wrapped his arms around me, and tucked my face against his bare chest.

"Do you want to… to be with other people?" I said, forcing my voice to sound unconcerned.

"I want *you* to have whatever you want," he said. "And I want…"

"What?" I looked up at him, but he was staring past me, out the window.

"Things I can't have," he said.

"What do you mean?"

"It doesn't matter." He looked at me again. "Right now, pretty bird, you're the only one I want to kiss, the only one I want to make love to. But I can't promise you that won't change. Right now, I can't promise you anything." He leaned away, cupped my cheek, and stroked my face with his thumb.

"And I'd hate to think you want me only because you

haven't tried fucking anyone else." He grinned his most wicked grin, but it was missing something. Conviction, maybe.

"That's not –" He put his fingers on my lips and I frowned at him.

"Do you like him? This handsome werewolf?"

"His name is Dag," I said, pushing his hand from my mouth. "And I don't even know him."

"You didn't know me."

"That was different."

"Because you had visions of me? Pretty bird, if you want him, go fuck him. Then if you still want me…" He didn't finish the sentence.

"You said you felt a connection with me," I said. "At the Abbey. Even through the wards, you knew when I had a vision that distressed me." But before I could finish the thought, or explain what I meant, or ask him what the rest of his sentence was going to be, there was a clatter at the outer door, and Kiernan was stepping away, bending to pick up the blanket, and wrapping it around his waist.

"It sounds like our hosts are home," he said. "You should probably introduce us."

As it turned out, I didn't have to, because Moira came in and did it for me.

"Ah, you're up," she said. "I'm Moira and the big, lurking presence in the doorway is Col."

"And I'm Aeric." A small, messy-haired boy pushed past his enormous father into the room and stood staring at Kiernan.

"And Aline," said a girl who looked just like her brother, pushing into the room and staring just as he had.

"You're awfully small for werewolves," Kiernan said, pretending surprise and looking at the two children with eyebrows raised.

"Well, you're kind of short for a fey," retorted Aeric.

Kier laughed. "That's because you're used to Alfar, who are long and skinny. I'm Sidhe."

"Well, we're children," said Aeric. "So of course we're not big. Not yet."

"Also, half human," said Aline.

"Me, too," said Kiernan, and the children looked at him with more interest.

"All right, you two, go play," said Moira, and she herded the children out the door.

Kiernan turned to Col and held out a hand. "Thank you," he said. Col clasped his hand briefly and let go. Next to the huge werewolf, Kier looked almost as childlike as Aeric and Aline.

"You put out the fire that hag at the Abbey sent into my forest," Col said.

"She was aiming at us," Kier said.

Col shrugged. "Moira says you near burned yourself hollow stopping it. That means something."

"Well, thank you anyway. Especially…" Kiernan glanced at me. "Especially for him."

Col nodded, then excused himself and left. Before I could ask what Kier meant, Moira returned and handed me a cloth-wrapped bundle. "Tea," she said. "For pain. And salve for bruises. You use some of both yourself." Then she turned to Kiernan.

"Sit down," she said, indicating the bed.

He sat, looking amused.

She was tall for a human, not quite towering over Kier, but certainly looking down at him. She had thick, curly, reddish-brown hair and eyes a silver that she assured me were a shade darker than mine. She had an air of authority – maybe from raising children, or maybe from having a werewolf for a husband – that made one want to do as she instructed.

I unwrapped the bundle she'd given me to find a clay pot of salve and a package of dried leaves.

"Put the kettle on, will you, love?" Moira called, and I heard the grunt of Col's reply from the other room.

"Now, let's have a better look at you," she said to Kiernan, and turned him so he sat with his back to her. She prodded the bruise gently and he winced and hissed under his breath. "Next time you leap off a tower and land on your back, I suggest you remove your sword first."

"I'll try to remember that," Kiernan said, glancing at me and grinning.

"You're lucky you didn't break your spine," she said, then stepped around him. "Salve," she said, looking at me and pointing to Kiernan.

I nodded and pried the lid off the jar. A sharp but not unpleasant smell wafted out and I dipped my fingers in and spread some gently on Kier's back. He grunted but held still so I could reach every edge of the bruise.

"Let me see your arm," Moira said, and Kiernan looked at her.

"My arm?"

She didn't explain, she just reached out and took Kiernan's tattooed wrist in her hand, lifting it into the light from the window.

"My arm is fine," he said.

"Yes it is," she replied. "But I wasn't sure your tattoo would be."

He cocked his head and looked from her to the green designs. I couldn't see his face, but I could tell from his posture when he figured out what she meant. He suddenly leaned forward, away from me, and at first I thought I'd hurt him, spreading on the salve, but then I realized he was examining the inside of his forearm.

"Goddess Below," he said softly. "Look, Fionn."

I leaned over his shoulder to see, and followed with my eyes as he traced the tendrils and leaves on his arm. I blushed to think of how I had inspected his tattoo when I first saw him naked in my infirmary, how I had looked at it so long I knew every twist and line of it.

"Oh!" I said, when I saw what he had noticed. There was a new little tendril, curling off the design on the inside of his arm, that had not been there before.

He looked over his shoulder at me, eyes shining.

"You're very lucky," Moira said. "That you didn't burn yourself hollow with all the magic you were throwing around."

Kiernan rubbed a palm over his arm and Moira let go of his wrist.

"But your tattoo would have faded if you were hollowed." She pointed at the design. "Instead, it grew."

"I'll recover," Kiernan said, looking at her. I couldn't resist putting my arms around his neck and hugging him.

"You'll recover," said Moira. "And you'll be stronger."

15
Kiernan

Satisfied that I was going to be all right, Fionn took himself off to Moira's weaving shed, leaving me to help with the household chores.

Moira took no pity on me for having spent half my life in a royal court, where everything was done for me, and half in a fortified castle, where nothing was done at all unless one of the soldiers' wives got sick of the mess and a hired cook made sure we ate. I did, at least, have experience living alone in the forest, so she set me to skinning and cutting up rabbits for stew, and when I finished that, I put my knife skills to work peeling and chopping root vegetables.

"I thought you'd have refused to do such menial tasks," said Moira, as she set an immense pot of water over the hearth fire and began shoveling in the results of our work.

"Why would I do that?" It might not have been work I was familiar with, but I refused to think of any work as beneath me; that would make me too much like my mother. "You helped us when you could have left us to the Abbess; I'll do anything I can to repay your kindness."

I scowled at an especially oddly-shaped turnip and decided to cut the vexing thing in half before trying to remove the rest of its skin.

"Col's happy to displease the high and mighty Abbess in any way he can," she replied. "Do you know how different the werewolf view of the Lady of the Moon is from the way the Alfar sisters see her?"

"I wouldn't think werewolves would follow a sexless virgin goddess," I said, and she swatted me like I was one of her children. She was smiling and it was an affectionate gesture more than a punishing one, and it caught me a little off guard. I wasn't used to affection, especially not so easily expressed.

"I only meant you're fey, and from a Monarch's court, no less," she said. "I didn't think your lot did anything for themselves."

I finished cutting the turnip and added it to the pot. "I wouldn't be much use to anyone if I couldn't feed myself," I said.

"Is that your whole ambition in life?" she asked, looking at me curiously. "To be useful to others?"

I considered that as I picked up my turnip peels and put them in the basket for taking to the compost pile. "I suppose it's the only thing that's ever gotten me anything worth having," I said. I suspected, from the way she had said "Monarch's court" and not "royal family," that Fionn had kept up my pretense, and I was thankful for it. The last thing I needed was for someone to think they might gain by reporting my whereabouts to my mother. The longer I could stay away from her court, the better.

"I know we're an imposition on you," I said, taking the bundle of carrots she handed me. "For Fionn's sake, I'd like to stay longer, but we should probably move on soon."

She paused in her chopping of some kind of savory-smelling greenery and looked at me. "For Fionn's sake?" she asked.

I studied the carrot in my hand. It was such a pale orange it was almost yellow, and it smelled sweet. "I suppose we'll have to go to the Eyrie," I said. "But he… I don't want to take him from one place of isolation to another without letting him see how other people on the Isle live, without showing him that there is good and kindness and love in the world, that living doesn't just have to be about existing." I looked up and met her eyes. They were almost steel-gray, but had the same silvery brightness as Fionn's, as every seer I had ever met.

"You want him to feel cared for," she said. "But what of yourself? Do you want nothing of your own?"

I ignored her questions and focused on the statement instead. "I want him to have the chance to learn about being a seer from someone who will take into account what *he* wants, and not just how they can best use him."

She resumed chopping. "If it were up to me, I'd have Col build him a house next door," she said. "If he wanted to stay." She scraped the herbs into the pot and pulled another bunch out of a basket.

"I won't take him to the Eyrie if he doesn't want to go," I said. "But I also don't want to force him into the life of an outlaw."

"Which you would be – which *he* would be – if anyone were to learn of his existence."

"Yes." I wasn't used to being so serious, or to putting someone else's needs before mine, but something about Moira encouraged the unburdening of the soul. It was, I think, part of being a seer. I had always felt comfortable being open and honest with our seer in Morven Forest, and Fionn made me want to bare every flaw to see if he would still want me.

"Does he know?" she said, adding more herbs to the pot. The water was coming to the boil, and it was starting to smell delicious, even though it would be hours before it was ready to eat.

I glanced up from the carrot I was dismembering. This one was almost purple and left a red stain on the wooden board. "I told him we'd be hunted and taken to the Vogel Monarch if we didn't go on our own, yes."

She shook her head. "That you love him."

I stared at her, unblinking, not wanting to admit she was right – not *able* to admit she was right – but unable to deny it, either. I had only known Fionn for a handful of days and nights; I couldn't love him. Could I?

"I can't…" I said.

"Can't love him, or can't tell him?" She raised an eyebrow.

"Take your pick," I said, chopping the carrot so violently I almost chopped my own finger, and I hadn't cut myself on anything since I was a child and learned how to handle a blade.

"Why?"

"If he knew, he might… he might let it affect his decisions. Of where to go, what to do now," I said. "And I can't… I can't give him any kind of life. In my mother's court, he would be seen as a lesser being. She would – maybe – let me keep him as a servant, but never as an equal. And that's if she chose not to turn him in to the Vogel King or try sacrificing him to the Moon herself."

I put the knife down and scooped up the carrot pieces. "My father doesn't allow anyone not at least half-human into his stronghold at all. And most who aren't full human don't stay, because of how they're treated."

"Like lesser beings?" she said, borrowing my phrasing.

"Like animals," I said.

Moira sighed and leaned on the counter, watching as I added my carrot to the pot, one piece at a time. "There are other places to live, Kiernan Druison."

"And thus, back to being outlaws," I said, watching each small splash as I aimed my carrots.

"You may find, young Prince," she said, and I looked up and met her eyes. So she *did* know who I was, whether she guessed or Fionn told her. "If you embrace what is in your heart, you will be happier for it." She added a palmful of salt to the pot and stirred it with a long wooden spoon.

Then she laughed. "Even if it means your life will be harder." She seemed to be speaking from experience, and I resisted the urge to ask her about her own life. Maybe someday I could pass through here again and have a proper visit.

"It's not *my* life I'm worried about."

She touched my shoulder and I tensed for a punishing grip full of claws such as my mother would have done. But she only squeezed gently. "He is of the age of majority," she said, drily. "He's capable of making his own choices."

"He's an innocent," I said. "He's only known the Abbey of the Moon. If I could spare him any hurt, I would."

"Perhaps," she said. "But he is intelligent, and I think he understands more than you realize." She squeezed my shoulder again, then turned to cleaning up the mess of vegetable peelings. "Don't treat him like a child, or you *will* lose him."

"I'm going to lose him anyway," I said, holding the basket for her to scrape the peelings into.

"You might, you might not," she replied, turning back to the hearth to reach for the kettle and pouring hot water over herbs in a teapot. "But that seems to me to be all the more reason not to waste the time you have."

I picked up my belt from where I'd hung it on the back of a chair and slung it around my waist, settling my knives into place and doing up the buckles across my thighs. My sword I left propped in a corner near the door.

"How did you know?" I said.

She shrugged. "Col thought, at first, that you were just fucking him. He's beautiful, and desperate for comfort." Then she met my eyes and it felt like she could see right into me. I tilted my chin up and faced her directly; I might not have the most honorable past, but I wouldn't hide. I would let her read all of me if she wanted to.

She smiled at my defiance. "I didn't need to do any more than look at the surface of your thoughts, Kiernan nicFia. Your feelings for Fionn are there for even the least sensitive seer to see. Which you may want to keep in mind if you're going to be near any hostile beings who can read emotions."

"Can he? See my feelings?" The thought of Fionn knowing how I felt, even though I refused to say it, was at once comforting and unsettling.

"I expect he may, but he wouldn't believe what he saw, for fear that he was only seeing what he so desperately wants to see."

I nodded and turned for the door.

"Tell him, Prince of Morven Forest," she said. "And you'll both be happier for it, whatever comes after."

But I couldn't tell him, could I? For all that I felt protective, felt a deep, strange connection, felt love, how could I know if it would last? If I told him how I felt, then stopped feeling it, it would hurt him, badly, and the last thing I wanted to do was hurt Fionn.

He deserved so much better than me.

Which was why, when I reached the weaving shed and

poked my head around the corner and saw a big handsome wolf man leaning against the wall, watching Fionn measure a length of cloth, I almost turned and walked quietly away.

But something in the set of Fionn's shoulders, the slight hunch in the way he leaned over the table, made me pause. As I watched, the werewolf straightened up from the wall and leaned over Fionn. He put his hand on the small of Fionn's back, running his thick fingers through the feathers there.

I knew exactly what it felt like, to touch Fionn that way. I knew how fine and soft his feathers were, and how warm the skin underneath. And I knew exactly how he would arch his back, just slightly, to lean into the touch.

Fionn looked up and I saw not heat, but uncertainty, in his eyes. "Dag, please," he said, his soft voice a shade huskier than usual. "I need to get this finished."

"I wouldn't mind if you kept wearing this blue frock," the werewolf said. There was no denying the sexual undertones in his voice, and if it had been directed at me, I'd probably get hard just from the deep rumble of it. "I like being able to look at your legs.'"

He *was* right; Fionn had spectacular legs.

Fionn held very still as Dag brushed his hand down over the base of his tail feathers and shifted sideways to stroke his thigh, then dipped under the feathers to touch his ass. I had to clench my teeth to stop myself from knocking Dag into the wall.

"I don't —" Fionn said, and the wolf suddenly pulled him around, pulled him close, and silenced him by kissing him. It's something I would have done, to some pretty thing, before I'd met Fionn and had my heart ripped out.

I heard the wet sound of their tongues sliding together and I was sure I felt something snap in my thoughts. I stepped away from the door, intending to leave them to whatever they decided to get up to. I'd told Fionn right out to go after Dag if he wanted to, that I wouldn't interfere. And he deserved better than my jealousy. He deserved the fucking world.

He hadn't made any promises to me, and I'd promised nothing to him. But I still couldn't deny that it hurt.

As I turned my back and stepped away, I heard their breathing as they pulled apart.

"Dag, no. I don't want –"

The sound of kissing again, just as I would have done if a lovely lad or lass had only tried to stop me with words. I hated that Dag was so much like me; so much like the man I had been. But then, as clearly as if someone had spoken in my ear, or grabbed my heart and twisted, a feeling of overwhelming confusion and distress. Fionn was conflicted, he had changed his mind, and I could feel it.

I turned back and stepped through the door.

"Oh, sorry," I said, loud and forcefully cheerful. "Didn't mean to interrupt."

Dag had Fionn pinned against the table. He turned his head without moving his body.

"Then go away, elf boy," the werewolf said.

Elf. The favorite word for humans to refer to fey in a derogatory way. I had never really figured out what was supposed to be so demeaning about it, but I knew how it was wielded.

"That's Sidhe man, to you," I said, and leaned my hip in the doorway and crossed my arms.

"Whatever," he said. "You *are* interrupting, so leave."

"I'll leave if Fionn wants me to leave," I said. "If *he* tells me to fuck off, he's all yours."

Dag ran a slow hand from Fionn's neck over his chest and belly and stopped, finally, at his thigh. "You don't like to share, fey?"

"My name is Kiernan, and Fionn isn't mine to share or not share."

Fionn's eyebrows drew together into a little frown, but he didn't say anything.

"No, he's not yours." The werewolf leaned over and licked Fionn's neck. Fionn stared at me, silver eyes wide and unsure. "He's mine." And Fionn's eyebrows crowded together again.

"Fionn?" I said, ignoring the werewolf, even as he turned away from Fionn, keeping between us, and towered over me. Counting height and build, Dag must have been at least twice my size, maybe three times.

"Kier," Fionn said, voice barely above a whisper. "I…"

I smiled at him. "Tell me what you want," I said. "Do you want me to go? Or is this big hairy beast bothering you?"

"You think I'm beneath you, don't you, you fey shit?" Dag took another step towards me. I didn't move; I just kept leaning against the doorframe as if he meant nothing.

I met his eyes. "I fucked a werewolf once," I said, and had to pretend not to notice Fionn flinch as I said it. "As I recall, *I* was beneath *him* most of the time. On my knees, on my back, on all fours." I could have lied just to sting him, but it was all true, though that particular story had a decidedly *not* happy ending, due to my cousin finding me beneath that particular wolf man.

Dag's eyes narrowed. "Are you offering yourself in exchange for this little seer? You're attractive, I'll give you that, but you're not as pretty as he is." And then I knew what was making Fionn uneasy; he suspected the handsome werewolf wanted him because he was pretty, not because he was *himself*. Dag took a step closer, close enough he could have easily reached out and touched me.

I looked him up and down, taking my time, studying him. To Dag, it probably seemed like I was sizing up his sex appeal.

And I was, but I was also watching how he moved, how he held himself, and figuring out what kind of opponent he would be.

"Kiernan," Fionn said. "It's okay. I'm fine. Dag was just… being friendly." It stung a little, that he didn't want to tell me how he actually felt, but he was probably trying to de-escalate the situation by being diplomatic. Maybe he was worried I would get hurt because Dag was so much bigger. He edged backwards, away from the table, putting a large spinning wheel between himself and the werewolf, so I knew that despite his words he wasn't comfortable with the big man so close. Or touching him. Or kissing him.

"Yeah, just being friendly," Dag said. He raked his gaze over me. "You want me to be… friendly… with both of you?" he said. "Together?"

I smirked and spoke to Fionn instead of Dag. "What do you think, pretty bird, do you want to fuck us both at once?" It might have been cruel, to ask such a thing, but I couldn't figure out what Fionn wanted me to do. His words said one thing, but the distress I felt, and the way he was edging away from Dag, said something else. I don't know what I would have done if he'd said yes. Fucked them both, I suppose.

Fionn's cheeks turned bright pink. "No, Kier. I –" He suddenly pushed past Dag and past me and out the door. I let him go, but when the werewolf moved to follow, I straightened up and put myself in his way.

"Move, elf," he said, and I showed him my teeth. They might not have been as impressive as a werewolf's, but they were as long and as sharp as a fox's and he knew exactly what meaning I intended to convey.

He bared his teeth back at me and leapt.

He was fast, considering his bulk, but I was faster. Werewolves like Dag tended to rely on their wolf speed and brute force, and were useless against blades. I, obviously, had no brute force to rely on, though I wasn't a weakling, and I had trained from a young age – with fey teachers and human – in a variety of forms of combat.

Dag found himself face down in the dirt in front of the weaving shed before he even knew what had happened, one of my knives against the side of his neck, and my knee between his shoulder blades.

"I don't think he wants your attention," I said, calmly.

"Fuck you," he spat.

"I would," I said, sheathing my knife and getting up. "But I don't think he wants you to have *me*, either, and I have this peculiar desire to do whatever Fionn wants."

And that was when I underestimated him. He twisted around and leapt up, and instead of flinging himself at me as I expected, he just swung one long arm and his reach was enough that he backhanded me across the face.

I moved, but not fast enough, or far enough, and I felt his knuckles connect and the crunch as he dislocated my nose. And I tasted my own blood. A calm settled over me.

"Good hit," I said, smiling with my teeth showing and letting blood drip down my chin. He looked taken aback, like he wasn't used to violence after all, despite his bluster, and the fact that I hadn't crumpled at the first blow worried him.

"You better hope the next one takes me down, wolf, or you might find yourself missing the essential parts for fucking anybody ever again."

He glanced down, as if expecting his tackle to be missing already, and I took the opportunity to drop him to the ground again. Then I walked away, knowing he wouldn't follow.

I FOUND FIONN SITTING on a rock next to the stream, his arms wrapped around his knees and his back hunched. Col sat on the ground next to him, dangling a fishing pole into the water.

When I stopped next to them, Col looked at me, swore under his breath and laid the pole aside. Fionn hunched farther into himself and didn't look up.

"Your nose is broke," Col said, and even then Fionn didn't look up.

"Just dislocated, I think," I said, realizing my voice sounded a bit odd because of it. I didn't move when Col got up, looked down at me, then reached out with both hands, felt my face, and suddenly wrenched, snapping my nose back into place with a crunch and a shooting pain that made me stagger.

"Put cold water on that," he said, and nodded at the stream. "Tis not as cold as ice, but not too far off." He handed me a handkerchief from his pocket, picked up his pole, and walked away.

I sat where he had been and soaked the cloth in the stream and pressed it to my face. It *was* cold, and it helped.

"Kier?" Fionn said, tentatively.

"You okay?" I asked. "Should I not have interfered?"

"Am I – Kiernan, he broke your *nose*." He took the handkerchief from my hands, dipped it in the water, and leaned closer to wipe away the blood.

"I've had worse," I said. "And I heal fast."

He didn't meet my eyes, but carefully wiped my face and neck and then rinsed the cloth, folded it, and pressed it over my nose. "Hold it here," he said, so I did.

He turned and stared out over the stream, so I did, too. Dragonflies darted over the water, hunting small insects, and the two tree serpents swooped, hunting dragonflies.

"I thought about what you said," he said, after a while. "About… about fucking Dag if I wanted him."

"Did you?" I said, gently, and even I wasn't sure if I was asking if he'd thought about it, or if he'd slept with the werewolf.

"I… I thought I wanted to until… until he was there and kissing me and all I could think about was how different he felt from you."

"Different isn't bad." I tried not to sound jealous, but I was. I burned with it.

"And then… when you said those things to him and he… he didn't want *me*, he just wanted… someone pretty. And you…"

I leaned against the rock he was sitting on. "I said those things to get him to move away from you," I said. "I could *feel* your emotions, Fionn. I could tell you weren't comfortable."

"But you weren't lying," he said softly.

"About fucking a werewolf?" I tilted my head so it rested against his leg and he stiffened, but didn't move away. "It was a long time ago."

Then he put his hand on my hair and I relaxed, closed my eyes, and let myself rest against him.

"I… I didn't run right away. I saw him hit you, and you just laughed."

"I've faced worse."

"You scared me," he said, threading his fingers through my hair, and it felt like a stab wound to the gut.

"I'm sorry, Fionn. I don't want you to be afraid of me."

"It was only for a moment." His fingers found the base of my right antler and traced the irregular bumps there. I sighed and pressed my face against his thigh. "But you were… you were defending me because you…" He stopped, but I didn't tell him not to say was he was going to say. He changed the words anyway. "Because you care about me. Because you care about what *I* want."

"I'm yours, Fionn," I said, and I wasn't even sure any words actually came out of my mouth until he was on his knees in front of me, kissing me fiercely.

16
Fionn

WHEN I LEFT THE WEAVING shed, I didn't have any place in mind to go; I just needed to get away.

Except how childish must I seem, and how much weight would it lend to the idea that I was incapable of making my own decisions?

I stopped at the first bend in the path and turned back. I heard a grunt and a thump and peered around the trees just in time to see Kiernan land on Dag's back in a graceful leap, and a knife seemed to appear in his hand like magic.

"I don't think he wants your attention," Kier said, his voice sounding nothing like he'd just taken down a man more than twice his size. He sounded calm and reasonable and somehow it made him even more frightening. And more beautiful.

I put both hands over my mouth to keep from making the noise that threatened to work its way up from the sick feeling in my belly.

"Fuck you," replied Dag, spitting out dirt and words.

"I would, but I don't think he wants you to have *me*, either." Kiernan stood gracefully up from where he'd been crouched with his knee between Dag's shoulder blades. The knife vanished back into its sheath. "And I have this peculiar desire to do whatever Fionn wants."

He said the words so simply, but they hit me like a jolt to the heart. Maybe he wouldn't say he loved me, but wanting me to have everything was the same sort of thing, wasn't it?

I clamped my hands tighter on my face and held my breath. I started to back slowly out of sight, though I don't think either of them had noticed I was there. It was only my clasped hands over my mouth that kept me from screaming when Dag found his feet again and struck out at Kiernan. I heard a crunch and saw blood.

Kiernan was rocked back on his feet but didn't fall. He smiled, and there was laughter in his voice when he said, "Good hit," as if he was actually impressed that Dag had managed to strike him. Blood flowed out of his nose and over his lips, staining his teeth, before dribbling down his chin. He hardly seemed to notice.

Dag looked slightly horrified and a little afraid, but nothing like the fear that settled in my belly. I didn't even know if it was fear *of* Kiernan, or fear *for* him. It made me twitch inside my sheath, and I realized I was getting aroused by two handsome men fighting over me. A hot flush spread up my neck.

"You better hope the next one takes me down, wolf, or you might find yourself missing the essential parts for fucking anybody ever again." Kier's voice was still calm and reasonable, but so cold I shivered.

For only a second, Dag glanced away, and then he was on the ground again and I turned and ran, not wanting to see what was going to happen next.

I slowed when I came out of the trees and saw Col sitting next to the stream, fishing. He didn't appear to have caught anything and was staring contemplatively out over the water. I sat on a rock next to him, and even perched up higher than he was, I felt small and young.

"Okay, lad?" he said without looking my way. His voice was very deep and gentle.

"Yes," I said, then realizing how miserable that single word sounded I added, "Just confused."

He made an understanding noise in his throat, and tugged at his fishing pole, causing the line to make a ripple on the surface of the water. "Dag gets too forward, you let me know," he said.

My neck felt warm, and it crept up to my cheeks. Had everyone seen how much attention Dag was paying to me? Could they also see how tempted I was, and how guilty I felt?

"It's okay," I said. "He's okay." I wasn't sure I quite meant it; if I had, Kiernan wouldn't be back at the weaving shed right now, defending me. He'd have left me and Dag alone, and I didn't even know if he'd care.

Another noise, like he understood more than I'd said. "Still," he said. "You let me know."

"Okay."

We sat quietly until Col suddenly said, "Your Kiernan cares more than he lets on," and tilted his head a little, towards where I could just hear the soft shushing of careful footsteps in the long grass.

I couldn't look up, too ashamed that I had run off and left him to fight for me. I couldn't even look when Col swore under his breath, and stood, and did something that made a sickening crunch and Kier hissed in a breath. I didn't look at Kiernan until he took Col's place next to me and I heard the werewolf walk away. Kier dipped a handkerchief into the stream and started dabbing at his face with it. I leaned down, took it from him, turned his face towards mine with a touch on his chin, and gently wiped away the blood. He sat patiently, eyes closed, letting me tend to him, and then pressed the cloth to his face when I told him to.

When I confessed how I thought I had wanted Dag until I changed my mind and it was too late, he listened, and didn't seem to be judging me.

"When you said those things," I said, "And it turned out he didn't want *me*, he just wanted someone pretty. And you said…" I had to stop because thinking about him telling Dag he'd fucked a werewolf before hurt too much. And remembering how he asked me if I wanted them both at once made me flush with shame and embarrassment. What if I had said yes? Did Kiernan want that? Me and Dag both? Together?

I was too busy feeling miserable to hear what he was saying until he said, "I could feel your emotions, Fionn. I could tell you weren't comfortable."

And how could I be angry with him then, no matter how much it stung to think about him fucking someone else, about him *wanting* someone who wasn't me? He hadn't meant to hurt me with any of the things he said; he was always trying to make me happy, to protect me. I touched his hair, hesitantly, then ran my fingers though his curls until he leaned his head against my leg.

Admitting to him that he had frightened me was even harder than admitting to myself that I was jealous, and he sighed when I said it, when I told him I'd been afraid of him. My fingers found the base of his antler and I stroked it and he sighed again, but this time with pleasure. I wanted, badly, to tell him I loved him, but now that he wasn't telling me *not* to, I couldn't get the words out.

I just traced the shape of his antler with my fingertips until he said, so softly I almost didn't hear, "I'm yours, Fionn," and for a moment I couldn't breathe.

And then, suddenly, without really knowing I was doing it, I was kneeling on the ground, reaching for him, kissing him, and he was laughing and pulling me down to him, on top of him.

I kissed him hard, desperately, wanting him to feel all the things I couldn't say out loud, until my teeth bashed into his and my nose bumped his nose and he flinched. When I pulled away a thin trickle of blood flowed out of one nostril.

"I'm okay, pretty bird," he said before I could apologize.

I sat back, took the handkerchief, and wetted it in the stream.

"You can hurt me if you want to," he said, his voice teasing. He poked me in the ribs. "I kind of like it."

I pushed his hand away and wiped the blood off his face.

"I don't want to hurt you," I said. "I don't like hurting people."

"Not even if I asked you to?" He poked my ribs again, and tickled me until I pushed him away, but I couldn't help returning his smile.

"I don't think I'm capable of hurting you on purpose," I said, wringing out the cloth and pressing it gently over his nose. It was starting to swell.

He touched my face. "I don't think you are, either," he said. "You're so kind. So gentle."

I turned away, settled on the grass, and looked out over the stream. Smoke and Flame had tired of chasing dragonflies and were now splashing among the rocks.

"Would you rather I was bolder?" I said. "Harder? More forceful?"

"Oh, you're plenty hard when you need to be," he said,

and grinned when I shot him an exasperated look. "I like you just how you are," he said, and took one of my hands in both of his. He traced my finger from the first knuckle to my fingertip, sliding his touch over the claw-like nail and then underneath to brush over the pad of my finger and up to the palm of my hand.

My breath caught.

"You're perfect, pretty bird," he said, and brought my hand to his lips to kiss my palm and trace my fingers again, this time with his tongue. It suddenly felt very difficult to breathe and I wished we were somewhere private.

"I'm not perfect," I said. I watched the tree serpents splashing for a moment and resisted the urge to pull my hand away. I wanted to find his bare skin to touch, so it was better he keep my hands occupied, even if it meant his tongue sent tingles all over my body.

"You are," he said, his lips brushing my skin as he spoke.

"My wings are stunted," I said. "And bird folk are supposed to be bright colors. Greens and blues and reds and yellows, with skin like dark honey. I'm as colorless as… as a cave fish."

I felt his smile against my palm. "Have you ever seen a cave fish?" he asked, lifting his head from my hand and clasping our fingers together in his lap.

"I've read about them. All pale and eyeless and weird."

"I've seen them," he said. "Once. There's a cave in Morven Forest where initiations are held. Deep inside the earth there are pools of clear water with tiny fish in them. They catch the light like snowflakes under the full moon, or like the facets of a cut gemstone in the sun." His voice was soft with wonder and memory. "They were… they were so beautiful I cried, Fionn. Like magic given secret life deep in the land."

"I think you see beauty in everything," I said, but my voice felt thick with emotion, touched that he had shared something so meaningful.

"There *is* beauty in everything." He let go of my hands and leaned back on his elbows. "Or nearly everything." He looked up at me. "Obviously, you *are* pale, and your wings are small, and maybe that's not what a bird man is supposed to be. But it is what *you* are. And you are so beautiful, Branfionn. And you *are* perfect. To me."

I knew I was blushing, probably glowing pink, and I had to look away. "You're just saying that so I'll let you fuck me again," I said, trying to make my voice light when his words hit me so deeply, to be teasing so I wouldn't end up crying.

He laughed, as if he knew I needed to be a little silly. "Yes," he said. "Absolutely I'm saying it so you'll fuck me again. But I'm also saying it because it's true. And I'll keep saying it until you believe me. And even after you believe me, even if you never let me touch you again."

I knew, then, that he was telling me he loved me in as many ways as he could without saying those exact words. Why he couldn't just say it, I didn't know, but maybe it didn't matter if he *meant* it. I let myself smile and something painful relaxed in my chest.

"I'm not afraid of you," I said, even though we hadn't even been talking about that anymore.

"No?"

I shook my head. "No."

"Good."

"I thought Dag was going to kill you," I said. He snorted. "Or that you would kill him."

He touched my hand. "I wasn't intending to do much more than show him he couldn't push me around," he said. "I don't think being too pushy towards you is really a killing offense. Now if he'd actually forced himself on you…" He left the sentence hanging and somehow I thought maybe that would be an offense that brought worse than killing. I didn't want to think that Kier might be capable of inflicting deliberate, cold-blooded pain, but it also gave me a forbidden thrill that he might do so for *me*.

We sat for a while longer, watching the serpents play, until Moira called out that supper was ready.

After we ate, Kiernan and Col went out to chop wood for the hearth, and I settled down with a needle and thread and the clothes I had cut out earlier. Moira settled the children with some toys and then took the trousers from me and we sat and sewed together.

"When you go," she said, "Remember what I taught you about finding out how your magic works, and never forget that a seer *asks* the Realms for help rather than commanding the magic to do their bidding."

"I will," I said. In only a few days, Moira had taught me more about magic than thirty-three years in the Abbey, listening to the Abbess and scouring the library. Then a thought occurred to me. "If all seers must serve their monarch, by the law of all the Isle, how are you here in a werewolf village?"

"I was wondering when you'd get around to asking that," she said. She sewed for a few moments before answering. "More seers are born among humans than to any other people of the Isle," she said at last. She tied a knot in her thread, then measured out another length and threaded the needle.

"But human seers tend to be less powerful, both in magic and in *seeing*, than seers among other peoples. So, when I was born and my mother saw my seer eyes, she decided no one need know what I was capable of, even if I turned out to be powerful. And I did, both in magic and in *seeing*, but as soon as

I was old enough to understand, which was right around when I developed my abilities in the first place, she taught me to act as if I had very little power."

She laughed. "And because low-magic seers are normal among humans, and seers so common, no one thought to test me. And no one objected when I married Col and moved to an obscure little village. They didn't know they were losing anything, and I believe I have done more good here, among these humble folk, than I could have done anywhere else."

"Would that have worked if you were fey?" I asked, finishing off the seam that connected one arm of my new shirt to the body. "Or Vogel, or… or anyone else?"

"I don't think so," she said. "Seers are much rarer among the fey, and almost always powerful. And among the bird folk… There hasn't been a seer for centuries. Until you."

"So, there's no point in trying to convince the Vogel King that I'm a terrible seer? Even if it's true?"

"No point at all, child. You're unique, and he will insist you serve at his court, even if you were to never *see* ever again."

I felt tension creep into my shoulders. "So my life will never be my own?" I said, pulling too hard on my stitch and snapping the thread. My eyes burned and I thought of how happy I had been sitting by the stream with Kier, just holding hands and watching the serpents splash.

She smiled, but the expression was sad. "I wouldn't lose hope yet," she said. "There are always many possible paths ahead, even if you can only see one in the immediate future."

"I wish…" I said, then stopped.

She put a hand on my shoulder and squeezed gently and I wondered if my mother had been someone like her. "Follow your heart as best you can," she said.

"My heart says to go wherever Kiernan takes me," I

whispered.

"And his tells him to follow you." A teasing note crept into her voice and I let a small smile show.

I re-knotted my thread and began to attach the second sleeve. "So we'll just follow each other in circles?" I said and laughed. More seriously, I said, "We *do* have to go to the Eyrie, don't we?"

"Perhaps."

"Otherwise, the Vogel King will be looking for me, or the Alfar, or… I don't want to be always running away."

The door burst open, making me jump, and Dag stepped through. I stood, knocking over my stool.

"Have you forgotten how to knock?" Moira said, voice mild but full of strength.

"You have to hide," Dag said, directing his words to me, as if Moira wasn't even there.

"What?"

Col and Kiernan crowded in behind him and the wolf children moved to their father, each wrapping their thin arms around one of his huge legs.

"What's going on, lad?" Col asked, carefully detaching one child and handing him to his mother, then lifting the other into his own arms.

"I was having supper with Mam," Dag said. "And Ben came home." He glanced at me. "My brother," he explained. "He and his buddies came back from Streamside just now and there's King's men there, looking for two fugitives from the Abbey. They're offering a reward."

I felt for my stool, suddenly feeling weak, forgetting it was on its side on the floor. Dag and Kier both saw my motion, and both stooped to retrieve the seat at the same time. It was Dag who backed down and let Kiernan help me sit.

"Okay, pretty bird?" he said gently. I nodded.

"You have to hide," Dag said again. "There's caves not far. We can bring you food."

"No," said Kiernan, and everyone looked at him. He rested a hand on my shoulder. "If they find you hiding us, hiding *him*, the King's men will show no mercy." His voice was hard. "I know him, the Alfar King. I know how he rules. No fey soldier would hesitate to raze this village to the ground if their monarch thought you were deceiving them." He blew a gust of air out his nose and squeezed my shoulder when I shivered.

"We have to leave," he said. "I won't put you in danger, and I won't risk them finding Fionn."

"We can keep Fionn safe here," Dag insisted.

"You can't," Kiernan said. "You couldn't even protect yourself against one Sidhe half your size armed only with knives. How can you face a troop of armored Alfar on horseback, armed with swords and spears and crossbows?"

Dag growled. "I could take you, elf. You didn't give me a proper chance."

Kiernan made a dismissive gesture. "Do you think *they'll* give you a chance?"

Col put his arm around Dag and steered him towards the door. "You and Ben and your friends get out in the woods, keep watch. If they come here, we need to know."

"Kiernan's right," I said, suddenly hating the thought of letting events just happen around me. "We can't put you in danger. We have to go. Now."

"Surely you can wait till morning," Moira said.

I shook my head and looked at Kier. His face was set. Hard. He looked so beautiful I could have wept.

"We best go now," he said, looking at me for confirmation, for my opinion.

"Yes," I said, standing. I looked at the cloth in my hands.

"It's too bad I couldn't have finished this. I'm not really dressed for travel."

Kiernan rubbed my back between my wings. "You can work on it when we stop to rest."

Moira took the fabric from me. "It's almost finished," she said. "You lot get ready to go. Col will find you an old cloak, food, blankets." She looked at her husband as she spoke and he nodded, put the child he was holding down, and began to move around the room, gathering supplies and dividing them between two sacks.

Moira put down the other child. "I'll get these done up in no time."

"We can't take your food," I said.

"You've already done too much for us," Kiernan added. "And we haven't had the time to pay you back."

"Don't matter," said Col. "You can and will take what we give you." He stepped into the other room and returned with a huge cloak he shoved into my arms. He gave another, smaller one to Kiernan, who slung it around his shoulders as soon as he finished fussing with the straps of his sword.

"Those'll do you for blankets, too," he said, pausing to adjust Kiernan's hood like a concerned parent.

Moira stood up from her chair and handed me a now-finished pair of trousers just as Col gave Kiernan what looked like a wide roll of soft leather.

"This is too much," I said as I stood in the middle of the room. I looked at Kiernan for support, but he was busy putting things in the sacks as Col handed them to him.

"Hush, child," Moira said, and put her arms around me. At first, I didn't know what to do, but then I relaxed and returned the hug. "We'll meet again," she said. "I've *seen* it." Then she sat back down and turned her attention to finishing the sleeve on my shirt.

"Okay," I said, not knowing what else to say. I slipped my legs into the trousers, and pulled them up, shoving the hem of the blue tunic out of the way and tying the waist securely. They were constructed so they'd dip under my tail and they fit well, considering how hastily they'd been made.

"Sit down, pretty bird," Kier said, and I sat automatically. He knelt in front of me and took one of my feet onto his knee. He wrapped it gently in soft linen, then began to wind the strip of leather that Col had given him, leaving my long claws free, but protecting the pads of my toes and the soles of my feet.

"We haven't time for this," I protested.

He just took my other foot and wrapped it the same way.

Moira handed me the shirt. "Take a spool of thread and a packet of needles, in case you need to repair anything," she said, then left me to change shirts and drew Kiernan to one side. Perhaps, as a human, she didn't realize my hearing was at least as keen as a werewolf's, but I heard her say, "Keep him safe."

"Of course," Kiernan said.

"Not only because you care for him," she said.

I could hear the smile in Kier's voice. "Because you care for him, too? Even after so short a time? He does have that effect on people."

"I do, but not only that." Her voice dropped so low I had to strain to hear. "I've seen several possible futures," she said. "And you *must* let him make his own choices. If you always tell him what to do, he will let you, and you will for sure end up losing him."

I could hear Kiernan's breathing change, so I knew Moira's words affected him. "I understand," he said.

"Perhaps," Moira replied. "But also, in almost every vision I have *seen* where the two of you are together, he… becomes a symbol."

I turned, tucking the new shirt into my trousers, and met Kiernan's eyes over Moira's shoulder.

"Keep him safe, Kiernan Druison," she said, urgently. "Because he will come to mean the possibility of a better future, not only to bird folk, and for seers, but for *all* the peoples of the Isle."

17

Kiernan

I HADN'T REALLY THOUGHT the Abbess or the Alfar King would send anyone after us once we escaped into the forest. But I'd forgotten – and you'd think thirty-six years off and on in a fey court would ensure I'd always remember – that fey rulers do not like to be thwarted. And few could hold a grudge like fey nobles.

I suppose I should have expected them to at least attempt to find and eliminate Fionn quickly, because once news of his existence made it out into the world, it would expose the Alfar Monarchy's plotting and their violation of one of the few sacred Isle laws: that a seer belongs to their own monarch.

If we could escape cleanly and make it to the Eyrie safely, I didn't think the Alfar would keep pursuing us. They would dare break the law secretly, but doing so in open defiance would set all the peoples of the Isle against them, and without the boosted magic Fionn's sacrifice would have given them, they didn't have the strength to prevail.

So now we just had to escape.

We parted with Moira and Col at the door to their house.

"I'll make sure you're compensated for helping us," I said. "Somehow."

"No need, lad," said Col. "No need to repay us doing what's right."

"I know," I said.

"We know you can't spare much," said Fionn. "And we wouldn't have you face hardship because of us. It's also right for *us* to help as we can." I squeezed his hand and he squeezed back.

"We will see you again," Moira said. "Someday."

We left our farewells at that and turned into the darkness. Smoke and Flame appeared, chittering at us that we should all be asleep, and finally settled on Fionn's shoulders, under the hood of Col's borrowed cloak.

"Quiet, now," I said softly to all of them, and led Fionn upstream.

"You're taking me to Morven?" Fionn said and I paused, pulled him close, and touched his face.

"I'm taking you away from here," I said. "We'll plan where after that." I didn't tell him, yet, that I was definitely *not* taking him to Morven, because werewolf ears are keen and someone might overhear. But if it *looked* like we were heading toward my mother's court, so much the better.

"I'm frightened," Fionn said, so quietly I almost didn't hear, and I'm not sure he was aware of saying it aloud. I took his hand again, held it tightly, and led him along the path.

"So am I," I said.

"I didn't think you were afraid of anything." He stumbled in the dark, so I pulled him closer and made better sure of letting him know where there were rocks and branches to be stepped over. I could see just fine in the faint moonlight that came through the trees, but apparently bird folk didn't have much in the way of night vision.

I stopped to guide him around a fallen tree that blocked the path and took the opportunity to adjust his pack to sit better across his shoulder, and to kiss his cheek. I wanted to blurt out, "I'm afraid of losing you," but I kept silent. He didn't need *that* to worry about, as well.

I smelled a werewolf not far ahead – one in sore need of a bath – and pulled Fionn behind a tree and put my fingers on his lips. He froze.

A wolf man crept along the path, looking around him but focusing on the way ahead. It was Dag.

"I heard you, little seer," he said. "I just wanted to let you know we haven't seen any King's men yet."

I touched Fionn's hand, hoping he would understand I wanted him to stay where he was, and stepped out onto the path, behind Dag.

"Were we making so much noise?" I said, and he jumped and spun around.

"Where is he?" Dag said.

I ignored his question. "Listen, wolf," I said, keeping my voice low, so only he and Fionn would hear. "If the King's men question you, don't lie. Tell them exactly what you did and what you saw."

"I'm not going to betray him," Dag said, and I noticed, as I'm sure he meant me to, that he'd said nothing about betraying me.

"If you lie," I said, "And they find out – and they will find out, because they probably have a seer with them – they'll not only kill you, they'll punish your whole village."

Dag scowled. "So I just give him up?"

I shrugged. "We'll be gone. It won't matter. Just answer truthfully and keep your village safe. Tell them you gave us shelter, not knowing who we were. And tell them we ran when you told us we were hunted. Tell them you saw me here in the woods, heading towards Morven. Be *truthful*." I emphasized the last word, in case he was still not understanding me. "And keep Moira and Col and their children safe. Keep your mam and your brother safe."

I gripped his shoulder and he scowled but didn't pull away. "Let *me* keep Fionn safe."

"We meet again, elf," he said, "And I will take you down, and I'll take your pretty little seer away from you."

"You're welcome to try." I let him see my teeth. "But right now, look out for yourself and your village."

He scowled deeper, then nodded and gripped my shoulder briefly, before turning down the path back to the wolf village.

I hoped he would listen to me, not only because cooperating with the King's men was the only way to be sure the village didn't suffer, but also because I wanted him to tell the Alfar he'd seen me come this way.

"Come on, pretty bird," I said and Fionn stepped out from behind his tree. I took his hand again, and we followed the path until it diverged from the creek and turned to head towards a large stream half a day's journey away, where the town of Streamside was.

I took us instead along a deer trail that followed the creek, and after a long stretch of picking our way over rocks and fallen branches, we came on a spot where a large tree had come down right across the creek. I could feel how full of questions he was, in the same way I had sensed his distress before, but he kept silent and followed as I climbed up onto the log and used it as a bridge.

If I was correct, and the Alfar were behaving as I thought they would – as I would have directed them to, if I were leading them – there would only be a small number of men stationed at Streamside, asking questions and looking threatening. They knew we may have gone there after fleeing the Abbey but were unlikely to go back.

If I was right, there would be men both upstream and downstream of the path to Streamside, and they would visit all the villages in the area, patrolling the route between Aven Forest and Morven Forest, and between the Abbey and the Eyrie. Those were the two likeliest ways we'd have fled – the only possible ways unless we did the unreasonable thing and doubled back to flee inland, right into the heart of Alfar territory.

The best thing we had going for us was that the Alfar preferred travelling on horseback, and horses disliked moving at night. They were also likely to assume that we would prefer to travel during the day, because bird folk couldn't see well at night. So, I would move us in the dark, and find somewhere to hide during the day.

With luck, it should only take a couple of days – three at the most – to travel to the Eyrie. I refused to think about how that meant I only had three more days with Fionn.

The hardest part would be slipping past the King's men who were almost certainly waiting for us downstream. I hoped to slip past them tonight, and worried that I might have wasted too much time heading upstream first, to throw them off. Once past them, we needed all the time we could get to stay ahead.

When we climbed back down from the log, I pulled Fionn close again, nestling into his warmth and putting my mouth close to his ear. "You must do your best to be quiet now, pretty bird," I said. "If they hear us, we're lost."

He nodded and stared in my direction, eyes wide and pupils dilated, trying to see me in the dark.

"I can't say for sure yet, but I think we may have to pass very close to the King's men." I cupped his face in both hands, feeling the slight tremble he tried to hide. I could feel his terror in my bones, in my heart, but he was holding it back, not letting it get the better of him. I wanted to tell him how proud I was of him, but I just said, "I'll keep you safe."

Then I closed my eyes and felt for the Realms above and below and around me, for my own connection to the forest, even if this wasn't *my* forest. I had been afraid the magic wouldn't respond, that I was still hollow, but it was there. Not so strong as it had been – the connection was still damaged – but it was there.

I breathed a little easier and then, as if I were appealing to the Lady of the Forest herself, I asked for help. And the forest responded, sending shadows curling around us, making us blend into the trees, into the darkness between and under and around.

"Quietly, now," I said, and took Fionn's hand. His fingers were cold. I led him down a deer trail heading downstream, following it until it vanished as deer trails do, then down another, and another. We climbed onto a log and used it as a road across a stretch of rocky, branch-strewn forest floor, followed along another deer trail, and the whole time the shadows kept us hidden.

As we made our way carefully down yet another deer path, one of the serpents poked her head out of Fionn's cloak and hissed. He put out a hand to soothe her, and I stopped us, and listened, and smelled the air.

Wood smoke. The fires were small and well-tended, and most townsfolk wouldn't have noticed the scent at all. But I had been well-trained to my mother's use and my father's both, so I did notice. I heard a horse snort, not close enough to worry about, but still there.

I touched Fionn's shoulder and felt around me through my magic, asking the forest for a temporary hiding place. And there, just between the trail we had been following and the stream, was a fallen tree with a deep, fern-lined hollow at its base. I led Fionn there and pulled him down to crouch among the ferns and roots.

I leaned close to speak softly in his ear. "Wait here. I need to scout ahead." He hugged his knees and looked at me with wide, frightened eyes, but he nodded.

"You guard him," I whispered to the serpents. They poked their heads out of Fionn's cloak and looked at me like I was stupid.

We guard, said Smoke.

We keep safe, said Flame.

I hated to leave him, but I needed complete silence, and I needed all my senses focused on one thing. I wasn't worried about the Alfar men camped just over the rise to the left of our path, nor about the guards who leaned on their pikes around the perimeter of the camp.

I was worried about their scouts, the silent men they'd have at intervals farther out from the edge of camp, watching and patrolling, waiting for us to try to sneak by.

I had trained for that exact job myself, and before my mother had decided I'd be more use in a diplomatic role, for my ability to lie, I had spent a lot of time patrolling Morven Forest. I knew exactly how unlikely it would be for Fionn to sneak past me, and that it would be just as unlikely that he could sneak past whomever the Alfar had assigned to watch.

I found the first of them almost right away and was glad the serpents had alerted us when they had. I should have been far more cautious, because without that warning, we'd have walked right into the Alfar scout.

He was cocky, though, and self-assured, and simply watched the deer trail. Presumably, he assumed it was our only way past him, and for Fionn, it would have been.

I thought about slitting his throat to be sure he wouldn't

discover us, but I needed to avoid bloodshed if I could. It would be best not to cause an incident between the Alfar and the Sidhe courts. Our peoples had enough grudges between them already.

The second scout gave himself away when he suddenly stood up from the tree I'd been about to slip behind to relieve himself noisily in the leaves. He was sloppy, but if not for the shadows cloaking me, he'd have seen me. I needed to be more careful.

I picked out a third scout by asking the moonlight to show me hidden things, and a fourth when an owl landed on a branch and immediately startled away from the Alfar perched there already. I didn't see any others, but I still moved carefully as I made my way back to Fionn along the creek bank.

It was a risk, following the creek, as our footprints would show anywhere we had to walk across sand or gravel, and it was possible Fionn would trip and give us away with the sound. But it seemed the better choice. There would be more light for Fionn to see by, and the scouts all seemed to assume we'd follow game trails in order to stay within the shelter of the woods.

Fionn couldn't stop the squeak he let out when I suddenly appeared next to him and, without thinking, I pressed my mouth on his to keep him from making any more sounds. He tucked his cold fingers into my hair and held tight until I gently pried them away.

"No sounds," I said. He nodded and got up and I smiled when he managed to get out of the tree-root hollow without even making the ferns rustle. He was learning, and learning fast, and it might be enough to save his life tonight.

I led him to the stream bank and along it, choosing our route carefully to avoid as much open sand and gravel as possible, and to keep us from going too far out into the open, where the shadows couldn't conceal us.

The forest kept us cloaked and the light from the waning moon seemed to avoid falling on us, and I saw the exact moment Fionn realized I was using magic when I turned around to help him balance on a narrow log.

His eyes opened wide and he parted his lips as if to speak, but closed them quickly. His eyebrows drew together, and he looked down to concentrate on the log and his balance.

And I had to bite back a shout when I saw the figure appear out of the darkness behind him, nearly invisible in his own cloaking shadows. The scout had a knife at Fionn's throat before I could even react and if the Alfar hadn't still wanted to capture him alive, to salvage their sacrificial ritual, Fionn would have been bleeding at my feet.

One of the serpents hissed and my own knife left my hand and appeared in the scout's right eye almost in the same moment. Fionn's eyes widened again, and a tear slipped down his cheek, and then I was past him, catching the scout before his falling body could make too much noise and alert his companions. I let his body slide quietly behind the log and retrieved my knife.

Fionn was still staring straight ahead, frozen in terror, but when I touched his shoulder he looked at me and nodded, just a slight movement of his head. He followed me off the log and across a stretch of slippery rocks.

By the time we had skirted the Alfar camp and I was comfortable that we'd avoided the rest of the scouts, the moon was gone and so was most of the night. I moved us away from the stream and back onto deer trails, and let my magic slip away. I could feel Fionn's exhaustion deep in my belly. He was strong, but not used to the sustained physical effort of travel, the strain of keeping silent, of staying hidden from hostile eyes, and it was beginning to show.

I hated to do it, but I had to keep us moving for as long as the night lasted, to get as far away from the King's men as we could.

When he stumbled over a branch he couldn't see in near total darkness and fell to his knees, I relented, and found a fallen log for him to sit on.

Smoke and Flame emerged from his cloak and launched into the air. They didn't seem to have any trouble with the darkness.

We scout, said Flame.

Keep watch, said Smoke.

Fionn leaned against me. "I'm sorry," he whispered. "I just need to rest."

I settled my head on his shoulder. "I shouldn't have pushed you so hard, pretty bird."

"You killed him," he said, and I was surprised here was no anger or even concern in his voice. "For me."

"I would do it again," I said, and he rested his face against my hair.

"You shouldn't be using magic," he said, and I felt his breath against my scalp. "You're still healing."

"Shh," I said, stroking his fingers with my own. I tucked his hands into mine, trying to warm him.

"I couldn't bear it if…" He let the sentence trail off and buried his face deeper in my hair.

"Without magic, pretty bird, we'd be the ones who were dead beside the creek. Or captured for killing later." I rubbed his hands between mine. "And I'm fine. This kind of magic isn't much of a strain."

"Still," he said.

"I learned to use magic from a seer," I said. "Not from a magic-worker."

"Asking instead of commanding," he replied. "That's what Moira said."

"The forest is happy to help, even against Alfar. I ask, they command. The forest prefers to make its own choices." I rubbed his fingers some more, finally feeling heat come back into them. "Can you keep going now?"

"I think so." He sounded so tired I wanted to give in, to make a nest at the base of the log and let him sleep. But we had to keep going, at least until sunrise.

I got up and he followed, letting me lead him down another deer trail, and another, until birds began to sing and slowly the world turned from black to deep blue, to gray, and brown and green. And morning was on us. The serpents returned, happy to have left the Alfar behind.

I called on my magic one more time, asking for a place we could hide until night came again. The forest offered logs and fallen trees and then, a little way downstream where the water had undercut a rock outcropping on the opposite bank, a cave entrance.

If it was obvious, a cave would be worse than curling up under a log, but if it was well-hidden it would be the perfect place to rest, to eat and sleep, and plan what to do next.

I led Fionn along the stream to a place opposite the rock. I couldn't see anything. Trees and brush grew right to the waterline, finding root in every crack and crevice, branches overhanging the water. I reached out to the magic for a hint of where to find the cave and almost laughed.

Under the outcropping was a deep pool, full of small brown fish and black tadpoles, and there under the overhanging trees, knee-deep under the water, was the entrance to a large otter den.

I went in first, clearing debris and branches from the entrance. A big otter stared at me when I popped my head into her home, then slipped past me when I apologized and asked if we might borrow her den.

It's always difficult to say exactly how intelligent any given animal is, how much of what you tell them they really understand, but I think she understood we needed shelter. She snorted and slipped out the entrance into the stream, giving me leave to use her home.

I ducked back under the water to fetch Fionn, grateful that the bags Col had given us were waterproofed. Fionn was staring after the otter as she swam away.

"It's going to be a bit damp," I said. "But we'll be safe here for the day."

Inside the den, we both called up wisplights and discovered there was more room than expected, with a deep bed of dried leaves we immediately burrowed into.

"Get some sleep, pretty bird," I said, as Fionn curled against my side.

"You must be careful using magic," he said. "Kier, promise me."

I didn't say anything for a few heartbeats, then the words came out more fiercely than I intended. "I'd burn myself hollow using magic if it would save your life, pretty bird."

18
Fionn

I EXPECTED TO LIE AWAKE for a long time, but I slipped into sleep almost as soon as my eyes closed. The pile of leaves was surprisingly comfortable, and Kiernan was warm and I didn't even take the bag from around my shoulders before I relaxed and drifted away.

I woke when I thought I heard someone call my name. Our wisplights had gone out so I called up a new one in the palm of my hand, thinking about the first time I'd done it, up on the roof of my tower in the Abbey. It seemed so long ago now – that version of me was inexperienced and naive – but it was few enough days I could still count them on my fingers.

Kiernan was asleep, curled in the leaves like a forest animal, his hands tucked under his chin. I couldn't resist brushing a curl of hair off his cheek, and he sighed.

If someone had called out to me, it must have been a dream, forgotten as soon as I woke.

I looked around. I had been too tired to notice much when we first crawled in here, and I saw that while the space was obviously an animal den, with a layer of dirt on the floor and the pile of leaves, it was clean, as if the otter who lived here didn't like to leave food remains or feces strewn about her home. It was a small chamber of stone, carved out of the rock outcrop by the action of water, not by an animal.

The ceiling was low, with just enough room for me to sit up in the pile of leaves. Across from us, on the other side of the pool of water that marked the entrance, the ceiling dropped even lower but didn't quite meet the floor. I didn't have enough control over my wisplights yet to float one over to light up the area – if I let it out of my hand, it would vanish – so I shifted onto my knees and crawled awkwardly over, almost falling into the entrance hole.

I still couldn't see the end of the cave so I stretched my arm out into the low crevice as far as I could and saw that it became a sort of passage, so low it would require crawling on my belly to get in, and then curved away until I couldn't see any more.

I heard the leaves rustle behind me and turned around. Kiernan's eyes were open.

"Is something over there, pretty bird?" he asked. "Did the otter leave a pile of bones or a nest full of babies?" He stretched.

"I think the cave keeps going," I said, and Kiernan sat up, summoned a wisplight, and floated it past me into the passage.

"It's nearly sunset," he said. "We should keep going."

Then I heard it again, a sort of whisper that wasn't in my ears or even in my mind, exactly. Instead, I could *hear* it the same way I *saw* visions. And it wasn't my name at all, but somehow still seemed to refer to me, as if I had a kind of name that couldn't be expressed by sound, and that could only be understood by seers.

"I think… something's calling me?" I didn't mean for it to

come out as a question.

Kiernan slung his sack and waterskin over his shoulders and crawled out of the leaves and past the entrance until he was on hands and knees beside me, peering deeper into the cave. His wisplight floated back out, around the bend, and I let mine go out so I could rest with both hands on the floor.

"Do you want to go look?" he said. "It's a tight squeeze, even for one as slender as you." He put his hand on my arm. "What if your wings get stuck?"

I flattened my wings against my back and stared into the passage. "We should keep going," I said, knowing we had no time to spare if we were to keep ahead of pursuit.

"Maybe," Kiernan said softly, and I looked over at him. He was studying my face. "Something really is calling you," he said, and I felt the tug of that not-sound that was not quite my name. "I can almost feel it," he said. "Pulling at you."

"You can?"

He nodded. "Every time I feel what you're feeling, it gets stronger." He touched my hand. "Do you want me to ignore it? To try to shut you out?"

I looked at his hand, grimy fingers touching mine, just as grimy, and then back at his face.

"You might not want me knowing how you feel," he said. "It's okay."

I shook my head. "It's… it's nice." I moved a little closer to the crevice.

"Let's go see," he said. "The cave entrance is well hidden, and if they do find it, they'll see an otter den, like we did. We can be safe here for a while. Maybe even until they stop looking for us."

I knew we didn't have enough food to last that long, but the urge to go farther into the cave was getting stronger, so I didn't say so. "Okay," was all I said, then I flattened onto my belly and wriggled forward.

Kier sent wisplights floating ahead of me, and they made the tight space feel more open somehow and chased off some of my fear of getting stuck.

"I'm right behind you," he said. "I'll pull you out by your feet if you get wedged in there."

I reached back with one of those feet, planted it gently on his face, and pushed. He laughed.

It was a slow process, wriggling forward on my stomach, and it didn't help that the tree serpents slipped forward easily and disappeared around the bend, making me feel even more awkward.

Partway along, my stomach suddenly growled and Kiernan said, "You're going to bring the whole cave down on us with your echoes." He grabbed my foot before I could push it on his face again. "We'd better stop and eat once we get out of this passage."

"Mmm," I answered, and kept wriggling. Another moment or two and I could push up onto my hands and knees. Then, ahead, the wisplights zipped out into more open space and soon I could stand. I would have kept going, moving faster now that I could, but when Kiernan crept out of the narrow passage behind me, he stopped me with a hand on my shoulder.

"I meant it, pretty bird," he said. "You need to eat. And drink." He passed me a waterskin and stared at me with raised eyebrows until I drank. Then he rummaged in his bag and pulled out bread and cheese.

"I can eat and walk at the same time," I said, and he smiled.

"Okay. Lead the way."

There was only one way, a single tunnel leading into darkness. That was probably a good thing, because the thought of being lost down here, of wandering endless passages like the hapless characters in a fairy tale I read in the Abbey library was not a comforting one.

And though the passage we followed appeared to be entirely natural, carved out by long-ago water, the floor was even and flat, save for a dip in the middle like a channel. A thin trickle of water ran along the bottom, leading us deeper in.

Every now and then the walls opened out and we passed through a larger space. Columns of white stone hung down from the roof and rose up from the floor and sometimes made fantastical shapes. The water that must have formed them was long gone, except for the trickle along the passage, and the dry depressions in the floor looked eerie in their emptiness.

The whole time, the nagging feeling of being called tugged at me.

It was silent here underground, which seemed to amplify whatever it was that urged me on. Kier's quiet breathing was a comfort, letting me know he was there, right behind me. His footsteps were barely audible, while mine shuffled and clicked.

I felt like I belonged here – which was a disconcerting feeling because how could a bird person, made for the sky, belong in a place so confined and so deep in the ground? But I also felt too noisy, too uncouth, for such a place. Because, despite its evident natural cause and its emptiness, this place felt sacred.

Kiernan laced his fingers through mine, making me feel less lost, and I squeezed to let him know the contact was appreciated. We walked on, both quiet save our footsteps and our breathing. The serpents had not returned from scouting ahead.

And then, suddenly, the whole floor dropped away, the ceiling vanished upwards, the walls opened out, and we looked out over a huge cavern. It appeared as though it had once had water all through it, pools and streams and waterfalls. Now there was only the little trickle at our feet.

"Goddess Below," Kiernan said, in an awed whisper.

"Look." I pointed and he followed my gesture across the open space to the far side. "There's a spring there. And a pool."

"Is that steam?"

"A hot spring?"

"Fancy a bath, pretty bird?"

"Yes," I said. "But can we spare the time?"

"I think we're safe here," he said. "I think we can take as much time as we want, now."

The serpents swooped out of the dark to play with Kier's wisplights and chirp at us. Then they swooped away again, chittering happily.

We climbed down, and though there was no evidence that the stone had been deliberately worked, there was a path that descended to the bottom of the cave, where it split many times, meandering away among the columns of stone, leading who knew where.

"Does this look like a lantern to you?" Kiernan said, pointing to a stubby column next to the path that had a hollow in its top. He called up a flame in the palm of his hand and dropped it into the hollow. Some remnant of fluid caught fire and flared up. "They're all along here," he said, and made a gesture, sending little flames out to light our way.

We walked across the floor between rows of fire. Something deep and sacred built up in my belly and swelled my heart.

"What is this place?" I whispered, but I thought I might know.

Behind us, whatever fuel had been left in the column tops burned low and one by one the flames went out as we walked hand-in-hand across the cavern towards the spring. I felt like I was participating in a ceremony but had no idea what it might mean.

All the flames had gone out by the time we reached the spring, and we were left with Kiernan's wisplights. The water was indeed hot, deep, and clear, with a continuous flow from under the stone, like the Abbey bathhouse. We needn't worry about our bathing making the water dirty.

"Is this where the voice called you to?" Kier asked, unslinging his bag and letting it drop to the floor next to the pool. He started to work on the buckles of his sword rig.

"It wasn't really a voice," I said. "And… maybe. I can't feel it now." I dropped my bag next to Kier's and sat down to unwind the leather from around my feet. When I looked up, Kiernan was already naked, stretching in the flickering wisplights.

He held out a hand to help me up, tugged my shirt over my head, and reached for the tie on my trousers.

"I thought you wanted a bath," I said, tugging on his left antler.

He grinned. "Last time we had a bath together, I wasn't allowed to touch you." He let go of my trouser tie and the garment slid down my legs to puddle around my ankles.

I pushed his hands away, playfully. "Maybe you won't be allowed this time, either." I raised an eyebrow at him.

He grinned wider. "Okay," he said. "You can touch me instead." Then he bent down and slipped into the water and held out a hand for me to follow.

"Oh," I said, as I slid into the water and into Kiernan's arms. "This is lovely." The water was the perfect temperature, hot without being too hot, and it felt like it contained salts or something else that made it soft on the skin.

"Yes, it is," Kiernan said, sliding his hands down my back.

"And so are you."

"Are you sure they won't follow?"

"Smoke and Flame will let us know if there's danger," he said.

I put both hands on his chest, then suddenly pushed him and laughed as he fell back into the water, surprise and delight on his face. He submerged and disappeared. He stood up suddenly, streaming water, eyes wide with excitement.

"There's another passage under here," he said.

"You're not going to go in there?" I said. But I could feel excitement of my own, building in my belly, and the call that wasn't a call told me this was where I was meant to go. "What if there's no air?" I said, still nervous.

He grinned, and kissed me, and was gone under the water again. I waited, terrified, and impatient. I knew he could hold his breath for a long time, but what if he got stuck? What if there was a current in the water and it sucked him under? What if there was an animal?

When he came back, all my worries fled, and I felt a pull in my gut. His face was full of wonder.

"You have to see this, Fionn," he said.

I followed him under without a word. He made wisplights for me, and I swam after him, through a narrow passage that would have stopped me from going any farther if I hadn't seen the look on his face or felt the pull in my belly. We came out in a small pool, barely big enough for both of us. I stood up, and stared.

Kiernan had summoned a whole crowd of wisplights and they danced and drifted around the chamber. There was another, larger pool, almost a perfect circle, with a stubby flat-topped pillar on the other side of it. Small objects, like offerings, glittered on the flat space, and steam drifted up from the pool. All around the cave, crystals projected from the walls, sending the lights from the wisps in all directions and breaking them apart into a rainbow of colors.

For a moment, I couldn't breathe. Then all my breath rushed out at once.

"It's a shrine," I said.

"It reminds me of the cave in Morven Forest." Kiernan's voice was soft, reverent. "The one with the cave fish."

"There was a book in the Abbey library," I said. "The oldest one I ever found, written just after the founding of the Nine Monarchies." I climbed slowly up onto the floor, fanning my wings for balance, and Kiernan followed.

"What did it say?" He reached for my hand.

"It said there were once shrines all over the Isle, in caves and forest groves, on mountaintops and shorelines."

"There still are," he said, voice hushed.

"These were hidden," I said. "Sacred to the spirits who were here before our Goddesses, before most people were even here." I stepped closer to the pool and saw how there were crystals lining the bottom, turning the whole into a huge glittering gemstone in the wisplights.

"Some of them were taken over and given to the deities of the fey and the humans. Some were destroyed." I squeezed his hand. "And some... some stayed hidden."

"Who built them?" he asked.

"No one. They were all naturally formed."

"Then who worshipped there?"

I licked my lips and stared down into the pool. "Before the humans and fey came to the Isle..." I said and stopped.

He pulled his hand from mine and rested it on my back instead, stroking the feathers just above my tail. "There were already people here," he said, softly.

"They say... the book said, the sea people were here, and the plains folk and..."

"The bird folk."

"They were here already, and the three lands were divided between us. Or maybe shared is a better word. There were others here, too, the wild folk like werewolves and dryads."

"And then the fey came, and the humans, and carved it all up into the Nine Monarchies."

"This shrine could be older than history," I said.

"The nearest people now are bird folk, "Kiernan said. "And the Eyrie is very old, too, they say." His fingers found the skin beneath my feathers. "This could be an ancient Vogel shrine."

I knelt at the side of the pool and dipped my fingers in. Kiernan put his hand lightly on my head.

"Do you think it's okay to touch it?" he said, crouching next to me.

"I think it was meant for bathing in," I said. "For purification, perhaps, or… I don't know, but it feels welcoming." My seer senses were urging me to get into the water, to float in it and let it… transform me? I looked at Kiernan and he smiled and touched my cheek.

"You're almost glowing, pretty bird," he said.

I looked back at the water, sat on the edge of the pool, and slipped in. It was barely waist high, but it felt right to be in it, somehow. I faced the flat-topped pillar and raised my hands.

"If there are any spirits here," I said, "Know that we honor you, and we thank you for allowing us to be here."

"So we do," said Kiernan, using the traditional response for fey rituals that had, I suspected, been borrowed from earlier rites than theirs.

I turned back and held out my hand.

"Are you sure?" he said.

I nodded, so he took my hand and slipped into the pool next to me. We knelt so the water reached our necks, and I pulled him closer, suddenly needing him to touch me, to kiss me. When his lips met mine, the not-voices swirled around me, through all my senses, welcoming and joyous.

"Are you sure?" Kiernan whispered again, lips brushing mine.

"Sex can be holy, too," I said.

"Did you read that in the Abbey library?" He traced the side of my neck with his tongue.

"In a book the Abbess would have burned if she knew it existed."

He smiled and closed his eyes and kissed me again, and let me push him gently away until he was floating on his back with me between his thighs.

"Fionn," he said, and the cave echoed my name back to me until he might have been saying it over and over directly into my ear. I started, because none of our other words had echoed so. Then I saw that he was aroused by me so close between his thighs, so I leaned down and took him in my mouth.

His moan echoed, too, bounced around the chamber until it seemed like the cave was full of Kiernans, and I was pleasuring them all.

"Fionn, look," he said suddenly, and there was no echo. I opened my eyes and he was pointing upwards. I slid my mouth off him and looked up.

The ceiling of the cave was flat and painted to look like the sky on a slightly cloudy day. In the sky, amid a flock of feathered serpents, was painted a bird person, wings spread, tail wide, soaring.

"He looks like you," Kiernan said, voice low with awe. The figure had wings much bigger than mine would even be, but Kier was right. They were pale-skinned, silver-and-white-feathered, and their long hair streamed out around them.

"Why do you say 'he'?" I asked. "It's difficult to tell except by feather patterns. Except when…" and I blushed.

Kiernan laughed softly, respecting the sacredness of the place. "I'm pretty sure he's showing off an impressive boner."

And he was right about that, too.

"Maybe this is a fertility shrine," he said.

"Wouldn't there be a woman, too? And maybe not a seer?"

"A sex shrine?"

"You have sex on the brain," I said, but pulled him close again.

"So did he," Kier said, gesturing at the ceiling. "And so do you." He curled his fingers around the erection I hadn't even felt slide out of my sheath.

"Do you think we should?" I said.

"You started it," he said. "You tell me." He kissed me, but I was the one who slid my tongue into his mouth.

We knelt in the hot pool, hands caressing, mouth fierce on mouth, for what felt like a long while. And every caught breath, every soft sound of pleasure, was echoed back to us.

Then I pulled away and looked into his eyes. "Kiernan," I said, and his name echoed around the room.

"Fionn," he replied, and my name echoed, too.

"I feel like there's something I should be seeing. One more element that I haven't figured out yet." I looked around the chamber but kept my hands on his skin.

He looked, too. "Does that look like an ass print?" he said, suddenly, and I choked.

"What?"

He pointed. Just below the stubby flat-topped pillar with its offerings was a sort of double hollow on the edge of the pool.

"Look," he said, hoisting himself out of the pool. "It fits." He leaned back against the pillar.

I laughed. "So it does." I moved closer. He was at exactly the right height for me to put my mouth on him again, so I did.

He made a noise deep in his throat and buried his hands in my hair. And even though the sound wasn't the sort that should echo, it did, returning to my ears over and over and making me want to pull more such noises out of him. It was so erotic my erection twitched.

"There are footprints here, too," he said, when he caught his breath.

I lifted my head to look and there were smaller depressions on each side of him, shaped just like a bird-person foot, with a long sole, two big toes on one end, and a single toe on the other. Kier held out his hand, mischief and desire in his eyes. I took it, gripping his fingers, and let him pull me up to crouch astride his lap. My feet fit into the depressions like they had been meant for me, and the pillar had perfectly-placed handholds.

I stared into his eyes. "Do you think we're imagining this?" The call I had felt swirled around my senses until I felt dizzy.

"It seems too perfect," he said, stroking my erection and making me gasp. The sound bounced around the room and into my ears again.

"Kier?"

"Mm?"

I slid my hand down my belly, dipped my fingers into my sheath and pulled them out again, covered in lubricant. I rubbed it onto Kiernan and his little sounds of pleasure surrounded me.

He studied my face, watched my eyes as I guided the tip of his hardness against my anus and rubbed. His hands tightened on my hips, keeping me balanced. "Oh, pretty bird," he said and a hundred Kiernans whispered it into my ears.

His eyes slid closed as I lowered myself onto him, impaled myself with his erection, and his moan echoed deep and needy in my ears.

I braced myself on the pillar, lifted myself with my legs and lowered myself again, feeling him slide inside me. When he moved one hand from my hip to stroke my hardness I cried out and it echoed and echoed and I pulsed so suddenly I wasn't expecting it. Semen splattered up his belly and onto his chest.

"Goddess Below, Fionn," he said. "You feel so fucking good."

I lifted and lowered onto him, one hand clutched on the pillar and one tangled in his hair, and I pulsed again, this time shooting thick white fluid all the way up to his neck.

"Spirits," I said. "I don't think our goddesses are here."

"Spirits," said Kiernan and moaned again. The walls carried it back to me and I pulsed in Kiernan's hand and splattered his face.

He arched his back and tilted his head back against the pillar. He licked my semen off his lips.

"Spirits," he whispered again. "I'm going to come really fucking soon."

"Yes," I said, then, "Please don't stop."

"Don't stop," echoed around me, and he must have found a ledge under the edge of the pool to brace his feet on, because all at once he was thrusting up into me, his hand stroking me in time to his hip movements.

"Don't stop," I whispered and heard my voice echo as I cried out. The fourth pulse hit me and I ejaculated hard, spurting into Kier's hair and right to the top of the pillar. He started to move his hand back to my hip, to brace me to thrust harder into me, but I grabbed frantically to keep him where he was, to keep him stroking me.

"Don't stop," I begged again. "Please."

He looked at me though eyelashes spangled with white threads of my semen and then his head tilted back and his body arched under me and I felt his cock throb in my ass and he seemed to come forever, his gasps and moans echoing and echoing.

And a fifth pulse ripped through me, just as I felt the tightness of *seeing* behind my eyes and I thought I might topple over backwards into the pool as I finished my orgasm violently and a vision hit me at the same time.

I think I screamed.

Slowly the room came into focus and Kier's arms held me steady and my whole body thrummed and vibrated with the aftermath of the most intense orgasm I could imagine.

And I was full of knowledge I couldn't put into words. Magic swirled through me. The spirits of this place had spoken to me as I had my fifth pulse, but they had not spoken in words or even pictures.

They had told me, showed me, what had happened to the last seer of the Vogel, had told me why I was how I was and what it meant.

I knew so much, was so full of knowing, and it was seeping away faster than I could hold onto it.

Kiernan held me gently in his strong arms as I wept into his hair.

19
Kiernan

I WASN'T SURE IF I LOVED or hated the sex shrine.

For one thing, I'd just had the longest and most intense orgasm I'd ever had in my life, *and* I'd given Fionn one with five fucking pulses. But for the other thing, my sweet gentle lover was now sobbing in my arms like his heart was broken.

I didn't try to get him to stop, or to talk to me; I just held him, stroked his back, and murmured nice things about how lovely he was. When I could breathe properly, I eased over the side of the pool and into the water, letting the heat soothe and relax him.

When he finally went limp against me, I leaned back and stroked away the hair that was sticking to his face. He looked at me, stared, and suddenly laughed.

"You've got semen all over your face," he said. "And in your hair."

"And whose fault is that?" I kissed his nose and unwound one arm from him so I could rinse my face. When I surfaced, he was still smiling. I was relieved that my after-sex state could give him some amusement.

"I'm sorry." He wet his hand and worked at a bit of spunk still stuck in my hair.

"For making me come so hard I almost dislocated my hips?"

His lips curled up a little more. "For… for crying." His cheeks turned pink. "Right after you…" He licked his lips and looked away.

"I counted five," I said, wrapping my arms securely around him again.

"Goddess Above, Kier. That was…" He shook his head and looked at me, his pink tongue caught between his teeth.

"Toe-curling?" I said. "Amazing? Mind-blowing?"

"Oh, yes. All of those things." He tucked his head against my shoulder.

"But you had a vision." He turned his head so his face was buried in my neck. "It wasn't a vision. Or it was, but…" He made a frustrated noise. "It was like I was filled with knowledge, like the spirits here flooded me with magic and… It was like my fifth pulse tore me open and they… I was so full of knowing it was too much to bear."

"Is that why you cried?" I pressed my face into his hair.

"No," he said, his voice gone soft. "No, I cried because it was wonderful and then… it all started to drain away, and I couldn't hold onto it."

"Is it all gone? Everything the spirits filled you with?"

"No, not all of it. But there was so much. I knew who I'm meant to be, and I knew why the Vogel have so few seers, and I knew how to do so much magic. And… even what's still in me feels distant, like I know it's there but I can't reach it."

I kissed the top of his head. "I know what this place is," I said.

"A shrine." He laughed into my shoulder and some of the

sadness seeped away. "A mind-blowing sex shrine."

I laughed, too. "It is that. But remember I said this place reminded me of the cave in Morven?"

He nodded.

"The Sidhe use that cave when we first come into our power as children. We're taken there and presented to the Lady of the Forest. It's… it's like being examined by someone who can see right into your being, only you can't see them at all." I paused to shift him in my arms, to settle into a more comfortable position.

"Seers aren't taken there until they have their first vision," I continued. "And then, I'm told, they're left in the cave until they have a second vision, one that will show them the direction their whole lives will take. Our seer, my mother's seer, said she felt something like you described, like she was filled with knowledge that drained away when she tried to look at it. Like she was filled with and then lost a lifetime of *knowing*."

"It hurts."

I kissed his hair again. "She also told me that nothing is really lost. It seems to vanish, to seep away the more you try to hold it, but she says it comes back. Gradually, over time. Because if you tried to absorb it all at once, it would overwhelm you." I stroked his wing, made sure his feathers were smoothed down and not bent. "She told me that once in a while, the gifts of the spirits *don't* drain away, they stay, and the seer is so overcome it drives them mad. It's not a good end for a seer, pretty bird, so I'm glad that knowledge didn't stay with you."

He sighed into my neck. "So this is a place of initiation?"

"No, I think it's more than that." He lifted his head from my shoulder, and I kissed the end of his nose. "The cave in Morven is a place of initiation. This… this place is… I think we were right and it *is* a sex shrine. Or… a place for inducing stronger visions using… well, sexual ecstasy."

He blinked at me and understanding grew on his face. "That book I read, abut the ancient sites of worship, it said sacred sex could be used to raise magic and bring visions even to those with little power."

"So there you go. We accidentally figured out how to use a sex-powered magic enhancer created by your people at the dawn of time." I felt relieved when he smiled and it lit up his whole face.

"Will you be okay?" I didn't want to let him go, but we couldn't stay in the water forever, no matter how soothing it was.

He nodded. "They won't let you stay with me at the Eyrie, will they?"

"I don't know, pretty bird. They say bird folk are very private, that despite being a vassal Monarchy, they don't even let visiting Alfar royalty stay in the palace, and have a residence for them in the city instead." I cupped his face with one hand and felt a tear trickle down his cheek.

"I'll stay with you as long as I can," I promised.

"I don't want to give you up," he whispered, burying his face against my collarbone. "Kier… I can't… I can't do this."

"It will be okay," I said, knowing it might not be. "Let's go get some sleep. I promise I won't make you go anywhere you don't want to."

When we surfaced out of the hot spring on the other side of the passage, the two tree serpents were zipping frantically around, and flung themselves into Fionn's hair as we climbed out of the pool.

Where? said Smoke.

You left, said Flame.

"We're fine," I told them. "Did anyone follow us down

here?"

No one.

Safe.

We got as comfortable as we could on the stone, leaving our damp clothes draped over rocks to dry, and curled up skin to skin.

"I have to go," Fionn said. "Don't I?"

"I won't make you."

"But I can't run forever. I have to go to the Eyrie and meet my King, my people. It's what I was born for. I'm a symbol, Moira said. I… maybe I can help them find a better future."

I sighed and smoothed his wings, checking to make sure he was comfortable. "I don't know. We're told we're born for our Monarchs, for our people, that our futures are already chosen. But you're a seer, you know the future is changeable."

"It's the law, though. If I don't go, you'll be blamed."

"Maybe."

He was quiet then, and I thought he'd fallen asleep. But he rolled onto his back, tucking his wings carefully under him, and stared up into the dark. I had kept one wisplight hovering nearby in case he needed to get up to relieve himself, but otherwise the huge cavern was cloaked in shadows. It was eerily silent; even the water in the spring made no sound as it flowed through the stone.

"Take me to the Eyrie," he said, finally.

"Okay." I said it reluctantly even though I knew it was the best choice. The only real choice.

"And Kier?"

"Yes?"

"Thank you for letting me come here."

"We're in this together, pretty bird. I don't get to choose for you."

"I'm glad you're with me."

"Me, too."

"I'm glad… I'm glad you could fuck me one more time before…"

I pushed myself up onto my elbow and covered his mouth with mine. He parted his lips for me, drew my tongue in with his own, and left me hungry when I pulled away. "Don't say it," I whispered. "If you say it, I won't have the strength to hand you over to your King." I pressed my mouth on his again, and felt his fingers slide into my hair.

I pulled away again and he nodded.

"We could stay here a little longer. A day or two. We have enough food for that. If we find an exit, I could hunt." I knew I was sounding desperate, but I didn't care. "We can stay as long as you want."

He combed his fingers through my hair. "I think it will be harder, if we wait."

I swallowed hard. "Sleep then. Rest. Tomorrow we'll see if we can find a way out without going back the way we came."

"There is a way," he said quietly. "The spirits showed me."

"After you…?"

The corner of his mouth twitched up in mischief, chasing away some of the melancholy. "After I covered you in more semen than I knew I could hold in my body? Yes."

I snorted in surprise at his bold words and looked more carefully at his face. He still looked sad, but there was wickedness in his eyes, too.

"Want to do it again?" I leaned over and kissed him. He bit my lip, but not hard.

"I don't think I can," he said, licking where he had just bitten. "I'm completely dry." He met my eyes and I saw the naughty gleam. "But you're welcome to splatter *me*."

I laughed. "I'm not sure I can, either. I'm not even sure my legs will hold me up."

The silly sex talk made both of us feel better, and for the second day in a row, we fell asleep together, curled up in a cave.

WHEN I WOKE, I reached out carefully to my magic, to find out what time of day it was, and discovered it was the middle of the night. We'd spent a whole night and day and half the next night underground. Longer, if you counted the day we spent sleeping in the otter den. Considering what we'd done with the time, I refused to call it wasted.

Fionn was already awake, sitting with his feet in the water, chewing a bit of dried meat. I sat next to him, taking the food he held out to me. It was flavored with herbs and despite its chewiness, it was delicious.

"One more bath before we go?"

"Eat first," he told me. "And don't forget to drink." He held out the waterskin and gave me the same look I'd given him the day before – or was it the night before – when he would have hurried into the cave and ignored his growling belly. I grinned at him and stuck out my tongue, but I drank.

I wanted to think of a clever remark, something that would make him smile and forget where we were headed next, but everything weighed too heavily. So I ate and drank some more, and dangled my feet in the hot spring.

When Fionn would have stood I put my hand on his thigh. "Let me make you feel good, pretty bird. Let me make love to you before we go." I didn't say, "one last time," though I was thinking it, and from the feeling of sorrow I felt from him, he was, too.

"Is it making love, now?" he said, teasing. "I thought you

liked fucking."

"I do like fucking. And I like being fucked. But right now I want to touch and taste and tease every part of your body, slowly, so you understand exactly how I feel about you."

He let his eyes slide away from mine. "I'm frightened." His voice was strong and determined, despite the words, and I knew he wasn't talking about sex.

"Me, too."

We sat, just looking at each other, words we couldn't – or wouldn't – say hovering between us. I thought of Moira, and how she'd told me to say what was in my heart. But if I said it, I would never let him leave this cave, and if I somehow did get him to the Eyrie, it would hurt him so much more when I left him there.

"Come here," I whispered, and he let me pull him close, and kiss him. His mouth was desperate on mine, his tongue ready for mine, drawing me in. I wanted him to devour me, or at least make me forget everything but the taste of his mouth.

When I could stand to lift my lips from his, I buried my face in his neck, followed the muscle to his collarbone, and stroked my hands across his smooth chest. He was so strong under the softness, and I wanted to memorize every plane and curve.

His skin tasted salty from the minerals in the hot spring and underlying that was his own sweetness. I wanted to overwhelm my senses with him, with the taste of his skin, the scent of him – musk and honey – the softness of his hair, the glow of his silver eyes in the wisplight, and his little noises of pleasure.

If I could have no one else ever again – and I couldn't imagine even *wanting* anyone else after him – I wanted to remember all of Fionn.

He arched as I traced my lips, my teeth, my tongue over

his belly and teased open his sheath until his cock slid out, hard and slick and sweet tasting. He clung to my antlers as I pleasured him with my mouth, so slowly he begged me to suck harder, faster. I gave him four slow, delicious pulses of orgasm, each one more intensely sweet than the last, while my wisplights danced around us.

When he had caught his breath and could move again, I made him sit up and drink from the waterskin. Then he rolled me onto my back to trace every one of my muscles with his fingers and his tongue, and by the time he finally nudged open my thighs to kiss the crease where they met my pelvis, my voice was hoarse with moaning.

He kissed and nibbled between my thighs, sucked each testicle into his mouth for a moment and then stopped to look up at my face.

"Don't stop touching me," I said. "Please, Fionn." I looked down at him, crouched between my legs, wings raised a little above his back. He looked otherwordly in the wisplight.

"Tell me what you want me to do to you," he said, his voice gone low and growly.

I panted and arched my back, desperate for him. "Goddess Below, Fionn, please."

"Tell me." He ran his nails down my thighs. "Say the filthiest words you know."

I stared at him. "You like it when I talk dirty," I said, finally realizing and wondering why I hadn't noticed before how he had always wanted me to tell him what I wanted to do to him.

He flicked out his tongue, barely touching the tip of my erection and making me gasp.

"Put your beautiful mouth on my cock," I said, and he lowered his head, slid his hot mouth over me, and dug his nails into my thighs.

"Suck me." I groaned, groping for his hair. "Suck hard, pretty bird." He did and I couldn't hold in the cry, didn't want to hold it in. "Make me come," I growled. "Fuck, Fionn. Fuck!"

I tried not to pull his hair too hard when I climaxed, but a few pale strands clung to my fingers after.

We lay together a while, hands stroking gently, as if unwilling to stop touching. Then we washed in the spring, dressed, and it was time to leave.

I let Fionn show me the path he had *seen* in his vision. He took my hand and led me through the cave as I had led him through the forest.

"Once you told me there must be a better way to live," I said, as we departed the huge cavern through a smaller tunnel nearly opposite from where we'd come in.

"Yes."

"I agree. There must be." I breathed slowly, letting the scent of the cave fill my nose so I would remember it always. "I'm going to find it."

He glanced back at me, and I saw neither hope nor defeat in his look. "I hope you do."

We walked a long way, sometimes having to squeeze through narrow crevices or wriggle on our bellies, but Fionn never faltered, even when the passages branched, and we might have been walking through a labyrinth.

Once, he got a wing caught in a crevice and I had to wriggle back through, squeezing past his feet, to reach it and carefully pull it open so he could get free. I felt his fear in my belly, edging close to panic as he tugged and struggled, so I made a silly comment about his pointy toenails and cold feet and how they had kept me awake all night and he laughed. The panic subsided, and I pulled his wing free, and we carried on.

One perfect flight feather had caught on the stone and pulled out. I picked it up and tucked it in my vest.

"I can't imagine how people with bigger wings could possibly get through here." He rubbed his wing over his shoulder then flipped it back into place.

"They must have been very determined to have mind-blowing orgasms." He bopped me in the face with the same newly-freed wing, so I pinned him to the wall with my body, pulled his head down so I could reach, and kissed him soundly.

And finally, as our third day of flight dawned, we found the exit from the caves and stepped out to the sound of wind and birdsong. The tree serpents were delighted, swooping and soaring in the open air, letting updrafts carry them high above us then plunging down again.

We had climbed up inside the caves, slowly but steadily, and now we looked out over a spur of Aven Forest from halfway up a large hill. And there, tantalizingly close, was the sea.

To our right, the hill we were emerging from joined a range of other hills, small mountains really, that curved around the forest to drop in steep cliffs down to the sea.

Just visible where cliff and sea and sky met, an ancient sacred site where all three Realms touched, was the Eyrie.

From here we couldn't see details, only the pale cliffs, but it shone like a beacon, and I heard Fionn's breath catch when he saw it, and speed up like he had run a long distance to be here.

"That's it, isn't it? In the cliff?"

"That's the Eyrie." I touched his hand. "The ancient stronghold of your people."

He leaned back against the edge of the cave mouth, like he could draw strength from the rock, and he reached for my hand.

"When I had the vision of my mother, it was there." He pointed to the line of sand than ran next to the sea and vanished below the cliff. "She was on that beach, and there was a flock of feathered serpents around her, listening to her sing." His voice was soft and sad.

"She was singing to you," I said, even though I had no idea, *could* have no idea.

"I think she was." He sighed. "I was still in the egg. It would have been months before her body absorbed the shell and I was born." I stroked his hand with my thumb and his fingers gripped mine tighter. "I wish I could have known her."

"I wish you could have, too."

"I like to think she was wonderful," he said. "But I know not all mothers are good mothers."

I looked at him sharply but said nothing.

"Do you think your mother loves you?" The question was unexpected, and hurt more than I would have thought possible, after so long.

"In her way," I said. "I suppose she *thinks* she does."

"I had no mother, and you had a cold one." I don't think "cold" was the word I would use, but I let it pass and didn't interrupt. "I wonder which of us was worse off." He stared in the direction of the Eyrie, but I'm not sure he was seeing it.

"I don't know." I let go of his hand and stretched. "And I'm not sure I care."

He dragged his attention away from the view. "Oh." He bit his lip. "I shouldn't have said that. I'm…"

I bumped my hip against his leg, and he stopped speaking. "Don't apologize," I said. "It was a perfectly reasonable question. And anyway, our seer treated me as if I was her own son, since my mother wouldn't allow her a family."

"What's her name? Your seer?"

"Siona," I said. "It means 'fox' in our language. She has

copper-red hair, like the embers of a fire." I smiled, then frowned, the expressions twisting my face into what felt like a grimace. "My mother's hair is red, too, but darker, like the flowers of the strangler vine."

"Seer Siona." He looked back out over the forest. "Perhaps I'll meet her someday."

"I'd like that. She's why I kept going back to my mother's court, you know, after she sent me away, and even after I ran away on my own, when I was thirteen. Siona gave me comfort and kindness when I was a child, and I think… I hope I do the same for her, when she feels trapped by her obligations to the Monarchy."

"I think your Seer Siona was your true mother," he said, looking at me again, silver eyes catching the sun. "The mother of your heart."

I smiled. "You may be right."

"Will you tell her about me? When you return to your forest?" He sounded wistful, and I knew it was time to keep going, before we both fled back to into the cave to die together, happy and hungry.

"She's the only one I will ever tell about you," I said. "You're too precious to share with anyone else."

"Am I precious?"

"You are more precious than any jewels my mother could offer me. More precious than a real place in her court."

"More than being her heir?"

"Far more."

"More than the sword of your ancestors?" He reached up and tapped the hilt that projected over my left shoulder.

"Much more than my sword, than even the legendary Sword of Dragons that they say will bring about a new age on the Isle and beyond."

He laughed at that, though it sounded bittersweet.

"Let's get out of this cave." I pulled his hand to my mouth and kissed his fingers before letting it go.

"Is it safe to travel during the day now?"

"We'll still be careful, but I don't think we need to worry about the Alfar King's men anymore. They can't have expected us to burrow under the hills."

I stepped away from the cave entrance to look for a path down the hill. And saw we had a new problem. We had come out of the earth halfway up a sheer cliff.

It would not have been a problem for the ancient bird folk who had used this shrine. But it was decidedly a problem for one wingless Sidhe and one bird man with wings that he couldn't fly on.

"Well, fuck," I said.

20
Fionn

A FEELING OF MELANCHOLY had settled over me and I couldn't seem to make it dissipate. I wanted to be cheerful for Kiernan, to make it seem like I was looking forward to arriving in the city of my ancestors, to meeting others of my kind.

And I was, but I couldn't summon any kind of excitement when I knew that going to the Eyrie meant leaving Kiernan behind. All I could feel was a horrible sickness in my belly, no matter how I tried to be positive.

We had only known each other a short time, but it was as if that double handful of days was standing in for as many years. And it wasn't fair that we had found each other after – for me – a lifetime of visions only to have to part again so soon.

Life wasn't fair. I supposed life had never been fair to either of us; why should it start now?

So when Kier looked over the edge of the cliff and saw only a sheer drop, I wasn't even upset. It was a setback, a delay, but a delay meant more time together. I would take every last moment I could get.

I crouched next to him and looked down. Not only was it a sheer drop, but the cave entrance was an overhang, projecting out over the rock face below, making it impossible for Kiernan to climb down, even if there had been handholds.

"I guess we go back in." I looked at him, watched him contemplate the hillside. "And try to find another passage out."

He sat back and hung his feet over the edge. "I could use magic."

"You could *over*use magic and lose it forever." I sat next to him. "I can make it to the bottom without breaking anything." I fanned my wings, blowing his hair forward into his eyes. "But I can't carry you. We almost died falling off the tower. We would have if your magic hadn't been at full strength."

"Would you go on without me? Would you go to the Eyrie and send someone back to fetch me down off this cliff?"

"I won't leave you until I have to."

Something shifted in the way he looked at me, but I couldn't read it. He looked away and leaned his head on my shoulder.

I wanted to pull him into my lap, to kiss him, undress him, and make love to him again. Our time together was up, but this delay might give us more. Just a little more time.

Instead, I put my arm around him and kissed one of his antlers. "If only we had rope." I was glad that we didn't.

"Maybe..." He shifted against my side.

"Maybe what?"

"The sacks Col gave us are linen. They're strong, and the waterproofing makes them stronger. We could make them into rope. Neither of us is very heavy. We only need to get down to that ledge and I think we could climb the rest of the way." He pointed and I leaned over the edge to look. There *was* a ledge.

It was too far to jump down to, even if the cave mouth didn't overhang it, but with a rope... Maybe.

I didn't want to tell him he was right because, even though I was the one who insisted we shouldn't loiter in the caves, I suddenly didn't want to leave at all.

"Maybe," I finally said. "But where do we tie the rope?"

We turned around, and of course there was a convenient chunk of upright rock just outside the cave mouth. I scowled at it.

"Pretty bird?" Kiernan touched my shoulder and I started, feeling guilty. "Have you changed your mind about going to the Eyrie?"

"No." I leaned into him, tilted my forehead against him, and closed my eyes. "No, I still have to go. I just want as much time as I can get before –"

His kiss stopped the rest of the sentence. It felt as desperate as I did, and I knocked my teeth against his in my hurry to get my tongue down his throat.

"Goddess Below, pretty bird. I'd kill to feel you inside me one more time." His voice was rough and low and so intense it made me shiver.

"Don't say it like that." I bit his ear, and I wasn't gentle. "Like it will never happen again."

He abruptly pulled away and started unbuckling his sword, his knives, his belt.

"Kier, what?"

His breathing was ragged as he turned away from me, dropped to his knees and leaned against the rock face. His trousers slid down over his thighs, and I stared as his perfect, sculpted buttocks. "Please," he said.

I slid to the ground behind him, put my arms around him, and pressed my chest to his back. When I moved my hand down his belly, I found him hard. "Please." He didn't ask, he *begged.*

My own erection pressed against the inside of my sheath, and I wanted to cry. "I can't do this, Kier."

"You can't…?" He drew in a breath that sounded so close to a sob it threatened to break my heart. "Okay." He reached for his trousers and started to pull them back up.

"No." I pushed his hands away. "That's not what I meant." I curled my fingers around his erection and felt him push against my grip.

I tore at my own trouser tie with my other hand, struggling with the knot until I wanted to reach for one of Kiernan's knives and cut it. But finally it came free and I could press my thighs against his buttocks. I relaxed my sheath muscles and my erection slid out to poke against his back.

His breathing went even more ragged. "I don't deserve you." He pressed his hands into the rock and leaned his forehead on them. "I've never deserved anyone like you."

"Shut up." My voice came out fierce, angry. "Don't say that." I sat back on my heels and slid closer, pushing his thighs apart, trying to get under him. I was so much taller.

"It's true."

"No." I let more anger slip into my voice, suddenly so full of rage at the whole world that I had to let it out or go mad. I was angry at whomever made him think he didn't deserve good things, at being stuck on this stupid hill, at the simple fact that we didn't get to be together after all we had shared.

My gentleness was gone, fled, chased away by rage and I spread his cheeks open, aimed, and shoved into him.

"Oh fuck." His fingers tightened against the rock face. "Take all of me."

"*You* take all of *me*," I snarled into his ear and shoved into him again.

"Yes," he said. "Fuck, yes."

It wasn't like me to be so angry, so forceful, so rough, but I just wanted to pound against him, into him, so he couldn't ever forget me.

I pulsed hard and felt him clench briefly around me. He pushed against my hand, so I stroked and rubbed and tugged at him, harder maybe than was comfortable for him but he didn't complain.

"Tell me you want me." His voice was barely audible.

"You know I want you. I want you so fucking much." The swear word didn't feel daring anymore, it just felt like the truth, and I pulsed again as I said it, and I wasn't even sure the last word came out.

"Tell me… Goddess, Fionn, tell me…" He couldn't get the rest of his words out, either.

I knew what he wanted me to say; I could feel deep in my belly what he *finally* wanted me to say, and I couldn't. Not because I didn't feel it anymore; I felt it so strongly I could hardly breathe with it. I couldn't say it because I was sure he wouldn't be able to say it back, even if he *felt* it.

"I'm yours, Kiernan," I whispered in his ear instead, and pulsed again. And it was as if my third pulse relieved something in me, and I felt less urgent, and slowed, worried that I'd been hurting him. I didn't ever want to hurt him. I stroked him lightly, fucked him gently, and he leaned back into me.

"I'm yours, Fionn." His breathing had eased. "Always."

When Kier throbbed in my hand and spurted onto the stone wall, my fourth pulse came, slow and delicious, rolling over me in gradual waves until I felt lightheaded. When I was done, when *we* were done, I held him against my chest, breathing in the smell of him, listening to his heartbeat.

In my head, I told him I loved him, would always love him, but out loud, the words still didn't come.

Finally, we pulled apart, set our clothes and gear back to rights, and he turned to face me. His eyes were shiny and there were wet trails down his cheeks.

"Were you – ?" He put his fingers on my lips, and I scowled. He was always stopping me from speaking.

"I –" But he couldn't get words out either, even without someone holding his lips shut. "Let's just get this over with." He picked up one of our bags, dumped the contents out, and set to cutting it into strips.

I THINK YOU SHOULD go first, pretty bird," Kiernan said, tugging to make sure the makeshift rope was securely tied. "I can lower you down."

I peered over the edge. It didn't look *too* far.

"Fuck, maybe I should go first." He leaned over next to me, lowering the rope to make sure it was long enough. "In case it breaks."

"If it's going to break, it's better it breaks on me. Wings, remember?" I fanned one of them in his face.

He raised his eyebrows.

"So I can't *fly*." I poked him in the chest with a wingtip and he tugged my feathers. "But I can break my fall enough I won't die."

"And I can use magic to not die." Satisfied with the length of the rope, he pulled it back up.

"And end up hollow." I stepped away from the edge. "No."

"Fine. You go first. Once you're safe and we know the rope will hold, I'll climb down after you."

"The rope won't break." I wanted to argue more, but I knew I was only trying to delay us, to steal a little more time.

I let him tie the rope around my waist, and kiss my chin, and help me over the side. I spread my wings and tail, ready in case the rope broke, and he began to lower me. The serpents swooped around me, chittering encouragement.

Then a strong gust of wind caught me, lifted and twisted under my wings, and slammed me into the cliff face. I was glad the rope was tied around me because I wouldn't have been able to hold on.

I managed, somehow, not to cry out when my right shoulder and wing took the brunt of the blow, but for a long moment I couldn't even breathe. A unpleasant tingling shot down my arm to my elbow, and my wing kept wanting to droop.

"Fuck. Are you okay?"

I looked up to see Kier leaning over the side, hands strong on the rope, fear making his eyes wide.

"I'm okay." I lifted one hand – my left – to wave at him. "Just bruised."

He looked at me a moment longer. "Maybe keep your wings tucked."

I snapped them against my back, feeling the sore one twinge and want to droop again, and I folded my tail close to the backs of my legs. "Okay." I felt the rope jerk and he lowered me some more, and some more. I hoped my arm wasn't going to be too sore that I couldn't climb the rest of the way down the cliff, because being stuck on that ledge would be worse than being stuck in the cave mouth.

I dangled, close enough to the cliff that I could feel the sun's heat reflect off the stone, but not quite close enough to touch the cliff. Lower and slowly lower I went.

A gust caught me again but this time, with my wings tucked in, it only made me sway on the end of the rope. And then my feet were almost level with the ledge. I looked at it, just out of reach.

"You'll have to swing," Kiernan called down. "Find something to grab onto."

I swung and didn't quite make it. I swung again and managed to put a hand on the rock face, but there was nothing to hold on to. The ledge was there just below my feet, but I couldn't stop the swinging in order to untie myself.

I let the momentum ebb away until I was dangling again and looked up at Kier. "I'm going to have to untie myself first, then jump off.

"No. It's too dangerous. There has to be something to hold on to."

"There's nothing."

"Fuck."

"It's okay. Wings, remember?" I flapped them and regretted it as the updraft caught me and spun me around. I snapped them shut and the right one shot a barb of pain down to my back. "It will work."

I shifted the rope around my waist until I could untie it, keeping it wrapped around me, but only held there by my grip. Then I swung again. At the last minute, I couldn't let go. I let the swing peter out.

"Okay, pretty bird?" Kier was watching me, concern and fear on his face. And so much love I felt dazzled.

I swung again, and again, until my shoulder touched the cliff face, and then I let go. The rope pulled free, then suddenly caught, tangled in the waist tie of my trousers. I teetered on the ledge, my toes just barely touching the rock, hands scrabbling for something to hold. I refused to scream.

Then my weight won the tug-of-war and the rope pulled the rest of the way free, and I landed on the ledge, found my balance, and leaned gratefully against the rock. And the knot at my waist slipped the rest of the way undone, dropping my trousers to my ankles.

I stared down at them. Over my head, Kiernan was making a strangled noise and I looked up to see him, his hands clamped over his mouth, eyes wide. He was *laughing*.

"I almost fell to my death, and you're laughing at me." I crouched awkwardly to reach my trousers and pull them up, managing not to fall off the ledge.

"Sorry." Kiernan snorted, breathed deep, and cleared his throat. "You just… Your face." He started laughing again and I pointedly ignored him until he got his breath back under control and pulled up the rope. It reappeared in front of me a few moments later, a bundle of our cloaks and supplies tied to the end.

I fought with the rope, which had pulled too tight to easily undo. I couldn't cut it, because then it wouldn't be long enough for Kiernan to climb down, and anyway, I didn't have a knife.

I tried to lift the bundle, to take the weight off the knot, but it kept slipping and threatening to knock me off balance.

"I'll pull it back up and re-tie it." Kiernan watched me struggle.

"I almost have it."

"I don't want you to fall."

"I've got it." And then I did, and the whole bundle landed on my face and for a terrible moment I couldn't tell which way to lean to keep from falling over the side.

But then I felt the rock face at my back and relaxed into it, clutching our bundle of gear.

Above me, I heard the scrape of Kier's boots on rock as he tied the rope around himself and stepped to the edge.

I let out a breath, sucked another one in, and lowered the bundle to the ledge so I could see. I watched his feet and legs appear over the edge, and then his muscular backside, and finally the rest of him. He had tied the rope to his wrist, giving him more length and letting him climb more easily.

Smoke landed on my shoulder. *Look*, she said.

Look look, said Flame, curling in the air around Kiernan as he climbed carefully down the rope.

I looked, not sure what I was supposed to be looking for, or even where I should be looking.

Above me, slowly moving closer, Kiernan said, "Birds? They're very colorful."

I glanced up to see him looking towards the Eyrie, so I turned my gaze towards the pale cliff over the sea and saw what he saw: two shapes, one with wings of green and blue, and one in red and golden yellow. I might not be able to see at night like Kiernan could, but my distance vision was excellent.

"Those aren't birds."

Something in my voice must have alerted him because he stopped climbing to look again.

Pretty, said Flame, twisting around Kier's neck.

Like you, said Smoke, rubbing her head against my cheek.

"Bird folk." Kiernan's voice was awed, and nervous.

I watched the shapes, saw how they held themselves, lean honey-gold bodies stretched to the air, and huge wings spread as they soared. I flexed my own wings in unconscious imitation and wanted to weep. I hadn't realized how it would ache, to see what I should have been, but could never have.

"They're coming this way."

"Have they seen us?" Kiernan climbed faster, lowering himself quickly down the rope and abandoning caution for speed.

"I don't know, but they're coming." As they came closer, I could see more details. Each had a sort of feathered skirt that matched their wings. I had to assume it was a garment, unless I was deficient in that respect, too, because I had only a thin layer of downy feathers to cover my sheath, and nothing but my tail over my buttocks.

Each figure also had an elaborate arrangement around their head, in their cropped-short hair, and sprouting from a mask or helmet that covered their face with something that looked like a gleaming gold beak.

"They have to have seen us." I pulled my wings close to my back, suddenly not wanting them visible, ashamed of my stunted appendages.

Kiernan had reached the level of the ledge and was swinging himself closer. I caught him when he was near enough and leaned back against the rock as he struggled with the knot. The waterproofing that had made the makeshift rope stronger also bonded the knots more tightly.

It seemed only an instant, then, before the bird folk were closer, too close, heading directly for us.

"It's fucking stuck. Fucking rope." Kiernan struggled and I clung to him, pulling him as tightly against me as I could.

"Cut it," I said. "Just cut it."

The bird folk swooped past us, so close I could feel the air stirred by their wings. They didn't call out or even gesture; they just *looked*, and passed by, turned and passed again.

"This is not how I imagined the first meeting with your people would go."

"I can't hold you, Kier." I struggled to keep my balance on the ledge, to keep his weight on the end of the rope from pulling me over the side.

"I've almost got it." He twisted, yanking at the rope, and the bird folk soared past again. One called out, but I didn't understand the words or even recognize the language. And the world seemed to slow down as I watched everything happen.

I slipped and lost my footing and had to let go of Kiernan or else break his wrist or pull him down with me.

I opened my wings, felt a pinching grip on my shoulders tugging me suddenly upwards, and I thought Kiernan had somehow caught me but I was being pulled away from him.

He reached out with his free hand and caught my hand and for a moment I hung suspended between one grip and another.

There was terror in his eyes, and longing, and regret, and a thousand other things I couldn't name. And right before the world returned to its normal speed, I finally found my voice. I squeezed his hand, then let go, and said, "I love you, Kiernan."

I heard him scream, "Fionn!" as the grip on my shoulders tightened and the world spun and blackness gathered at the edge of my vision.

"Smoke," I said. "Flame."

Here.

With you.

"Stay with him." And I blinked away the darkness and watched the hill recede in the distance as I was carried towards the Eyrie and, I supposed, my destiny.

21
Kiernan

I DANGLED FROM ONE WRIST, watching the bird folk carry Fionn away. They would take him to the Vogel King, to the Eyrie, and he would be where he should have been from the moment he was born.

And I would… what? Go back to my mother's court and play the good prince, go where she sent me, to lie for her because full-blood fey can't lie?

Before I'd gone to the Abbey of the Moon, it had seemed like the best life I could hope for, and a better life than most people got. I could travel, see new places, and meet new people. Fuck my stupid ass off. I had been born from an alliance between two noble houses to stop a war; it was fitting I spend my life smoothing over conflicts and squabbles among other such families.

I hung there until my fingers went numb and then I yanked free a knife, cut the fucking rope, and jumped. I somehow landed on the ledge instead of plunging over the side to my death, though in that instant, I didn't really care either way. I sank down onto the stone and watched the little specks of the bird folk vanish into the distance, first bright against the dark green of the forest, and then blending into the paler colors of the sand and sea and cliff.

As they faded away, two other specks came into view, dark blue and green and a splash of vibrant red. The feathered tree serpents were returning.

I watched them come arrowing back, not twisting through the air with the sheer joy of flying as they usually did, but heading straight for me. Both of them barely slowed as they reached me, and burrowed under my vest, into the folds of my shirt, churring soft noises and bumping their heads under my chin. I stroked them automatically, and they settled, droning a rumbly little purr I hadn't heard from them before.

"You should have stayed with him." I rubbed a finger under Smoke's chin and her purring intensified.

He sent, she said.

Said stay, Flame added, bumping her sister's head away for her share of chin rubs.

"Still. You should have stayed with him."

You need more, they said together and settled against my neck. I didn't think that was true, but I didn't try to argue.

I stared into the distance, but I wasn't seeing the forest or the sea or anything else in the landscape. I was seeing Fionn's face as he was snatched away. Confusion, as he felt himself pulled off the cliff. Then understanding and fear and... loss? Then he'd smiled that beautiful smile that made me catch my breath and his fingers tightened on mine before letting go. And he said the words we'd both been dancing around for days. The words he'd already said once, in sex-muddled half-sleep, and that I'd kept telling him not to say again.

I should have fucking said them back. I should have screamed those words for all the world to hear instead of just helplessly shouting his name.

My breath had gone shaky, and I felt hot tears slide down the side of my nose.

I could count on the fingers of one hand the number of times in my life I could remember crying.

One: as a child when my mother tore my little spike antlers off and sent me to live with a father I had never met.

Two: when my delight at learning I had an older brother – my father's first son – had turned to dread and sorrow when he hated me and would taunt me for my pointed ears and the antler scars on my forehead and beat me whenever he thought he could get away with it.

Three: when I ran away from my father's stronghold and returned to Morven Forest and our seer had defied my mother's orders and took me to the caves where I was re-introduced to the spirit of the Lady of the Forest – our Goddess Below – and saw the cave fish.

Four: this morning when I was feeling lost and broken and Fionn had held me and fucked me, exactly as I needed him to.

And now, five: when the man I belatedly realized I loved more than my own life was snatched away before I could say goodbye. And I hadn't even had the presence of mind to tell him, even as he'd said it to me, so clearly and full of certainty, "I love you."

It hit me like my older brother's fist in my gut when I was too young to understand resentment. "I love him." The serpents stirred at my throat, rearranging themselves when I toppled onto my side and curled up as tight as I could on the ledge, as if that could make me a smaller target. But the hurt was coming from inside this time, and there was no escaping it, no making it less by making myself tiny.

Smoke and Flame nestled more closely against me,

purring fiercely, as if their contentment could drive away my pain if they expressed it loudly enough.

We love, said Smoke.

Dark and bright love, said Flame.

I let the tears come, let myself wallow in misery until I was choking on it. Until an insistent rasp against my cheek, and another on my nose, roused me enough to force my breath back to something resembling normal. The tree serpents were licking the tears from my face, their sandpaper tongues chafing on flesh still tender from my nose being flattened by a werewolf.

No cry, said Smoke, and I wondered if she really even knew what tears were. Did serpents cry?

I sat up. My head hurt from weeping and my wrist stung from the rope. I hadn't put my arm guards back on after we had bathed in the cave, and I was regretting it now.

My hands felt rough on my face as I scrubbed the tears away. I had thought, maybe, that letting out the despair would make me feel better, but it didn't. I just felt achy and dry.

"What the fuck do I do now?" The serpents didn't answer.

There didn't seem to be a whole lot of point in trying to get to the Eyrie now. The chances had already been negligible that the Vogel King would let me stay with Fionn. Now that I'd be showing up alone, the likelihood had dropped to nothing.

I had no doubt he would try to convince his guards, his King, anyone who would listen, to come back for me. But I had just as few doubts that anyone would comply.

So by all the rules of logic, and no matter which way I approached the problem, I should climb down from this Goddess-forsaken cliff and make my way directly back to Morven Forest. I would do whatever diplomatic – or underhanded – tasks my mother, my Queen, had for me and eventually she would marry me off to whomever would give her the most advantage. Assuming anyone worthy of her notice would take me.

What a dismal fucking prospect. I had no illusions that I was destined for great things; as I'd told Fionn, I had serious doubts about the whole notion of destiny. But Fionn had done more than make me fall in love. He had made me want more than to just survive. I wanted a life of my own choosing, with a partner of my own choosing. Nothing grand, just a small cottage in the woods, hunting and foraging, with a pretty silver-eyed seer by my side.

If Fionn would even want a simple life after tasting the pleasures and beauty of the Eyrie.

Clouds drifted across the sky, and the Eyrie seemed to brighten in the distance as the sun struck it. What had the serpents said about light? They loved both dark and bright? I laughed. I had thought, when they said it, that they were happy to offer affection equally during bad times, dark times, as during good, bright times. But I realized I had mistaken them, thinking their intelligence was less refined than it was.

"Dark" was me: dark haired, darker-skinned, creature of the forest at night. Even my name translated into Islish as "shadow."

And "bright" was Fionn: silver of hair and wing and eye, pale-skinned, stubbornly cheerful, dweller in sunlight, whose name meant "fair."

Moon and sun, night and day, cynical and optimistic, jaded and innocent, dark and bright, Kiernan and Fionn. Me and him.

I didn't want a life without him in it.

How the fuck I could achieve such a life, I had no idea, but it started with staying as far away from my mother as possible. Let her find out where I was, and she'd come after me herself. So I couldn't let her find me.

I stood up and stretched, and as I bent to untie the bundle of gear I'd lowered down, a large silver-white feather slipped free of my vest and fluttered over the edge into open air. I grabbed for it and missed and almost went over the edge myself. And just as I resigned myself to watching it fly away from me, just as the man who'd lost it had, one of the serpents slipped out of my vest after it, grabbed it in mid-air as it was starting its downward spiral, and brought it back.

To remember, she said. *Silly fey.* And she curled around my neck again.

"Thank you, little friend." She purred and it tickled my collarbone.

I looked at the feather, gleaming and pure next to my grimy fingers, just like Fionn himself was. It made me feel unworthy, but it also made me determined to find out what *he* wanted, and to see if I could give him whatever he asked for.

So now I just had to get to him, because there was no point in planning a life where we could be together if he had no wish to leave the Eyrie.

I unslung my sword and drew it partway from its sheath. The feather fit nestled against it, quill slotting perfectly into the fuller down the blade, and it didn't even catch as I slid the sword home. I settled it back over my shoulder and snugged the straps so it fit fight against my back. I could feel the long bruise where I'd landed on it, but it didn't hurt too much. It reminded me of what Fionn and I had already achieved together.

"I'm coming, Fionn," I said, and the serpents stirred against my neck. "I have no fucking clue what I'll do when I get there, but I'm coming."

Along the shore, the bright sand and stone dimmed and brightened and dimmed again as clouds drifted across the face of the sun. I didn't have Fionn's keen distance vision so I couldn't see all the details he would have. But I could pick out where a river came out of the forest, split into many smaller streams, and joined the sea. I followed it back through the forest, where it was visible more as a change in the texture of the trees than as an actual strip of water. It originated just to the left of the hill I was on.

If I could get down this cliff, I could follow the river through the forest to the sea, then turn at the ocean and follow the beach to the Eyrie. I hardly needed a river to navigate through a forest under any circumstances, but there was a good chance there would be more game trails there, which meant easier – and faster – passage.

This side of the Eyrie's cliff didn't appear to be inhabited, but there had to be a way to the city at the cliff's base on the other side. Most of the peoples who traded with the Vogel didn't have wings, after all.

"Let me know if any bird folk come along, will you?"

Smoke and Flame stirred against my neck and slid out, one on each shoulder.

We watch, said one.

We fly, said the other, and they flowed down my arms and into the sky.

I turned to the bundle of gear, freed the smaller of the two cloaks and put it on. Then I cut the larger cloak into a square of cloth I could use to wrap the food in. I put on my arm guards and tied the bundle and the waterskin to my back and started to climb over the edge.

Almost as soon as I found my first foothold, I realized I would never be able to climb down in boots. So I hoisted myself back up, took off my boots, and tied them next to the waterskin. I felt about as graceful as a tortoise tipped over on its back, but with my feet bare I could dig toes and claws into crevices in the rock. And I'd always preferred bare feet, anyway.

From there it was just a matter of feeling out places to cling and gradually lowering myself down. And trying not to lean over and look with every step to see how much closer to the ground I was.

Once, I put my foot in a crevice full of dirt and small plants and as soon as I leaned my weight on it I slipped and skidded downwards, descending several times my own height much too rapidly.

I had, stupidly, relaxed my handholds as I leaned on my foot, and I only managed to stop when my fingers caught a projecting spur of rock, and I dug my claws in. I felt one nail split and start to tear, but I stopped sliding.

When I had caught my breath and found more secure hand- and footholds, I held up my hand and saw blood dripping down my wrist. I stuck my finger in my mouth like a child. It helped. I sucked until it stopped throbbing and withdrew it to examine it more closely. My claw was split almost to the base of the nail bed, but it hadn't actually torn away. It was going to hurt for days and would certainly make getting down off this cliff a lot harder.

I twisted and looked down. At least I was a lot closer to the bottom.

Smoke and Flame flitted around me, making sure I wasn't going to slide again.

"All safe?" I asked.

All safe, replied Smoke.

Some humans, added Flame.

"What kind of humans?" I felt for a toehold, and made sure to test it, and *not* let go with my hands, before putting my weight on it.

Grow plants, said one of the serpents.

Peas, said the other. *Earth daggers.*

I puzzled over that for a moment, testing a handhold, then a foothold, and lowering myself a little more. Then I snorted. "Carrots. The earth daggers are called carrots." Another careful step down. "So the humans are gardeners if they grow a few vegetables, or farmers if they grow a lot."

Fish, said one serpent.

Drying on sticks, said the other.

So these humans fished the river and grew peas and carrots. "Is there a village along the river?" I hadn't seen any obvious signs from above, but some humans were nearly as good as Sidhe at blending into the landscape.

Houses.

Some.

"How many is 'some'?" I wondered if serpents could even count. Another toehold, another careful step lower. My arms were aching, even though I had been careful to keep most of my weight on my legs.

As many as… wings, Smoke said.

"Your wings? Or yours and Flame's together?" The cliff seemed finally to be getting less sheer, and the top of a tree appeared over my shoulder. I had almost made it down.

Only mine.

"Six then." Another step down, and another, and I was able to turn around and skid down on my ass. "You have six wings. Three pairs." I could almost hear her thinking. Would she remember any of this? Did she understand it? I wondered, suddenly, if anyone had ever tried to train serpents beyond using them as hunting companions as the Vogel did. I wanted to ask Fionn if he'd ever read such a thing, in his explorations of the Abbey library.

I'd have to make sure our little cottage in the woods had room for plenty of books.

"Unless you count your tail as a wing." Tree serpent tails

ended in a wide, flat array of feathers that they used in flight almost as much as they used their actual wings.

Tail not wing, said Flame and I could hear her disgust at my ignorance and almost laughed out loud.

"So six houses. Six humans? Or six pairs of humans? Or families?"

We visit?

"No. I think we'd best avoid them. The fewer people see me, the better."

Shadows?

So the serpents knew I called the shadows when we were fleeing in the forest. I looked around. It was afternoon, but under the trees there were shadows. Not as dark or thick as they would be at night, which would make borrowing them more obvious.

"Not unless I have to."

Good. That was Smoke, usually the more opinionated of the two.

No hollow, said Flame.

Bright bird would cry. It was the most compete thought I'd heard either of the serpents express and it made me think they were far more intelligent than anyone had previously assumed.

"Yes, he would," I said, softly. I slid down the last slope of the hill and onto the forest floor. It was blessedly cool under the trees. "Quiet, now." As if humans could hear the serpents speak, anyway.

The river would be around the hill to my left, but heading that way was too much like backtracking. And besides, I hardly needed it to navigate. I'd never been lost in the forest, even as a small child. Instead, I'd meet the river where it curved toward the sea and the Eyrie.

I found a deer track and started to walk, ignoring the bundle banging uncomfortably against my bruised back until one of my own boots kicked me in the ass. Then I stopped, grumbled under my breath, and pulled them away from the bundle and shoved my feet into them. I hated not being barefoot in the forest, but wearing my boots was easier than carrying them, and I'd need them once I got to the city.

I flexed my toes and scowled when my claws scraped against leather, and I thought about how Fionn liked me to touch his feet but pretended he didn't. I had told him he had pretty feet to tease him, but it was true. They were like bird feet, a little, but warmer and softer, and decorated with iridescent silver scales. I loved the way he curled his toes into a sort of fist when I tickled him, and how he stretched them out long when I rubbed salve into his soles.

And I especially loved how he got turned on when I slipped a finger between his two big front toes and gently stroked.

Fuck. I was turned on when I touched between Fionn's toes. I was turned on *now*, just thinking about touching him. I would never have thought feet would make me horny, but Fionn had such lovely feet, like he had lovely everything, and I really was lost for him, wasn't I?

Soon I could smell the river, damp and cool, full of water draining from the mountains. It smelled lush, fertile, full of fish. This would be a good place for people to settle, or at least to visit and spend some time catching and drying the bounty.

If I didn't have someplace to be, I'd have stopped for a day or two myself. Few things were better than fresh-caught fish cooked in a hot pan and eaten in the forest. But I did have somewhere to be, and I didn't have a frying pan.

Just across the river was a small house, neatly built of logs and roofed with sod. A thin trickle of smoke rose from the riverstone chimney, and I caught the faint sharp scent of winterleaf tea. I stayed inside the cover of the trees as I passed, listening for inhabitants. If anyone was close, they must be inside.

Three more houses clustered together around a bend in the river, where a deep pool shaded by fallen trees made an ideal spot for young fish to shelter. There was a garden dug into a flat stretch on its bank where trees had been cleared to let in the sun. The rich dark soil nurtured healthy-looking plants, including peas and carrots, just as the serpents had said.

A tired but contented looking woman pulled weeds from between the plants and as I peered out of my safe place in the trees, she stood and stretched. A moment later, three men came around the bend carrying fishing poles and bundles of shining trout. The oldest of the men smiled and kissed the woman while the younger two – their sons, if I had to guess – took the catch into the nearest house. Something painful shifted in my chest watching them, so content in their simple lives.

I left them behind and carried on, feeling like an intruder in this idyllic scene. Could I ever have a cozy house in the forest like they did? Would Fionn want to live this way? Hunting and fishing and gardening and foraging? Maybe we could keep a few sheep and he could spin and dye and weave their wool into lovely blankets and cloth we could sell to buy him books to read on the long winter nights.

I shifted the bundle on my back and winced as my sword dug into the bruise. I shook my head. There was no point in wishing for things I might never be able to have. I didn't even know if I would see Fionn again, let alone convince him to share my life. I shook *that* thought away, too. I needed to focus on getting to the Eyrie first.

One insurmountable task at a time.

I skirted two more houses and several more people, going

about their quiet lives as if I wasn't even there. And to them, I might as well not be. I wondered how much of their catch they had to pay in taxes, and to which monarch. I wasn't sure if this section of forest, so close to the Eyrie, fell under the rulership of the Alfar King of Aven, or the Vogel King of the Eyrie. Perhaps, because they were human, it was the human monarch who would make sure they never had enough to be anything more than poor.

In Morven, there was little mixing of peoples, but here in Aven, everywhere I'd been seemed to have both human and fey, plus other peoples who didn't have a share in government, like the werewolves. In Morven, the Sidhe ruled the forest, the Hirsch had the plains, and the humans had the floodplain of the Great River. Each was ruled and taxed by one of the three Monarchs, and everyone else paid tribute to whomever's land they dwelled on.

It was why my mother and father's alliance was supposed to usher in a new age of cooperation in Morven. And while it had stopped the war, it had failed to unite the two monarchies. If Father had been in a more direct line to the throne, maybe they would have had more success.

I thought, often, that the failure to unite the two monarchies was the reason neither of my parents had wanted me around for long when I was younger. I was a reminder of the grand change they were supposed to bring about, and of the fact that they couldn't stand each other after the first three years of their marriage.

My mother wanted to forget that the marriage had even happened, and I was an inescapable reminder that it had. By finally deciding to take control of me, she could, in a way, take control over the result of her alliance.

To my father, I was a reminder that the beautiful woman that he was still smitten with – obsessed with even as he hated her – had grown tired of him and had sent him away before their child together had even left the womb.

There had to be a better way; Fionn was right about that. What that way was, though, I had no idea. And I was so lost in thinking about it, I almost walked out onto the beach without looking to see if it was occupied.

Fortunately, the serpents were there to hiss at me, and save my ass again.

I had followed the rightmost stream in the estuary, both because it saved me from having to cross, and because it tended toward the cliff and the Eyrie. I was small enough that when the trees gave way to brush, I still had plenty of cover.

Now, all I would need to do was follow the shining stretch of sand to the cliff and find a way over or around or through to the city below the Eyrie. Unless I could climb into the ruins I could now make out dotted across the near side of the sheer face.

It must have been a glorious sight, once, and I assumed the other side must still be intact, must still be a glorious sight, because I had heard recent accounts of the beauty of the Eyrie from the diplomats my mother had brought to the forest for me to learn from.

When the serpents warned me not to stride right out onto the strand, I stopped.

A group of bird folk dressed in simple homespun tunics, their long legs bare and tanned deep gold, worked to pull a net from the water. For some reason, it had never occurred to me that there were Vogel peasants, but of course there were. Even the Sidhe had people my royal siblings referred to as "lower class," who farmed and fished and paid taxes to the crown and sometimes died from starvation in a bad year.

Two other Vogel, guards dressed in feathers and gold masks like the ones who had taken Fionn, kept getting in the way. One of them kept trying to tug the net out of reach, like he meant to free the fish, while the other used his spear to trip the fisher folk. They were both laughing.

The peasants didn't appear to react to the taunting, except one who looked like he was speaking urgently, pleading with the guards, even as he kept his hold on the net. I could hear their voices, but I couldn't understand the words. My mother had not seen fit to educate me in Voglish, and they weren't creatures of the land so I couldn't use magic to understand them.

Then a brilliantly stupid idea came to me, and I pushed those thoughts aside. They would all speak Islish, and even if they didn't, they would understand from tone of voice when they were being insulted. I grinned, and unslung the bundle of gear from my back, and stepped out onto the beach.

22
Fionn

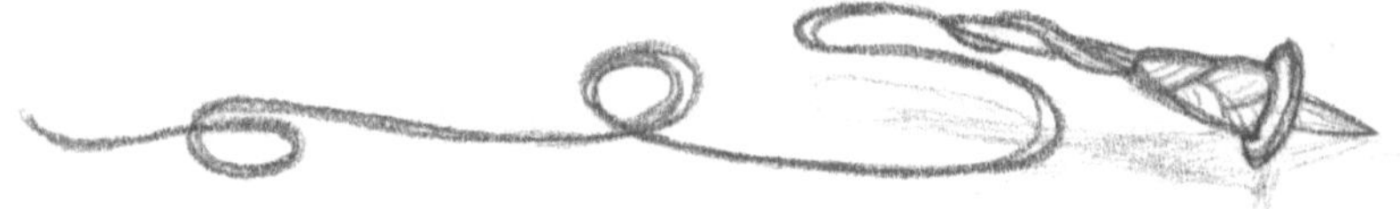

As my captor turned and banked away from the cliff I tried to twist in his grip, to keep Kiernan in sight. He hung from the rope, one arm outstretched towards me, green eyes huge. He was afraid, but not for himself.

I struggled against the talons gripping my shoulders, heedless of the fact that if they let go, I would fall, and with an injured wing, I probably wouldn't even be able to slow my descent much.

"Stop!" I yelled, raising my uninjured arm, and grasping my captor's ankle. "Go back!"

He didn't respond to my grip or my words and I couldn't hold myself twisted around to look behind us any longer.

"Take me back!" I yelled. "Or bring him with us. He saved my life!"

Both guards ignored me. "Please." My voice sounded broken, even to my own ears.

The tree serpents had ignored my instructions to stay with Kiernan and flew alongside me, twining around my legs and chittering.

"Go back," I whispered to them. "Please, Smoke, Flame. He needs you more than I do. Go back and you can help him find me later."

They alighted on my shoulders, one on each side, and bumped their heads under my jaw, nuzzling with their cold noses.

We love, said Flame.

Dark and bright, said Smoke.

"Please stay with him."

We go, they said and slipped off my shoulders and away and I couldn't turn and watch them go.

BEING CARRIED THROUGH the air, high above Aven Forest, should have been a joy, *would* have been a joy if I weren't heartbroken at leaving Kiernan behind, and injured, besides. At last, I was doing something I should have been born to do, but never could. I was with my own people, and flying, after a manner of speaking.

But there was no joy. Instead of soaring, wings outstretched to catch the wind, I dangled like a sack of potatoes from a painful, pinching grip on my shoulders that soon had my fingers tingling and numb. I tried, once, to open my wings to feel what flying really was like, but the wind buffeted me as it had on the cliff, and my sore wing twinged and throbbed, and the guard carrying me jerked his feet and said something that was probably a swear. So I snapped my wings closed again.

"Go back and get him!" I yelled again. "He saved my life, the life of one of your own people!"

The guard carrying me still ignored me and when I craned my neck to look up at him, all I could see was the bottom of his jaw and the golden bird mask.

"Will you fucking listen to me!" I yelled, almost screamed, and the guard glared down at me and said something I didn't understand. I felt shame that I didn't even know the language of my own people. I had been raised with Islish and Alfar, and could read a little Sidhe, but the Abbess had not bothered to teach me the language of the Vogel, and the library hadn't had so much as a dictionary I could look at.

I might be able to use magic to understand; after all, bird folk were supposed to be able to communicate with birds and serpents – and even dragons, according to some sources – so why not with their own kind? But I was too unsettled, sore, and frightened to even try magic. If I had grown up learning magic as I should have, as Kier had, no doubt I would be able to use it under nearly any circumstances, but I was still practicing children's tricks and had to concentrate to even keep a wisplight going.

"Goddess damn you!" I yelled, and the other guard circled around and dropped closer to me. I think he studied me for a moment from behind his bird mask, and then spoke.

I didn't understand him any better. I wanted to cry. I would *not* cry.

"I don't understand," I told him. "Can you not speak Islish?"

He made a disgusted sound. "I said a seer such as you are should watch how you sling curses around." He looked away, and then back at me. "You are Vogel. How do you not speak our language?"

When I started to answer, wondering how to fit a long story into something suited to shouting across the wind, he cut me off with a gesture. "We take you to the King. *Your* King."

"I know." I raised my voice to be heard over the increasing wind. "But you must bring my friend, too." It felt wrong, calling Kiernan "friend," though of course he was. But he was so much more than that. But I didn't quite dare call him my lover, my beloved, in front of these strangers.

"No fey may enter the Eyrie. Vogel only." He tipped his wings to bank away, then returned, and his voice was a little gentler. "If it is as you say, you may ask the King and perhaps he will send someone to fetch your friend to the City Beneath the Cliff."

I felt hope drain away in a trickle and tried to hold on to some of it at least. Surely the King would listen? I was only one insignificant Vogel man who had grown up far away, but I was also a seer, and if Kiernan was right, I was the only Vogel seer born in seven generations. I was worth something to my people, to my King. Surely that would be enough to let me bring one friend to the city. Surely that wasn't too much to ask.

By the time the guard had left me to dangle from his companion's talons again, we had nearly reached the end of the forest. We flew low over a river estuary, where the clear water of a winding stream met the rich soil of the shore and divided into many smaller streams.

The spaces between were lush with berry bushes and long grass, and hundreds of birds took flight as we passed over. I could see fish in the water, silver scales flashing as the sun passed in and out of the clouds. A group of bird folk cast a net into the sea, just where the river emptied, and I watched them haul it back in, bursting full.

I wanted to enjoy this, to take in as much as I could. I wanted to feel the wonder I knew I would have felt under other circumstances. Kiernan wouldn't be upset if he knew I was enjoying myself while he was left behind. He would *want* me to be happy.

But how could I? I hung miserably from aching shoulders and tried to ignore the throbbing in my arm and wing that got worse with every heartbeat. I had to make myself observe as much as I could as we passed over, because I didn't know what might prove useful later.

The fishers glanced up when our shadow fell across them, and one pointed. They all turned to stare and one by one, they fell to their knees and held out their hands, even though some of their catch took the opportunity to wriggle free of the net and flop across the sand to the water and escape. I envied those fish.

"What are they doing?" I didn't realize I'd said it aloud until my captor spoke.

His voice was deeper than the other guard's, gruff and hard. "They see a miracle, a seer of Vogel kind. To the peasants, a seer is a religious icon they have not seen for hundreds of years. It is as if our Goddess Above sends a messenger to speak to them. To speak *for* them." Then he was silent again and we banked to follow the bright sand of the beach along the shore towards the shining sandstone cliff.

As we passed over, I tried to pick out the spot where my mother had walked in my vision, where she had stood to sing to the sea, to her flock of feathered serpents, to the unborn fetus that was me, curled tightly in my flexible eggshell inside her swollen belly. The spot where she had been murdered and her eviscerated corpse left to the sea and the scavengers.

But the beach had changed in thirty years, the sand had shifted, and the forest grew closer to the shore. There were cottages and platforms for drying fish that hadn't been there in my vision, and everything looked different from above, anyway.

As we approached the cliff, my guards beat their wings to gain height and my captor grumbled something in Voglish that probably had to do with how heavy I was. I could see clearly, now, the ruins in the cliff face that I had spotted this morning and closer up they looked tragically beautiful. Once, there had been balconies and windows and turrets, all built in a graceful style comprised of long curves and pointed arches, flowing shapes suggestive of wings and delicate uprights that didn't look like they'd have been capable of supporting weight even when whole.

I peered into the shadows, trying to see if there was anything still visible of the inside of the ruins, and if the whole parts of the city could be seen through the gaping voids. But the contrast between bright daylight and the inner darkness defeated my eyes. Surely, they would have walled off the broken areas from the other side, though, and not let the wind and the rain into the sacred city through its broken parts.

Then we were swinging out to sea, still climbing, and we passed over the place where the beach ended and came to a point against the cliff face, and only water lapped at the base of the stone. As we came around the jutting face of rock, I began to see what the ruined city had once looked like, centuries ago when it was all intact.

Here, the balconies were unbroken, the windows still glassed, and towers small and large still perched on any outthrust of stone, creating something that looked like a magical city out of a fairy tale.

"Goddess Above," I whispered. It was breathtaking, the gleaming stone hollowed out and built upon to create a palace in the very bones of the land, perched on the fringe of the sea, and reaching into the domain of the sky.

I could see why the Vogel would want to keep outsiders away. Here was an ancient place that sat at the meeting of the three sacred Realms. Magic must be close to the surface here.

But the more I looked, the more I noticed signs of decay.

The uppermost reaches of the Eyrie, built into levels of stone that were untouched on the other side, were in pristine condition. The stone and glass gleamed with the care that had been taken to clean and maintain them. The lower levels, by contrast, had places where the stonework had been repaired and patched by unskilled workers and many of the windows were grimy with bird droppings and other unidentifiable filth. It was as if only the top few levels – separated from the rest by an expanse of uncarved, uninhabited stone – were worth the effort and expense of maintaining properly. I knew, without being told, that those upper levels would belong to the royal palace, and the lower to less important officials and workers.

As we came around the final curve of the rock I could see the City Beneath the Cliff, crouched at the foot of the Eyrie. It was bright with color and bustled with people. Perhaps we were too high up to attract notice, but I saw no one look up as we passed over one corner of the City on our way.

Clinging to the Eyrie, one above the other, were two huge semicircular balconies, like grand entrances. The lower one was unoccupied, its door closed and dark from the shadow of the balcony above, even though a large expanse of unadorned white stone separated the two. It was the upper balcony we were headed for, and it jutted out from the lowest level of what I had assumed was the royal dwelling.

When we reached the broad expanse of stone, one of my guards landed, and my captor followed, hovered a wingbeat, and dropped me.

I hit the stone hard, twisting an ankle under me and gasping out involuntarily. I looked up to find seven gold-beaked masks turned my way, eyes gleaming from within their shadows. I wanted to sink into the floor and disappear. My guards stepped close to each side of me, and each took one of my elbows and pulled me to my feet. I yelped when the guard on my right pulled too hard and my shoulder shot pain down to my wrist.

"You are injured," he said. It was the kinder guard, and he eased off on his grip. I saw his beaked head turn to look behind me and I realized my wing was drooping, too. I tried to tuck it against my back, but it wouldn't stay.

"I hurt them climbing down the cliff," I said, and the gruff guard hissed at me to be quiet.

"The King will send for a healer," the kinder guard said.

I bit my lip and said nothing, not wanting to be chastised by the gruff guard again.

We waited and I took the opportunity to look around. The balcony was edged by a low railing of reddish metal, worked to look like climbing plants and tree serpents. Evenly spread across the back wall were the guards with their gold masks. Each was dressed only in the mask and a skirt of feathers, and they were all tanned deep honey-gold.

Each guard carried a long spear, and they alternated in color: first one with blue and green feathers, then one with red and yellow, then blue and green, and so on. Their wings and tails were so large they touched the ground, even when held up above their shoulders.

Next to their bright splendor I looked like something that had crawled out of a cave to blink stupidly in the sun.

I remembered Kiernan's deep, smoky voice telling me about the wonder and magic of cave fish, but I was something far less magical. A cave worm. A cave slug. I wanted to hide.

The wall of the Eyrie, protected by its seven guards, had a huge door in the middle of it and a row of half-round widows above. Each window was colored glass and represented a different constellation. The massive door was wooden, carved and embellished with paint and metal into the semblance of two dragons, rearing up face-to-face. Their eyes were some kind of gemstone that caught the light and gleamed orange-red.

I could never have imagined such a place existed outside of the fairy stories I had read in the Abbey library. And this was only a small taste of the outside. I was filled with awe and wonder and fear, and I wished more than anything that Kiernan were here next to me, holding my hand and lending me his strength, sharing in the discovery.

The thought of Kier reminded me of magic, and that reminded me that I was helplessly unable to speak the language of these people. *My* people. To be sure, most of the bird folk probably spoke Islish, at least a little, but I'd be at a disadvantage if I couldn't understand their native tongue. *My* native tongue.

So while I waited, I closed my eyes and breathed as Kiernan had taught me, reaching up to the sky, down to the land, and out to the sea, drawing them to me, though me, making myself a conduit for them to mingle. And the magic leapt to my reaching, so strong I nearly gasped out loud. For a few heartbeats, I just basked in the rush of power through me. I wondered what amazing things I could accomplish if I knew how to wield it. But I remembered Moira's teaching: a seer asks and does not command. So I asked to understand the Vogel tongue, to know it and speak it and read it.

The Realms answered and when I opened my eyes and a new person came through the huge door and began to speak, I understood.

<You found a seer!> said the newcomer. They were tall, as tall as the guards, who were each at least a full head taller than I was, making me feel small. I had expected myself to be average among my kind, not tiny. Kiernan would have looked like a child next to them.

The newcomer was dressed in a flowing tunic of some

kind of silken cloth in pale blue that matched their wings and had an elaborate arrangement of feathers around their face, but no bird mask.

<The King said fly towards the cliffs above Aven Forest. We found him there,> said one of my guards, the gruff one whose talon prints were probably visible on my shoulders as abrasions and bruises.

<Was he the cause of the surge in magic the King felt?>

I felt my guard shrug. Had there been a surge in magic? If Kiernan had felt one, he hadn't said. But then I realized there *had* been a surge, because we had caused it, Kiernan and I, in the cave shrine beneath the hills. I blushed to remember what we had been doing.

The blue-clad person came closer, step by step, inspecting me as they came. I met their eyes with a defiant stare. Theirs were the same pale blue as their wings and tunic, and they crinkled at the corners with amusement.

<Fierce little thing, are you?> they said.

<Do I need to be?> My voice came out shakier than I liked, and the other smiled. My guards both looked at me in surprise.

<You are a seer, but we have heard no news of a Vogel seer's birth.> I noticed they ignored my question. <How old are you?>

<Thirty-three this past solstice.> Another surprised glance from my guards. I was being judged, I could tell that, but I wasn't sure why, or by what criteria.

<So not a boy, after all. You're small for thirty-three.>

<I'm also colorless and have stunted wings,> I said, saying the last part without thinking, and wishing I hadn't when the person stepped around me to look at my stupid diminutive appendages.

<And rude,> they said, with amusement. <Though I

suppose that is understandable, under the circumstances.> They stepped back in front of me. <Did your mother hide you in shame at your deformities?>

The word "deformities" hit me like a slap. I was used to thinking of myself as somewhat useless, with unremarkable visions and wings that couldn't carry me, but *deformed?* To the other bird folk, I supposed I was. Would Kiernan still think I was beautiful, still perfect, once he saw me next to these magnificent people?

<My mother was murdered,> I said and they recoiled. <I was cut from her body, still in the egg, and taken to the Abbey of the Moon, where the Alfar kept me hidden to use for a sacrifice once I reached my majority.>

<And yet you live.> They had recovered from their shock at my mention of murder and now watched me carefully.

<I was rescued. Your guards left him behind when they snatched me off the cliff. I would appreciate it if you would send someone back for him.>

They looked from me to one of my guards, then the other. The gruff one only shrugged. The kinder one said, <There was an Alfar boy with him. Obviously, we couldn't bring him here.>

<He's Sidhe, not a boy.> I jerked my arms free of my guards, careful not to put too much weight on my twisted ankle and wincing at the twinge in my shoulder, and they let me go. "He's older than I am." I switched back to Islish, suddenly annoyed at all the questions. I was here. I was obviously a seer. What more could they want of me?

"You may speak to the King and perhaps he will allow your rescuer to stay Beneath." They switched languages without hesitation, and spoke in perfect, unaccented Islish.

"When may I speak to the King?" All I really wanted was get this over with so I could sit down, rest my wing and my arm and my ankle, and sink into despair about never seeing Kiernan again. I would ask, but I had less hope the longer I was here. I wanted his laughter, his strong hands, his inappropriate comments, his tongue flicking over the most sensitive parts of me. I wanted him safe and near.

"He is on his way. Do you have a name, boy?"

I declined to remind them that I had not been a boy since the solstice dawned. "Branfionn."

They blinked at me. "That is a Sidhe name."

"It is the name I have. The Abbess of the Moon found it amusing, I think, to give me a name from the enemy they planned to defeat first, using the magic they stole from my sacrifice."

They snorted. "You are a cheeky thing. I like you. But you best learn politeness quickly. Our King likes his subjects docile and obedient."

I looked at my feet. "Yes… um, what do I call you?"

"I am Councilor Rocsh. You may address me that way, or simply as Councilor."

"Yes, Councilor."

"I suggest you choose a proper Vogel name, or else the King will assign you one, and you may not like it."

"I speak Vogelspek only through magic," I said. "I don't know what an appropriate name might be, Councilor."

The kinder guard stepped forward. <If I may?> he said, looking first at me and then at Councilor Rocsh.

The Councilor shrugged and made a gesture of permission with one hand.

<Tokka means "silver." It is an uncommon name, but would suit you, my Seer.>

An odd thrill went through me at being called "my Seer," and at finally being addressed kindly in what so far felt like a hostile place.

<Silver? That does suit me. But that's not Voelspek.> I smiled tentatively at the guard. I couldn't tell if he smiled back, but he nodded before stepping back to his place.

<It's Trillka, the ancient language of our people, from before we adopted a shared language with the other original peoples of the Isle. It's only used for names, now.> The Councilor smiled. <Tokka will do nicely, if you like it, my Seer.> And it suddenly felt as if the whole feeling of the place had shifted when the guard, and then the Councilor, had called me "Seer" as if it were a title and not merely a description.

<Thank you,> I said, and my guard nodded again.

Then there were footsteps, echoing out of the open door, sounding like something huge must be making them, and as one, every guard sank to one knee, and the Councilor bowed their head. Not knowing what to do, I bowed my head also.

Straightening, Councilor Rocsh put one hand on my arm – my left, fortunately – and drew me forward a step.

<My King,> they said. <May I present Seer Tokka, stolen from us in the egg, but now returned.>

They stepped away a step, bowed slightly, and gestured. <Seer Tokka, meet your Monarch, King Sarkot tanEyrie, Lord of the Three Realms, and Sovereign of the Vogel.>

III: THE EYRIE

23
Fionn

THE KING STALKED across the shining white floor of the balcony and I felt like a prey animal that sees its own death coming but is too terrified to flee.

He was even taller than his guards, by a fingerwidth or three, and had wings of deep blue and blue-green. He wore a tunic similar to Councilor Rocsh's, but in purple trimmed with gold, long enough it flowed around his ankles. Like the rest of the Vogel I had seen, his legs were otherwise bare.

The feathers around his face were even more elaborate than the Councilor's and shone with iridescence. I wondered, absurdly, what bird they had come from. An argus pheasant, perhaps?

Where the Councilor had a pleasing face, the King was handsome, a little too sharp-featured to be beautiful, but still too attractive to be comfortable to look at for long. The eyes he examined me with were a deep, intense blue and I looked quickly down to avoid having to face them. The claws on his long toes had been painted deep purple, tipped with gold.

<My King,> I said.

<Seer Tokka.> He paced around me, and I resisted the urge to clamp my wings to my back in an attempt to hide them. He paused behind my right shoulder, and I flinched when I felt his hand on my injured wing.

<Relax, boy. I'm not going to hurt you.> He spread my wing out and I couldn't help the gasp of pain. <Who damaged you?>

Damaged me, like I was a commodity. I felt like livestock, inspected by a picky farmer at a fair.

<No one, my King,> I said, just managing not to jerk my wing out of his grasp. <I hit my shoulder and wing climbing down a cliff.>

He let go and I couldn't get my wing to fold at all; it just hung drooping from my back.

<Poor thing,> the King said, and I didn't know if he meant me or my wing. He lifted it gently, folded it, and held it against my back until I could get it to stay where it ought to.

<Councilor Rocsh?>

<My King?>

<Have the Queen's old rooms readied for him, and make sure there is a healer waiting.>

<Yes, my King.> The Councilor didn't move, as if he knew there would be further instructions to come.

The King took another step behind me and opened my other wing, stroked the feathers, then folded it again. <A pity they're so small,> he said. <They would be something to see were they not stunted.> He shifted position and ran a hand over my hair from the top of my head all the way down to where the ends brushed the top of my tail. <And *such* a pity we'll have to have this cut. I could kill the Alfar King for such a desecration.>

<My King!> said Councilor Rocsh, a note of warning in

his voice.

The King waved his hand dismissively. <No one here is unaware of how I feel about our blessed overlord Monarch.> He pronounced "blessed" as if it were filth between his lips.

<Shall I fetch the haircutter as well?>

<Not yet. Tomorrow is soon enough.> The King stroked my hair again, weaving his fingers between the strands. Then he dropped his hand to step the rest of the way around me.

<Find him suitable clothing and send a tailor to measure him for a wardrobe that befits his station.>

<Yes, my King.>

King Sarkot touched my face lightly and ran his fingers over the small feathers around my face. <Find him an attendant.>

<Yes, my King.>

<A *female* attendant.>

I caught the amused smiled on Councilor Rocsh's face as he bowed. He apparently had decided the King was finished issuing instructions because he turned and strode for the door into the palace.

The King stood in front of me, unmoving, and I finally dared look up at him again, to meet his eyes.

<You were to be sacrificed by the Alfar?>

I blinked and my surprise must have showed on my face, because he smiled. I felt heat touch my cheeks.

<I listened at the door before I came in.> There was laughter in his voice, and I had to look away or blush even more. He stepped closer and my two guards moved away as one, to take their places along the wall with their fellows.

<Do you understand what it means to be seer to a monarch?>

I focused on the middle of his chest because he was too close for me to stare at his feet.

<I barely understand what it means to be a seer, my King.> My voice was too quiet, and he leaned even closer. I felt heat creeping up my neck.

He lifted a strand of my hair in his fingers, just like Dag had done. <I will ask Councilor Rocsh to find you a tutor. There are no other Vogel seers, of course, but the humans have more than they know what to do with and have always been good trading partners with us.> He tipped my chin up with the hand that still held a strand of my hair and I had to meet his eyes again.

<You will have to go Beneath to meet with them, of course, but I will assign two guards to carry you there.>

And I realized, then, that the palace was inaccessible to those without functional wings, that I was trapped here unless someone carried me out. And that meant that even if Kier was allowed to stay in the city, I would have to get permission to see him.

<My King?> I tried to scrape together what courage I had left.

<Yes, little seer?>

<My friend… There was a Sidhe man who helped me escape the Abbey of the Moon, who saw me safely to the cliff and would have brought me to you if we hadn't been found by your guards.>

<I wondered when you would find the backbone to ask.> He sounded amused.

<Can you send someone for him, my King? To bring him to the City Beneath the Cliff?>

He looked at me a long time and when I would have looked away, he turned my face back to his.

<What is he to you, little seer?>

<My friend. My rescuer.>

His lips quirked. <I am called Lord of the Three Realms

because I am strong in magic of Land, Sea, and Sky, though for obvious reasons, air magic is my biggest strength. Among my skills, little seer, is reading truth and lies.>

<Yes, my King.> I could barely get the words out. <I did not lie, my King.>

<No, but you also did not tell me the whole truth. What else is this Sidhe to you?>

I blinked back tears.

<I'm not angry, little seer.> He ran a finger over my lips. <But you belong to me, and I insist that you tell me everything I ask.> His voice was gentle, but full of steel, and though it made me afraid, it didn't make me want to tell him my every secret. It made me want to hide even more.

<Seer Tokka? Was he your lover?> He traced a feather at my temple. <Your feathers, small as they are next to the adornments we Vogel wear now, tell me you prefer men. So?>

<Yes, my King.> I wasn't even sure why I wanted to hide my feelings for Kiernan. I wasn't embarrassed to love him, but I'd hardly been able to talk to him properly; I didn't want someone else to understand before he did. And maybe I just wanted to keep my thoughts of him for myself, and not bare them to this overwhelmingly handsome King, standing so close to me, filling me with confusion.

<There. That wasn't so bad. Were you ashamed to have dallied with a Sidhe?>

It stung, to have him think I should be ashamed. And "dallied" was hardly an appropriate word for what Kiernan and I had done to each other. *With* each other.

<Why would that matter, my King?> I finally said.

He stepped back and I felt like I could breathe again. <Because, though you may have been raised away from your people, you are still Vogel.>

I must have looked confused, because he added, in such a

calm, reasonable voice it took me a few heartbeats to realize what he actually said, <Vogel do not mix with Sidhe, or Alfar, or any other folk. We associate with them only when we must, and we do not taint our bodies with their effluent.>

I must have looked horrified, but I don't think King Sarkot understood which part of his words horrified me. It was that anyone would think having a lover from another people was somehow wrong, that it could "taint" a person. I was pretty sure he thought I was distressed at *being* so tainted, that I had allowed myself to be soiled.

<Don't fear, little one. There is a ritual cleansing bath that can restore your purity. Together we will make you whole again.> He touched my face again; he didn't seem able, or inclined, to resist touching me.

<Now, I will take you to your rooms, and tonight you will dine with me, and we can get better acquainted.> He draped his arm over my shoulders and directed me towards the door.

<And my friend, my King?>

His nostrils flared, maybe annoyed at my persistence, or maybe in disgust at the idea that I had had a Sidhe lover. <I will send someone to look for him, but Sidhe are fickle, little seer. No doubt he is long gone, hieing on back to Morven or whatever forest he was spawned in.>

<Yes, my King.> At least he had agreed to send someone. The King might not believe Kiernan would wait for me, but I knew he would.

<Tomorrow, I will present you to my council, and you will be instructed about your duties.>

<Yes, my King.> I followed as he led me to the door.

<And together we will plan how to announce you to the rest of our people. A parade, perhaps, or a festival. You are a cause for celebration, my Seer.> He drew me onward, towards the huge door, and into the palace.

THE BEAUTY OF THE DOOR into the Eyrie and the spectacular view I had been given of the palace's outside with its balconies and windows had done nothing to prepare me for what was on the inside.

The walls and floors, doorways and passages, stairways and windows, the whole palace had been carved into the living stone. It had been so skillfully done that no tool marks remained anywhere to be seen, but it was obvious from the lack of seams or joints that the palace had been hollowed out and not built up.

I knew that some parts of the Eyrie *had* been built, because I had seen the towers perched on every bulge in the rock, but there were none of those on the route we followed from the balcony entrance to the rooms that were to be mine.

The stone was mostly gleaming white but here and there it shaded into other colors – reddish hues, or yellows, and in one place nearly green. Every now and then, something had been uncovered, embedded in the stone, and the builders had incorporated such finds into their designs, so that one doorway had an ancient petrified leaf at the top of its arch, and a whole corridor was floored with the rounded shapes of long-departed insects.

I would have liked to stop and examine them, except I was also anxious to arrive at our destination so I could be alone a while. To sit down. To think.

The stark stone walls had been hung with tapestries and embroideries in rich hues. Some of those near the windows and balconies had faded with time and light, but those deeper in were vibrant still and depicted scenes with bird folk. There were hunting scenes and others I could only guess at, but which might have been stories from history or legend. I tried to remember where the most intriguing ones were located so I could go back later and look more closely, but the palace was large and sprawling, and my shoulder and wing and ankle had begun to ache again, so I was soon completely lost.

Every door and window was shaped in graceful arches with pointed tops, or in wing-like sweeping curves and crescents. Every window had some element of colored glass, from simple abstract florals in the tops of their arches, to complete scenes picked out in backlit hues. Everywhere I looked, there were depictions of bird folk, honey-colored skin, bright feathers, and enormous wings.

It was dizzying.

When we climbed the first stair, I tried not to limp too obviously on my twisted ankle. By the second stairway, I couldn't hide it, and by the third I could barely rest my own weight on that foot.

The King paused to wait, but didn't offer help, so I struggled on. Perhaps it was a test, to see if I was tough enough. Or to find out if I was too stubborn or too stupid to ask for assistance.

<We're almost there, little seer,> was all the King said when I pulled myself up the last set of steps by the handrail. <The healer will be waiting.>

<Yes, my King.> I suspected that was about to become the most overused phrase in my vocabulary. I hated it already.

Finally, we turned down a wide, empty corridor at the end of which a large set of doors stood open. There was sunlight streaming in, and I could smell the sea.

<I'll have someone bring tapestries to brighten up this hall.> The King walked a step ahead of me, but slowed enough I could keep up with my limping gait. <They were all taken

down when my Queen died.> He glanced back at me. <These rooms were hers.>

<I'm sorry,> I said.

He shrugged. <It was not a love match.>

I flushed in embarrassment, but he didn't seem to notice. <She provided me with two healthy children. I honor her memory for that.>

<Will you not remarry, my King?>

<What for? I have a daughter, should I need a marriage to seal an alliance, and a son who will find his own queen one day.> He looked down at me again. <But you don't know how to read our feather patterns, do you?>

He stopped and I bumped into him, stepped back hastily, and almost turned my sore ankle again. He caught my elbow and steadied me. <You needn't be afraid of me, little seer. Fulfill your duties to me, and I will be your best friend in the Eyrie.>

<Yes, my King. And no, I can't read the feathers. Is there a book I could study?>

He snorted in amusement. <Of course, being raised in an Abbey, your learning comes entirely from books.>

<I'm sorry, my King.> I didn't really know what I was apologizing for. My uselessness, maybe.

He laughed. <I will find you a book.> He touched the large feather at the top of his facial adornment. <This one says I'm King, Monarch of the Eyrie.> He touched the next ones down, one on each side of his brow. <These say I'm widowed. And these – > he touched the next < – say I have children.>

He stroked two large feathers just over his ears, and then two more. <Here it says I like to bed both women and men.> His lips curved into a smile and his fingers slid to the next set of feathers. There was something intensely erotic about the way he touched his adornment, though it was only long claw-tipped fingers running lightly over added feathers.

<These ones say I usually prefer men.>

He lowered his hands. <Obviously there is much more, but that's the most relevant information at the moment.>

He wanted me to know his preferences in bedmates. Did that mean he was interested in me? But how could he decide such a thing when I'd only just arrived?

And I remembered how Kiernan had started flirting with me the moment he woke up in my infirmary, before he could even see me. Perhaps some men were just like that, deciding who they wanted to fuck at just a glance. I wondered what Kiernan's feathers would tell me, if he had been bird folk. Did he like only men? I didn't actually know that, I had only assumed because he liked *me*.

But of course the King wouldn't be interested in me. Not when he was surrounded by tall, beautiful – colorful – people with large, functional wings.

I realized he was waiting for me, and I quickly limped after him down the hall to the large door.

Stepping though, I found a small room with a large chair, a table, and an ornate mirror that I avoided looking into, though I was curious, never having seen an actual mirror before. I didn't want to see how I compared to the glory of the Vogel King. I would look small, stunted, pale, and bruised.

A second set of doors also stood open, and through them was a sitting room. There was a large balcony projecting from the wall opposite, that looked out over the sea. Its clear glass windows gleamed as if freshly washed, as did the row of smaller panels above, each depicting a different flower in colored glass. I recognized some of the blooms, but others were unfamiliar.

Between the door where we entered and the balcony were several couches, upholstered in shades of green and purple, each with nearby tables for holding beverages or vases of flowers. The left wall was entirely taken up by an empty bookcase, and a huge fireplace served as a divider between the sitting room and the next area.

The King saw my glance, I think, because he said, <I'll see you have a key to the palace library. You may bring whatever books you choose here to your rooms.>

I bowed my head and followed him past two people who were vigorously cleaning everything in sight. The King didn't even acknowledge their presence, and when I tried to meet their eyes they looked carefully away. I smiled anyway.

Past the fireplace was a huge bedroom with its own door to the balcony, a couch in front of the hearth, a huge wardrobe on the inner wall and a small writing desk and chair on the outer wall. The bed was the biggest I'd ever seen, even larger than the one the Abbess had, that I had speculated could hold an entire family comfortably.

The bed was bare, but a pile of clean folded linens waited on a trunk at its foot. I hoped it would be made soon, so I could lie down.

Finally, we approached one more door and I had to stop and stare. It was a bathing room, all shining stone and bright tilework with an entire wall of colored and etch-frosted glass. I could hear running water; a sink and commode screened off by a panel decorated with thousands of tiny iridescent feathers in the shape of a firebird occupied one corner, and a huge metal bathtub with both hot and cold pipes running to it lurked at the far wall.

But it was the middle of the floor that made me stare. Sunk into the floor, its bottom tiled with colored glass to look like sea creatures on a sandy bottom, was a bath, steaming with hot water that flowed through it constantly. It was smaller than the bath at the Abbey, but neater and brighter and somehow more inviting. I glanced up and saw that the ceiling was painted to look like the sky, fluffy clouds and all. I half expected there to be a bird seer like the one in the cave shrine, huge erect phallus on display, flying against the painted clouds. I was relieved that it was just birds and feathered serpents.

I finally tore my gaze away from the bath to find there was a woman standing next to a long shelf of jars, sunk into a curtsey so deep her knee pressed against the floor. <My King,> she said and snuck a glance at me. <My Seer.>

<Healer,> replied the King. <I bring you your patient, Seer Tokka. He has injuries that need tending to.> He made a gesture and the woman stood, but kept her head bowed.

<Seer Tokka, this is Healer Kah.>

<Healer,> I said, and too late realized there was a mirror above the shelf where she had been working and I caught my reflection in it. I had been right; I looked washed out and pathetic next to the glory of the King. There were dark circles under my eyes like bruises and a scratch on my cheek I didn't remember getting. My eyes were far too big, too wounded, too *vulnerable*. I looked quickly away.

The King noticed and smiled. <You look tired, my Seer. Rest, bathe, let Healer Kah tend to you. Sleep if you can. I'll see you later in my rooms. Your attendant will bring you.> His hand, when he brushed it against the back of my head, felt intimate, and a flush rose up my neck.

<Yes, my King.>

When he was gone, the healer turned back to whatever she had been doing before we entered. I thought I could smell the herbs for pain relief tea. When I didn't move, she turned back to me.

<Into the bath, my Seer. The hot water will do you as much good as my healing.> She smiled. <I'm making you some

tea, and once you've soaked a while, I've a salve for your bruises and cuts, and a poultice for your ankle and wing.

I must have looked surprised, because she added, <I've been a healer a long time, my Seer, I can tell by looking at you where most of your pains are.> She turned back to her task. <And I have some healer's magic, as well.>

<Can you teach me?> I probably sounded too eager, too needy, but I heard only kindness and mild amusement in her voice.

<If the King allows,> she said.

I still hesitated, and she turned again, eyebrows raised. <I'm not going to ogle your pale little body, my Seer. Into the bath.>

<Yes, Healer.> My voice came out meek and she laughed.

<Not that you aren't pretty,> she said. <But as a Healer, I never seduce my patients, and besides that I have a very jealous guard who keeps my bed warm at night.> She laughed again. <And *you* don't like women in your bed, anyway.>

I wasn't sure I liked how everyone I met here could read at a glance what I liked and didn't like, while I couldn't read them at all. If the King didn't find me a book soon, I'd have to go in search of one on my own.

When the healer went back to her preparations, I took my clothes off, folded them neatly, and put them on a shelf by the door. Then I eased into the water. It was hotter than the baths at the Abbey, and I could understand why there was also a metal tub in which a bather could mix their own preferred temperature. It was, in fact, just barely on the right side of too hot. But as I sank in, I felt my muscles relax immediately, and I leaned my head back with a deep sigh.

"Goddess Above," I said, automatically reverting to Islish.

I was still confused, sore, and heartbroken, but if this bath was mine to use whenever I wanted, I might be okay.

24
Kiernan

It wasn't until I was closer that I realized how tall these bird folk were. I suppose I had assumed they would be similar in height to Fionn, but they were much taller, which meant they towered over me.

Not that I'd ever let a size difference stop me, in fighting or in fucking. So I sauntered up to them like the cocky little shit I was, and flashed them my toothiest grin. I tapped the nearest on the elbow and he left off harassing the fishers and scowled down at me.

"Why not pick on someone who can fight back?" I said and punched him right in his feather-covered skirt, which was at exactly the right height for me to throw all my weight behind the jab. I felt the muscles in his lower belly tense under my fist and then compress, squashing whatever he had in his sheath, and he dropped to the sand with a grunt, and stayed there.

The other guard swung his spear in my direction and said, "Mind yourself Alfar, and let the grownups do the talking."

Lovely. They thought I was a child.

The Vogel on the ground said something between clenched teeth and tried to stand. I kicked him in the neck before he could get very far, and he scrambled back.

"Not Alfar," I said. "Have you ever seen an Alfar with antlers? Horns, maybe, once in a while. Antlers, no." I danced away from the guard's spear. If I hadn't had an actual aim, this little tussle would be fun. "Also, not a child."

The guard looked me up and down and spat in the sand. "You're a little shit, whatever you are." Part one of my plan was a success: I had pissed them off. I just wished the first one hadn't gone down quite so easily.

"Yes. Yes, I am. Now are you going to arrest me, or just talk at me?"

The guard swept his spear around, aiming for my knees, and I hopped over it.

"Come on, you can do better than that. Surely your Monarch has provided *some* training. My old man fights better than you, and he's human." That was a bit of an insult to my father, really. He'd trained as a warrior his whole life and was actually an excellent fighter.

The guard snarled and advanced; no one not human likes being compared to them, which was honestly unfair, but I could use it to my advantage. He wove his spear in an almost mesmerizing pattern that had no effect on me at all.

"You carry a sword, little shit, why not use it and make this a fair fight?"

I laughed and danced away from his spear again. "I already outclass you," I said. "If I draw my sword, I'd end up killing you, and I'm not actually looking to be executed or tortured or whatever you lot do to murderers."

"We feed you to the fucking pigs," said the guard on the ground, who was using his spear as a prop to climb to his feet.

He succeeded, finally, and stood unsteadily, his bird mask askew.

The guard whose spear I was evading far too easily let go of his poker with one hand, pulled his bird mask off, and handed it to his companion.

His face was sharp-featured, high-cheekboned and handsome, with large dark eyes I wouldn't have minded gazing into under other circumstances. If I hadn't already fallen hard for a very different Vogel man and his bright silver gaze.

"You *are* a looker. You should take that mask off more often." I skipped over his spear again, and then slipped to the side to avoid his lunge. "Maybe you'd rather jab me with the spear you're hiding under your skirt than the one in your hands. You'd definitely have more luck getting it in."

"Fuck you," he hissed and lunged again. I let him get close enough that his spear shaft slid against the fabric of my vest.

"That *is* the idea." He growled and swiped, and I got out of the way. And I noticed that, while his efforts to strike me weren't skilled enough to connect, he *was* managing to herd me down the beach, away from the estuary and the fishers.

The sand became firmer underfoot, and with better footing, the guard was moving more confidently, making me think that whomever had trained these men really needed a reminder that not all battles take place on solid ground. With his long spear and his long reach, I no longer had much chance of hitting him. But that was okay; I wasn't trying to. I was trying to *get* hit. Captured. Dragged off to gaol.

When the other guard edged around behind me, still obviously in pain in his nether regions, trying to be stealthy and failing completely, I pretended not to notice him. I let the first guard herd me down the beach until I backed into his companion, who dropped his spear and his friend's mask to grab both my arms in a grip as solid and pinching as iron shackles. I was very glad I'd read him right, and he hadn't simply stabbed me in the back.

I did, however, decline to let the first guard, the one with the lovely eyes, hit me in the testicles with the butt of his spear. I was trying to get beat up and arrested, not gelded.

He brought the spear back around with surprising grace, perhaps remembering his training now that I couldn't get away so easily, and would have cracked me across the face if I hadn't twisted away. My face had taken enough damage for one moon. Instead, he got me in the shoulder with a stinging slap that would have been a lot worse if he hadn't also connected with his companion's rib cage.

The guard holding me said something in Voglish that had the right intonation and vehemence for a truly filthy curse, but held my arms tight. The lovely-eyed guard swore, too, and tossed his spear aside to grab at my shirt front. I head butted him in the chest – all I could reach, alas – and snapped my head up, catching him under the jaw with an antler. If he hadn't been so much taller than me, I might have done some actual damage.

He *did* catch me with a backhand across the face – always the fucking face – and clipped my still werewolf-damaged nose. I felt blood spurt and drip down my lip.

"Nice one," I said. I knew I must look horrific, blood staining my teeth and dripping off my chin. "Another one or two like that and you might actually hurt me."

Of course, he had already hurt me, but he didn't need to know that.

Instead of another backhand, he jabbed me in the solar plexus with the stiffened fingers of his other hand. The air whooshed out of my lungs, and I forgot how to breathe for much too long. I'd underestimated him, stupidly. I knew Fionn was ambidextrous, but it had never occurred to me it might be a common Vogel trait.

"There you go," I said, voice a croak. "You're doing better now. Pretty soon you'll be ready to fight someone your own size."

He aimed a kick at my groin, but I twisted away, and he ended up connecting with his companion's knee. The guard holding me wobbled but kept his feet. He said something that was probably very nasty to his companion, who grimaced.

"Shut up!" the lovely-eyed guard growled. He grabbed my shirt – actually managing to get a fistful of fabric this time – and pulled me out of his companion's grip. He lifted me off my feet so I dangled. "You are not worth my time." He flung me away so I sprawled on the sand, snatched up his spear, and barked something at his companion, who tossed him his bird mask.

"Aw, come on," I said, lounging back against the beach and crossing my ankles. "That was just foreplay. When do we get to the good stuff?"

The guard walked away, putting on his mask. Then he took three long running steps, leapt into the air, and flew.

"Fuck," I said. "I wish I could do that."

The second guard, whose tackle I'd crushed, hefted his spear, and looked down at me. I prepared to roll out of the way. If I hadn't underestimated him, I'd have realized his strike was a feint, but I had. So when he stabbed, I moved away from what I thought was coming and left myself open to what actually did. He whipped his bird mask off, and in the same motion, clubbed me in the temple with it.

I saw him turn and walk away before everything went black.

I CAME TO WITH A CIRCLE of curious Vogel peasants looking down at me. One of them was on his knees beside me, dabbing at my face with a cloth damp with sea water. The salt stung and I flinched.

"We are grateful you distracted those guards," he said, his Islish sounding awkward and formal. "But now they may return and do much worse."

I tried to sit up, but the nausea that gripped me made me lie back again, clenching my teeth to keep from throwing up. I pushed the old man's hands away, but gently. He was old and weather-worn, but his bright orange-gold eyes were sharp and intelligent. The short hair that fuzzed his head and the primary feathers of his large wings were a deeper version of the same color.

"They wouldn't bother you too much, would they? You're their own people."

The man shrugged and sat back. "They might, they might not. We are only peasants, yes? Those ones, they get selected for the guard and suddenly they think they're better than everyone else."

"So the ancient and glorious Vogel Monarchy is just as shitty as every other on this Isle. I suppose I hoped it would be better."

"We are a vassal monarchy. We get the shit from all sides."

"Better times come," said one of the other Vogel, an older woman dressed exactly as the men were, who looked their equal in strength. She had soft yellow hair and feathers and hazel eyes flecked with brown.

"I hope they do." I struggled to sit again, ignoring the throbbing in my temple and holding back the churning in my gut.

"A seer has finally come to the Vogel. It is a sign of peace and plenty for all our folk."

I looked up at her sharply, and I don't think she missed my reaction. If I had to guess, I'd say she didn't miss much at all. "You saw him? The Seer?"

The old man gestured to the sky in the direction of the estuary. "Two guards flew over while we brought in our first catch, and one of them carried another who gleamed of silver in the sun."

"Your seers only have silver in their eyes," the woman said, something like boasting in her voice. "Vogel seers are silver-winged, too." She was still watching my face carefully and I wondered what she saw. I know I felt a sharp stab of longing when she said silver-winged, and remembered Fionn on my lap, wings spread in ecstasy, moaning my name.

"It was a good catch this morning. Another good catch that the guards tried to spoil. He is bringing abundance already." Her voice was soft and full of awe, as if seeing her Seer and finding her nets full to bursting with fish were a religious experience. It amused me – probably more than it should have – that sweet, quiet Fionn was the cause. I mean, he'd given me a religious experience, too, though it was of a rather different nature.

"Did they take your Seer to the Eyrie?"

"Of course." The old man pointed up at the cliff. "This side is ruined now, but the palace is on the other side, and still as glorious as it ever was."

"You are a warrior, no?" said the woman, gesturing at my sword and my knives. "Do you come to assassinate our Seer? Or our King?" She sounded more worried about the former than the latter. I was pretty sure I could grow to like her.

"I came to make sure your Seer got here safely. I stole him from the Alfar who had him captive and brought him here."

"*You* brought him?" She looked doubtful and her voice echoed the sentiment.

"We got as far as the cliff in the forest." I twisted around and pointed in the general direction of the hill with its caves. "Then the guards came. They took him and left me."

"Why?"

"Because I'm not Vogel, I assume."

"No. Why did you do this? Bring us our Seer? And why did you defend mere peasants against our King's guards?" The old man studied me, just at the woman had. I was beginning to feel like an exhibit at a fair and had to resist making a face. "What do you hope to gain? Why not stay in your own forest and live your rich noble life?"

It was a lot of questions that didn't really have easy answers, as simple as they might seem on the surface. But it seemed important to answer as best I could. Fionn wanted a better world, and as far as I could see, the best way to gain that was to start by making things better for the humblest people, those who always suffered when the so-called noble classes squabbled.

And I could start, in however small a way, by being as honest with them as I could.

I shifted my seat on the sand and looked at my hands, thinking. The finger with the split claw was swollen and purplish. At least it was on my right hand and wouldn't interfere with my ability to use my sword. I closed my hands into fists.

"I brought your Seer here, as close as I could, because he asked me to. And I defended you because I can't stand bullies. I don't hope to gain anything except perhaps self-respect. And the respect of your Seer." I knew I already had Fionn's respect, but I still didn't feel like I deserved it.

"And I won't return to my Monarch if I can avoid it, because she holds me captive and away from her I am at least free to make my own choices."

They were simpler answers than the questions really deserved, but it was hardly the time or place for a deep philosophical discussion.

"Our Seer… he is your friend?"

I smiled and tried to keep the self-deprecation out of it, but the man and woman both frowned.

"He is…" I looked at my hands again, flexed them, and thought about the feel of Fionn's skin beneath my palms, the silk of his hair between my fingers. Then I looked up and met the woman's eyes. "He is my world," I said.

She put a hand on my shoulder and squeezed. She smiled and it made her face soft and beautiful. Her eyes were kinder than I probably deserved.

"You love him," she said.

I was saved from having to answer by the arrival of Smoke and Flame, who zipped several times around my head, scolding me.

Stupid, said Smoke.

Dangerous, said Flame.

I laughed and snatched them out of the air, making them coil around my wrists, one in each hand. I put them on my shoulders and they purred, nuzzling under my chin.

"They didn't even arrest me, after all that." I scratched under Smoke's chin, and then under Flame's. And I looked back at the bird folk to find them all staring at me, mouths open. "What have I done now?"

"You speak to serpents," the old man said. "You handle them, and they allow it."

"Only royalty and King's guards are allowed serpents," said the woman. "How is this possible?"

I shrugged. "They do as they please. They were his friends first. Your Seer's. I suppose they like me for his sake."

We love, said Flame.

Silly shadow, said Smoke.

"Are you heart-bonded?"

"With the serpents? I don't think so, but I don't know what that means, so maybe?"

The woman snorted. "With our Seer. Heart-bonded is like… like love, but more. Unbreakable even by death."

The old man made a disgusted gesture. "He is fey, woman. It is not possible for Vogel and fey to heart-bond. Only Vogel and Vogel."

"You don't know that," said the woman, mild disdain in her voice. "You only say it because the spoiled royal brats in the Eyrie decree it unlawful to even go to bed with non-Vogel. And obviously *that* isn't impossible." She turned away from the man as if to show him what she thought of his words. "That is not even *wrong,* and you know it."

Well, *that* was interesting. Most royals, of any people, frowned upon marriage between peoples. My parents had been a scandal in some quarters. But as far as I knew, fucking someone not of your own kind wasn't illegal; there were enough half-breeds like me to prove it. Except, apparently, in the Vogel Monarchy. They certainly took their isolationism to heart.

The old man just shook his head. "No matter. They are friends. It is enough."

"You were trying to get arrested, yes?" The old woman ignored the man.

I nodded. "I really didn't think they'd just beat me up and leave me on the beach."

"They seldom arrest anyone," the old man said. "It is too much effort to feed and house prisoners."

"I guess that was a bad idea, then."

"For what purpose were you trying this?"

"I wanted them to take me to the Eyrie."

The old man shook his head. "No outsiders are allowed in the Eyrie." I knew that, of course, I had just hoped… what, that I'd be an exception for no actual reason? "You would have been taken to the City Beneath the Cliff."

"At least I would have been closer. Could have seen him, maybe."

The woman shook her head. "The gaol is far from anywhere the royals would go, and no doubt they will keep the Seer close except to show him off to our people from time to time." She squeezed my shoulder again. "No, Hraf na Tokka, you would simply have rotted in a cell without seeing him ever again."

The old man frowned at her. "You give him a Vogel name, now? What next? Show him the path over the mountain?"

The woman only smiled.

"You *do* mean to show him the path. You'll be the death of me one day, wife."

"You would grow bored if I didn't continue to surprise you."

He snorted. "I will never grow bored with you." He looked at me again. "You know what this means, 'Hraf na Tokka'?"

I shook my head. "It doesn't sound Voglish, but I don't speak Voglish anyway."

"We call our language Vogelspek, and no, this is not in the language we speak now. It comes from an older tongue, from before recorded history, that we use now only for names. None speak it more than that, alas."

I nodded, as if I knew what he was talking about, and wondered if Fionn knew his people had a secret lost language. "What does it mean? Hraf na Tokka?" I said the words tentatively, but I must have managed the pronunciation well enough, because he nodded.

"It means Silver's Shadow."

"Silver shadow. I like that."

The woman shook her head. "No, no. Not shadow that *is* silver, but shadow that *belongs to* silver. 'Hraf' is 'shadow' or 'darkness'. 'Na' is 'of' or 'is belonged by'."

"'Owned by'," said the old man and the woman smacked his shoulder affectionately.

"'Tokka' is made of 'tok,' that is 'white,' and 'ka' which is 'shining'."

"Hraf na Tokka," I said again. "Silver's Shadow."

"So, you have a Vogel name now. We can help you and no one can say we weren't helping Vogel." She laughed and stood up.

"Tokka is Fionn, isn't it? Your Seer? And I'm his shadow." I smiled at that. I could definitely live with being the darkness standing next to my beautiful silver lover.

"What does this 'Fionn' mean?" The old man rose and stood next to his wife, holding out a hand to help me up. I considered not taking it; he was tall and sturdy, but old, while I was young and capable, if a little worse for wear. But fuck it, I wouldn't insult him by refusing help. I took his hand and let him pull me to my feet.

"It's your Seer's name. Branfionn. In my language, Sidhe, 'bran' is a sacred bird, and 'fionn' is 'fair' or 'white.' So Brannfionn would translate as 'White Bird'."

The woman nodded. "It is a good name."

"Now come quickly, in case the guards return. We should not have delayed so long talking." The man gestured to a path just down the beach, leading into the forest.

"No," I said. "You had to be sure I could be trusted."

"I'm still not sure," he said. "But you care for our Seer, so we will help you, Hraf."

"In my language, my name is Kiernan." I smiled and

found it turning into a grin. "It means 'darkness' or 'shadow'."

The woman laughed at that, a loud cheerful barking sort of laugh that made me like her even more.

The rest of the Vogel fishers headed back down the beach to return to their nets, while the married couple led me under the trees. I immediately felt better, as if the forest recognized my pain and soothed my injuries the way it could always soothe my soul.

The path ran away from the beach to a rock outcrop where a spring gushed out, creating a tiny waterfall surrounded by lush ferns and moss.

"May I drink?" I asked, and realized I had left the waterskin, and all my gear except my sword rig, back in the bushes near the estuary. We stopped and all drank, and the water was clear and cold and delicious and made my teeth ache in the best way possible. I splashed some over my face and it dribbled away red, but the throbbing in my nose eased.

Then we carried on, first directly into the forest, then gradually winding around to the left, and slowly, the land rose. At last, we came out of the trees onto a steep hillside. Across from us the Eyrie's cliff rose straight up, but there were cracks and fissures here, and places where trees and flowers had taken root and clung to the steep rock.

The old man pointed. "Do you see the tree with three trunks, twisting around together?"

"I see it."

"We call it the Dancing Dryads. Some leave offerings to the spirits there." I could see strips of bright cloth tied to many of the branches, and crystals catching the light.

"Look to the right, and you will see a shadow, long and straight, going up the cliff."

"A cleft in the rock?"

"Indeed. Go in there and go only straight in. When you

reach its end, you climb. At the top of the cliff, go just to your left and another fissure will lead you down again. Follow the trail, taking only left turns, and you will find the City Beneath."

"That sounds simple enough."

"Simple enough that some have gotten lost and were never seen again, yes."

"How do traders get to the city?"

"By boat, or else inland and through the Stricken Pass."

"And I don't have a boat."

"Or half a moon, I wager."

"So, straight in."

"Yes."

"What happens if I go left or right?"

"Right is only dead ends. Left…" He shrugged. "Caves. Miles of caves like the labyrinth in the fairy tale. They say our people once interred our dead there."

"Some say the caves join up with the lowest levels of the Eyrie," the woman said, a warning in her voice. "But you would be lost and die before you found your way. And anyway, those levels are in ruins and long ago walled off from the rest of the Eyrie."

I looked at the cliff, studying it. "Thank you," I said, finally. "May I know your names?"

The man and woman looked at each other and I knew exactly why they hesitated. If I were captured, I might tell someone who had helped me.

"Never mind," I said. "Thank you."

They nodded and left me standing there, staring at yet another fucking cliff.

25
Fionn

THE HEALER PRODDED my shoulder with her toe to get me out of the bath what felt like only a few moments later, but must have been a great deal more, because my fingers and toes were deeply wrinkled. I felt relaxed and much less sore than when I had arrived.

My heart still ached, but my body was already recovering.

Healer Kah handed me a tunic of soft, thick material to put on once I was dry, and then she sat me on a chair to apply ointment and healing magic to my bruises and scrapes and sore places. By the time she was done, even my wing was feeling better.

She handed me a cup of tea. <Drink this, and then to bed with you. Your attendant will wake you when it's time to dress to see the King.>

I sipped the tea and recognized most of the same herbs I would have put in a pain relief tisane, including a mild sedative. <I haven't met my attendant yet.> I drank the whole cup because I knew I needed rest, and there was no way my tumultuous thoughts would let me sleep without assistance.

<You will meet her when you wake. In the meantime, there are guards outside your door should you need anything.>

<Thank you, Healer.> She nodded and left, closing the door behind her, and I crawled into the enormous bed, now made up with crisp, soft sheets and a lightweight blanket of some luxurious fiber.

I slept and did not dream and woke clearheaded when a polite tap sounded on my sitting room door. I didn't even have time to answer before a thin figure slipped in and shut the door behind her. She was tall, as all Vogel were, and looked very strong but also elegant. Her hair was a deep brown so like Kiernan's that I wanted to touch it, and her wings matched, only her feathers had an iridescent shine and bands of black all down them, and black tips.

I pulled the sheet up to my chin and stared at her, before remembering where – and who – I was.

<Hello.> My voice was tentative, so I cleared my throat.

She curtseyed. <My Seer. I am to be your attendant. My name is Neeka.>

<Hello,> I said again. <Please don't curtsey.>

<I must,> she said. <If I don't show the proper respect, the King will have me disciplined, and someone else will be assigned to you.>

<The King is not here.> I mustered something resembling authority. <And I would not have you curtsey, or bow, or refuse to meet my eyes. You can save those things for when the King *is* here.>

She straightened, and smiled, and met my eyes with a bold look. Hers were amber and friendly. <I think I will like you, my Seer.>

<My name is Fionn,> I said. <I mean, Tokka.>

<If I call you by name, my Seer, I will get used to it and forget and *that* the King will notice.>

I frowned. <Could you at least call me Seer Tokka? 'My Seer' is too formal. I'm not royalty.>

<No, you are a seer.> She grinned. <That's better than royalty, so far as I'm concerned.> She held up a book. <Councilor Rocsh instructed me to bring this to you.>

<Oh!> I held out my hands and she crossed the room to hand me the thin volume.

<And this.> She fished in a pocket slung around her waist and handed me a large key. <For the library. When there's time, I'll show you where it is.>

I smiled and it felt good to have something to be happy for. <Thank you.>

I looked at the book, opened it and flipped pages. It was in Vogelspek but, thanks to my magic, I could read it, though only slowly. *On the Construction of Facial Adornments for Noble Vogel.* Presumably, there would be information on how to read – or maybe how to write – feather patterns.

<Are you planning on taking up a craft, Seer Tokka?> Her question was polite, but her raised eyebrows showed what she thought of the idea.

<Not *this* craft,> I said. <Though I should like a spindle and something to spin.> I set the book aside. <This is to help me learn to read facial feathers.> I touched my small natural feathers. <Apparently the magic I used to understand your language – our language – didn't include reading facial adornments.>

<Ah.> She looked at me a moment, then said, <You can practice with mine, later. Right now, we must get you dressed to meet with the King.>

<Am I to be joining a dinner party?>

She looked at me oddly. <I believe you dine with the King

alone.> She hesitated. <Did he not express his intentions?>

<He only said we should become better acquainted.> *Had* he said more? Was I to be interrogated? Tested as a seer?

Neeka disappeared into the sitting room and returned with a basket. As she lifted out a garment in midnight blue, she said, gently, <Perhaps we can find you a book on Vogel verbal innuendo.>

<I…> I blinked at her as I tried to sort through what she'd said. <Does getting better acquainted mean something… else?> I thought of Dag and how he'd just been "friendly" when he kissed me and tried to convince me to go to bed with him. My stomach clenched with sudden anxiety.

<Take off your sleeping tunic, my seer.>

I hesitated, then remembered Healer Kah's comments about her lack of interest in me, and pulled the fabric over my head, folded it, and set it on the end of the bed.

Neeka reached in the basket again and pulled out another piece of blue cloth, a shade lighter than the midnight blue, and handed it to me. I held it up to discover an undergarment, designed to cover my buttocks and sheath without interfering with my tail. I climbed out of bed and put it on.

<Neeka? What was the King implying when he said that?>

She helped me into the deep blue garment and settled it between my wings. It was a simple tunic, short at the back, ending just above my tail, and so long at the front I would have to be careful not to trip on it. Whenever I moved, it swirled around me, exposing a lot of my legs. A soft black leather belt with a pocket attached completed the outfit. I tucked the library key into the pocket.

<I could be wrong, Seer Tokka,> she said, turning to the basket and withdrawing a glass bottle of something that gleamed in the light, and a small, short-handled brush.

<Sit.> She pointed at the chair next to the writing table and I sat. She positioned herself at my feet and began to paint my claws a shining sky blue.

<What do you *think* he meant?> I held my foot very still so she could work.

<I believe he means to seduce you, my Seer.>

I almost jerked my foot away in surprise but managed to direct my agitation to my hands instead, twisting my fingers together until my knuckles ached.

Toe claws painted, Neeka pulled my hands apart and began to paint my finger claws with quick sure strokes of her brush.

<You're very pretty,> she said, laying my hand on my knee and picking up the other. She said it as if it were a simple fact. <And our King likes pretty things. Pretty boys, especially.>

<But I'm… I'm colorless and stunted and…>

She concentrated on her task until each nail was glossy blue, then laid my hand on my lap next to the other one. <Don't move until they dry.> She turned back to her basket.

<Your paleness is a novelty, and it marks you as a seer, something precious and rare. Our King likes unusual things, valuable things.> She studied the clay jar in her hands before looking at me. <And I wouldn't call you stunted, only small, and that… It makes you seem younger.>

<Oh,> I said. <*Ooooh.*> I felt a little sick.

Neeka straightened and had me tilt my head back while she applied a pink-tinted cream to my lips, then stepped back to look at her handiwork.

<They say our King is a generous lover. And skilled.>

<When he asked me if I knew what it meant to be seer to a monarch, did he mean that, too? That I would be required to share his bed?>

She shook her head. <I don't know. I know nothing of

how other monarchs treat their seers. But it does mean… It means you are *his*. You belong to him, so I suppose if he wants to take you to bed, then you haven't much choice.>

I stood and paced, suddenly too full of anxiety again to sit still. <Would he force me?>

She tucked her things back into the basket. <I don't believe so. But he will assume you will comply.>

"But I love Kiernan." I slipped back into Islish and she looked at my curiously.

"You have a beloved? He cannot be Vogel if you have never been to the Eyrie before. Is he Alfar?" Her Islish was smooth, with a pleasant hint of Voglish vowels.

"Sidhe. He's Sidhe." I paced across the room again. "He saved my life and he… he…" I stopped pacing. "The King said it is… that it tainted me to… to be with Kiernan." I met her eyes, expecting disgust. I saw only empathy.

"Not all Vogel think loving other peoples, bedding other peoples, is wrong. Many of us believe we are capable of choosing whom to love, or to sleep with, on our own, without outdated and meaningless laws to tell us what to do." She rearranged some of the things in the basket. "It is a point of contention between the royals and the lower classes. One point of many."

I studied my hands, turning them to see how the light caught the paint on my claws, then realized there was more to what she said than just a comment about love. "Is there much unrest among our people?"

"No." She shifted the basket in her grip, carried it to the bathing room door, and put it down just inside. "There is very little unrest, but considerable resentment." She paused, as if unsure what, or how much, it was safe to say, how much she could trust me. "As in other monarchies, sometimes the royals live richly at the expense of the common people."

She moved closer and adjusted the drape of the tunic over my shoulders and settled the belt more snugly around my waist. Then she moved behind me to gather my hair into a loose braid. "It will be a shame to cut this off." She worked slowly, carefully, and I wondered if this was what it was like to have a mother to care for you, except Neeka was a servant, and had no choice. Still, it felt nice. It felt like the way Kiernan would check to see my wings were comfortable when we curled up in bed together, or make sure to offer me a chair with enough room for my tail.

"In Vogel legends, in the fairytales we are told as children," Neeka said. "They say our people were not always ruled by kings. The Seers guided us, but it was the people, all of us, who made the laws and decided on policies. Only we haven't had seers for generations."

She finished the braid and moved back around me to arrange it over one shoulder. "Many of our people, especially those who live in the countryside, have been waiting for a seer to come and bring us a new future. They will look to you for that, to make all our lives better."

"I would if I knew how."

She smiled. "I believe you would." She touched my cheek gently, not a flirting gesture, but a comforting one. "Now you must spend the evening with our King. I believe he will understand if you don't succumb to his charms immediately, my Seer, but perhaps it is best not to remind him that you love a Sidhe man over your own King."

I took a deep breath and nodded.

<And remember to speak Vogel to him, Seer Tokka.> And with that, she ushered me to the door.

THE GUARDS OUTSIDE my rooms fell into step behind us as we came out, and I didn't know if they were there to keep me safe or to keep me from fleeing.

The way to the King's suite was short – putting him uncomfortably close – and too brief for me to formulate a plan of how to refuse him. When we arrived, my guards joined the King's guard to wait outside the door, while Neeka and I stepped into the waiting room after the King's attendant let us in in response to Neeka's polite knock.

The King himself opened the inner door, shutting it behind me, and leaving Neeka and his attendant in the waiting room. We were completely alone.

<My King.> I bowed my head.

<Seer Tokka. You look rested.> He led me farther into the room with a hand at my elbow. His sitting room was similar to mine, but the balcony looked out over the City Beneath and the space was larger. There was a huge desk covered in papers, and the upholstery was in brighter colors: red and oranges and yellows.

A variety of sizes and shapes of covered dishes filled a low table between two couches and my stomach rumbled at the delicious smells wafting out of them. I hadn't eaten since the dried meat and bread Kiernan and I had shared in the cave last night.

The King laughed at the sound and poured me something pale yellow out of a tall glass pitcher. I sipped cautiously.

<Apple wine,> said the King. Then he paced around me, and I felt like I was being inspected again. He brushed his fingers against the silken fabric of my tunic as he went, much too close to my sheath for comfort.

<The color suits you,> he said. <How is your wing?> He smoothed my feathers with one hand.

<Much better, my King.> I sipped the wine again to

distract myself from the heat that travelled from his touch to pool in my belly. I was suddenly very thirsty.

He laughed again when I gulped at the beverage and took it from my hand, setting it on a nearby table.

<Perhaps some water. As much as I would enjoy getting you drunk, I think tonight is not the time.>

<I'm sorry, my King.> I wasn't sure what I was apologizing for but I accepted the cup he handed me and drank deeply. The water was very cold and felt good on my throat.

<No need to apologize, little seer. But I expect you didn't drink much wine at your abbey?>

<No, my King. Only water and sometimes apple juice in the autumn.>

He touched my elbow and drew me closer to the couches. <Sit, little seer. Eat. You must be famished.>

I sat where he indicated and he sat on the couch opposite, mercifully leaving me alone. He lifted the covers off the dishes and told me what each one was, and I was so nervous I could only pick randomly at it, hardly tasting anything.

<Something is bothering you, Tokka.> I noticed he left my title off and wondered if it meant anything. He popped some kind of small red fruit into his mouth and watched my face.

Instead of answering, because I didn't know how without reminding him that I had recently had a non-Vogel lover, I tried one of the same fruits. I found it sweet, with just a pleasant hint of tartness. I quickly ate another and would have had a third, but the King put his hand on mine, twined his fingers together with mine, and rubbed his thumb over my knuckles.

<Tell me what concerns you.>

I hesitated a moment longer, then said, looking at our hands and not his face, <Only my friend, my King.>

<I see.> He lifted my hand to his mouth and kissed my knuckles gently, then let go. <My guards have seen no sign of him near the Eyrie or the City Beneath.> I looked up to meet his eyes and had to look quickly away again. He was obviously displeased with me. <Tomorrow I will send someone to the cliff where you were found, to see if they can determine where he went from there.>

<Thank you, my King.>

<I hope it won't wound you too deeply if we find he has left for his own lands, little seer. If he was bringing you to us, then he succeeded and has no more reason to linger.>

None, except that he loved me. *If* he loved me.

<I understand, my King.>

He looked at me a moment longer and I chose a slice of meat from a dish at random, to give my hands something to do. I put the food in my mouth to avoid blurting out that I didn't wish him to bed me, whether Kiernan came to the Eyrie or departed for Morven.

<You cannot keep him as your lover, little seer. It is forbidden, and even if it were not, it would be unseemly for you as Seer to this Monarchy to choose someone from another people over your own.>

I swallowed with difficulty and didn't look at him. <I know, my King.>

<Will you take the ritual bath with me? To cleanse you of him?>

The last thing I wanted was to cleanse myself of Kiernan. I very much wanted him all over me – his sweat, his saliva, his spunk. I wanted to be filthy with him for the rest of my life. But I couldn't say that to the King. And I couldn't *have* it, either. Not unless the world changed very much, very quickly.

<What does it require of me, my King?> I layered a slice of hard white cheese onto thin crisp biscuit and took a

tentative bite. It was delicious, and I couldn't help eating the rest quickly and trying a different cheese on a different biscuit. My appetite seemed to be shifting rapidly between uninterested in actually eating despite being ravenous, and determined to stuff in as much as I could whenever I forced myself to taste something.

<Try that cheese with the smoked trout.> The King made up a biscuit for me with his suggested items and held it out for me to taste. It was even more delicious, and I ate three before I realized I was eating directly out of his hand. I blushed and sat back on my couch.

<The ritual bath must take place in an ancient shrine deep within the caves.>

I swallowed and finally met his eyes. <Caves, my King?> My belly lurched, and I regretted eating so much cheese. Did the King know of the shrine to induce ecstatic visions, the sex shrine as Kier called it?

<Beneath the Eyrie, in the layers below ground are natural caves used by our ancestors for burials and worship and magic.>

I breathed a little easier. Of course a place so old, in a location so close to all three Realms, would have its own ancient shrine. And I was thankful I wouldn't have to go with the King to the shrine Kier and I had found; I could not imagine doing with the King what I had done with Kier and did not want to spoil that precious memory.

<One of those caves has a natural altar and a pool, and was once a shrine for ritual bathing, for purification before communing with the spirits our ancestors worshipped, before we came to the Goddess Above. I will take you there, and bathe you, cleanse you of any fey taint and you will be pure again.>

His soft, awed words reminded me of the Abbess as she

explained how my sacrifice would glorify the Lady of the Moon and the Alfar King. I shivered and hid it by reaching for my wine cup. This time, I sipped carefully. I had no more desire to be drunk than the King wanted to see me that way.

The King rose from his couch, skirted the table of food, and sat next to me, looking close into my eyes. I wanted to look away but felt trapped.

<Will you do this for me, little seer? Will you let me cleanse you, and free you to be our people's spiritual leader? Our salvation?>

He cupped my face with both hands. His skin was warm against mine, his eyes luminous.

I had to give him an answer, and I knew the only *safe* answer was exactly the one I wanted to avoid. So I said, <I will do what you require of me, my King.> I could live with that answer. I would do what I *had* to, but I didn't have to like it.

He didn't seem to notice my careful phrasing because he smiled. <Do your duty as my Seer, little one, and I will make sure you want for nothing.>

<Thank you, my King.>

He leaned forwards, tracing his fingers down my face, and brushed his lips against mine. I managed not to jerk away, but I knew he could feel my reluctance, my confusion. He ran his tongue over my lower lip and then sat back, taking one of my hands between both of his and tracing the shapes of my fingers.

<My King, I…>

<You are new here, and afraid. I can see that. I won't hurt you, little seer.>

<I know, my King.> I looked down at where his hands held mine.

<I can make you very happy.>

<I know that also, my King.> I bit the inside of my mouth

then turned my hand over in his, so it lay palm up and he traced the lines there with his fingers, making my skin tingle. I didn't want to give in to him, but I had to give him *something*.

I wanted Kiernan, desperately, with everything I was. But if I couldn't have Kiernan – and it seemed apparent I couldn't – could I, maybe, accept my King instead? He was handsome and had been gentle and understanding with me so far. If only he would give me more time to grieve.

<You still miss your little Sidhe bedwarmer.> He lifted my hand to his mouth to trace the lines of my palm with his tongue. <If you let me, I can help you forget him.>

It was difficult to breathe, and I was too hot, even in the thin tunic I wore. I wanted to walk outside in the night air and not think about any of this for a while. Perhaps Neeka would take me to the library on the way back to my rooms, to find a book I could be lost in.

<I know you will, my King.>

When he lifted his mouth from my palm, I touched his cheekbone with my free hand and he held very still while I traced the shape of his face, watching me, studying my eyes. He was so different from Kiernan. But Kier himself had said different didn't mean bad. And if I couldn't have Kier, I wanted someone different from him, as different as possible to keep my memories of him clear and fresh.

<I only need some time,> I said, my voice hardly above a whisper. <I need to know if he has abandoned me.>

<And if he has not?> The King continued to sit still as I ran my fingers over his face, and he didn't try to take my hand again when I placed it with the other in my lap.

<I do not know, my King.>

<Then let us see what my guards can learn in the morning. We will dine again in the evening, and perhaps I can do more than kiss you.>

<Perhaps, my King.>

When he leaned over to kiss me again, I started to pull away and he put his hand behind my head to prevent me. He was so careful, so gentle, his lips pressing softly on mine, his tongue probing almost tentatively, that I relaxed, and my mouth opened almost of its own accord to let him in.

I might not have stopped him, then, if he had continued to press me. But he sat back and smiled.

<Good night, my Seer.> And he stood and made his way into the next room, leaving me to find my own way out.

26
Kiernan

I LISTENED TO THE VOGEL couple's footsteps fade behind me as they made their way back to the beach. The day was drawing to a close and I was hungry, but eating either meant going back to the estuary for my gear or foraging in the woods, and I didn't want to take time for either. I ate a handful of early, and deliciously tart, berries from a nearby bush and then ignored my grumbling belly.

I would just have to wait until I reached the city. I still had a few coins in my pocket that miraculously hadn't fallen out. After that, I would decide what to do.

I moved carefully down the hill, knowing that a mossy slope could become a wild ride with one incautious step, and crossed a narrow boulder-filled ravine. I could hear water in the bottom of it, somewhere below the huge rocks that had tumbled from the cliff above, but it was too far down under too-heavy stone for me to reach, and sounded too small for fish, anyway.

The cliff was not as sheer here as it was closer to the beach where ruins clung to the sides. I peered upwards and could only see crevices and overhangs and trees. If there were ancient dwellings this far back from the sea, they were invisible from below.

The triple-trunked tree that the Vogel had called the Dancing Dryads was bigger than it had looked from the top of the hill. It had reddish bark that peeled away to reveal smooth, pale underbark not so different in appearance from skin. I laid a hand on it and it was warm from the sun and I would not have been surprised if an actual dryad smacked my hand away for being too familiar.

Every branch within reach of a tall Vogel was covered in offerings of homespun cloth, richly dyed and cleverly woven. From far away, I had thought the cloths were strips of fabric cut from a larger piece, like I had seen on offering trees in the human lands near Morven. Instead, every one appeared to have been woven to a specific width as if they had been intended as offerings from the moment the Vogel who left them had begun to make them.

The whole lot was like a catalogue of different weaving patterns, and I wondered if there was some significance to them, like one pattern for healing and another for good crops, or if they were simply chosen because they looked pleasing. Fionn would have loved to see this, and I imagined him examining each cloth to see how it had been made. I promised myself I would bring him here someday, if I could.

Among the woven bands were also lengths of bright braided wool and linen yarn tied with crystals of many colors, and with trinkets of wood and metal, ceramic and bone, shell and antler. I looked for longer than I should have, finding a deep joy in contemplating the heartfelt offerings of ordinary people. And I wished I had something to leave.

I stuck my hands in my pockets, thinking maybe one of

the coins would do, and found a key. It was not the key I had taken with me into the Abbey, that unlocked all the doors of Fionn's tower. Instead, it was Fionn's own key, that opened his sitting room and bedroom doors, and which I had stuffed in my pocket when preparing to leave so I could lock the doors behind me.

I held it up. It was tarnished and I had no way to polish it, but perhaps it would be enough. I tore a thin strip of green cloth from the bottom of my shirt, threaded it through the end of the key, and laid my hand on the tree again.

Fionn would have known the right words to say, which things were appropriate when approaching unknown spirits. I stood for a moment in silence, feeling the bark cool as the afternoon drew on and the sun slipped away behind the cliff. Finally, I reached up as high as I could and tied the key to a branch. It swung on the end of its cloth as I let go.

"Please keep him safe, spirits," I said. "And if it is in your power to let me see him again, so I can tell him..." I rested one palm against each of the two farthest trunks and tipped my forehead to press against the third. "Please let me have the chance to tell him I love him."

I had no way to know if they had heard me, or if they cared. And why would spirits honored by bird folk a thousand years ago care about one half-fey who happened by? But they *had* heard me – or heard Fionn at least – in the shrine beneath the hill. Maybe... But I didn't want to hope too much.

I stepped back and looked up into the decorated branches one more time and then walked away, heading to the cliff to the right of the tree to where the straight, narrow cleft split the face from bottom to top. It was no narrower than the tightest passage in the cave had been, so I stepped in and slid between walls of rock and felt the temperature drop because little sunlight would have touched here all day.

For the first while, there were no left or right passages, tunnels, or turnings to get lost in, and soon the cleft opened up enough that I could walk comfortably.

The old Vogel man hadn't said how deep into the rock this passage went, but presumably it would be less than half the thickness of the crag that held the Eyrie, because I still had to climb up, and then back down another cleft on the other side. It *felt* deep, though.

The first side passage opened on my right and it was easy to walk by, knowing it was a dead end. The bird woman should have told me they were all dead ends if she had truly wanted me to keep straight on. Another passage opened to my left and it was harder to just walk by. Some of those left-hand passages – or perhaps only one; I wasn't clear on that – lead to caves beneath the Eyrie. And some – or one – of those caves connected to the ruins of the ancient Vogel city itself.

I sternly reminded myself of the woman's warnings about getting lost and wandering forever, and continued on straight into the cliff.

The second left-hand passage was blocked by fallen rock and easy to ignore, but the third… I could see ahead to where the straight passage met a wall of rock that looked like it was made of handholds. It would be an easy climb.

But the passage to the left was a low cave entrance, half obscured by ferns and dripping warm water, as if it had come from a distant hot spring. I stared into it and even sent a wisplight in, finding myself unable to move past. Finally, I knelt on the ground and pressed both palms to the rocky floor of the cleft. I breathed deep, closed my eyes, and reached out for magic… and was almost knocked on my ass by the strength of what came to my asking.

I should not have been surprised; the Eyrie was a place where all three sacred Realms met and touched, and this spot was not far from that ancient place. I breathed slowly, and let the magic of land, sea, and sky flow through me for a few heartbeats, before slowly withdrawing. Pulling on too much magic too quickly – even with years of training – was the quickest way to burn oneself hollow, as I had nearly experienced personally.

I opened my eyes, hoping that touching magic would let me see the rock around me in different light. I felt for my connection to Fionn, still so strange and inexplicable, but also welcome because I could sense, distant and vague, his warmth, his emotions. And then I saw it, faintly, like a silver thread running away from me and into the dark of the cave. I knew it wasn't truly leading me that way, because it also led steeply upwards; it was only showing me which direction Fionn was in, relative to where I was. If I could have followed it directly, it would lead to him, but since I couldn't climb through air or wriggle through solid rock, it wasn't really much of a guide.

Still, I couldn't help but take that tenuous little thread of light as a sign that maybe my path didn't lead to the City Beneath the Cliff after all, but instead ran through the city of ancient bird folk. And I thought of the Vogel woman's warning again, and how stupid it would be to do exactly what she had warned me against.

"Fuck," I said. I sent my wisplight farther into the cave, until it illuminated a wall of pale stone, and a squat pillar, formed drip by slow drip in some far-past time. Like the pillars in the huge cave under the hill that had formed a path to the hot spring and the shrine, this one had a hollow top as if meant to hold fuel.

I stood up, brushing dirt off my hands onto my trousers – not that it made my hands any cleaner or my trousers any grimier – and walked into the cave. I only had to duck my head a little. There was sticky residue on the bottom of the pillar's hollow and when I summoned a flame, it caught and burned bright. Farther in, just within the circle of light it cast, was a second pillar. As I reached it, the flame from the first flickered and died.

Was this the path the ancient Vogel followed to lay their dead to rest deep under the Eyrie? There was always the chance that this path only led to a long-lost charnel house, a mausoleum for bird folk, and didn't connect to the other caves under the Eyrie at all. But surely those who lived in the Eyrie had brought their dead by a more direct path, leaving this back entrance to the peasants?

There was, of course, only one way to find out, and now that I had found signs of the long-gone Vogel I couldn't just turn around and leave. I only wished I had Fionn with me. This was *his* inheritance, not mine.

"Stay here, little friends," I said to Smoke and Flame. They grumbled but slipped off my shoulders and into the air. "If I don't come back out, go find Fionn."

We wait.

We find.

I summoned a flame again and lit the second lantern and saw a third just within the circle of light. And so I advanced slowly into the caves, one lantern at a time. At first, there was only a single path, but after the ninth lantern, more passages opened up and I was forced to choose.

I left a wisplight hovering over that ninth lantern and took a few steps down each of the other cave openings. Though I had never spent a lot of time underground, I had heard it was easy to get turned around, no matter how good your sense of direction above ground.

I determined quickly that the lanterns only followed a single path, which seemed just a little larger and a little smoother-floored than the others. That only meant it was a main route – the path to the resting place of the dead, perhaps, or to some other place of worship. It didn't mean the path connected to the Eyrie.

But if I was correct in my assumption that there would be a more direct route from anywhere important to the ancient city itself, which fit with everything I knew about cities and nobles and rituals, then this was the best path to follow.

At least if I kept following the lanterns, I was much less likely to get lost and end up wandering around in the dark until I expired. My stomach rumbled and I spared a thought for the half loaf of Moira's bread and the piece of hard, sharp cheese I had left behind with my cloak and other gear. There had been apples, too, small deep green ones that Fionn found too tart but kept taking bites from anyway, because he knew I loved them and would steal those bites out of his mouth with my lips and tongue.

I carried on and decided not to light any more lanterns in case I chanced upon someone else in the caves. Eventually, faint markings began to appear on the walls where more passages joined the main one, and the floor of the cave dropped more quickly, leading me far underground.

The marks were pictures of bird folk, as far as I could tell, but so damaged by moisture and time that I couldn't tell what they meant to depict. At least they told me I was getting somewhere, even if I still had no idea where that somewhere was.

And then, finally, the space opened up. The cavern I stepped into wasn't anywhere as grand as the one Fionn and I had found under the hill, but it was still very large. The walls had been worked into terraces and alcoves and shelves, and I realized suddenly that I was looking at the place where the ancient Vogel had brought their dead.

I knelt where I stood and bowed my head. I didn't see any

skeletons or offerings or any other signs that the cavern had been used, but it was damp enough that any remains would have crumbled into nothing. The people who had honored their departed loved ones here had lived so long ago they had left no traces besides the lanterns and the paintings.

"Blessed dead," I said softly. "May you find peace in whatever afterlife you dwell in." I hoped a modified version of Sidhe prayer to the departed would be acceptable to any spirits that might linger here. I felt a breeze pass over my skin and shivered. Then I stood and quickly crossed the floor. The only exits from the cavern that I could see were three openings directly across from where I'd entered.

I had felt sure I had made the right choice in following the lanterns this far, but now I didn't have such a clear option. All three openings were about the same size, and each had a stone lantern just inside it. As if conjured from a fairy tale, one passage slanted slightly upwards, one went straight and level, and one slanted downward.

The Eyrie itself was up from here, of course, but that didn't mean the upward-sloping cave was the quickest route there, or that it went there at all. I took a step into that one first, anyway, looking for clues about where it led. There were traces of paintings and something that I was sure must be writing – a row of symbols that could have deep meaning but only looked like bird tracks to me.

Next, I stepped into the level passage and found much the same. Traces of pictures and writing – a different combination of glyphs from the other passage – and no way for me to interpret them, even if they had been intact.

The third passage, the one that led downwards, also had writing and images, faded and crumbling. But it had one thing the others had not. It had a thin trickle of water running down from a crack in the wall that had made a little channel in the floor of the cave. I knelt and dipped my fingers in. It was warm, almost hot, and had that peculiar feel on the skin of water heavy with minerals.

There was nothing else to tell me which path to follow, but at least this one would give me an extra trail to follow back if I got turned around. Following where the hot water took me was better than choosing completely randomly.

Before I took more than a few steps I paused, touched my magic, and felt for Fionn. The silver thread was still there, shimmering in the near-dark, leading sharply up and into the wall.

I reached out and passed my fingers through it and felt them tingle. I wondered if he could sense me here, too. Or would he need to consciously search for me with his thoughts? Would he even believe I would follow him, or would he have assumed I'd headed back to Morven now that he was safely delivered to the Eyrie?

I shook my head and let the connection fade. I thought I could sense confusion, but was that his or only my own?

With nothing to do but go on, I walked ahead. The floor of the passage was even except for the little water channel, and it reminded me so much of the cave behind the otter den that I almost expected to turn and find Fionn walking behind me.

After a long stretch of heading nearly straight, sloping evenly downwards with only slight bends, the passage began to curve, then slant upwards. The trickle of water pooled and spread and vanished into a hole in the floor. When the passage dropped again, the water reappeared through a crack, and ran on it its little channel. Side passages appeared more and more frequently, some leading up and some down, and some even at head-height and going who knew where. I kept on following the little stream of hot water.

When I got thirsty, I stopped, cupped some of the water

in my hands, and sipped. I expected it to be bitter-tasting or metallic from the minerals, but it was almost sweet. I drained my cupped hands and scooped up more. At least I wouldn't die of thirst.

I noticed, too, that my damaged finger felt a little better after dipping it in the stream, so I splashed some on my nose and my cheek where the Vogel guard had hit me.

And then, as I was passing yet another side passage, I heard voices. They were indistinct, far away, but definitely not my imagination. I couldn't be sure, with the way sound echoed in the cave, but they seemed to be from somewhere ahead. I banished all my wisplights but one and, hoping I wouldn't regret it later, I took off my boots and continued, barefoot and silent. The one wisplight I let die back to almost nothing, keeping just enough faint blue light that I could see. To a daylight-eyed person, it would have been invisible.

I crept along the passage, listening, and the voices came again, closer. Two men, speaking Vogel. The passage opened into a small cavern, terraced like the mausoleum, but decorated with ornate carvings on each level. Perhaps it was where royalty was laid to rest? I caught the scent of burning candles and saw their faint flicker from an opening across and to my right.

My wisplight winked out beneath my palm and I went still. One man spoke, his voice deep and commanding, then another, lighter and maybe not a man's at all. I wished I had thought to study the bird folk's language, but it had never seemed necessary. The Vogel were too insular to invite visitors and when they – rarely – sent out envoys, they spoke perfect Islish.

I crept slowly, silently, closer until I was hidden behind a rock formation near to the passage where I could see faint light.

I waited, and the light grew stronger, and two men left the passage, one carrying a candelabrum with nine slender beeswax tapers. It was the lighter-voiced person who carried the candles, and they seemed to be lighting the way for the other.

The deep-voiced man was a striking figure, so tall I would look like a child next to him – even Fionn would look small – with midnight-blue hair and blue-and-green wings so big he had to hold them above his shoulders so they wouldn't drag on the ground. He wore purple and gold, and a thin gold circlet on his head glinted in the candlelight. His face was sharp and strong and handsome with a touch of superiority.

What was the Vogel King doing so far underground? Because the tall man couldn't be anyone else. He spoke to the other person, and it sounded like he was giving instructions. Of course, I had no idea for what, but one word caught my ear, a word I recognized. Tokka. Silver. Were they talking about Fionn or was it a more mundane conversation and they were discussing who to employ to polish their silverware?

They paused in the entrance to the cavern, then turned and took another passage out and away.

I almost called shadows around me and scurried after, because no doubt they were headed back up to the Eyrie and it might be my only chance to find the way there. But I was curious about the cavern they had come from, and only partly because the little stream of hot water I had followed this far ran directly across the cavern and through that passage.

So I waited for the footsteps and the voices to fade and then I waited some more. It must have been deep night by then. Finally, I got up and called a wisplight, keeping it dim just in case they came back, and I entered the cave. A long, low passage led inwards, and it looked as if it once had ended in a spot a bird man would have to slither on his belly to pass, but which had been crudely broken through with chisels and hammers. I wondered if the Vogel King had done it, or if he had found it that way.

I paused and knelt, because somehow it felt right to approach this place as a supplicant. Then I stood and took the last few steps. It was a shrine, more like the one I knew from Morven than the one Fionn and I had found, but there was no doubt it was the same sort of place.

There was a pool, to which the little stream ran, but it was smaller and deeper than the one under the hill, and devoid of the fish that swam in Morven. It looked like it might be for immersing oneself in before a ritual. Beyond the pool was a large slab of stone, like a row of squat pillars had grown together to form a long, narrow, flat-topped altar.

I looked up to see a ceiling painted like the night sky full of stars, with a bird seer flying, but it was too damaged to make out anything more than that. I tried to remember if the ceiling of the cave in Morven Forest was painted but had no image of it in my memory.

I walked around the pool, resisting the temptation to strip off and bathe. It *felt* like it would be okay, but I didn't want to offend whatever spirits might be here if it wasn't.

The altar, if that's what it was, was unadorned, looking exactly as it if had formed naturally, which it probably had. Beyond it, there were places on the floor with drips of candle wax, like someone had placed candles all around the cavern and hadn't cleaned up after.

Aside from that, there was nothing. I went back to the altar and placed a hand on it.

"What is this place?" I said softly and my palm tingled, not unpleasantly. I was not far from a mausoleum; could this be a place for cleansing and purifying the dead before taking them to their final resting place? It seemed likely, and I was suddenly glad I hadn't decided to take a bath.

I had the odd notion that it might be nice to lie down on the altar and sleep, suddenly followed by the thought that the spirits might be inviting *me* to my eternal rest. I stepped back.

"Thank you, but I'm not ready to go yet. Perhaps when I am, I'll return here." I glanced up at the painted ceiling and then made my way back around the pool. I felt at peace and knew it would end once I stepped back into the passage outside, but this was a place for the dead and their spiritual guides, not for me.

I left the cavern shrine and headed for the tunnel the King and his companion had taken to see where they would lead me.

27
Fionn

THE MORNING BROUGHT a new kind of dread. I was awakened early by Neeka, bathed, dressed, made up, and perfumed until I hardly recognized myself in the mirror.

Only the too-big eyes and the anxiety I couldn't seem to hide looked like mine. My cheeks had color, my face was surrounded by bright feathers, and my clothes swirled around me with every movement.

<I'm told the King is consulting with his favorite feather-worker to see if they can add to your wings and tail,> Neeka said as she smoothed my feathers with scented oil to make them sleek and shiny.

I felt a surge of dismay – that such a thing was necessary – and anticipation – that perhaps I might fly under my own power. She saw my look in the mirror as she adjusted the feathers around my face. Later they would be fixed permanently – only coming out when I molted – but for now they were made as a sort of mask that surrounded my face instead of covering it.

<They will only be decorative, Seer Tokka,> she said gently. <You won't be able to fly.>

My heart fell and I didn't know how to reply. What was one more disappointment, after all? Instead, I touched the feathers around my face. I had stayed up much too late studying the book on facial adornments.

<This one says I belong to the King,> I said, unable to keep the hardness out of my voice. I didn't like the idea of belonging to anyone. Even Kiernan had told Dag I wasn't *his*, I was my own.

I traced the elaborate feather in the middle. It was deep blues and greens and purples. The King's colors. Neeka had a similar, smaller one that showed that she, too, belonged to the King's household.

<And these,> my fingers brushed the next feather, <That I am unavailable for attachment.> That hurt to say, too, because what it really meant was that the King had claimed me and had forbidden anyone else from even considering me as a partner – of the bedding sort or the marrying sort.

<No children,> I said, touching the next feather. <And these ones…> I ran my fingers over the next few and frowned. <They should say I prefer men, but I don't know *what* they mean.>

Neeka straightened my tunic unnecessarily. <They're… well… blank.>

I frowned deeper.

<It means your preferences are private,> she said. <It's not a common signifier, but not unheard of.> She fiddled with the elaborate braided mass she had made of my hair. <It's usually used by those who prefer no one at all.>

<I see.> So it was the King asserting his claim on me, yet again.

<He will keep you safe,> Neeka said, understanding how

I felt without me having to say. <And provide you with everything you need or want.>

<Everything except the most important thing.>

She squeezed my hand. <Hold your beloved in your heart, my Seer. There he is yours and nothing can touch him.>

I blinked away the tears that wanted to come. I needed to be stronger, and if I cried now, I would undo all the careful work Neeka had done on my face, and we would be late to meet the King.

I refused breakfast, too nervous to eat, and followed as Neeka led me from my rooms and the guards stepped into place behind us, and we entered the bustle of the main part of the palace.

She moved swiftly behind me as we came around a corner, and how she knew I couldn't guess, but there was the King, waiting. I had thought he would meet us at the council chamber, but it seemed I was wrong.

<You look glorious, little seer,> he said, stepping forward to tuck my arm into his.

<Thank you, my King.> I kept my chin up and met his eyes with a calm I didn't feel. I would have to forge myself into a proper royal seer, to make Seer Tokka fearless and placid and as full of authority as mere Fionn had been full of uncertainty, and anxious, and afraid.

He smiled. <Growing bolder, I see.> He led me down another corridor to a stairway as his attendant and his guards took their places behind us. <I hope you will still be the timid boy you were in private.>

<I will be everything you require, my King.>

He frowned, just a slight crease between his brows and a downturn at the very corner of his lips, as if he could sense the tiny defiance in my choice of words. <Don't grow too regal, little seer. Your people need spiritual guidance. They need to

feel you are on their side.>

<Of course, my King.> It would not be hard to seem to be on the side of the ordinary people, because I *was*. I would do this, I would become the seer I was meant to be not for the King, but for the common Vogel.

For a moment, as we approached the door to the council chamber, I forgot how to breathe. It didn't feel like fear, though, it felt like… almost like elation and anticipation and love, deep in my belly. I would do this. I *could* do this. Even though I missed Kier like a stab to the heart.

The council chamber was much smaller than I had expected. I suppose I had been imagining something grand, something made for showing off the strength of the Monarchy. Instead, it was a more intimate, private setting for a small group of men – for the Councilors were indeed all men – to discuss the workings and direction of an entire kingdom and its people.

There was a large window looking over the City Beneath the Cliff, but no balcony, and a large oval table of gleaming wood that I wanted to run my hands over, it looked so smooth and satiny. A very large chair occupied one end of the table, dominating the room, and smaller but still very ornate chairs with plush seats were placed evenly around. All but the King's were occupied. Around the perimeter of the room, attendants waited on foot in case they were needed.

Almost as one, the Councilors rose from their chairs and bowed their heads, and the attendants dropped to one knee.

<My King,> they all said.

The King kept my arm tucked in his as he made his way to the head of the table and his chair. Once he was seated, the Councilors sat, too, and the attendants rose to stand against the wall, heads bowed.

I was left to stand alone, next to the King's chair, feeling utterly lost but determined not to let it show.

I felt the gentle brush of Neeka's fingers on the tip of my wing as she took her place against the wall, and it gave me the courage to keep my chin up and meet the eyes of each Councilor in turn. Councilor Rocsh gave me the barest nod as I met his gaze, and that gave me courage, too.

<Esteemed Councilors,> the King said and all eyes turned to him except mine; I looked straight ahead. <I am very pleased to present to you our long-lost Seer, Tokka tanKarshanka.> The way the King named me used the ancient word for the Eyrie, "Karshanka," which meant "cliff of the shining city." In effect, he was naming me Tokka of the Eyrie.

The Councilors all murmured quiet words of welcome and I bowed my head to acknowledge them.

<He has, owing to his upbringing, little knowledge of the requirements of a seer, but he is a quick study, and I have no doubt he will make us all proud.> I saw movement in the corner of my eye as the King turned to look at me. I kept my focus in front of me.

<A tutor is on their way, my King, my Seer,> said Rocsh.

The King only nodded to show he had heard.

<He is rather… small,> said a Councilor with extravagant facial adornments that told me he was married with twelve children. His feathers were shades of red and pink and his hair a deep garnet. <How old is he? Should we not keep him a little more… sheltered until he comes of age?>

Councilor Rocsh snorted and put an elegant hand over his mouth to cover his laughter. Now that I knew a little more about how to read feathers, I knew he was unmarried and not seeking a partner. The feathers that symbolized his sex were smaller than I had seen on others – the pink and red Councilor's were huge – and I wondered what significance their size had.

<Seer Tokka was thirty-three this solstice past,> Rocsh said.

<Then why is he so small?> asked another Councilor with feathers and hair an unfortunate shade of green.

Before anyone could answer for me, I spoke, keeping all emotion out of my voice and speaking as though I were simply stating facts. <I was born traumatically.> I met the green Councilor's eyes and he dropped his gaze to the tabletop in front of him. <I was still in the egg when I was cut from my mother's body and might have died there.> I let my gaze drift around the table again and they all looked quickly away except Councilor Rocsh, who hid a smile.

<I did not die,> I said. <But I was left small, stunted. But I assure you I *am* a seer. I have visions and healing magic and once I am properly trained, I will be perfectly adequate as our people's spiritual guide.>

<Well said.> The speaker was the one Councilor save Rosch who had – almost – held my eyes until I looked away. His feathers were so dark a green it was almost black, but his hair was deep blue and his eyes a soft brown.

I met his look again and he dipped his chin slightly. <It is unfortunate you have such small wings, my Seer,> he said, and I thought I detected genuine empathy in his voice.

<I'm having my feather-worker attend to that,> the King said. <He will still have to rely on his guards to get anywhere requiring flight, but I would not have him unattended at any time, anyway.>

They continued to discuss me for a little while longer, but eventually the talk turned to other things, like the upcoming harvest and how best to organize tithes that would improve on last year's methods. I paid attention as best I could, because I thought anything affecting my people should be my business, but it was difficult to stay focused because I knew so little about the politics of the Eyrie and the Vogel Monarchy.

Eventually, the King declared it was time for lunch, stood, took my arm again, and led me from the room. The guards who waited for us were not the same ones who had been there when we went in, and I hoped the others had had a chance to get breakfast.

<So, little seer, how did you like your first taste of government?>

<I understood very little. Is there a – >

He cut me off with a laugh. <I'm sure the library has many suitable books to help you learn.>

<Thank you, my King. When do I meet my people?>

<You just did.> He looked at me sidelong, a slight smile tugging at his mouth.

<I mean the common folk.> I turned and watched his profile, but his expression gave little away.

<Soon. We'll have your wings augmented first. And your hair cut. And you must first keep your promise to me. Then I will call an assembly Beneath and present you to whomever shows up to see you.>

<My promise, my King?>

<The ritual cleansing bath.>

<Yes, of course.> I looked at the floor. <May I walk in the City, my King? Once I am presented to my people?>

<We'll see,> he said, and drew me with him when I started to turn the corner to the corridor where my rooms were. <Have lunch with me.>

All I wanted to do was sit and think, to rest and study the feather book again, but I belonged to my King, and knew I didn't really have a choice.

<Of course, my King.>

Once we were inside his rooms, guards and attendants shut out, he dropped my arm, but turned me to face him with his hands on my shoulders when I would have sat on the couch in front of the low table of covered dishes.

<You did well, little seer.> His fingers held my shoulders tightly.

<Thank you, my King.>

<In these rooms, you may call me Sarkot.>

<I'm not sure I feel comfortable with that, my King. Perhaps when I know you better.>

<And if I order you?>

<Then I must obey.>

He snorted. <King Sarkot, then. Can you manage that much?>

<Yes, my… King Sarkot.>

<Good boy.>

I thought he would let go of me then but instead he stepped closer and moved one hand to my face, tilting it up to look at him as he gazed down at me.

<Little Tokka,> he said, and his voice dropped deeper, turned rougher. He pulled the temporary feathers from around my face and tossed the mask to the couch. <I do like seeing my feathers on you, but for today, I want you as I first saw you.>

<My king?>

He frowned.

<Sarkot,> I amended.

<Go wash this makeup off and take down your hair. This evening I'll send someone to cut it, but right now I want it long and loose.>

<Yes, King Sarkot.> He let go of me and I went through his bedroom, where I saw the sheets on his huge bed were rumpled and unmade and hoped he preferred them that way, and that no one would be disciplined for failing to tidy them.

His bathing room was even larger and more elaborate

than mine, with a central bath that could have held the entire Council and still had room. I went to his sink and washed my face, scrubbing away Neeka's hard work with the King's floral-scented soap.

When I was pale and colorless again, I raised my hands to my hair but could only get it half undone. It was simply too complicated an arrangement to manage by myself.

I bit my lip and smoothed my face into something blank, hiding my confusion and trepidation. Then I went back into the King's sitting room to find him sprawled on a couch in only his undergarment, eating cheese and fruit from a platter.

<I'm sorry, my King. I couldn't manage all the pins.> I gestured to my hair and tried to ignore his bare torso. He was golden and sculpted with long, lean muscle, and I didn't want to find him attractive, but I did. I supposed that would make it easier to give in to him, as I would have to do, but I didn't want to want him.

<Let me.> He stood and gestured for me to sit, then stepped behind me and began to work at the pins and braids until I felt my hair slip free from its confinement and drape around my shoulders. <You are magnificent, little seer.> His voice was husky. He buried his hands in my hair, and I felt his breath on my scalp as he bent his face close.

<King Sarkot,> I said, as he moved his hands from my hair to my shoulders, finding the clasps of my tunic and undoing them, so the garment fell to my waist. <Do you intend to take me to your bed?> I couldn't keep the slight tremor out of my voice.

He stroked his palms down my shoulders, onto my chest and lower, searching for my belt clasp.

<It's either that or take you right here,> he said.

For a moment I couldn't breathe, even though I had already known what his answer was going to be, if not the exact words. Even though I had known since yesterday that I would, sooner or later, have to give in to him.

<Your bed would be more comfortable, my King,> I said. I didn't move to help him, but nor did I try to stop him from unclasping my belt.

I felt his mouth on my neck and shivered. I was terrified, attracted, and repulsed, all at once. I was confused and wanted Kiernan to rescue me again, as he had from Dag, but he wasn't here, might never be here.

<But first, King Sarkot.> This time I couldn't keep the hesitation from my voice.

He straightened up behind me and moved his hands back to my shoulders. <You wish to know what my guards found at the cliff in Aven Forest.>

<Yes, my King.>

He pulled me to my feet gently and my tunic slid down my legs to pool on the floor. His eyes seemed to devour me for several long heartbeats. Then he met my eyes and his burned. I had to work hard not to look away, not to bite my lip like an uncertain child.

<It seems he descended the cliff and travelled to a small human settlement along the river.>

Hope bloomed in my gut, and I struggled to keep it hidden, to not let it show in my eyes.

<My guards spoke to the humans.> Regret touched his face, and I felt my hope begin to shrivel. <He begged supplies from them, and then turned north, heading for Morven.>

And disappointment crushed hope entirely. I willed away the tears that wanted to come, to cascade from my eyes and drown me.

<My guards tracked him as far as the road to the Abbey of the Moon, where his trail vanished into the forest.>

<I see. Thank you, my King, for sending them.> I wanted

more than anything to go back to my rooms to lose myself in sorrow and heartache, but that was not an option.

The King stroked the side of my face and something that might have been genuine sadness touched his face and was gone.

<Let me help you forget him,> he said, his voice low and urgent.

<Is it appropriate, my King?> I was determined to try one more time to put him off, if only for a day. <Before I am purified?>

He moved closer until our skin touched. His was hot and seemed to spread its heat into a flush on my own skin.

<We will take the cleansing bath together,> he said. <Tomorrow night, after your hair is cut and your new feathers attached.>

And with that my last hope at avoiding my fate was gone. Kiernan had said he refused to believe in destiny, but I didn't see any way to get out of mine.

<Yes, King Sarkot.> I didn't pull away when he pressed his lips to mine and felt for the tie holding my undergarment on.

I tried to turn off conscious thought, to just let my body react for me so I didn't have to think about what I was doing, about how the King was not Kiernan. I let him lead me into his bedroom and lay me down on the huge, sheet-rumpled bed.

<Are you still afraid of me, little seer?> he murmured into the skin of my neck.

<I am inexperienced,> I said.

<So your lover only had you once then?> He nuzzled my collarbone and slid a hand down my ribs to my hip. I didn't answer and he must have taken it for an embarrassed affirmative. <I will teach you, little seer,> he said, then sat up, straddling my legs so I couldn't have moved if I'd wanted to.

He looked down at me, studying me again. <So pretty and so young.> His voice was husky with desire, and I felt my breathing quicken. He leaned forward and placed both palms on my chest, stroked them slowly down and over my belly to linger at my sheath.

I was finding it hard to breathe and tried to keep myself detached, as if I was watching the King seduce someone else. I didn't want this, I wanted Kiernan, but my body responded with desire anyway. When the King dug his fingers into my seam and pried open my sheath, I closed my eyes. I didn't like how he rushed me, instead of waiting, like Kier would have done, for my erection to come out on its own. But I didn't need to see to know I was hard, that my manhood craved the King's touch even if I did not.

<Goddess Above, my Seer. You aren't so little after all.> My eyes snapped open in shock to see him staring down at me. He stroked my hardness with just his fingertips, and I gasped involuntarily. Then I looked where he was looking and saw my erection was as big as his was, even though I was a head shorter and more lightly built.

<Roll over, little seer,> he said, and I wondered if it was just that he was ready to fuck me, or if he didn't want to see the evidence that I wasn't the young boy he wanted me to be.

I rolled over and hid my face in a pillow. I almost cried out when he spread me open and pushed into me without asking to see if I was ready. Even aroused as I was, I *wasn't* ready, and it hurt. It burned and ached much more than when Kiernan took my virginity, because Kier had been slow and gentle, and I had been so turned on nothing he did to me could have been anything but pleasurable.

The King gripped my hips, his claws digging into the muscle, and with each thrust it hurt a little less and my body wanted him more. I tried to think of Kier, to imagine it was him fucking me, but the King felt too different and then it didn't matter anymore, because he was stroking me and I couldn't keep back my moans as he brought me to orgasm and I pulsed onto his bedsheets just as I felt him pulse inside me. He came in three rapid pulses, but mine were slower and he seemed almost impatient, letting go of me as soon as I gasped at my third and spurted onto his sheets again.

It was a good thing, I supposed, that he assumed I would only have three, because I was spared the embarrassment of having to tell him I was done.

<There, little seer. You see, I am not a monster.> He sounded amused. He sat up and stretched.

<Yes, my King.> I wondered if I should move away from the wet patch I'd made on the bed, or if that would be rude. How soon could I get up and dress and flee to my rooms?

He ran a hand down my back and looked at me fondly. <I think I like you inexperienced. You tremble so nicely, and your ass is so tight I could orgasm just by looking at it.>

I felt a deep flush up my neck, but it was shame, not heat at his teasing. <My King.>

He patted my tail where it spread over my buttocks. <Now go wash and dress and eat something before you go.> He stood up. <I need a long hot soak in the bath.>

28
Kiernan

THE TIME I'D SPENT in the death shrine and the longer legs of the bird folk meant the Vogel King and his companion were long gone when I entered the passage.

I kept my wisplight just bright enough to see and walked cautiously anyway, keeping my magic close in case I needed to ask the shadows for concealment at short notice.

This passage was marked by squat stone lantern-pillars just like the other had been, and its side passages were all narrow and damp, with undisturbed lichens growing on their walls and floors. It was the first time I'd seen anything growing in the caves and it made me wonder if these passages saw light at times, because I didn't think even the hardiest lichens could grow in total darkness. Unless they were magical. I didn't take the time to find out, I just moved quickly and silently, relieved when the floor began to ascend gradually, and a cool breeze lifted my hair from my face.

As I went, more and more paintings appeared on the cave walls, and they were soon in good enough repair that I could almost figure out what they were meant to depict.

Every one of them showed a tall silver-white Vogel of indeterminate sex. One, I was fairly sure, depicted a funeral procession, with the Vogel Seer leading the way, holding a staff with a glowing orb at its tip – like a wisplight caught in a gemstone – with their wings half spread. Another showed what looked like a corpse laid out on a large, rectangular stone that could have been the one in the death shrine. Three bird folk, shown smaller than the Seer, appeared to be washing and dressing the dead while the Seer oversaw the proceedings, again holding that glowing staff.

The quality of the painting looked very high to my untrained eyes; I was only familiar with textile arts and the tiny paintings that illustrated the books in my mother's library. But every object except the ones I had no context for was identifiable, and every figure was posed in a way that made the actions they were meant to be making clear.

I stopped when I came across a triptych that looked like a connected series of scenes. What it showed made my heart ache. In the first one, the bird Seer dangled a drop spindle and seemed to be spinning his own hair into thread. The spindle looked like the one I'd seen Fionn using, only the weight was near the top instead of the bottom of the shaft.

In the second scene, the Seer sat at a small loom, weaving with a long shuttle wrapped in silver-white thread. A narrow band of cloth formed on the web of the loom, and the artist had included subtle lines to show the band had a woven-in pattern that would be apparent when looked at from the right angle.

The final scene showed the Seer holding a narrow length of cloth – still with the thin lines to show its pattern – that had a glowing crystal attached to the end. They were standing in front of a reddish tree, a salt-leaf, and reaching up to tie the cloth to a branch.

I stared at the pictures for a long time, even reaching out a hand, but I refrained from touching the painting in case the ancient pigment crumbled away. Just looking at it made me miss Fionn so much my stomach ached. When had I fallen for him so hard?

At the Abbey, I had found his voice, his face, and then his body, very attractive, and I had only wanted him more after the first time we were together. In fact, each time we had fucked, or made love, or even kissed or held hands, I had wanted him more. And now, barely a nineday later, I couldn't imagine my life without him. It was like trying to imagine a life without magic.

And I was going to have to get used to being without him, because even if I was able to reach him now, to tell him I loved him, I wouldn't be allowed to stay. I'd be lucky to escape being executed for invading the sanctity of the Eyrie. But at the very least, I could keep myself out of my Queen mother's clutches, maybe even long enough to find a way to make the world a better place, or find a better place to make a life. Then I would come back for Fionn, if he would have me.

For right now, I just needed to find him, and confess my love, and find out what he wanted me to do next.

I started walking again and before much longer the walls closed in and I came suddenly around a corner to face an old brick wall. Had the King and his companion come a different way, after all? Perhaps the path I had been following really had been too easy.

I stepped close to the wall and carefully put a hand on it. It was sagging with age, but still solid. I looked one way and saw only stone. I looked the other way and saw a dim line of light. I sidled along the wall and found there was just enough room to slip through where the wall had sagged. It must have been a very tight fit for the Vogel King, but now that I knew to look, I saw splashes of beeswax and scuffs in the dust from their feet, and even marks that might have been from the tip of a wing dragging on the floor.

I peered cautiously around the end of the wall. The dim light was sunlight, filtered in from somewhere farther off. Which meant it must be morning already. I stepped out and found myself in the middle of a wide corridor hung with half-rotted tapestries and floored in dust and debris that might once have been furniture. The dust was marked with scuffs in both directions, but most heading towards brighter light.

I was looking at the ruined section of the Eyrie.

I followed the heavier scuffs and brighter light, padding quietly along the hall and gathering shadows to hide me. And hoping a moving patch of darkness wouldn't be too obvious to a day-dweller's eyes. To my own eyes, I'd have been as visible as if I were lit by glaring sunlight.

Another corridor intersected the one I was in, and another, and only the fact that I was familiar from childhood with the general layouts of both fortified strongholds and royal courts kept me from worrying too much about getting lost. Dwellings of any size tend to have a similar logic to their layout.

I rounded another corner and saw the source of the sunlight. It was a balcony, reduced to little more than a jagged opening in the rock scattered with chunks of broken stone, and it looked out over the beach, towards Aven Forest. It was very early morning.

A figure stood silhouetted against the light. Not the King, as I might have expected, but his slighter companion. I shrank silently back into the shadows.

"I thought I sensed someone following," he said, in unaccented Islish.

I didn't move.

"Come now, I know you're there. Fey aren't the only people on this Isle with magic. I, myself, am weak in most magics but I have a talent for detecting the intentions of others. Which means I am also good at detecting when others are present nearby, even if they are completely silent and very well hidden."

I still didn't move.

"I will have to tell my King you are here, but I haven't yet, and I won't for some time. He has gone to his bath and breakfast and doesn't like to be disturbed until after he has drunk at least one entire pot of tea."

I let the shadows drift away and the person turned from the window. "In addition, I very much doubt I could lay a hand on you. I was trained in diplomacy and management, not combat."

I still hesitated until he stepped out of the direct light and I could see him better, and he said, "He misses you, our Seer. It vexes the King most terribly, though he won't admit it."

Finally, I stepped the rest of the way around the corner and the Vogel man's eyes widened in surprise. "You're smaller and grubbier than I expected."

"Believe it or not, I'm considered tall for a Sidhe." I pitched my voice to be audible to him, but not much farther. "And I haven't had the luxury of a bath in a day or three."

He smiled. "You do have a pleasant voice and a handsome enough face." He looked me up and down and I prepared a response for the inevitable sexual comment. But he only said, "You are very determined to reach him. If your love matches your loyalty, I am not surprised Seer Tokka is so taken with you."

I just stared at him.

"Not a man of many words. I suppose that's understandable under the circumstances. I hope you know I wish you no ill. It is not my belief that liaisons between Vogel and non-Vogel should be forbidden. But I still cannot allow you to see him."

"Forbidden? Why? By whom?"

He shrugged elegantly. I suspected everything he did would be elegant. "Vogel law. It was our current King's grandfather, I believe, who enacted it, but it has been an unwritten principle since we were forced into vassalage under the Alfar Monarch. The belief is that we have suffered enough at the hands of others and should therefore be loyal only to our own kind." He said the last part with a very slight sneer he probably hadn't meant me to notice.

"I only want to tell him…" I stopped myself. I would not admit my feelings to some stranger before I told Fionn himself, even if that stranger already appeared to know. "I only need to say goodbye. Your guards took that from me."

"I am sorry for that. But surely you can see it is better for Tokka to have a clean end. To let him believe you have returned to your forest and abandoned him so he can begin a new life with his people."

I scowled.

"His people need him." The man's voice was so reasonable it seemed silly to contradict him.

I need him, I wanted to say. Instead, I said, "Why wait to speak to me? Why not just tell your King and let him catch me unwarned."

He shrugged again. "I find myself fond of young Tokka. He did not ask for this, nor for the King's attentions. And I suppose I was curious about you, and wanted to thank you as our King will not, for saving Tokka's life."

I nodded but refused to welcome his thanks in words. I had not saved Fionn for the bird folk, and in the end, I hadn't even done it to save the Isle from war. I had saved Fionn for himself. And maybe, a little, for me.

"If you're fond of him, as you say, will you… will you look out for him?"

"He is my people's Seer. I will watch over him for that reason alone." But his look softened. "I will do what I can to help him navigate his new position and all that it brings."

I nodded again. "He's stronger than he looks," I blurted out. "And he's so fucking smart." I flared my nostrils and licked my lips. "But he's also… He's gentle and kind, and I don't want that taken advantage of."

"As I said, young Sidhe, I will do what I can."

"My name is Kiernan," I said, impulsively. "Kiernan Druison."

He tilted his head. "A common enough surname among the Sidhe, and even the humans of Morven, if I'm not mistaken." His mouth quirked. "If I know fey as I believe I do, I would suspect you were only giving me part of your name."

I found myself smiling back. "You can hardly expect me to expose my vulnerabilities to someone I just met."

"And your name is a vulnerability?" He chuckled and waved his hand. "I won't pry. I am Councilor Rocsh, administrator of the King's household and of the Eyrie in general. I would we could have met under better circumstances. I think I might have liked you very much, Kiernan Druison."

"Likewise." I held out my hand and the Councilor looked at it curiously, then stepped forward and took my fingers briefly in his. Another man would probably have suspected me of deceit, but if he could read intentions as he said he could, he would know I was simply thanking him.

"And now, I am afraid I must go wait on the King to finish breakfast and report that we have an intruder in the ruins. You may wish to flee."

"And if I kill you to keep you from reporting?"

He eyed my sword and dropped his gaze to the knives strapped to my thighs. "I have no doubt that you could kill me before I could even get out a cry for help. But I do not think you will."

"I *have* killed for him before."

"For him, I will believe. But for yourself? And in cold blood? I can read your intentions, remember?"

I sighed and nodded. "Go tell your King as you must. I don't suppose you'll tell Fionn… tell Seer Tokka, that I was here?"

"That I cannot do. Farewell, Kiernan Druison." And with that he turned and strode down a passage. I waited a heartbeat, then another, and followed.

I T WOULD HAVE MADE sense to flee back into the caves and hide there until whatever guards the King sent after me gave up and went away. But I was full of urgency, and it made me stubborn. Or stupid. The same stupid that made me walk right up to the Abbey of the Moon and try to use magic to break through the wards. And we've seen how that worked out for me.

But in the end, even that had come out all right, or as well as it could have, and I'd escaped with Fionn. The chances of something similar happening this time were completely minuscule, but then I *am* known for thinking with my cock and not with my brain.

So I followed the Councilor until he reached a wooden door set into the end of a corridor and stepped through, locking it behind him.

I waited, then waited some more, then I picked the lock and followed.

The corridor on the other side was at an angle, with the door about halfway along its length, and it was the widest hallway I'd seen yet. Presumably it had once been a major thoroughfare in the Eyrie, but now it was dim and almost as dusty as the ruins. It was at least in good repair, with intact furniture and faded but complete hangings.

The only lights here were crystals and mirrors cleverly set in the walls to reflect sunlight from somewhere more distant. Curious, I followed them to a huge wooden door with a row of half-circular windows in a long row above. It looked like a main entrance.

I had to hide quickly, pulling shadows around me and darting behind a corner, when the door suddenly opened on almost silent hinges and two tall, richly dressed Vogel men strode through and away down the hall, two plainly-dressed bird folk scurrying in their wake. I started to follow but saw through the still-open door more Vogel arriving, their huge wings bearing them to the balcony outside and sweeping down to set them lightly on their feet.

I hid again and waited as they went by, and the huge door swung closed. Counting the first two, eight men of importance, each with an attendant, had passed me by the time the door clicked shut far more quietly than such a huge thing ought.

I followed silently behind until they all disappeared into a small, ornate entrance. Then I hid behind a large urn set in an alcove and waited. I hardly knew what I was waiting *for*, but something deep in my gut told me to stay still and watch.

Voices echoed down the hall and my stomach clenched when I recognized one of them. Well, two, but one was the Vogel King and he hardly mattered.

The other voice was soft, a little husky, and neither high nor low. It was a voice that made my skin tingle and my lips curl into a smile and then a stupid grin. It made my heart leap and my breath catch and then continue on too quickly.

I didn't know the language he was speaking, except to recognize it as Voglish – Vogelspek – but the voice I would know anywhere. I wanted to leap out of hiding and pull Fionn into my arms.

Instead, I crouched in shadows and watched as the tall, handsome Vogel King led my pretty silver beloved by the arm into the room where the other men had gone. Two other Vogel, more plainly dressed, followed them, while their guards took up places, two on each side of the door.

It took me a moment to realize Fionn had looked different. His hair was arranged in elaborate braids on top of his head, leaving his elegant neck bare, and his face was artfully painted, making him look older and more... untouchable. He had extra feathers in shades of blue and green and purple arranged around his face. I wondered what they said.

He had moved without hesitation, with grace and confidence; he had looked like someone far too good for the likes of me. But then I had known that already. Deep in my belly, though, I felt his anxiety, and I wished there was some way to let him know I was here, that... what? There was nothing I could do for him.

It also took me a moment – which was about three moments too long – to realize that the four guards were looking in my direction. They didn't see me, I didn't think, but they were suspicious about something.

I didn't move or even breathe when one of them left his post and started towards me. Then the other three fanned out behind him and followed. They couldn't possibly see me, but somehow they knew I was there anyway.

They advanced slowly, cautiously, long spears held at the ready. I wondered if they knew how easy it was for a single Sidhe to dodge around a spear and make a lot of trouble from close to. If they had the same training as the guards on the beach, they likely had no idea.

I contemplated my options. One: I could fight. But though I had no doubt I could handle all four of them, possibly even before the noise could attract the attention of the men in the room, I didn't want to kill them. Yes, they were King's men, but they were also just people. People like I had been, doing the job they were given with no notion that there might be other options.

Two: I could try to talk my way out of this. I had a reasonably smooth tongue when I wanted to – one reason my mother decided to start training me as an ambassador – even if I did have a tendency to crack dirty jokes at inappropriate times. Counting against that was the fact that no amount of clever talk could hide the fact that I'd broken into the Eyrie, where outsiders were forbidden, and even the Alfar Monarch who was their overlord wasn't permitted inside.

And three: I could run. It would defeat the entire purpose of my being here in the first place, but if could make it back to the caves, I could hide and wait for the guards to give up. And try again to find Fionn after that. In the end, it was the only real option.

So I stood, dropped my concealing shadows, and ran. And discovered that apparently Vogel guards aren't trained to *throw* their spears, because not one of them did. Sidhe are fast and I had been trained by a father obsessed with building the perfect warrior. Physically, I took after my Sidhe side almost entirely, which meant I was light on my feet. But Sidhe are built for the forest, where being small has distinct advantages, and can make one faster than someone with longer legs.

In the clear stone passageways of the Eyrie, though, long legs were better than short and small size was a liability. Still, by virtue of being better at going around corners, I stayed ahead of pursuit until we reached the deserted parts of the palace. Which, at this early hour, were no more deserted than what were presumably the busy parts. Either that or the Eyrie had very few actual occupants.

The final corridor, where the door to the caves exited, was wide. It was just broad enough for a Vogel to spread their wings, and the guards took full advantage, gliding swiftly after me. I had no chance of getting the door open before they reached me. I barely made it to the end of the corridor.

I zipped around a corner and sprinted and fetched up on a balcony overlooking the open ocean, with nowhere to go. I turned and put my back to the railing and watched my swiftest pursuer round the corner, tucking in his wings as he came.

I could have taken him out easily. One thrown dagger, or a quick stroke of my sword, and he'd have been on the ground, bleeding out or unaware that he'd just lost his head.

But I couldn't do it any more than I could have taken him down before the pursuit began. My father and mother had agreed – and they hadn't agreed on much since they first married – that although I was a skilled and efficient warrior, I was too kind-hearted, unwilling to kill or even injure someone unless they had it coming. And these men, for all their enthusiasm in chasing me, were just employees or conscripts, just doing a job so they could live a decent life and maybe support a family or aging parents. They didn't deserve to die for that, and I couldn't kill them.

One by one, the other guards came around the corner until they all stood before me, spears leveled.

"Okay," I said. "You caught me."

Maybe I could disarm them. Knock them out. And then

what? Tie them up and leave them to die of thirst in some forgotten back corridor of the palace? And besides, killing them would have been easy, but disarming and disabling all four without harming them was another matter.

I stepped back and felt the stone balcony press against the backs of my thighs.

The first guard spat in my direction, and I watched the blob of moisture sink into the dust on the floor. "Fucking fey. You're lucky the King wants you alive."

The next guard spat, too, and poked his companion in the ribs. "The King didn't say unhurt."

"Or intact," said the third.

The fourth guard held back, like he didn't really even want to be there.

I felt behind me with one hand, found the top of the railing, and leaned on it. It felt solid.

"I don't want to hurt you," I said.

"I'll go get the Captain," said the fourth guard. "And bring more men."

The first guard scoffed. "One little elf shit doesn't require the captain, or more men."

I leaned more casually on the rail. "I could kill you all," I said, using my most reasonable voice. "Only I really don't want to." I met the eyes of the fourth guard, the one who didn't seem to want to be there. "It would make your Seer unhappy with me, and I really don't like making him unhappy."

"You... you know Seer Tokka?" His eyes got very big behind his mask, and I realized he couldn't be much past his majority. King's guard – or maybe Seer's guard – was probably his first post after training. Poor boy.

"Of course he doesn't," said the second guard, voice full of contempt.

The third guard edged away from the first two, closer to

the fourth and I wondered if those two were Fionn's personal guard. I ignored the others and spoke to them.

"We escaped the Abbey of the Moon together and we were on our way here when your King's guards found us."

"Why are you here now?" the third guard asked. His spear wavered a little in his hand.

"To tell him goodbye," I said. "To make sure he's happy. That he's safe."

"Our King keeps him safe and makes sure he's happy. He doesn't need your kind." The first guard spat again and took a step closer.

I sighed. There was only one alternative to killing them all now, and it was probably going to hurt. A lot. And I *still* wouldn't have had the chance to tell Fionn I loved him.

I shifted my weight suddenly, thrust it all onto the arm I was leaning on, and used it to push me up and onto the railing. I balanced easily. I grew up walking on branches high in the trees, so this was nothing. I could hear the sea crashing against the cliff below. We were on the lowest level of the Eyrie, and I hoped it was low enough, that this balcony overhung the base of the cliff enough.

When the first guard snarled and leapt forward, sweeping his spear around to take my legs from under me, I smiled.

And I stepped off the railing into open air.

29
Fionn

I LEFT THE KING'S ROOMS as quickly as I dared but made myself walk slowly out the door so I wouldn't seem like I was fleeing – either to the King or to those who waited outside.

Neeka glanced up in surprise from where she was playing a card game with the King's attendant. They rose to their feet and the attendant said, <Does he require me?>

<He didn't say.> I looked back into the room. <He said he was going to bathe.> The attendant nodded and went through into the King's rooms.

Halfway back to my own rooms, I said, <Can we go to the library?>

<Of course, my Seer, but…>

I turned to find Neeka following farther behind than usual when it was just the two of us. She looked hesitant.

<What?> I was sharper than I meant to be, but she only raised an eyebrow. She seemed to be very good at sensing my moods and I wondered if it was simply her training as an attendant, or if she had some magical ability.

<Perhaps you would prefer a bath, first?>

I blinked at her and then I felt it, something wet and warm dripping down the inside of my leg. I flushed in shame and wanted to cry, but that would only have made everything worse.

She put her hand on my back. <I'll walk behind, Seer Tokka. No one else has noticed.>

I nodded, unable to say anything in my misery, and we continued back to my rooms. At every step I was terrified that I would leave a wet, smeary footstep.

Safe in my bathing room, I stripped off my clothes to find my undergarment soaked through with the King's semen and thin ribbons of blood. He had made me *bleed*. Some had seeped through the feathers of my tail, as well, and it had dripped down my leg.

I wobbled on my feet and would have slipped to the floor, but I felt Neeka's strong hand under my elbow. She helped me into the bath and sat down on the edge, behind me.

<Are you sure the guards didn't notice?> I felt the same deep shame I had felt as a child, soiling myself after eating too many overripe berries before a lesson with the Abbess. She hadn't let me leave my copying of a text to visit the latrine, and I couldn't hold it in. I had been scrubbing the sisters' worst-soiled laundry for weeks as punishment.

<No one saw, Tokka.> Her leaving out the honorific was almost as comforting as her hand stroking my hair. She seemed to want to say more but stayed quiet.

<You can say whatever it is.> I hunched my shoulders and buried my face in my hands. I could *feel* the King's leavings seeping out of me into the hot water. <You've already seen me dribble my King's spunk out my ass. You can't possibly say anything that will make me feel worse.>

She stroked my hair again, then slid into the bath behind

me, fully clothed, and wrapped her arms around me, holding me gently but firmly. I knew she had no interest in my body – her feathers told me she was unavailable and interested in women, and she had told me herself about her beloved who worked in the kitchens.

<I don't think I've ever heard you use words like that,> she said, amusement in her voice. <And you have nothing to be ashamed of.>

<I should have waited longer to leave. Or bathed first.>

<Did the King wish you to stay?>

<He told me to eat before I left, but I couldn't. He said *he* was going to bathe. I just wanted to get away.>

<Then you didn't have much choice. Did he hurt you?>

<No. Not intentionally.> I turned so I could rest my head on her shoulder.

<And… has *that* happened before?>

I snorted. <Soiling myself after?>

<You didn't shit yourself, my Seer.> Her hand smoothed my hair again and I sighed.

<No. That's never happened before. Kiernan… we always lay together after. Feel asleep together, usually. Except once and that time I…>

I could feel her smile against my hair. <You had *him*.> She said it as if it were a simple fact and not something to be embarrassed about.

<I don't remember him *leaking*, after.>

She chuckled. <Next time you go to the King, I will make sure you have a very thick, soft undergarment. You might leak, but nothing will show.> I could feel her trying to hold in laughter and eventually I started to laugh, too.

<I shall be like an old man,> I said when I finally stopped. <Diapered like an infant. Perhaps the King will find me repulsive, then, and the problem will be solved.>

<Did you not enjoy yourself?>

<I… I suppose I did, in the end. But…>

<He wasn't the one you really wanted to be with.>

<He wasn't.>

She poked my shoulder. <Well, in the meantime, let me solve this problem for you. We women know a thing or two about leaking and blood.>

<I don't need to know *that*,> I said, and she laughed at me again.

THE VOGEL KING'S LIBRARY was smaller than the one in the Abbey – much smaller than I had hoped – and every volume I examined was in the Vogel language.

The room was in the center of the Eyrie and lit by crystals and mirrors reflecting distant sunlight. Without thinking, I summoned a wisplight to add to the illumination and Neeka stared at it like it was the deepest sort of magic.

<What?> I looked at her. <It's only a wisplight. Children's magic.>

<You learned this as a child?>

I flushed, remembering my own first sight of such small magics. <No.> I knew I sounded sheepish. <Kiernan taught me.>

I looked around and noticed the two guards – my original two, returned from their lunch break – also staring, but trying very hard not to *look* like they were.

I smiled at them. <Come here.> They stepped cautiously closer and let the library door swing shut behind them. <Sit.> I sank down onto the rug in the library's entrance, and Neeka and the two guards sat facing me. <Will you let me teach

you?> Neeka and one guard nodded eagerly. The other guard only looked at me. <Take off your masks, then.>

I took a deep breath, had them close their eyes, and then talked them through connecting with the Three Realms, as Kier had done with me. I had them imagine the wisplight in their cupped hands and watched as one by one, flickering blue lights pooled against their fingers.

Then I told them to open their eyes and watched the wonder dawn over their faces. Even the older and sterner of my two guards looked at the light in his hands with delight.

He looked up at me, and his light faded to nothing. <I don't know if we should do this. What if the King learns of it?>

<Is magic forbidden?> I held out my hand and managed to make my wisplight float up over it without going out.

<Few Vogel are taught magic.> Neeka closed her hand over her light, and opened it again, summoned a new one, and grinned at me. Then her face went serious. <Unless a child shows an undeniable aptitude, magic simply isn't discussed.>

The younger guard spoke up shyly. <The children of nobles are tested to see what magics they are naturally good at, and then given appropriate instruction.> He looked too young to be wielding a spear in service to his King, and he had been sneaking glances at me the whole time we were in the library, like he was checking to see if I was real.

He stared at the wisplight in his hand. Of the three of them, his had come most quickly, and glowed the brightest. <I wish I had been taught this sooner.>

<Perhaps it would be best to keep this to ourselves, then.> I let my light fade and got to my feet. <But if you like, I will teach you other things.> I smiled, letting it twist in mild self-deprecation. <Not that I know that much magic myself yet.>

The guards stood, put their masks back on, and took up their spears. Neeka summoned a wisplight into each hand and grinned at me before letting them both die out.

<If someone catches you and seeks to discipline you, I will take responsibility.> I stretched and looked around at the crowded bookshelves.

The guards looked at each other, then at me.

<I believe even the humblest of my people should be allowed magic if they are able to call it. If they want it.> I said the words with defiance and they both nodded.

<Thank you, my Seer,> they said together.

<Now.> I looked around again. The number of books was a little disappointing, but perhaps they were all of high quality. <Who's going to help me carry these back to my rooms?>

<All of them, my Seer?> said the young guard. The other jabbed him in the ribs and I laughed.

<Only the best ones.>

<Perhaps if you made a pile on the table, my Seer,> said the older guard, pointing to a big slab of wood in the middle of the room. <Then we can divide them between us.>

I smiled and began walking along the aisles, running my fingers over the spines, and reading random titles to see how the library was arranged. Then I thought about what I most needed to know.

In the end, I realized that every volume had been selected with care, and I would want to read them all sooner or later. I chose the ones that seemed the most basic so as not to throw myself in too deep and ended up with a relatively small selection covering the history of the Vogel Monarchy, the specifics of government in the Eyrie, treatises on fishing, farming, and agriculture in Vogel lands, and several collections of fairy tales and legends.

The prize was a thin volume on the original, ancient Vogel language, which I discovered was called Trillka, meaning "shining speech." We divided the pile into four and were about to leave for my rooms, so I could set to reading as soon as possible, when I noticed one shadowed corner I hadn't investigated. I set my books back on the table and hardly noticed when the two guards divided them into their own stacks.

Neeka followed me, grinning as she summoned a wavering, pale wisplight to help me see. There was a single small bookcase here, next to a curio cabinet full of dusty odds and ends that made no sense to me as precious objects.

The books on the shelf had no titles on their spines, only worn numerals scrawled in ink. I pulled the first one from the shelf and discovered it was a journal, written in a sprawling hand I had trouble deciphering at first. I frowned at it, and as I began to puzzle out the characters, I realized it was describing the ruined sections of the Eyrie. The cabinet, it dawned on me, was filled with items that had been found there.

On the other side of the cabinet was a lectern, turned to face the wall, holding a huge old book, fragile-looking and dusty. It was open to a page of cramped writing, a mix of Vogelspek and something that looked like tiny bird footprints. I closed the book carefully and hefted it. It was very heavy, but I was intrigued, determined to bring it to my rooms and figure out what it was. I placed the first volume of the journal on top and lifted them both.

<Are you sure you want that dusty old thing?> Neeka said, blowing on the book and creating a cloud of filth that made us both sneeze.

We came out of the dark corner laughing, and I thought I saw my guards smile under their bird masks. Then we all laughed together, because every one of us was burdened with books, and no one had a free hand to open the door.

That problem was solved when the door opened from

outside and we all stared, wondering if we were about to get caught and disciplined for being too familiar. I knew if that happened, I would not be the one to get the worst.

Councilor Rocsh came through the door, looking at us with raised eyebrows, and stepped all the way into the room. The older guard caught the door with his foot to keep it from closing.

<Councilor.> I stepped forward to bring his attention fully on me. <We were…>

He held up a slender hand. <No need to explain yourself to me, my Seer.> He looked at the guards, then at Neeka. Though all three belonged to the King's house, they were directly responsible to Rocsh, as administrator of the King's affairs. <You three may go. Take the books to the Seer's rooms and wait for him there. I would speak to him in private.>

<Yes, Councilor.> The guards and Neeka spoke in perfect unison and slipped out the door. Neeka glanced back once, and I nodded to her. She nodded back and the door closed behind her.

Councilor Rocsh looked at me, head cocked. <You seem to have made quite an impression.>

I lifted my chin. I would not apologize for being kind to my guards. <They are good people.>

He smiled. <I would advise you not to grow too attached, but I can't fault you for simply being who you are. You will have all your people madly in love with you if you continue on in this way.>

<Is that… not desirable?> I put the huge book on the table and Rocsh looked at it curiously.

<It will make you popular among our people.> He ran a hand over the cover of the book. <Just be cautious that our King doesn't use their love of you against them.>

I looked at him sharply, but he didn't elaborate.

<This is an interesting choice of reading.> He tapped the smaller book with one finger.

<I only thought it unusual. I don't even know what it is about.>

He looked away from the books and met my eyes. <This one> – his hand moved back to the cover of the huge volume – <Is almost certainly the oldest book in this library. Older than these journals by centuries.> His fingers returned to the smaller book. <The man who wrote these was an ancestor of mine, and he found the ancient book in the ruins, but never said where.>

<You've read them?>

He nodded. <The journals, yes. I have not yet attempted the other, only read what he had to say about it.> He looked at the books again, brushed his fingers over their covers.

<He wrote that this volume contains all that was then known – those generations ago when it was written – about seers among our people.> His fingers traced the deep embossing, following the geometric shapes.

<I was told there hasn't been a Vogel seer for seven generations.>

<Indeed. Do you know how many years that is?>

I shook my head.

<Nor do I, but we are a long-lived people, so it must be a millennium at least. Since soon after the humans and fey came to the Isle and the Nine Monarchies were founded.>

He sighed. <I believe it will be good for you to read this, but perhaps not so good for the King to know you're reading it. He does not wish to learn from the past, only to use it to make the future *he* wants.>

I stared at him, and he looked up at me with a smile. <Oh, I do not plot behind my King's back, never fear.> His smile twisted slightly. <But I do not always agree with him.>

He surprised me by lifting a strand of my hair and letting it fall again. <I do what I believe is best for my people, for *all* my people.> His smile turned sad. <And now, for my Seer.>

I didn't know what to say to that, but I hoped he was telling me I could find an ally in him.

He straightened from the table and turned to me. <I came to tell you our King has sent for his hair-cutter and his feather-worker to attend to you this evening instead of tomorrow.> He frowned, just a touch to his features that made him look stern.

<I see.> I twined a bit of my hair around my finger, wondering how it would feel to have it all gone.

And Rocsh surprised me again by taking the strand from between my fingers and severing it with a little knife I hadn't even seen him draw.

<What?> I said, alarmed.

He coiled the piece of hair, lifted the cover of the book, and tucked the strand inside. <You never know when you might wish to remember.>

<I…> But I had no words.

<The King will take you for your ritual bath late tonight.> He tucked the knife away up his sleeve. <In the morning, he will present you to your people.> He moved away, running his fingers over the spines of the books. He smiled at them fondly, and I wondered how much time he spent here, reading.

<I believe he will allow you to walk among our people, under the watch of your guards.> He paused and added, <If you please him well enough.> He looked regretful, and my stomach clenched. He turned back and fixed me with his pale blue stare. <I might suggest you visit the unfortunate souls in the gaol. It would look good to our people to see your compassion for those who strayed from the path of the law.> He looked like he might want to say more, but he didn't, he only looked at me with a very serious face until I nodded.

<I will do that, thank you, Councilor Rocsh.> I felt like I was being examined, but not in the critical way the King had done. The Councilor seemed almost hopeful.

He sighed, then, and seemed to relax a small amount. <Child, I will help you as I can, but do not expect me to move directly against the King.>

I had no idea what he was implying, so I just said. <I am not a child, Councilor, though our King might wish I was.>

His lips curled up and sympathy touched his eyes. <Of course, my Seer.> He looked at me a moment longer, then nodded and left.

WHEN I GOT BACK TO MY ROOMS, my guards were in their places outside my door. The younger one smiled under his mask – I could just see the edges of his jaw move – and I smiled back. The older didn't change expression that I could see, but he opened the door for me and closed it quietly once I passed through.

Neeka waited in my sitting room with two others, presumably the hair-cutter and the feather-worker, though I had not expected them until later. She stepped quickly forward to take the books from me and I dusted off the front of my tunic.

<Councilor Rocsh informed me that you would be stopping by.> I faced the two strangers calmly.

The hair-cutter, or so I assumed from the two pairs of shears sheathed at her belt, stepped forward and bowed. <Apologies for arriving early, my Seer. We thought it best to get this done so you have time to get used to it.>

<You will need to adjust your balance to your new

feathers, my Seer,> said the feather-worker, dipping his knee closer to the ground and then straightening. He reminded me a little of Councilor Rocsh, with the same tall, slight build, and similar coloring, but there was something unpleasant in the way he looked at me that made me uneasy.

<Shall we begin with my hair, then?> I had to make myself refrain from touching the long strands.

<I can examine your wings while it is cut,> said the feather-worker.

The hair-cutter bowed again and lifted an empty basket that had sat by her feet. <In the bathing room would be best, to make for easy cleanup.>

I nodded and led the way. I sat on the same chair Healer Kah had sat me on to tend to my injuries. It felt like moons since that had happened, but it had only been a day. Two days? Three?

The hair-cutter stood behind me and pulled my hair back from my face and over my shoulders while the feather-worker unfolded my right wing and had me hold it out so he could measure. He made what sounded like disparaging noises with his tongue on the roof of his mouth.

I knew cutting my hair wouldn't hurt, of course, but I still winced at the first snick of the shears. The hair-cutter was quick and had me trimmed down to within two finger-widths of my scalp before the feather-worker had even finished taking his measurements.

While she used a smaller pair of shears to tidy my hair and make it look pleasing, the feather-worker left to begin selecting my new feathers.

<You may wish to bathe.> The hair-cutter brushed off my shoulders. <The small ends can be itchy if they work their way into your clothing.> She lifted her basket, now full of my hair, bowed, and walked out.

I sat still for a few heartbeats, trying to get used to the feel of air across the back of my neck. Neeka poked her head in the door and stared.

<Oh,> she said.

I stood up slowly, keeping my back to the mirror. <Is it terrible?> I reached up and touched the short fuzz left on my skull. It was still soft, but it felt strange.

She shook her head. <It's not terrible, but it *is* different.>

<I don't know if I can look.>

<It will be less obvious once your facial adornments are on. You can do that first. The feather-worker is ready for you.>

I turned, still avoiding the mirror, and looked at the feather mask I had worn earlier, sitting on the shelf of lotions and medicines. Then I took a deep breath and looked up. My eyes looked even bigger and my cheekbones sharper without my long hair to soften them. Even my ears seemed to stick out more and the tiny feathers around my face seemed to disappear.

I rubbed my hand over my head, remembering the feel of Kiernan burying both hands to the wrist in my hair, making fists to pull me closer to kiss me, to thrust harder against my mouth when I pleasured him. I suddenly felt weak and had to lean on the shelf.

<Seer Tokka.> Neeka's voice was gentle, her hand strong under my elbow.

<I'm okay. I was just remembering.>

<Your beloved liked your hair.> Her voice was audible only to us two.

I smiled sadly at her in the mirror. <He would say he likes me as I am, even without hair.> My smile grew, then faded. <He would probably say he likes me bald.>

She leaned her head on my shoulder, then said, letting a

wicked smile touch her face, <Was he better than our King?>

I tapped the top of her head lightly with my palm. <Never less than four.>

She snorted and started to choke, trying not to laugh.

<And the King?>

<Three.> I let my smile grow again, briefly, and straightened my spine.

<Three is good.> She stepped back from me.

<But it's not four.> I turned away from the mirror <Now let's get the rest of this over with.>

The feather-worker waited in my sitting room, feathers spread over every surface except a single chair, which he indicated I should sit in.

<We begin with your face.> All the feathers were the King's colors: blues and greens and a few purple. The smell of the glue was unpleasant, and I tried not to breathe deeply. Fortunately, he was very quick and sure with the brush and was soon stepping back to check his work.

<Are they the same as the others? The temporary ones?>

<Very similar. The King asked for a few changes to better reflect your unique status.>

He had me stand then, and began to attach long feathers to my tail, until I could feel them brush the floor whenever I bent my legs to shift position. Next, he turned to my wings and by the time he was done, the smell of the glue had left me lightheaded and Neeka was opening the balcony door and every window she could reach to let more air in.

<Many of these were our King's own feathers.> The feather-worker had me spread both wings to make sure they matched perfectly. They felt heavier than they should have, but perhaps it was only the air resisting their passage. <Some of the smaller quills are from his children.>

He stepped back. <You may wish to save your own

feathers when you molt. If you can collect enough, I can create your new wings from your own feathers and you will be all silver, as a Seer should be.>

<Thank you.> I didn't really feel grateful, though; I felt drained, empty, like someone had taken me apart and put me back together with pieces that weren't mine.

He bowed, cleaned up his baskets, and departed, so encumbered that he looked like a peddler going to market in an illustration of a fairy tale I'd seen in the Abbey library.

When he was gone, I tried to sit down and almost ruined his work. <How do you sit with these cursed things?> I said in frustration as Neeka smoothed the bent feathers back into place.

<You'll get used to them. In the meantime, move slowly.> She hid a smile.

I went to the waiting room mirror, which was longer than the one in the bathing room, and stood myself in front of it. A stranger looked back. They were my eyes, my face, but the rest was not me; I was looking at Seer Tokka, not Branfionn.

Jewel-toned feathers surrounded my face, making me look even paler. They told anyone who cared to look that I was my King's and subject only to *his* commands, that I was untouchable and wanted no one but my Monarch. The feathers were fewer than the temporary ones had been, with less to convey, but each was fancier, with sweeping thin wisps and elegant long quills, round bright ones to catch the eye and that one larger multi-colored plume in the middle that matched the King's.

I swallowed and stared, as if I could face myself down. I turned to look at the grand sweep of my wings, blue and green sprouting from beneath silver-pale, with purple accents added to my upper wing and tail coverts. I spread them and they filled the small waiting room. I snapped them shut and felt them catch the air and wondered if it was true that I couldn't fly on them. Perhaps the glue was not strong enough.

I felt off balance, my head too light and my wings too heavy. <How do I do this?> My voice sounded small and lost.

Neeka took my hand and led me back to the couch, then helped me arrange my wings and tail so I could sit.

<One day at a time.> Her voice was gentle. <You do it like the rest of us do. One day at a time.>

30
Kiernan

I was getting very tired of waking up in places I didn't know, and not knowing how I got there.

I remembered stepping off the balcony and falling towards the sea. I didn't quite make it to the water before one of the King's guards caught me, talons digging into my shoulders until they drew blood.

I rubbed one shoulder and winced. The blood had crusted, but the wounds were deep. Why had I thought they wouldn't follow me? They had fucking wings after all.

My captor had had to work hard to carry me. I was small, but solid, and I didn't have the hollow bones I was more and more convinced the Vogel had.

He only made it to the beach than ran alongside the City before dropping me. Unlucky for me, he dropped me from high enough to stun me. I was neither quick enough to call magic to soften my landing, nor rested enough to be agile, so I landed flat on my back. Again.

My sword slammed into the ground, and then into the

long bruise it had left the first time around. For much too long, I couldn't move, nothing but agony in my brain, in my body.

"Fuck." I shifted one leg with effort. Well, that was good, at least. Nothing seemed to be broken. I sat up and if I'd had anything in my stomach I'd have lost it onto the sand. I was wrong; at least two ribs were broken, and something grated against something else and shot sharp pain through me. I'd probably have screamed if the two Vogel guards weren't advancing down the beach towards me, spears lowered.

Only two. That was good. I could manage two. They both had red and yellow feathers and not the blue and green of the two who had almost believed I knew their seer. That was not so good. These two would be happy to maim me in their effort to bring me to their King alive.

I staggered to my feet and thought about drawing my sword. I even raised my left arm, hissed at the sting of stretching the punctures in my shoulder from the guard's claws, and then realized I still didn't want to kill them. That was probably going to be the death of me, someday. If I made it out of here alive, I would have to find someone who could teach me disarming techniques.

It's only in the heat of a fight that you realize where your deficiencies are.

"How about you arrest me, and I'll come quietly?" I said, raising my hands, palms up.

"What, no more lies about how you know our Seer?" one guard said. He moved forward quickly and swept his spear at my legs. I jumped over it but when I landed a stabbing pain shot though my ribs and knocked me to one knee. Dropping me on a hard-sand beach had turned out to be the best move these guards had made so far.

I forced myself to my feet again and this time, when the guard swept his spear at me I stepped quickly backwards. And

I tripped over nothing and fell on my back again.

This time I couldn't keep in the scream when my sword dug into the bruise on my back.

"A little sore, are you?" The second guard jabbed down at me with the butt of his spear, and I twisted aside, just enough to keep him from crushing my tackle. Instead, the wood shaft hit me in the hip, carrying the full weight of the Vogel and the force of his muscles. My whole leg went numb.

I tried to scramble backwards but my limbs didn't seem to want to work quickly enough. I kicked out with my good leg and the first guard sprawled in the sand. But it hadn't been a hard enough hit to do more than briefly knock the air out of his lungs.

I was starting to think I might actually be in trouble.

In the meantime, the second guard had stepped around behind me and swung his spear shaft at my head. I saw bright sparks dance in front of my eyes when it connected, and gray gathered at the edges of my vision.

It was agony, but I made myself curl into a ball and tuck my arms over my head, and then I let the blackness pull me under.

And I'd woken here, on the most uncomfortable wooden bench on the Isle, lying on a back so sore I wanted to scream again. Gingerly, I pushed myself up, almost passing out three times as broken ribs stabbed at me, my head pounded like someone was using it as an anvil, and, fuck, my right arm was broken.

At least it wasn't my sword arm, though not having my sword anymore, it hardly mattered.

I wasn't surprised to find myself in a gaol cell. They hadn't been trying to kill me, after all. It was damp stone, and the only light was sunlight filtered in from somewhere – not via crystals and mirrors, but the simpler way of bouncing off pale stone and getting dimmer with distance.

Still day then. Or was it day *again?*

I tested the inside of my mouth with my tongue. It was dry and I was thirsty, but I wasn't quite desperate for liquid. I still managed to produce enough saliva to rinse some of the blood from my tongue. I probed some more. Plenty of blood, but I still had all my teeth.

I studied my cell, but there wasn't much to see. Stone floor, three stone walls, wooden ceiling, wall of bars with a door. Easy to pick lock.

The second lock on a chain through the bars would be less easy to pick. I patted myself down left-handed. I had nothing to pick locks with anymore, anyway.

They had taken my sword and my knives, of course. They had also taken my wrist guards and my vest and would probably have taken my boots if I hadn't left them behind in the caves.

And as for things left behind, I wondered how Smoke and Flame were, if they had given up on waiting for me and left to find Fionn.

I stuck a hand in my pocket and was not at all surprised that they had taken my coins. Unless the coins had fallen out while the guards beat me. I hoped that was true, because I didn't mind a Vogel fisher finding them and maybe being able to buy his family a little extra bread and cheese, but I really didn't want those two guards getting a pint of ale on me.

The bench I was half-sitting up on and a bucket in one corner than smelled like it hadn't been emptied after the cell's last occupant left completed the decor. All I could see of the rest of the gaol was the damp stone hallway.

While I watched, a guard dragged a thin, scruffy-looking Vogel man past by his arm. I heard bars clang and a lock snap to. I guess the poor fellow had broken some law or another –

by the look of him, he'd probably tried to steal an apple from a fruit vendor – and got himself locked up for his trouble. At least they'd give him something to eat. Probably.

The guard walked back in the other direction and spit onto my cell floor as he passed. If he was aiming for me, his sense of direction was bad.

"Are you going to tell me what I'm charged with?" I said, not expecting an answer. Most city guards in most parts of the Isle didn't bother charging anyone with anything before locking them up. Unless they were a noble or very wealthy.

He paused and looked at me, tipping back his bird mask so I could see his sneer. "Treason," his said, his Islish thick with a Vogel accent, even on the single word.

"I'm pretty sure it's impossible to commit treason against someone who isn't your own Monarch," I said. "And besides, I didn't go anywhere near your King." Which was only true if you had a very precise definition of *near* that didn't include "close enough to smell his terrible perfume."

"Fuck you, fey shit," he said, and started to walk away again.

"You can try," I said. "But your friends beat the crap out of me, so I'm not sure I can get it up yet. Unless you like fucking people who can't respond."

He snarled and pulled a key out of his pocket and moved to fit it into the lock. It couldn't be *that* easy, could it?

Then I heard a voice I recognized and swore under my breath. Not Fionn this time, alas. Though I wouldn't have wanted him to see me in this state, anyway.

The Vogel King said something in his own language and the guard scowled.

The tall, handsome bird King held out his hand as he came into my line of sight and the guard handed over the key, scurried off, and returned with a chair. Then he stood against the wall, stiff and straight, his mask pulled back down over his face.

The King looked at him, eyebrow raised, and said something else. The guard started to protest, and the King interrupted him. This time, the guard left.

"So, you're the Sidhe who has my Seer weeping into his pillow," he said. I refused to believe Fionn would let this man see him cry.

He unlocked the padlock and slipped the chain from the bars, letting it dangle when he opened the door. Interesting; the main lock on the door was either broken, or the key had been lost.

"If you made him cry," I said, voice as calm and reasonable as if we were speaking about the weather. "I'll fucking hurt you."

He laughed and moved the chair into my cell, blocking the door. I wondered if he knew that would only stop me from leaving because I could hardly move.

"I don't think you're in any shape to hurt me, little fey." Okay maybe he did know.

He sat on the chair and stared at me. I stared back. Perhaps he expected me to break down under the scrutiny, to begin a babbling confession or beg for my life. I had seen other nobles use the tactic quite effectively, but not on me. I had been raised among royals far haughtier than he, and rough soldiers, too. It took a lot more than a superior stare to break me.

"What do you want, Vogel King?" I said.

"Only to tell you you will never see him again."

"You had me beaten and arrested for that? Why not just kill me?"

He shrugged and it was an impossibly elegant gesture. "I wanted to see your face first."

"So, no thanks for rescuing him from the Alfar who planned to slit his throat as a sacrifice to their Lady of the Moon?"

He waved his hand, all elegance again. "I might have considered thanking you, before you invaded my Eyrie. And before I learned you defiled him before bothering to rescue him."

"I *what?*" I sat up straighter and immediately regretted it but managed to turn my shriek of agony into a long hiss between my teeth.

He stood up and towered over me. If I had been standing, I'd be staring at his lower chest, he was so much taller. "You tainted him, you fucking little fey shit. Soiled and defiled him." Spittle flew from his lips and I almost recoiled. He had gone from serene to furious more quickly than I'd ever seen anyone do besides my Queen mother.

I breathed slowly, careful to show no reaction. "Oh, that," I said, so calmly he blinked at me and sat down again, crossing his legs and folding his hands in his lap, the very picture of calm.

"You mean I fucked him." His eyes narrowed at my word choice. "Yes, I did do that." I scratched my crotch thoroughly and gave him my biggest, wickedest grin.

"Has he turned you down, then, King? Because he begged me for more."

He was as quick on his feet as he was to shift emotions, but he could have been moving in slow motion and I still wouldn't have been able to avoid the backhanded blow he aimed at me.

My nose crunched and blood spurted, and I'd have puked if I could have. I worked my jaw carefully, and watched him sit back down, as calm as if he hadn't even moved. I felt my face and found my nose shifted into what was definitely the wrong angle. I held his eyes, gripped my crooked nose tight, and yanked.

I think I blacked out briefly after I heard the crunch, but I did get to see the Vogel King's look of complete horror. I wiggled my nose to test it.

"Why do people keep breaking my fucking nose?" I said, as if inquiring about the time of day. "It's a nice nose. I like it. Having it broken is getting tiresome."

"Perhaps it's because you keep pushing it where it's not wanted." His face was blank again.

"Fair point. But I seem to have touched a sore spot with you. Did I guess a little too close to the truth?"

"You slander him," he said, observing me like I was an especially slimy slug he'd just found on his salad.

"You think wanting good sex is a bad thing? I can't say I've heard anyone but the Abbess of the Moon express that opinion. He liked what I gave him. Or are you just upset you couldn't do the same?"

His mouth curled up unpleasantly, and I braced for another blow, but he simply looked at me. "Don't worry yourself on my account, Sidhe. I had him yesterday, and he did not leave my bed unsatisfied."

That one hurt, I had to admit. Not that I expected Fionn to abstain, or to pine over me for the rest of his life. Fuck, *I* was the one who'd told him he should fuck whomever he wanted. But it still hurt, and far more than it should have, but I didn't let it show on my face. I hated talking about Fionn this way, as if he were just another conquest, but I wouldn't let on to the King that he'd wounded me.

"Tonight, he will be cleansed of your filth and I will show him what it really means to be claimed by a King."

"I'm not following you," I said. "But you do whatever you need to to feel like you're in control."

He smiled again. "He tells me you only had him once, so it will not be difficult to best you, to make him forget you and love me instead."

I wanted to punch his stupid smug face for talking about "having" Fionn, as if Fionn had no say in the matter, as if Fionn hadn't *had* me as often as it was the other way around.

"Is that what he told you?"

He looked unconcerned. "He confessed he was inexperienced, and I told him I would teach him."

I knew I should keep my mouth shut; I already had what I needed from the King. I knew that if Fionn wanted the King to think we'd only been together once, I should leave him to think that, but he was so fucking smug I couldn't leave it. Like I've said before: I'm not known for thinking with my brain.

"How many pulses, King?" I said and watched his eyes widen before he recovered and his face smoothed back to serene. He probably assumed I'd have no idea about Vogel orgasms, like he thought I could only have given Fionn a single pulse, not knowing any better, which would leave the King sure in his belief that he was better in bed than I was.

"Two?" I said and his lip curled slightly. "Three?" His face smoothed again. "Four, maybe?" His eyes twitched, only slightly, at their outside corners.

I smiled with one side of my mouth. "Three, then."

He scowled and almost looked like he might get up and hit me again. He was very good at appearing calm, but not so good at keeping his emotions off his face when startled. He should have had a mother like mine to teach him.

"If you know what a pulse is, fey, then you know that three is an excellent orgasm." He seemed not to like the word "orgasm" and I almost laughed.

"I do know," I said, meeting his eyes again. "I also know that four is mind-blowing and leaves him limp as waterleaf in my arms afterward."

His nostrils flared, but I think he suspected I was trying to provoke him.

"And," I said, scratching my crotch again, "Five very nearly makes him pass out."

I let the words hover in the air for a couple of heartbeats and added, "But then I'm half human and I could be lying."

His face was still, but his eyes were stormy. They were nice eyes, except for the fact that they looked at me like I was a turd he'd found floating in his bath.

"You know nothing about Tokka," he finally said.

I shrugged and tried not to show how much it hurt to do so. "I've known him less than a ninenight, it's true. But you've known him even less than that."

"He is a Vogel Seer, and I am his King. That is all I need to know."

"Why did you come here, Vogel King? Why come here and glare at me, break my nose, and try to convince me your Seer is in love with you? What the fuck is the point of this meeting?"

"I owe you no explanation."

"You're right, you don't. So fuck off."

"Don't you want to know your fate here, little Sidhe?" He stood and moved the chair back out of my cell. He stood in the door, looking down at me.

"I assume you'll either have me killed or leave me here to rot."

"So, you're not as unintelligent as you look." Then he stepped out, locked the door, and left with the chair.

When he was gone, I opened my right hand, which throbbed with every heartbeat from my broken arm. I looked at the key in my palm and started to laugh.

IWAITED FOR NIGHT, expecting every moment that someone would notice the key was missing, but no one did. I didn't think very highly of the quality of the guards in this gaol.

A guard passed by, and I could smell the porridge and water he carried, but he didn't stop to give any to me. Presumably, the King had opted to let me die of thirst.

I couldn't have tried to escape any sooner if I'd wanted to, because every time I moved, pain from somewhere – or multiple somewheres – shot through my body and I nearly passed out. Once or twice I'm pretty sure I *did* pass out, which at least helped the time pass more quickly.

From the minimal amount of noise I could hear outside, the gaol was not near a main road. I hoped it was at least in the city, because even if I could manage to drag my wounded ass out of here, there was no way I could get very far on foot. I wasn't even sure, yet, if I could stand, let alone walk.

So I waited and tried to rest, calling on magic to ease the pain. I didn't have healers' magic, though, so I could only dull it a little. I considered my options.

It said a lot about how shitty I felt that I even thought about revealing my identity and letting the Vogel King summon my mother to fetch me – because there was no way she would trust me to make my way home by myself now, and she couldn't trust anyone else to be able to control me. I think it galled her sometimes, that her half-human son was stronger in magic than most of her court.

My sisters could do it, but my mother couldn't trust *them* not to kill me.

Returning to my mother's court in Morven Forest meant giving up any hope of a future of my own making. The price for her to declare me legitimate was one I would never have chosen to pay now, though it had seemed a small sacrifice at the time.

Legitimacy was a vital part of how Sidhe politics worked, of how all fey politics worked. A monarch was required to formally declare a child legitimate, no matter how obvious it was whose offspring they were. So even though my mother had given birth to me, she could have chosen to disown me entirely. As a child, I assumed that she would, and only waited for her to announce I was not hers and condemn me to living with my father and having the shit kicked out of me every day by my human half-brother.

But even when she sent me to him, she still had not renounced her maternity, and eventually I proved useful enough – when I wasn't fucking my way through her entire court and most of the nearby countryside – that when I reached my majority at thirty-three, she had offered me a deal. I should have known it sounded better than it was. Because even if fey can't lie, they sure as fuck can manipulate.

But by the time she made the offer, I was so desperate to be wanted that I took it without looking too closely.

She offered me legitimacy, a place in her royal lineage as third in line to her throne, and work to do that would benefit my Monarchy and – supposedly – my people. It made me feel that my existence was worthwhile, which was all I had ever desired from either of my parents.

All I had to do was surrender my freedom.

It had seemed such a small thing, at the time. After all, if I was going to be working for my Monarch, why would I need to be free of her? For three years it had seemed like I had made a reasonable trade. I did as she told me. I learned diplomacy and lied when she wanted me to. I learned to kill without leaving a trace and eliminated men who had it coming. And I learned seduction – and not merely fucking – and pried secrets out of those who would rather not have told them.

And then I turned thirty-six and she sent me to a remote abbey in Aven, to prevent a blood sacrifice that would have caused a long and bloody war for all the peoples of the Isle. And I had thought I was just seducing the pretty young man I found there, showing him that touch could mean pleasure as much as it could mean pain.

I thought I was seducing him, but instead he was seducing me. Not on purpose, but effectively just the same. So instead of killing him – which I could never have done to such an innocent, anyway – and instead of delivering him to my mother, I had asked him where *he* wanted to go. And we obeyed the law of the Isle and travelled to meet his own monarch.

Who proceeded to take all of his choices away.

I was left with the deep certainty that my life would mean nothing without Fionn in it, that I had fallen hopelessly in love with him. And that I would rather die than return to being my mother's tool.

If I was identified as the Prince of Morven Forest – and all it would take was for someone to recognize the green magic-infused tattoo on my back – she would come and take control of me again.

And she would, no doubt, find some creative way to punish me for defying her. If I was very lucky, she would marry me off to someone useful, an ancient, powerful fey witch, perhaps. She would gain a magical ally, and I would spend the rest of my life as a crone's sex toy.

If I was unlucky… well, the less I thought about that, the better.

So I waited for night, and then I stood up slowly, to see if I could. I didn't black out, but stabbing pain hit me in so many places I felt like an archery target.

It was not hard to open the lock. I simply asked the air to muffle sound for me, inserted the key, turned, and slipped off the chain. I pulled shadows around me and stepped into the corridor. To one side, a row of cells stretched out, some standing open and others locked. To the other side were more cells and a patch of dim light where a corner turned. I heard faint snoring and smelled cold porridge.

I crept down the corridor, slow for silence, but also because I simply couldn't move any faster. When I reached the corner, I gritted my teeth against the pain, crouched, and peered around from just above floor level. The door out stood wide open to let in the breeze, and a guard sat at a table, leaning back in his chair.

I almost laughed out loud. The snoring was his.

I slipped into the room and wrapped an arm around his skinny neck, and he hardly struggled at all as I stole his breath and left him unconscious. I'd have liked to let his head hit the table with a thump, but I needed silence, so I laid him gently on the wooden surface. I put the key right where he would see it when he woke.

I didn't see my sword and knives anywhere in the small room, so I pulled the shadows tighter around me and walked right between the two guards outside the door and into the night.

31
Fionn

I HAD EXPECTED TO BE woken late at night, but I hadn't expected to be woken with a kiss.

I'd been dreaming of Kiernan rescuing me from Dag, only instead of me running off, Dag had been the one who left, while Kier stayed to kiss me and caress me, and gently fold me over the worktable. So, when I woke with lips pressed to mine and a hot tongue in my mouth, I reacted not in alarm, but by parting my lips to let him probe me deeper, by reaching for him, and moaning softly when he pulled away.

<Well, that was a pleasant surprise, little seer.>

I opened my eyes to candlelight and the King looking down at me. I made a different noise then, but he thought it was only another sign of arousal, not of the distress it really was.

<My King.> I forced my voice even and unemotional, but I couldn't force the pressure behind my sheath muscles to go away.

He sat on the side of my bed and smoothed the feathers

around my face. <I like my colors on you, Tokka.> He smiled. <It's too bad we have somewhere to be tonight. I would have liked to have seen where that kiss led us.>

<Yes, my King.> I looked down at the bed and did my best to sound regretful.

He stood and held out a hand. <No need to dress.> I noticed he was also clad only in a simple sleeping tunic and didn't even have his crown perched on his head.

I took his hand and let him lead me from my bedroom and out into the hall. His two guards and mine – a different pair from my daytime guardians – fell in behind us and followed us through the palace. When we reached a door set into the middle of an absurdly wide corridor, the guards took up positions, two on each side.

We passed through the door and the King locked it behind us. I looked around, saw dust and broken things and ruined wall hangings, looking sad and forgotten in the dim candlelight. I wanted to summon wisplights, but I was not inclined to share my magic with the King, no matter how much my body wanted to feel him touch me.

<We're in the ruins.> I spoke quietly, as if there might be ghosts to overhear.

<We are.> He took my hand again and led me down one corridor after another until I had lost all hope of ever finding my way here by myself. Had the ruins seemed so large from outside? Perhaps he was taking me by a circuitous route to confuse me on purpose. Finally, we came to a brick wall, sagging away from the stone, but still apparently solid. He showed me how to slip around one end of it, where it didn't meet the rockwork anymore, and we stepped into a natural passage, carved not by ancient Vogel, but by time and water.

I gasped when I turned away from the wall, though it wasn't really an impressive tunnel. It was simply its existence that thrilled me, even though the King had already told me of it.

<Caves,> I whispered, then snapped my mouth shut. I would not tell him about the caverns Kiernan and I had found under the cliff in Aven Forest.

<The base of the Eyrie is riddled with them, deep into the land.> He stroked my cropped hair and smiled down at me. <Your wonder is intoxicating, little seer. It makes you look so young.> He bent and brushed his lips on mine and made a noise that might have been a repressed moan. I shivered, and it was not from arousal. He confused me so much.

He began to walk along the passage, and I followed. <See the paintings.> He gestured, but I had already been staring around us at the pictures and bird-track symbols on the walls. Every image showed a bird Seer. Spinning and weaving were the focus of one set of images, and I would have liked to stop and look at them, but the King hurried me along. Another image, glimpsed quickly in passing, looked like a funeral procession, a silver Vogel leading the way with a glowing staff.

I needed to come back here on my own, to study the images and try to determine what they meant. In the meantime, maybe the journals and the huge ancient book I had found in the library would be able to tell me something. I had only just begun to read the journal before I'd fallen asleep.

<This is…> I didn't have the words. And I didn't really want to share them with my King, anyway. I would have given anything for it to be Kiernan here with me. Nothing I could have said would have expressed what I was feeling but Kier would have known without me having to say.

And I began to think a lifetime of captivity in the Eyrie might be worth it, to be able to study these pictures, these undeciphered texts left behind by my ancient forbears.

I stared around me as we walked, but the King was in a

hurry and wouldn't let me linger even the slightest. He pulled me along by the hand as we dropped deeper and deeper into the land until, finally, we came out in a small cavern. On all sides were shelves and alcoves, natural arches and pillars of white stone, their shapes enhanced by graceful, intricate carving. It was empty but must once have had some significance. It just *felt* momentous, and I shivered.

<This way, little seer.> The King led me away from the cavern, down a side passage marked by a squat stone pillar, hollow like the ones Kier and I had seen. And I had to duck into the opening, take several steps bent over, until it opened out. The ceiling, which would once have had us slithering on our bellies, had been chipped out and made tall enough for a Vogel King with chisels and picks. I had seen such desecration nowhere else in any of the caves I had visited.

I put my hand on the chipped stone, and the feeling of wrongness intensified. <Who did this, my King?>

<I had it done. No King should have to crawl on his belly like a commoner to visit a shrine of his people.>

I remembered Rocsh telling me the King wished to *use* the things of the past, not learn from them, and I thought it was worse than that. He wanted to use them, yes, but he also wanted them altered for his convenience. It felt blasphemous, disrespectful to our ancestors. To *my* ancestors, who had led our people in worship here.

I followed him past the ruined stone and into a shrine and had to stop and catch my breath. The ceiling was painted, though much damaged, with a soaring Vogel Seer, silver wings spread against a black sky spangled with stars. I drank in the sight, trying to commit it to memory, and had to drag my gaze away to look at the rest of the cavern.

In the floor in front of us was a pool with hot water running through it, just big enough for a tall person to lie full-length. Steep steps led from the floor down into the water and the bottom was tiled with black glass, as if to reflect the ceiling and leave the bather afloat in the night sky.

Beyond the pool was a huge slab of white stone like an altar, formed naturally from the slow deposition of pale rock.

The king set his candle on the floor and slipped off his tunic. His skin gleamed in the uncertain light, and I thought I could see his sheath bulge. I looked away.

<Come now, little seer. It is time to keep your promise.>

<I'm not sure...> I shook my head. This didn't feel right.

<This is a place of purification. Let the waters cleanse us together. You and I are destined to bring glory to our people, little seer, to usher in a new age.> His voice was low and calm, but underlying it was a deep fervor, as if he really did believe what he was saying. Or as if he needed to convince *me* that he believed.

But I knew Kiernan's thoughts on destiny, and I knew my own experience with visions of the future. It was always changing. I bit my lip, and he reached out to brush it with his fingers.

It *did* feel like a place of purification; I believed he was correct in that. But I wasn't convinced it was a place for *us*. Or more specifically, for *him*. I hadn't had a chance to look closely, but I didn't recall seeing a king in any of the wall paintings we passed. Only a Seer and ordinary people.

But I couldn't tell him any of that, even if I'd been able to find the words. So I took off my tunic, folded it, and placed in on the floor next to the candle.

I took a deep breath and put my hand in the King's and let him walk with me to the edge of the pool and down the steps. The water was not as hot as that in my bathing room; it was well above skin heat, but cool enough to feel pleasant.

I swallowed and let him turn me so my back was to him,

and he held me close to his chest and lowered us both into the water until we floated full-length. I stared up at the ceiling, at the Seer who mirrored my position in paint as if he were flying over me, leading me on a journey. The King's touch faded, and I floated in the dark night sky, my spirit drawn away to follow the painted Seer.

Then the King submerged us and I stared through the blur of water that didn't even sting my eyes and felt like I was floating away from here, away from my body, drawn on to another place where spirits peered down at me in confusion and looked at each other, speaking in silent voices.

Then something cold seemed to brush against me, and the spirits stared at me again, and made gestures with their half-visible hands, as if telling me to go, to hurry, and something probed at my mind, pulled at my spirit, sharp and cold, and I tried to scream.

Hot water flooded my mouth and I almost breathed it in, but the King was standing up and pulling me with him, apparently unaware of what had just happened. The presence was gone. I could still feel spirits around me, but I could no longer see them.

I let the King lead me out of the water, climbing the steps to stand before the altar.

<That wasn't so bad, was it, little seer?> He smiled at me and stroked a hand down my chest, lingering over my belly. I realized he had experienced none of what I had. He had not seen the spirits, or felt himself drawn into the otherworld, or had something try to drag him from his body.

He tucked a hand around my waist and pulled me closer, turning me to sit on the altar. <Lie back, my beautiful boy, and let us see how well the shrine has cleansed you of your past.>

As he eased me back on the stone and I fought against how wrong this felt, a tightness gathered in the back of my skull and my spine convulsed. Vaguely, I thought about Moira, and how she told me seers aren't supposed to have seizures when visions come, which was one more thing that made me different, that made me *wrong*.

<A vision,> I managed to gasp out before my twisting back threw me to the stone and only the King's quick reflexes kept my head from slamming against the rock.

And the cavern was gone. The King was gone. It was dark and I was half curled up, somewhere warm, blankets piled around me. A candle in a shaded holder flickered on a table nearby, but all it showed me was vague shadows of unfamiliar furniture.

I pushed back my hair, grown out just long enough to fall into my eyes. A warm arm tightened around me, and a smoky voice said, "Can't sleep, pretty bird?"

"A dream," I said, turning over to face him. "I didn't mean to wake you."

"You didn't. I don't sleep much these days."

I knew he could see me better that I could see him, but even in the dim light I noticed the dark circles under his eyes like bruises. I wondered what he saw when he looked at me.

He lifted his arm to touch my face, then reached behind me to stroke my nearest wing. He paused when his fingers found the edges of my added feathers, but he didn't comment, he just smoothed his hand over me again. "Are your wings comfortable?"

"My everything is comfortable."

He smiled. "That's good."

"Why don't you sleep much?"

He sighed and rested his forehead on mine. "It aches, Fionn." His voice was raw. "It aches constantly, and it only stops when Siona draws magic through me."

"I'm so sorry, Kier. If I had known…"

He shook his head. "You make it all worthwhile."

"Stop."

A smile touched his lips again. "You do. Especially when you kiss me."

So of course I had to kiss him. He opened his lips for me, slid his tongue alongside mine, and his breathing sped up, and so did mine.

I ran a hand down his arm, and back up, reveling in the way his skin slid over his muscles. I stroked my palm over his chest, hard with muscle but skin soft under my fingers. In response, he ran fingers over my ribs, brushed his hand over my hip, my thigh, under my tail to grip my buttock. I wrapped my leg over him.

"That's nice," he said and kissed my collarbone. His fingers curved around my butt cheek, found the dip between and traced along my crack until I moved my leg to open myself for him. Then he traced his fingers gently over my anus, circling and massaging.

I made a noise in my throat, and I saw the flash of his teeth as he grinned. "You make the prettiest little love noises," he murmured and pressed his lips to mine as he pressed his fingers harder against me, dipping inside me just a little.

I grabbed his hair and pulled his mouth harder against mine.

And the vision yanked me away, wanting him, needing him, and dropped me somewhere else.

Dark again. I heard frogs somewhere nearby, water burbling in a stream. I smelled trees, moist earth. I could hardly see at all. I crouched in the branches of a tree, wings and tail folded tightly, toes gripping and holding me firmly in place. I held a knife in each hand, familiar and comforting, and though the leather of their hilts was shaped to hands broader and shorter-fingered than mine, they still fit my grip perfectly.

Kiernan's knives felt like an extension of my own hands. I stared into the dark and heard my target approaching below.

I was wrenched away again, only this time I stood in the bright sun of early morning streaming through my balcony. I looked at the King, felt his hair between my fingers and he appeared surprised by something, by me. There was the silver flash of a sword in the sun wielded by a shadow I could only half see, and I thought maybe there was blood, but then I was flying. Somehow, I was flying, my own ragged, small wings spread against the sky, bright against the sea below me and I shouted in glee.

And I was wrapped in blankets again, in Kiernan's arms again, his mouth on mine, our bodies pressing together, our erections rubbing together as we thrust and left each other gasping.

And it was all gone except the pressure in my sheath which vanished in the cold that enveloped me. I was lying on stone, my head in the King's lap, my wings bent awkwardly under me, and a headache starting behind my eyes.

I didn't move for a long moment, and then I struggled to sit up. The King helped me, supported me while I swung my legs over the side of the altar.

<A vision, little seer?>

I nodded and rubbed my forehead. <I... nothing made any sense.>

<Will you tell me?>

<Once I get rid of this headache and can figure out what I *saw*.>

I shivered.

<You're ice cold, little seer. Let's get you home.> He sounded disappointed, like he wanted me to tell him that no, I was fine, and really I'd much rather he ravished me first.

But I was not fine.

I let him help me up, and lead me around the pool, and pull my tunic back over my head. While I waited for him to dress, I wrapped my arms around myself to stop the shivering. I couldn't shake the feeling that what we had done, what the King had intended to do, was not how this place was meant to be used. And while I stared into the dim, figures took shape. A Vogel Seer in the pool, saying words I couldn't hear over someone who floated there. Someone *dead* who floated there. He lifted the body out and carried it up the steps to lay it on the altar where three other bird folk began to dress it while he watched.

I shivered more violently as the figures faded and others took their place. Other Vogel, other bodies, other ritual cleansings. And then, at last, a lone figure standing next to the altar, small in stature, his hand resting on its surface. He smiled and said something inaudible. Then he stepped away, walked around the pool and directly through me and I almost cried out. These were glimpses of the past, shown to me by the spirits I felt crowding around me and the last one…

Kiernan had been here. He had come looking for me. Was he as dead as the long-ago people the spirits had also showed me? Was that what they meant to tell me?

I must have made a noise after all because the king looked up from tying his belt and touched my shoulder. I was still shivering.

<Little seer? What is it?>

<I saw… spirits. Ghosts.> I tried to still my body, but it only got worse, I was so cold. <This is a place for the dead.> I said, understanding rising in me, like a memory surfacing. <This is not a place for purifying the living.> I stared at the King, willing him to understand. <My King, this is where our ancestors prepared the dead before leaving them to their final rest in the cavern.> I pointed down the passage we had come

in.

<The pool is for purifying the *dead*.> I felt something like hysteria building and I couldn't stop it. <The altar is for dressing corpses before interment.>

I was shivering uncontrollably now and couldn't stop the words that poured out. <We should not have come here. We should not have bathed in the pool. Not for this. Not for you to fuck me in whatever cleansing ritual you made up for us to play out here.>

I stopped when his palm cracked against my face, but I couldn't react because I was shaking so hard. I was so cold. I felt myself falling and I was vaguely aware of him catching me, throwing me over his shoulder, and carrying me from the shrine.

I don't know how he got me past the brick wall without help, but I was aware, at least somewhat, when he passed my limp body to my guards and they dragged me, an arm over each of their shoulders, back to my room. My daytime guards were waiting outside my door, and I felt their shock on seeing me. They set their spears aside to take me from the night guards.

<Get him to bed and make sure he's ready to be presented to his people after morning meal.> I was barely aware of the King leaving. I was concentrating too hard on keeping my teeth from chattering.

<He's freezing,> said the younger guard as he eased my arm over his shoulders and the two of them helped me through the door and into my rooms.

<Get him into the bath,> the older guard said. <No bed will be warm enough.>

The younger guard looked at my face, tried to brace himself against my violent shivering. <Did he hit you, my Seer? What did he do to you?>

<None of that,> said the older guard sharply. <The King hears you and dismissal is the very best you can hope for.>

They carried me between them into my bathing room and the older guard held me while the younger guard climbed into the pool. I felt like a small child, passed between them.

The younger guard eased me into the water, sat with me on the bench, and I kept shivering, despite the heat of the water.

<Stay with him,> said the older guard. <I'll fetch Healer Kah.>

<No,> I managed to say, though I couldn't have come up with a reason I objected to them calling the healer. <I'll be fine. I only need to get warm.>

They looked at each other. The younger guard wrapped both arms around me and held me against his chest, as if he could stop my shivering through the strength of his grip.

<Please,> I said. I looked up at my older guard. <May I know your name?>

<Konta, my Seer.>

<Please guard my rooms for me, Konta. I don't wish any visitors. Only Neeka, when she arrives.>

He frowned, but nodded and went reluctantly back to his post.

<And your name?> I managed to ask the young guard, who held me carefully, as if I could break if I knocked into the tiled side of the pool. I could finally feel heat seeping into my limbs and the shivering eased.

<Trikta, my Seer.> He tucked my head against his shoulder, and I closed my eyes.

I returned his embrace, unwrapping my arms from my own torso, as if he was the only thing keeping me from flying into tiny pieces. Him and my vision of Kiernan, of myself wrapped in his strong arms, because it had been a *seeing* of the future, which meant we had at least a *chance* to be together again. Which meant he wasn't dead.

I could tell by the way Trikta held me that he felt more for me than he should, and I knew I should move away, establish an appropriate distance between us, because letting him think I returned his affection would only cause trouble later. For both of us.

But I was selfish, and my heart ached for Kier, and I was afraid again. So I let him hold me, even after I stopped shivering.

He touched my hair, tentatively, and I lifted my head from his shoulder. His eyes were soft green, not deep and dark like Kier's, but alike enough I could almost pretend.

His lips brushed mine and I let them linger before gently pulling away.

He pressed a hand to his mouth, eyes wide. <Goddess forgive me, my Seer, I should not have done that.> When I didn't reply, he blurted out, <I'm so sorry they cut your hair,> and it was so absurd I laughed.

I shook my head. <It's okay.> Whether I was referring to the kiss or my hair, I didn't know.

I put a hand on his chest and then moved away, sliding down the bench to create room between us. <Thank you.>

<It is my privilege to serve you, my Seer. In whatever way you want me.> Then he seemed to realize what he'd said and he flushed from the roots of his hair, down his neck, and across his chest. He looked down at the water.

I touched his shoulder and he jumped. <Thank you, Trikta.> I bit my lip. <Becoming… involved with me would not be wise. I am learning that our King is a jealous man.>

He touched my cheek, just a brush of his fingers, then stood and climbed from the pool.

<Did he hit you, my Seer?>

<It doesn't matter,> I said. <It makes no difference to anything.> I rose and got out of the bath. I wanted to strip off my soaking wet tunic, but it seemed a bad idea to do it in front of my young guard, after what had just occurred.

He handed me a towel and began to dry himself. <Do you love him?>

I rubbed at my hair with the towel. <It doesn't matter if I do or do not. I am his.>

<It's unfair,> he said, and I smiled, remembering how I had once said something similar to Kiernan. How did I feel so much older in so short a time?

<It is, but do not let the King, or anyone else, hear you say so. Not even Konta.>

<Yes, my Seer.> I could see he wanted to say more.

<What is it?>

He looked at his feet, flexed his toes, and spoke to the floor. <You had a friend.> He laced his fingers together, then relaxed them and let his hands fall to his sides.

<I had a lover,> I corrected gently. <He is Sidhe and forbidden to me now.>

<I saw him.>

My stomach turned to ice, even though I had seen the past shadow of Kier and knew he had to have been in the Eyrie.

<What?> My voice came out hard and Trikta flinched.

<He was in the palace. I think... I think he saw you go into the Council Chamber.>

He saw me walking arm-in-arm with the King.

<We chased him, Konta and me, and the King's guards. He... he escaped out a window.>

My breathing sped up, so fast I felt dizzy and had to sit in the chair I'd had my hair hacked off in, to send to the Alfar Monarch as a tithe.

<Tell me.>

<The King's guards flew after him. Konta and I went back. The King said we must say nothing to you or we would be disciplined. He said he would punish our families if you found out.>

<Stop,> I said.

<He was here. He wanted to tell you goodbye, to make sure you were happy and safe. He loves you, my Seer.>

<Stop!>

He stared at me, eyes huge, and far too young for this job.

I forced my breath calm and pushed myself to my feet. <You should not have told me, Trikta. And you must never speak of this again, do you understand?>

He nodded but looked unsure.

<You should not have told me but thank you.> I put a hand on his shoulder and squeezed. <I am glad you told me, but I won't have you or your family punished for me. So you must never mention this again, even to me.>

<Yes, my Seer.> He looked so confused that I couldn't help putting my arms around him. He was tall, like all the guards, and my head tucked neatly under his chin. For a heartbeat he didn't move, then his arms closed around my back.

<Thank you,> I whispered.

<My Seer,> he said, confusion gone and determination taking its place. <I may not be allowed to… to court you, but I can still love you in my own way. I am your guard, and anything you need, only ask, and I will do it.>

His voice was full of something like religious awe, and I knew there would be no dissuading him.

I stepped out of his arms and smiled. <I hope I can be worthy of your devotion, Seer's Guard Trikta.>

He grinned. <You already are, my Seer.> He conjured a wisplight and set it to floating about my head.

32
Kiernan

THE GAOL, I SOON DISCOVERED, was located on the outer edge of the City Beneath the Cliff, up against a stone wall than ran from the cliff itself, in a broad curve around the city, to the beach.

It looked like it had once been a strong, fortifiable defense, but it was now pierced by so many gates and denuded of its best stone in so many places that all it really did was draw a line between the city on one side and the countryside on the other.

The only reason it was in good repair near the gaol was because it formed the building's back wall, and letting it go to ruin would mean all the prisoners would escape and there would be nowhere to store thieves.

I found an alley to lurk in, far enough from the gaol I didn't feel I'd be captured at any moment. Assuming anyone noticed I was gone. Like most cities I'd visited, the City Beneath was almost as active at night as it was during daylight, only the activity was quieter, more secretive. And since I didn't know my way around, I would have to be careful not to make myself a target.

Fortunately, even though I was far from my forest, the shadows seemed content to hover around me, without me having to use much magic. Since childhood I had found darkness friendly, when I'd frequently needed to escape one sibling or another.

The alley I had chosen ran next to a tavern, and I listened to people as they passed by, hoping to learn something of the character of the City. Naturally, most people spoke the Vogel language, but there were enough non-Vogel around that I overheard Alfar and Islish and even a little Sidhe.

I learned plenty of gossip about people I had never heard of and would almost certainly never meet. I discovered that the price of shellfish had become too high for most people to afford – despite its once having been considered a last resort to eat – owing to its current popularity among the rich. And I found out that, while most citizens considered King Sarkot to be the handsomest royal in several generations, they didn't think so well of him as a ruler. In hushed tones with many glances around for guards, more than one passer-by expressed the opinion that he was too interested in returning to some forgotten golden age of Vogel rule, and not interested enough in basic things like making sure his people had enough food or repairing the City's crumbling stonework.

I leaned against the side of the tavern, thinking, trying not to stand in any of the puddles of piss and worse that alleys near drinking establishments invariably had – I *was* barefoot, after all – and longed to just sit down somewhere. A cup of cider would be nice, too.

My leg ached and my hip where the guard had poked me with his spear-butt was so tender even my trousers brushing across it was torture. And I was starting to think I might have been hurt worse by the fall to the beach than I had thought. Or maybe from the beating afterwards, which I had been mostly unconscious for. Something didn't feel right inside, though my head also wasn't clear enough to have described what with any sort of accuracy.

I was just thinking about looking for an out-of-the-way corner – not filled with piss puddles – where I could sit undisturbed and wait out the rest of the night, when a word caught my attention.

"You going to go gawp at this seer the King dredged up from somewhere?"

I edged closer to the street. The speaker was a lean, weathered-looking Vogel man with dull brown feathers, who spoke Islish with a thick accent.

"You suppose he's even real, and not just plucked and dressed up in some sea-bird's feathers?" The second man was smaller, human and painfully thin under a battered leather coat. His nose was even crookeder than mine had been before I yanked it back into place.

The Vogel laughed, a wet, unhealthy sound. "You give the King too much credit for thinking," he said. "Though if it were, I don't think you'd get close enough to tell. Royal platform's a little high above the square."

"Fishers are saying they saw the Seer fly over, all shining in the sun, like. *They* believe, at least."

"Fishers is superstitious."

"Reckon I'll go have a look, anyway. Might be some good coin to be made."

"Don't get caught lifting no noble's purse, you. I hear your cousin were hanged for it."

"Nah. Got his hand cut off is all. He just learned to pick pockets with the other."

The Vogel laughed again. "I bet he sits on a street-corner

and begs, too, showing off his stump, like."

"Not one to waste an opportunity, him." The human took a packet of leaves from his pocket, selected one, and put it in his mouth. He offered them to the Vogel, who refused.

The sluggish breeze brought the sharp, dry scent to my nose and I almost sneezed. The man was chewing spunk, a highly addictive stimulant that, unfortunately, was all that got some overworked peasants – and pickpockets, it seemed – through each day. It was named, I had heard, for the way it tasted, as much as for the energy it imparted.

"They say he's going to walk through the city after, to show he's not above the common folk like us." He snorted. "I reckon I could maybe get close enough to tell if he's real or not."

"Look him in the eyes, like, and see if they're silver, too?"

They both laughed, then shook hands and went their separate ways.

I leaned on the wall and tried to breathe normally. They were talking about Fionn. The Vogel King was planning to show him off in the morning and maybe I could get close enough to… what, scream, "I love you" and get speared by a guard for my trouble?

It didn't matter. I coughed and for a long few heartbeats I couldn't stop. It bent me double and every injury, inside and out, stabbed into me at once. I felt myself sliding down the wall, gray gathering at the edges of my vision.

I dug my claws into the soft wood siding of the tavern, somehow staying on my feet. A sliver jabbed into my infected finger, right under the split nail, and I threw up all the water I had drunk from a public fountain just after leaving the gaol.

There was blood in the water I puked, and when I wiped my mouth on my sleeve, it came away stained dark.

"That's probably not good." I straightened up, clenching

my jaw so hard I thought my teeth would crack, and managed to stand without crying out as my ribs stabbed me, something in my back popped, and my leg tingled unpleasantly. I was definitely in worse shape than I had thought. I guess even Sidhe can't heal quickly when there's that much to heal.

The public square the thieves had mentioned would probably be directly under the Eyrie – somewhere the royals could make appearances and pontificate to their people without actually having to mingle with them. I eased out of the alley and looked around, and up. Even at night, the Eyrie cliff was ghost-pale.

I began to walk that direction, keeping close to the edge of the road, making use of alleys when I could, and holding my shadows close. I moved slowly, carefully; I couldn't have gone quickly if I'd tried. It was a good thing I still had most of the night to get where I was going, because it was going to take me that long to arrive.

I roused when something soft slid against the back of my neck and a tiny voice chirped in my ear. I lifted my head from my knees with effort and smiled when Flame's little dragon-like face appeared over my shoulder. She slithered onto my knees and bumped her head against my chin. I managed to lift a hand on the second try and scratched under her jaw and she purred.

I find, she said.

"Yes, little friend, you found me." I looked around. Morning had arrived and people were moving about getting ready for the day. I smelled food of several varieties and knew I should be hungry, but I couldn't find any interest in eating.

"Where's Smoke?"

Find bright bird.

"He'll be over there before long." I tried to point, but my arm didn't want to move. Flame looked where I was looking.

We go together?

"No, little one. I can't go with Fionn. Not anymore."

You love, she insisted.

"Yes. I love him. But… I can't."

She cocked her head at me, shifted half her length to one side, then then other, examining me from several angles.

Dark hurt, she said, and draped herself around my neck again. *Don't like.*

"I don't like it either," I leaned my head back against the wall I was sitting against. I had no idea how I was going to stand up, let alone follow Fionn when he came down to walk through the City. But one problem at a time.

I love, Flame said, nuzzling under my ear.

"I know you do." I said. "I love you too."

I help. She purred in my ear, and it shifted into something like a rhythm, a rising and falling song with no words, a vibration that started in her tiny body and shifted into my jaw and spread until it felt like my whole skeleton was shivering. And the pain eased away. It didn't vanish, but it became bearable. I had no conception of how long I sat there with a vibrating serpent around my neck, but when she stopped humming and my bones stopped vibrating, the sun was bright on the side of the cliff, and the square was full of people.

"Thank you, Flame," I whispered. "I didn't know you could do that."

Have secrets, she said, and sounded very smug.

"You certainly do." I pushed myself to my feet slowly, to stand atop the wall I'd been sitting on, and leaned against the one behind me. I knew that whatever Flame had done, she hadn't healed me, only took away some of my pain. I hoped it would be enough.

The people around me gave me odd looks, but no one spoke to me, or told me I shouldn't stand on the wall, or pointed me out to a guard. The square was soon crowed with people waiting to see the promised seer, and I was glad I had chosen a spot higher up, even if it was far away from the royal platform.

There was a trumpet blast and the whole crowd fell silent.

Bright bird, said Flame, and as she said it, a pale figure stepped out onto a balcony high above. Two green-and-blue feathered, bird-masked guards flanked him, leapt into the air above him, and lifted him by his raised arms between them. I thought I spotted a tiny, sinuous shape curling through the air around Fionn's legs.

They descended, followed by more guards, and then the tall figure of the King himself.

And one by one, they landed on the platform across the square.

I couldn't breathe and I didn't know if it was my injuries or just the sight of Fionn. He had blue and green and purple feathers around his face, and more added to his wings and tail. He looked unearthly.

I felt him tremble, deep in my belly, as the guards set him on his feet and then landed beside him, and I saw one guard touch his back, brief and fleeting, before stepping back to his place.

A deep longing ache stabbed through me, and I could feel his anxiety. I could also feel his determination, stronger than I realized he had.

"Goddess Below," I whispered. I swallowed hard. It hurt. Everything hurt. My heart hurt most of all.

He looked over the crowd, eyes searching, as if he knew I

was here somewhere, and I knew, I felt it, when his eyes found me, and his lips silently shaped my name.

"I love you Fionn," I whispered, so softly no one but Flame could hear me, except somehow I think *he* heard me. He placed a hand over his heart.

He loves, said Flame.

"I love," I said.

Yes. Bright and dark. Love and love.

The King moved up beside Fionn and spoke to the crowd, but I heard none of it; I wasn't even aware if he was speaking Vogelspek or Islish. I just drank in the sight of Fionn, calm and serene in a way the King had only pretended to be when he visited me in gaol. He was afraid, uncertain, but able to push his worries aside to be his people's Seer. I knew – somehow, I *knew* – that he was finding his way.

"He's going to be okay," I said softly, and Flame stirred around my neck, and nuzzled under my ear.

I don't know how long I stood and stared; time was becoming a concept my mind just couldn't hold onto anymore. That probably wasn't a good thing, any more than coughing blood had been.

Eventually, the crowd began to break up. Many people wandered away to go back to the usual tasks of their day, while others crowded forward to get closer to where their Seer would walk. The guards stepped down from the platform and cleared the way for Fionn. He glanced my way, then at the King, who was leaning to speak into his ear. Fionn nodded, and the King departed with a pair of guards, leaping into the air above the heads of the crowd to circle back up to the Eyrie.

I slipped into the nearest alley and followed Fionn's path as best I could, looking for somewhere I could intercept him. I only needed a few minutes, and after that it didn't matter what happened to me.

Go there, said Flame and I looked up from watching where I placed my feet, and saw a small tea house on the corner of two very clean-looking streets.

"They'd never let me in there," I said. "I look like I crawled out of a garbage heap, and I smell worse."

Go, insisted Flame.

I didn't have the strength to argue with her, so I sighed, limped out of the alley I'd been following, and crossed the road.

"You!" said a sharp voice.

"Fuck," I said, and turned. A blue-and-green feathered, bird-masked guard pointed his spear at me. I raised my hands. There was no way I could run. I could barely walk.

"I only wanted to see the Seer," I said.

The guard approached, lowering his spear. I saw him tip his head to look down at me, at the feathered tree serpent on my shoulder. He pushed his bird mask to the top of his head and smiled. He had moss-green eyes and looked too young to be a King's guard.

"My Seer would like to buy you a cup of tea," he said. He was one of the guards who had chased me in the palace, the one who hadn't seemed to want to be there.

He gestured to the tearoom door. "Please? Before the rest of them catch up."

Flame purred and poked her head into the side of my neck. I nodded and walked, as dignified as I could – which wasn't very – into the tearoom. I stood between the neat little tables, not sure what to do. I couldn't sit down. I had so much filth on my clothes – on my skin – that the poor tearoom owners would never be able to wash it out of their seat cushions.

So I stood, and waited, and watched as the guard lowered the sun blinds on all the windows.

A thin man, taller than me but shorter than the guard, emerged from a back room to look at me curiously. He had the fair skin and delicate pointed ears of an Alfar, but his broad, handsome features and large hands must have come from the human sailors and fishers of the coast of Tronven.

"My Seer's eyes are sensitive to light," the guard said, and the man smiled.

"Of course." He turned his smile at me. "Will you sit?"

I gestured to my clothes and winced as something twinged, stabbing through the magic Flame had worked on me. "I would not wish that terrible fate on your furniture."

His smile grew wider, and I thought I saw empathy in his eyes. "I will prepare the tea then."

The guard turned back to his task and when he was finished, he looked at me. "You don't look well," he said.

I laughed, which turned into a cough, and that almost had me on the floor. I'd have fallen, but the guard's strong hands held me up until I recovered, though I nearly screamed when he gripped my broken arm.

"Goddess Above, you're hurt bad." Horror grew in his eyes. "Did the King's men do this to you?"

I leaned on his arm and wiped my mouth on my sleeve. More blood. "It doesn't matter. I'm sure I had it coming." I tried to smile.

Noise outside the door had us both looking that way and I suddenly, desperately, wanted to sit down.

"That's them," the guard said.

"Tell me your name." I heard voices outside, now, along with the footsteps. Someone spoke instructions in a clipped tone, and then I heard the soft husky voice I knew better than my own.

"Trikta," the guard said. "I'm a Seer's guard, not a King's man."

"Trikta." I pulled my gaze from the door to look at him. "You care for your Seer?"

He straightened his spine and lifted his chin. "I do." Two short words, and I could read all his feelings. He would have to learn to hide himself better, but I smiled. He more than cared for Fionn.

"He's going to need friends. People he can trust. Are you one of those people?"

"Yes." His conviction filled the word, made it bigger than it was. I nodded.

The door opened and another guard stepped through, holding it for the person who followed him.

And the Seer of the Vogel Monarchy stepped through into the tea house. I'd have sunk to my knees to worship him, if I could have.

He was… he was Seer Tokka of the Vogel, straight-spined and regal, worthy of his people's devotion. Worthy of *all* people's devotion.

The door closed behind him, shutting out the rest of the guards and the people who followed, and I still couldn't breathe.

He stopped just inside the door and looked at me, lips slightly parted, fingers twining together in uncertainty. He looked like he couldn't breathe, either. Under the bright feathers, the elegant clothing, the makeup of Seer Tokka, I saw my Fionn, sweet and shy and gentle.

I took a step towards him, and it was like a spell breaking. He closed the space between us and wrapped his arms around me, pressed his lips to mine and I didn't even care that agony stabbed through me from uncountable directions.

"Goddess Above, Kier, what did they do to you?"

I wanted to tell him I was okay, that I'd be fine, but I wouldn't let our last moments together be tainted by lies.

"What did they do to *you?*" I retorted and he laughed.

"I don't look like myself, do I?"

"I see my pretty bird under there." For just this moment, I could pretend everything would be okay.

"He told me you left, that you went back to Morven." He spoke softly, but there was more in his words that he couldn't say out loud.

"I'd rather die than go back to my Queen," I said. "And besides, I couldn't leave without saying goodbye."

He put his hands on either side of my face and looked deep into my eyes. I wanted to drown in silver. "You're in pain," he said. "I can feel it."

"I'm not doing so good," I admitted. I didn't know how much longer my legs were going to hold me up. Whatever magic Flame had worked on me was fading now.

"I'll get you a healer."

I shook my head. "Your King won't allow it, and you mustn't try. Don't make him angry, pretty bird."

He started to protest, and I used some of my last strength to kiss him. Softly at first and then desperately, needing him to know how much I wanted to stay, how much I needed him.

I pulled away. "Listen, I know what the King intends for you. Don't fight him. Please. Stay safe. I can't bear this if I don't know you'll be safe."

He rested his forehead on mine. "I had a vision, Kier. Of us. Of the future."

I smiled. Even my face hurt. "According to a very clever seer I know, visions of the future are only possibilities."

He smiled back. "But possibilities can be made reality." He turned my chin up so I had to look at him. "Tell me you'll come back for me," he said. "Tell me that and I will endure whatever I have to until we're together again."

"Fionn…"

"Tell me."

I wanted so much to give him what he asked, everything he asked, but I would not lie to him. "If I could, Fionn, I would come back from the shores of Tir na n'Og for you. I love you, pretty bird, so much I can't imagine life without you."

He caught his breath, kissed me, and pulled away smiling. "I love you, Kiernan." He waited for me to smile back, but I didn't seem to be able to move my face. He looked at me, and I saw the moment understanding came into his eyes. "You'd come back from Tir na n'Og? From …*death?*" His voice broke.

"I'm sorry, pretty bird. I tried." I felt my legs start to buckle and tried to cling to him, but he slipped through my hands.

"I'll get you a healer."

"It won't be allowed. Your King wants me dead. I think he's jealous." I tried to laugh, but only a croak came out.

Fionn's arms held me up. "He would not want you dead if he knew who you were. He wouldn't dare start an incident between Monarchies. Between *Triarchies.*"

"Please don't, Fionn. I can't go back there. I love you more than life, but I'd rather die than go back."

He kissed my forehead gently and my knees buckled completely. He held me, lowered me carefully to the floor, and held me in his lap.

"Trikta. Konta," he said, and his guards moved into the graying edges of my vision.

"Please don't, beloved," I said.

That stopped him for a moment. "Beloved," he repeated. A tear slid down his face, making a pale line in the makeup. "I need to ask you for something. It will be the hardest thing you've ever had to do, but I need to ask it from you before I let you go."

I sighed and relaxed in his arms. He meant to let me go. I

could die in peace. I could die loved and wanted. "I would do anything for you."

"I need you to live." And as the gray turned to black in the edges of my sight, I felt him pull up my shirt, push down the waist of my trousers, and turn my back to the guards.

I heard one of them swear.

"I'll get the King."

"I'll fetch Healer Kah."

"I love you, Kier."

And then it all went away.

33

Fionn

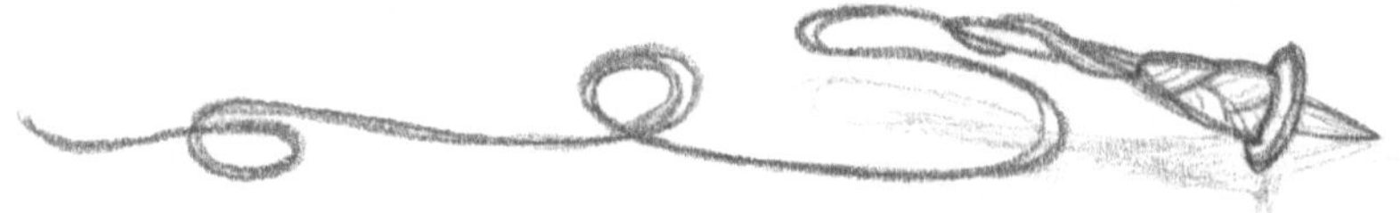

King Sarkot, Lord of Three Realms and Monarch of the Eyrie, swore at me. He ranted at me, stormed though my rooms knocking things to the floor, smashed my writing desk by slamming his hand down onto it, and put his foot through the firebird screen in my bathing room.

And finally, he walked over to me where I stood calmly in the middle of my sitting room and towered over me. <You deceitful little shit.> His spittle hit my face and I wiped it away with the hem of my already soiled tunic. <Why didn't you tell me?>

I looked up at him from under my lashes, let a tear slide down the side of my nose, and bit my lip as if uncertain how to reply. <I'm sorry, my King,> I said in my softest voice. <I didn't know what it meant. He only told me it marked him as belonging to his Queen.>

<It marked him as belonging to the royal fucking family of Morven fucking Forest.> He seldom swore, so I knew he was still furious, but he no longer looked like he was going to hit

me.

<Why did you meet him in the tea house?> He took both my hands in his and stroked his thumbs over my skin.

<I enjoy, tea, my King.> I flicked my gaze up to his and away. <I wanted to give my custom to one of my people, to begin to build relationships with the community so they may get to know their Seer.>

He growled under his breath, but he had agreed, even last night, that allowing myself to be close to my people would make them revere me more. <Did he harm you?> He looked down at the blood – Kiernan's blood – on the front of my tunic. His face softened and I knew I had won. He might be able to tell truth from lies, but he was unable to detect a more subtle deceit.

I hated dishonesty in all forms. It made my mouth feel wrong to pronounce a lie, and my stomach hurt when I was anything but truthful. From birth I had been punished for lies. But I had realized, finally, in the moment I had drifted into the otherworld in the death shrine, that to do more than just to survive here, to *thrive* here, I would have to find a way to get the King to do what I wanted. All while thinking I was doing what he wanted.

It would mean letting him have me, completely, and the thought made my stomach turn, now that I had seen what he was. But I had *seen* my better future, and now that I knew it was possible, I would do what I had to in order to get it.

<My King…> I peered up at him through my lashes again, playing shy.

He put a finger under my chin and tilted my head up, so I had to meet his eyes directly. I knew he was looking for lies. <Yes, little seer?>

<Is there… Is there a way I can apologize to you?> I licked my lower lip, then pulled it between my teeth, knowing

it made me look childish, knowing he liked it.

His fingers tightened on my chin, and I thought I had made a mistake, but he only leaned closer and pressed his mouth on mine.

<I'm afraid,> I whispered against his lips.

<Of me, little seer?>

<Of angering you, my King. Of… doing the wrong thing. Of touching you wrong.>

He moved closer still, pressing me to him with a hand behind my back. <I'll tell you if you do anything wrong,> he said. <And if I punish you, it will always be for your own good.> His voice was rough.

<What would you have me do?> I brushed my mouth against his neck and felt his throat move as he swallowed. <To make up for my error?>

He leaned away, smiled, and put both hands on my shoulders. <You may start by getting on your knees, like a good boy. Please me well enough and I will begin to forgive you.>

<Yes, my King.> I let him push me to my knees, let him pry open my mouth with his thumb and even moaned when he pressed down on my tongue, and I put my mouth where he told me to, sucked when he told me to, and swallowed when he told me to.

The tears I let fall were only partly for his benefit.

<You are such a beautiful innocent, my little seer,> he said. <It will be a shame to take that from you, but I will enjoy it just the same.> Then he pushed me away, put his clothes back in order, and left.

I heard the lock snap shut after he went. He hadn't even let Neeka come in to attend me.

I went into my bathing room and leaned over the sink, jammed two fingers into my throat, as far as I could get them, and vomited stringy white fluid into the basin. I rinsed it down, and did it again, and again, until all that came up was froth.

Then I stripped out of my clothes, stained with Kiernan's blood and whatever awful things he had been subjected to while wandering alone through my city, mortally injured. I climbed down into the bath, scrubbed makeup off my face, and then leaned against the side and closed my eyes.

"I love you, pretty bird," he had said. And even though I had already known, had felt it deep in my gut, it had still hit me like a punch to the chest, stealing my breath and making me want to cry out in joy.

"I love you, Kier," I whispered to the air. And I banished the memory of the King's touch, the King's mouth on mine, his cock in my throat, by thinking about Kiernan. About my beloved.

I was almost not surprised to feel the tightness in the back of my head, in my scalp and my forehead. I hauled myself out of the bath so I wouldn't drown, and tried to jam a folded towel under my head so I wouldn't brain myself on the stone floor.

And I let the vision take me away into the dark, where a candle burned in a shaded holder on a nearby table, and warm arms held me close.

"I love you, Fionn," he said, his green eyes reflecting the candlelight.

"I love you, Kier," I replied and smiled at the way his whole face brightened when I said it.

I tightened my fingers on his hardness, felt silken skin slide under my grip, and my breath sped up to match his.

He tightened his grip on my erection in response and stroked me until warmth spread through my limbs.

"What do you want me to do you, pretty bird?" he asked

in his smokiest voice.

"Make me forget him," I said. "Make me remember only you."

He kissed me, hard, poked his tongue into my mouth, and pressed me back against my pillow. Then he pulled away far enough to look into my eyes. "Tell me what you want me to do to you," he said again.

I smiled. "Be mine."

"I am yours."

"Only mine."

"Until I die."

I brushed my lips on his, then pressed harder, pushing him back onto his pillow. "Don't leave me," I said, knowing it couldn't be true, not yet. Knowing I would have to leave *him* soon.

"Never again, beloved."

"I want you to fuck me."

He slid his hand off my erection, his fingers coated with my lubricant, and gently pushed my thighs apart. I gasped when his fingers slid between my cheeks and found my anus.

"Is this okay?"

I rolled flat onto my back, and spread my legs wider, pushing my pelvis up against his hand. "Oh, yes."

"Do you want my fingers inside you?"

"Fuck yes. Put your fingers in me."

He complied, sliding two slippery fingers into my ass, slowly, gently. He curled down over me, ran his tongue over my cock, slid his lips over me, and sucked.

I buried my hands in his hair, found an antler under my fingers, and clung to it. "Wait," I said, when the pleasure started to nudge me over the edge.

He raised his head, smiled, and waited.

"I want you to fuck me."

His smiled widened and his fingers slid out of me. He put himself between my legs, bent my knee up to my chest, and stroked his hand down to caress the skin on top of my foot.

"Put me where you want me."

I reached down, dipped my fingers into my sheath, and spread my fluids onto Kier's length, grasped him, and pressed his tip between my legs, against my circular muscle. I rubbed him against me, and he moaned into my chest.

"Please," I said, and he kissed the skin below my collarbone and pushed himself against me, into me, and at the same time, he slid his finger between my toes, and it was my turn to moan. "Goddess Above," I breathed. "Kier."

He thrust against me, his belly muscles sliding against my hardness, his finger caressing the absurdly sensitive place between my two big toes.

You wouldn't think there could be very much difference between having one man's erection up your anus and another man's, but there was. There was a world of difference, so much that it might not have even been the same act.

I came to on my bathing room floor, a towel half under my head, wings sprawled out across the stone, and my hand curled around my erection, stroking.

"Spirits," I whispered as my back arched, with pleasure this time and not from a vision seizure. I pulsed three times, one right after the other, and had to try hard not to cry out with them. I wondered if he could feel me, and if he would think I was with the King.

For a long while I continued to stroke myself, almost sure a fourth pulse was coming, but it faded as the vision faded and I stopped and lay looking at the stained glass upside down. Then I crawled back to the bath and washed.

I dressed, cleaned up the mess the King had made of my rooms, and sat down on the balcony with a book on the government of the Eyrie, waiting for someone to come and tell me what was happening in the world outside.

I WAS NOT ALLOWED to see Kiernan, nor had I expected to be, and the King grew angry whenever I asked after his health.

But one noonmeal Councilor Rocsh arrived with the trays of covered dishes.

<I thought perhaps we could eat together,> he said, and I gestured for him to sit.

The King had still not allowed Neeka to return, perhaps thinking to punish me by making me turn down my own bed and dress myself. I don't think he knew that the real punishment was the lack of her company.

<I've asked for a new desk to be found for you,> the Councilor said. <And a screen for your bathing room.>

<Thank you, Councilor.>

<He won't lock you in here forever.> He reached out to take the lid off a dish. It was poached shrimp in a savory sauce, with tiny forks to spear them with.

<Only until the Prince of Morven is gone, I suppose.>

He lifted the lid on another dish. Thinly sliced raw fish in a deep shade of pink had been laid over soft sheep cheese on thin biscuits. I reached for one and ate it, careful not to scatter crumbs. I had lost weight since I came to the Eyrie, and I had already been thin. I had to try not to lose any more or I would waste away.

<Did you really not know who he was?> the Councilor asked, selecting one of the fish and cheese biscuits. Before I could say anything, he said, <No, don't answer that. I don't need to know.>

<Is he… Is he well? Is he healthy?>

<It's a wonder he was still alive. He's very determined, your Prince. But yes, he is healing. It will be some time before he will truly be well.>

<But he will recover?>

<Healer Kah has done what she can. The rest is up to him. Or, perhaps, to healers of his own people.>

<The Sidhe have more healing magic than we do,> I said, though I knew that was at least partly due to the Vogel policy of only testing the children of the wealthy for magical ability, and only training them if they had a lot of it.

<They do.>

I investigated more dishes, wondering what would happen to the food we didn't eat. I hoped it went to someone who needed it and didn't end up in the midden. I told myself I must remember to ask Neeka, and make sure the leftovers went where they were needed.

<His mother… his Queen is on her way here?> I chose a slice of baked fowl and nibbled at it.

He nodded. <She will be here within a ninenight. Sooner if the winds are good.> He wiped his fingers on a napkin and reached for the pitcher of water. <You will attend a ceremony of farewell when they depart. The King expects you to behave.> He looked amused.

<I will not disappoint him.>

He regarded me, head tilted. <I wonder what you are up to,> he said.

I set down the forkfull of roasted root vegetables I had been about to eat. <Today, tomorrow, and for the near future, I am only trying to survive. After that, I mean to make sure my people survive.>

He looked at me a moment longer then nodded. <How did you know to meet your Prince in the tea house?>

I smiled. <I didn't, Councilor. I didn't even know he was in the city, though I suspected I might find him in the gaol.> I looked at him from under my eyelashes and his lips quirked slightly, but he didn't comment. <The serpents guided us together, even told me to send a man ahead to meet him.>

<Tree serpents? I had no idea they were so intelligent.>

I shrugged. <I suspect they reveal themselves only to those they trust.>

<And where are they now?>

<With him. They're watching over him for me, but I believe they will stay here when he goes. They don't like what they've heard of his Queen.>

He laughed. I still had no idea if he was an ally, a spy for the king, or had motivations all his own. For now, at least, he seemed to be on my side.

I DIDN'T KNOW THE QUEEN of Morven Forest had arrived until my door unlocked and Neeka bustled in, her arms full of cloth and a basket slung over her wrist.

She waited until the door closed behind her, then flung her burden at the nearest couch and grabbed me in a hug.

<I missed you, too,> I said, laughing.

<You scared me, Tokka. I thought… I don't know what I thought, but you scared me. No one would tell me why I wasn't to attend you anymore.>

<I'm sorry, Neeka, I'd have told you if I could. I wasn't even allowed to speak to my guards.>

<Did you really fall in love with the Prince of Morven Forest?>

<Shhh.>

She poked my chest. <You only told me he was Sidhe.> She sat on top of the pile of clothing she had brought. <Goddess Above, my Seer. First the King, and now a Prince.>

I pushed aside some clothing and sat. <There is a considerable difference between them.>

<Yes. You don't love the King.>

<Shhh.>

She pressed her lips together, pinching them closed with her fingers. <And now I'm supposed to get you ready for the big farewell as if nothing has happened.>

<Have you seen him? Does he look well?>

<Of course I've seen him! Everyone has seen him. He and his Queen mother were given a huge banquet when she arrived. We all had to help serve. He didn't look so well *that* night, but a Sidhe healer has been with him every moment since. And *she* was magnificent, the Queen. She's tiny, you know? Even smaller than your Prince.>

<There was a banquet?>

<And a whole bunch of ceremonial meetings and political speeches. It was all very boring.>

<Why wasn't I invited?>

<I think our King is saving you for last. To show you off.>

<Or he still doesn't trust me.>

<Well, you'll be at the farewell, which is soon, so they can set out with the tide. She came on a ship, you know, around the coast. And what a ship! It's small but so pretty, so elegant, like her.>

<Neeka.>

<And she brought gifts. White deer and golden dishes and dryads. Have you ever seen a dryad?>

<Neeka!>

She stopped suddenly, as if only just realizing she was babbling. <Sorry, my seer.> Her bright smile didn't fade.

<She brought dryads? As in magical people who are kin to trees? As *gifts*?>

<Apparently, they're considered… less intelligent and commonly used as… um…>

<Pleasure slaves?>

<Some of them are…> Her voice had gone very quiet.

<The fey think of *us*, of the Vogel, as less intelligent, too. As barely sentient.>

<*Oh*. I mean, they won't be used for *that*, not here where it's forbidden to fuck someone not Vogel, but…> Her eyes were wide. <Goddess Above. I never thought of them as *people*. That's horrible.>

<Yes.> I looked at my hands. That was one more thing to add to my list of things to accomplish: freedom for captive dryads. It would be difficult, as dryads needed to periodically root in the soil they were born in, but if the Queen of Morven had got them here, I could get them out.

<Well,> I said. <Best get me dressed and made up and turn me into Seer Tokka.>

<You *are* Seer Tokka.>

<Of course.> I was because I had to be, but I wished that tonight I could just be Fionn, and that the Prince of Morven Forest could just be my Kier.

I ARRIVED IN THE KING's receiving hall before anyone except the King himself and his nine Councilors, carried down from the palace by my guards and set on my feet in front of the door to the only part of the Eyrie that was accessible from the ground.

I lifted my head high, felt Neeka behind me, Trikta and Konta to each side, like strength-giving beacons, and walked serenely into the hall, pure white moth silk tunic swirling around my ankles.

The King's eyes burned when he saw me, but he simply nodded. <My Seer.>

<My King.> I had walked across the room to take my place with my hands clasped at my waist. Now I unclasped them to hang by my side, and I dared to brush a finger against the back of the King's hand. <I've missed you,> I said, so that only he could hear.

<Have you?> He returned the touch, briefly, then shifted out of my reach.

<Am I ever to be forgiven?>

<We'll see how well you behave.> He looked at me sidelong. <Come to my rooms for the evening meal.>

<Yes, my King.>

Then the doors opened wide, and four King's guards strode in and took their places halfway down the hall. After them came four Sidhe guards, dressed in green and gray and rust, leather and linen and moonsilver. Next to the King's guards, they were tiny, but they moved with more grace and had a kind of feral strength.

The stood to each side of the door, swords bare in their hands. The ones on the left carried their blades in their left hands, and the ones on the right wielded right-handed.

And then the Queen of Morven Forest came in and it was hard to look at anything else. She was even smaller than her guards but carried an aura of immense power. She was delicate-looking, but her green eyes were harder than steel. Her hair was so long it nearly reached the floor, and it was the deep red of dried blood. Instead of a crown, every tine on her magnificent set of antlers was tipped with moonsilver and inscribed with intricate, twisting designs.

Next to her, his arm tucked in hers, walked the Prince of Morven Forest. He looked paler than he should have, with his bronze complexion, and there were smudges like bruises under his eyes, only partly hidden by the green tattoos. But he held his head high and looked at everyone in the room like they were beneath him.

His unruly hair had been cut, trimmed close to his neck at the back, and left somewhat longer on top, where it curled around his antlers. His tines, too, had been tipped with engraved moonsilver.

He wore deep green and moss green and earthen brown to match his mother and his sword was in its place across his back, his knives strapped to his muscular thighs, only the sky blue of their leather hilts appearing out of place.

He looked up, sparing the King barely a glance, and surveyed the Councilors, the guards, and me, and not a flicker of anything passed over his face or touched his eyes. My stomach lurched.

<This ceremony is a simple farewell, Seer Tokka,> said the King quietly. <Take their hand when it is offered, bow over it, kiss their fingers. Express your wish for a safe journey. They will reply in kind.>

<Yes, my King.>

The Queen and the Prince approached down the long aisle, and I kept my chin up and my expression indifferent. The King stepped down to meet them and presented his Councilors one by one to bow and be bowed at. Kiernan looked bored.

Then the King gestured to me, and I stepped from my place to meet the Queen.

"And at last, good Queen, I present my Seer, Tokka tanKarshanka. He was returned to me partly through your son's good work at the Abbey of the Moon, and I am most grateful."

I wanted to hide rather than face Kiernan's mother. How much did she know about Kier and me? Had he told her anything? But she simply regarded me emotionlessly with her hard green eyes and held out her hand.

"Safe journey, Queen of Morven Forest," I said, and bowed over her hand, placing a quick kiss on her fingers.

"Good health to you, Seer Tokka," she said, and her voice would have made me shiver with its coldness but I held myself carefully still. She bowed, brushed her lips over my knuckles, and moved on to speak to the King again.

And then I was face to face with the Prince.

"Safe journey, Prince of Morven Forest," I said, and caught a glimpse of something raw in his eyes just as I bent over his right hand. He shifted his fingers in mine, used his thumb to push a wide silver ring on his middle finger down to his knuckle, and I drew in a breath a little louder than it should have been. Around his finger, where it would be covered and secret, was a thin circle of shining white.

I pressed my lips to his fingers, hard, and the circle flexed under my lips, brushed against them like silk.

He had a ring braided of my hair hidden on his finger. His middle finger on his non-dominant hand. It was, if I remembered the forbidden book at the Abbey correctly, the finger of promise; he had hidden a promise to me under the ring avowing his loyalty to his Queen and his lineage.

I felt his breath on my ear as he leaned slightly closer. "I'm yours, beloved," he said, so soft only I could hear.

I straightened and looked at him coolly as he bent over my hand, knowing I must show nothing that could be seen by the King. I almost ruined it by gasping when Kier's tongue flicked over my knuckles, but I managed to react only by tightening my fingers on his. I wanted to laugh, and cry, and scream. I only said, so softly even *I* couldn't hear, though I knew he would, "Beloved, I'm yours."

He didn't smile when he straightened up, met my eyes, and said, "Good health, Seer Tokka," but I could feel his joy deep in my belly, and I knew he could feel mine.

As he walked away, two slender shapes descended out of the air high up by the ceiling to drape themselves across my shoulders. The King looked at me, raised an eyebrow, but said nothing.

Smoke nuzzled one ear, and Flame the other.

Dark and bright, said Smoke.

Love and love, said Flame.

About the Author

NICO SILVER LIVES like a hermit on the edge of the woods, but haunts used bookstores like a wraith. They fully expected to be found someday as a mummified old corpse crushed under a toppled to-be-read pile, but the rise of e-books has made that somewhat less likely, though the books will always outnumber even the dustbunnies. Nico will read just about anything, including the instructions on the back of medicine bottles, but has a particular fondness for good stories with a hint of magic. They write dark, sexy urban and romantic fantasy, and sometimes dream in black and white.